ZOOLOGICA FANTASTICA

ZOOLOGICA FANTASTICA

AN ANTHOLOGY OF STRANGE CREATURES IN CLASSIC CRYPTOFICTION

Chad Arment, Editor

COACHWHIP PUBLICATIONS
Greenville, Ohio

Zoologica Fantastica, edited by Chad Arment
Copyright © 2013 Coachwhip Publications
All rights reserved. No claims made on public domain material.

ISBN 1-61646-163-2
ISBN-13 978-1-61646-163-8

Cover: Locust © Sergey Goruppa

CoachwhipBooks.com

CONTENTS

A PLACE OF MONSTERS
Thomas P. Byron
1911

I

It was a trail through the treetops—a rift in the forest through which the sky stretched straight away as far as the eye could see, like a blue band on a dark-green canopy. When we found it we were hopelessly lost in the maze of jungle that lies between the two republics; so we followed the strip of sky that blazed through the ragged gap, in the hope that it would lead us somewhere, and for two days it had led us as straight to the northeast as one might go.

Don Innocencio called it The Sky-Trail, but the Railroader rechristened it The Trail of a Thousand and One Torments. They were there—the torments—in biblical legions, buzzing their endless song and gorging themselves on our blood. Each one was barbed, each one was poisonous, famished—insatiable.

We could see them coming to the feast in dense clouds; there were a thousand and one varieties, and a million and one of each variety. They put the jungle venom into our veins, too, and made us part of the great scheme. We were no longer men, but, with our swollen, distorted features, were become monstrosities that Nature had built in a debauch, as she had created the rest of the place.

Every bush, every leaf, every atom of that cunning, creeping jungle was alive. It was one vast, palpitating thing, of which we were a part and you could see its lifeblood flow in a mammoth, blighting current such as you may have noticed in examining a bit of protoplasm under a microscope.

Lars called it a place of ghosts. At times it fairly rang with noise, and then again it was weirdly silent. We could hear the cries of birds and the roar of beasts, but they hushed at our approach. We could hear great monsters crashing away ahead of us, but never once did we catch a glimpse of them.

It gave us shivers—this abject fright, of which we were the cause. It was as if there were some horrible thing about us that we ourselves could not see. We looked at one another suspiciously— to search out who might be the accursed one.

We had joined forces back at Lake Peten the day that a white man staggered in from the jungle dying of fever and some strange poison. He had raved of things that crawled upon him and stung him, of things that chased him and coiled about him, and—of an island of pearls in the middle of a swamp.

And clenched in his hand when he died were five enormous pearls.

So we five were hunting for the island.

The Railroader was an American tramp; Lars, a runaway sailor, who looked like a Viking; Don Innocencio, a manikin carved from a grain of coffee and steeped into animation; the Enigma was a short, fat, hairless sphinx; and I—I was myself.

Toward the evening of the second day we were fighting our way through the brush, when the Railroader, who was leading, sang out.

"There's an open space ahead," he said. "I believe we are com- ing out somewhere."

Full of hope, we struggled on through a dense thicket, and emerged into a blinding sunshine, where the whole world was spread out before us. We all blinked and stared silently.

We had happened upon a great, gorgeous-colored, prehistoric monster lying in his lair.

The lair was a gray, loathsome swamp—a fen such as might have produced huge reptiles when the earth's crust was still hot and steaming.

The monster was an island gorgeous with the flaring colors of tropical vegetation, and it lay on the edge of the swamp. A jagged mass of white rock formed a hideous head; elsewhere it was covered with arborescent flora of dazzling hues, with stripes of green grass running over it. A great wing stretched out into the swamp, and off to our left was a long tail that broke into a fork at the end.

It looked like a great beast that had lain sad-colored and dormant in the fen that had given him birth, and then, chameleon-like, had shone in a thousand glaring hues when the first sun burst through the bank of clouds that encircled the steaming earth. Through a thin mist that hung over the swamp it seemed to tremble, as if it breathed and shook itself now and then. Only the fierce glare of the sun and the cloudless sky gave the lie to the primordial aspect of the monster and its dank, gray lair,

"It's a place of snakes and alligators," said the Railroader.

"The swamp—yes," said Don Innocencio; "but the island is a place of gorgeous things. Perhaps it's the island of pearls."

The Enigma pointed. Beyond the island was a silent, gray lake, on the farther shore of which a forest stood down to the water's edge. At a break in this, spirals of smoke, clearly distinguishable through the mist over the swamp, rose in the air. "There are men there," he said.

Lars was staring, with a strange look on his face.

"What is it, Lars?" I queried.

"Is it a mirage?" he asked in a troubled voice. "Not the island—the tree! Is it a mirage?"

We all looked. At the head of the island, among the white rocks, a single, enormous, heavily fronded palm stood out green and feathery against the sky.

It was the only tree of any size on the island.

"It's no mirage—it's a palm, all right," said the Railroader. "What about it, anyway?"

"It is alive," answered Lars.

We burst into laughter, and then stopped short and stared.

"Seems to me I can see something bright there," muttered the Railroader.

"You see the bushes," replied the Enigma.

"It's even brighter than the bushes, and it seems to move."

"The mist from the swamp causes that. The island seems to move, too."

"It's alive," insisted Lars, and he and the Railroader continued to gaze at it uneasily.

"We'll soon find out," said the Enigma. "The swamp is full of open and dry places. It's a regular network of trails, and it will be no trouble to cross it. We have two hours before sundown, and we'll rest on that green grass to-night. There ought to be fresh water there."

"And pearls," I added.

We picked up our packs: and started, Lars holding back.

"I don't like it," he said as I passed him. "It looks as if there were dead men there."

"The jungle is breaking your nerve, Lars," I answered, laughing.

As the Enigma had said, the swamp was composed of paths of hard, sun-dried mud that crossed and crisscrossed in every direction between sections of slimy morass and stagnant water, where grew tall reeds and great clumps of saw-grass that cut the clothing like razors.

Now and then we saw mottled snakes gliding in the reeds, and the place was full of mournful, drab-colored little birds that ran about crazily—here and there and everywhere, like Chinese mice—as if they were searching for something. They never rested, nor did they pay the slightest attention to us, and their feet made a curious soft pattering on the hard mud.

The grass and reeds were higher than our heads, and only occasionally could we get a glimpse of the island or the jungle we had quitted; but we turned to left or right as we judged it necessary to bring us to our goal.

At the end of three-quarters of an hour we came upon a *cul-de-sac*, and another deep, silent, mud-colored pool.

We tried more roads, with the same result, working feverishly, and without due judgment in the effort to get across before nightfall; and soon we were so thoroughly lost that it would have been a matter of equal difficulty to gain either the island or our starting-point again. The paths were so narrow—with the reeds and grass swishing in our faces—and they were all exactly alike.

Suddenly we emerged upon the shore of the lake perhaps a quarter of a mile from the head of the island. The open water reached straight from us to the white rocks, and beyond to the break in the forest, where the smoke was rising.

The island thrust another wing out into the lake on the other side, giving it more the appearance of the monster than ever, and we could see that it was not really an island, since there was no open water between it and the swamp.

"The palm-tree!" ejaculated Lars. We stared at it in silence.

The last rays of the sun sinking in the swamp glittered on it, and all at once the top of the tree seemed to quiver, unfold, and shake itself violently, shining in the most gorgeous colors. And then from across the lake there came booming a distant roar, as from a multitude of throats.

It was faint, wild, full of a brazen ring, and seemed somehow to give one the picture of lank forms and working throats.

"There's many a throat off yonder," said the Railroader slowly. "I'm glad we've got plenty of cartridges."

As he spoke he drew his hand across his own throat, and I saw that his face was white.

"I wish we had a boat," said Lars, still staring at the palm-tree. "We could be at the island in fifteen minutes, and see what is in the palm."

"We might paddle our way thither on a log, if we can find one," I suggested.

"No—no!" cried Don Innocencio. "That gray water may be alive with reptiles. It would not do to trust ourselves to it."

"We can't stay here all night."

"The last pool we came to had an open space sixty feet or so across," said the Enigma. "Suppose we go there. We can sit in the middle."

"That's the trick," approved the Railroader. "I, for one, don't want to go exploring about this swamp at night, nor yet to stay here with the saw-grass slapping my face. It's too easy for things to spring out at us."

This was the unanimous opinion, and we were back at the spot in a jiffy.

It was as round as a bull-ring, dried by the sun to a consistent hardness, and bordered on a small pool that we tried with a long reed and found to be bottomless, as far as our measuring apparatus was concerned.

The reeds and grass about were not so high, however, and we could see the island plainly when standing. The Railroader had brought a canteen of water from the lake. It was fresh and sweet, in spite of its warmness and grayish color; and before we had finished our short meal twilight was upon us.

"This is a sad place," said Lars. "Saddest of all at twilight. I am curious about the palm-tree. I will not be able to rest until I find out what it was."

He had risen and gone to the edge of the open space, and stood perhaps a dozen feet from the saw-grass, looking toward the island. In the dim light his form, silhouetted against the sky, seemed gigantic.

Suddenly a long, dim bulk swung like a flash from out the reeds and struck him fairly in the side with a crunch, knocking him twenty feet away to the edge of the pool. The thing reared up until it seemed to tower in the sky, fell its whole length forward, and was upon his crumpled form.

The Enigma was shooting on the second, and Don Innocencio and I were only a breath later, screaming to each other as we fired. Some of our bullets went home, I'm sure.

But the creature had yawned half its length and seized the sailor. There was a great splash, and only the agitated waters of the pool remained to show where man and monster had disappeared.

The Railroader cried out: "What was it?"

"It was the devil!" chattered Don Innocencio.

"It was a monster crocodile," said the Enigma grimly. "It struck him with its tail and knocked him to the edge of the pool. Then it seized him and plunged in."

"Can't we do anything?" cried the Railroader desperately.

"We can only stay in the middle of the open space," answered Don Innocencio. "The swamp may be alive with them. We had best sit quiet here—and back to back."

We followed his example, and in a moment more the last streaks of light were gone and it was as black as pitch.

"Listen!" whispered the Enigma. "The place is alive!" A light wind had sprung up and rustled in the reeds like the hissing of a thousand serpents. We could hear things crashing in the rushes, and the splash of heavy bodies in the water.

Lone night-birds called shrilly now and then, and all about we could hear the endless pattering of the drab-colored birds. It was a ghostly sort of clamor, and it was soul-shriveling work sitting there, thinking that the darkness was full of cunning monsters waiting for us to come within the sweep of their mighty tails.

The Railroader was the first to break the silence.

"Poor Lars got his," he whispered.

"It was a blow that would have killed an ox," replied Don Innocencio. "They can swing their tails like lightning. Like enough, it almost cut him in two. Those scaly tails are like knives."

"What was that?" demanded the Railroader suspiciously.

From the pool had come a soft, gurgling sound.

"Bubbles," said the Enigma sententiously.

We understood, and shuddered.

The thing was tearing our companion to pieces on the bottom of the pool and devouring him.

II

We waited for the moon to rise. It was on the wane and was due to come up about ten o'clock.

I was facing the east and the island, and over the tops of the reeds I could see the sky glow faintly and then brighten into a heavy red as if all the world were afire beyond and one could see the blaze through heavy banks of smoke

The Railroader, who was back to back with me, suddenly rose to his feet. The rest of us heard it, too, and Don Innocencio and I were on our feet, clutching our carbines.

It was a steady flapping that seemed to circle about us, sometimes near and sometimes far.

Suddenly a draft of wind struck me full in the face. To my raw-edged nerves the shock was like that of a blow. I dodged instinctively and Don Innocencio and I tumbled together upon the Enigma, who had not risen.

While we struggled in a heap we heard the Railroader's voice in a scream of terror. "Hold me! Shoot!" he cried. "It's got me—"

The words ended in a tiny gurgle. We could hear something dragging heavily through the reeds. And then all was as silent as the grave—even the swamp had ceased its clamor as if to listen.

We clutched each other and shouted to the Railroader, and at the sound of our voices, the swamp, as if reassured, began its noise again.

We struck lights and peered about the open space. It was vacant as ever.

The water of the pool was silent and unruffled, the mud on the edge was clawed up where the crocodile had dragged Lars with him, and the sailor's hat lay near the edge. But the Railroader had vanished as completely as if the earth had opened up and swallowed him.

"Better sit down," advised the Enigma. "It may come back."

"Yes," whispered Don Innocencio. "I was knocked flat by something—a wing I think. And while we were struggling on the ground I was bitten on the foot by something."

We struck more lights and looked about for snakes and examined Don Innocencio's foot; on the instep was a tiny puncture around which the flesh was slightly discolored.

While I held a match the Enigma slashed it with a sharp knife and squeezed as much blood as he might from it. It flowed clear and red, there was no discoloration, and Don Innocencio felt no pain other than from the cut. Whatever it had been had bitten right through the boot.

"It doesn't amount to much," he said at last, and then, shrinkingly: "But what took the Railroader?"

"It was something that flew," answered the Enigma. "It must be what we saw in the palm. We'll shoot it tomorrow."

"No, no. Let's get out of this swamp tomorrow as soon as we can. There's something strange about the place, and I don't want any more of it."

"We'll settle that tomorrow. But in the meantime we had better keep quiet until the moon rises. It may come back."

We huddled down as close to earth as we could, and watched.

A golden rim had crept up over the rocky head of the island and the swamp seemed to be filled with a luminous pinkish haze that became brighter as the moon, red as blood, slowly rose.

The fronds of the single palm-tree shone against it for a moment like a great spider on a red egg of molten metal, and then—they seemed to twist and contort as if the spider had been shriveled up by the egg's heat and was writhing in his dying agonies.

The agitation lasted for a second, and then ceased as the moon rising higher swung free from the palm and brightened from a sullen red to a whiter hue. And it seemed to me—I knew—somehow—that the Master of the Swamp was back in his perch. He to whom the lank men on the lake shore had shouted a salute at sundown.

The moon broke through the haze all at once and poured a flood of quicksilver over the swamp that seemed to fill every nook, and coat with glistening white every blade and leaf. We could see the reeds sway and bend, and even the drab birds, now white, that pattered about continuously. It was a welcome sight, and the night was robbed of half its terrors.

We stood up and gazed about in every direction, but nothing met our glances save the waving expanse of silver-limned swamp and the dark line of the forest beyond.

"Not a sign of him," said the Enigma at last. "But if it comes back, we will be able to see to shoot, anyway. That is one comfort."

"It won't come back," I said dully.

We sat down again and fell into a silence that was only broken by brief inquiries concerning Don Innocencio's foot, and the monotone of his reassuring reply

Fatigue began to fight with fear and wonder. Now and then I nodded, and I seemed to see Lars and the Railroader fighting with uncanny monsters. They always seemed far away, as if I were watching them through the wrong end of a telescope, and always I roused myself with a start.

I felt Don Innocencio jerk uneasily at times, and I wondered if he, too, were having the same experience.

A dull rage crept into me at the constant strain. I watched the struggle of the two with calm philosophy, and would have closed my eyes upon them in indifference had I not known that it would be all over as soon as I withdrew my gaze. Why did thy not give up and have it over with and let me go to sleep?

The monsters in the swamp—the thing in the palm! Let them come! I was tired and was going to close my eyes at any cost. So I closed them.

Then I saw the twain coming back after it was all over—shadows who looked at me with reproachful eyes.

This was the worst of all, and I started up in horror to flee, and found that I was awake and that it was bright day.

It took me a moment to get free from my cramped position and look about. The sun had risen over the island, scintillating in all the colors of the rainbow; the swamp steamed like a caldron. The Enigma was getting food out of his pack, and Don Innocencio was on his feet, staring. Following his gaze I, too, regarded the palm-tree long and carefully.

"There's nothing in it," he said at last.

"How is the foot?" I demanded.

"The least bit swollen, but no pain. It doesn't amount to much."

"'Twas some insect that crawled in your boot," said the Enigma.

"No, there is a puncture in the boot. Perhaps it was some kind of a thorn, though."

We ate silently. The Enigma was as sphinxlike as ever, but Don Innocencio had gone to a sickly paleness under his dark skin, and it gave him an unhealthy look. His face was drawn, and his large, dark eyes were abnormally great for the rest of him.

"It was horrible," he said, when we had finished eating.

"Yes," I answered. "The crocodile that took Lars was bad enough—"

We all stared a moment at the pool.

"The other thing is some great, flying thing," said the Enigma. "It roosts in the palm-tree. We'll shoot it, if it appears today."

"I suppose there's no use—" I began.

The Enigma waved his hand.

"I thought I heard something dragging through the bushes at the time, but you can see that not a reed is out of place. I'm afraid there's no use in looking for him."

We all took a drink of *aguardiente* and started. The day was very bright, the sun had burned up the mist, and only a filmy haze through which the island monster was trembling as before hung over the swamp. The strings of smoke were still rising at the break in the forest.

The lake gleamed with a grayish sheen, in the jungle parrots were screaming, but the swamp was silent save for the endless pattering of the sand-colored birds that rushed about frantically in their eternal search for something they were never to find.

We set to work scientifically to find the way to the island.

The first road we tried led us to a point where at a distance of some seventy yards from where we had camped the reeds on both sides were broken down and smashed as if a heavy body had been dragged across struggling. We stopped and looked at each other.

What was coming next?

"See how the reeds are broken," I said. "It came from where we camped and went toward the island."

The Enigma threw down his pack. "I'm going to have a look in there," he declared.

"I am, too," I replied.

The *don* hung back and we started, pushing the reeds and saw-grass to one side with our guns. It was a regular quicksand where one sank at once over the ankles and continued to sink, if he did not keep moving.

The reeds were thick in the sticky mess, and here and there were clumps of saw-grass that seemed to afford more solid footing, but were too narrow to stand upon.

Suddenly we stopped.

Twenty feet ahead of us on the surface of the terrible, filthy slime there was a white face.

It was the Railroader. His limbs and body were sunk beneath the mud, his tangled yellow hair had caught on a thick broken reed and had kept his head from following.

His face was shrunken to less than half its former size.

It was white—dead-white, wan, and drawn, with the blue veins standing out rugged all over it. He looked as if the last drop of blood had been drawn from his veins, leaving only skin and dry flesh. And yet his face had something calm and peaceful about it.

"It must have been a vampire," said the Enigma slowly.

"Let's get out of here quick." I shuddered.

It was high time.

In the brief instant I had stared at the face I had sunk to my knees. Another moment or two and we had kept the Railroader company.

I had to clutch a bunch of saw-grass and work like mad to free myself, and when the Enigma advanced to loosen the Railroader's hair from the reed, I had to sit on a clump and pull him free from the clinging embrace. Otherwise he, too, would have gone down.

When we turned for a last glimpse, the face was gone, the slime was smooth and placid.

III

We told Don Innocencio of it while we cleaned the filth from our legs. It had a sweet, nauseating smell and, in spite of his tremors, the little Guatemalteco walked ahead of us to be free from it.

The very next trail we tried curved and zigzagged about for a while and finally led us straight to the middle of the island, perhaps half a mile from the head. When we emerged from the grassy maze and stood in the clear again, we found that the brilliant colors had dulled marvelously.

In place of the monster of flaming scarlets and pinks and emeralds that sunlight and distance had shown us, we found a long mass of white, quartz-like rock covered with bushes of brown and heather-like purple, and grass of dull green. It was in the shape of a cross, and here and there were detached rocks.

A collection of these last formed the head where stood the palm. It was now hidden from us by a high pinnacle, but we worked our way thither without delay.

The tree was ringed about on three sides by great rocks, on the other was a sheer drop of thirty feet to the lake.

We came upon the place suddenly after passing the rock that cut it off from our view.

The tree was empty: its fronds shone bright green in the sunlight; below, among the rocks, it was rather gloomy. Beneath the tree was a great flat stone. We stepped quickly to the lake-edge.

The water was full of driftwood, logs so water-soaked that only humps here and there rose above the water; they were as close together as in a mill-pond, and one could have walked about on them with the greatest of ease. There were hundreds of them.

"All the driftwood of the lake must collect here," said Don Innocencio. "There must be a—"

He stopped with a yell, and if the Enigma had not seized him, I believe he would have fallen in the lake.

The Enigma had kicked a stone into the lake, and suddenly each log had become a yawning, red-eyed monster in whose gaping jaws, set with three rows of enormous teeth, the little Guatemalteco might have disappeared bodily.

We all jumped back, and Don Innocencio and I shook like aspens.

"They seem to be expecting us," said the Enigma.

A sudden rage seized him.

"I wish that thing would come back," he snarled. "I want to kill something. If I had cartridges enough, I'd sit here on this rock and never stop shooting as long as there was an alligator in that cursed lake."

"So would I," hissed Don Innocencio.

They glared about for something on which to vent their rage. The *don* ran to the center of the flat rock. Suddenly he uttered a hoarse cry.

"Look! Look!" he babbled.

He was kneeling on the rock, and plunging his hand in a cavity, he brought it up filled with things that glittered white as milk and dropped back again with a musical rattle.

The next instant the three of us were pawing them up in great handfuls and roaring with excitement.

We had found the island of pearls. The hole in the rock was full of them. We laughed and cried and talked all at once.

"There's enough of them," stammered Don Innocencio incoherently, "to buy the Five Republics."

And we laughed like madmen at the thought.

The Enigma was the first to come to himself.

"There's a pearl fishery in this lake somewhere," he said slowly, "and this rock is someone's storehouse. Who put them here? Who were the ones that shouted last night at sundown? What was it that—"

"Look there!" he broke off suddenly. "Look there!"

From the break in the forest where the smoke was rising a fleet of canoes was coming out toward the island.

IV

We jammed the pearls into a bag, seized our guns, and never ceased running nor stopped to look back until we were across the swamp and stood on the edge of the jungle again.

Don Innocencio was limping.

"I am done," he gasped feebly. "My leg has started to swell, and already I can hardly walk."

We stared back at the island a moment and then gave him *aguardiente* and urged him to press on. But before we had made two miles I was obliged to stop and help him. Each time we rested the Enigma poured *aguardiente* into him, and soon he was either drunk or fever-stricken, for he began to rave.

He talked of jungles and swamps and treasure, and declared one moment he was the president of the Five Republics, the next he begged us to take the pearls back. But never once in his madness and gibberish did he cease to struggle on as long as an atom of strength remained to him to get as far as possible from the swamp and the island.

We had walked perhaps six miles when he gave out entirely, so we made a camp where the lianas and other parasites grew thickest about the trees. The place was so shut in that we were invisible twenty feet away, and we had no fear of pursuit, for to find a man in that jungle would have been equal to the task of finding a needle in a haystack.

Don Innocencio's foot was like that of an elephant, huge, discolored.

We washed it with *aguardiente* and water, and then poured liquor into him until he was stupefied, and lay still, breathing heavily. We decided to remain where we were until he was better and then endeavor to make our way back to Petén.

We ate and drank and rested and took turns watching over him until after midnight.

Then, as he lay quiet, and all seemed well, we both fell off to sleep.

I was awakened by a fierce grip on my shoulder, and sprang to my feet, for I had dreamed that the thing that had taken the Railroader had seized me.

The Enigma, wild-eyed, was shaking me, and it was day.

"Gone!" he cried bitterly. "Gone!"

"The pearls!" I gasped.

"Yes, and Don Innocencio."

"Where can he have gone?" I muttered.

"Heaven knows. He is crazy from fear. He has tried to get farther away, and he will wander until he drops, and we will never find him. Who could find a man in this jungle?"

"No," said I. "He has gone back to the island."

"Back to the island! That is just where he would not go. He is mad with fear of the place."

"Nevertheless," I answered calmly, "that is where he has gone."

We gripped our carbines and started out to overtake our mad comrade. He had left his own gun behind him.

We ran and walked by turns, fighting our way through the tangle like eager bloodhounds, stopping to drink each time we came to water, for the country was full of little rivulets that emptied into the swamp. Once the Enigma stopped and pointed to a stone.

It was daubed with a stain, and we knew that Don Innocencio had stepped there with his poisoned foot.

But we did not speak a word until we had broken out of the jungle and could look across the swamp again.

Everything—swamp, island, lake—was quiet; the palm-tree was motionless; nothing was shining or moving there. But away out in the center of the swamp we could see a tiny white speck.

Dazed though he was, Don Innocencio had taken the right trail, and was heading straight for the island.

Hardly stopping for breath, we dashed on with new energy at the sight of him.

V

Almost to the island there was a slight rise—a hump in the swamp beyond which the trail—straight for a couple of hundred yards, was girt in by reeds and grass at least ten feet high.

Topping this rise we came upon him.

The squat, white little figure was limping on ever so slowly.

He held the bag of pearls in his hand and toiled on, putting his swollen foot to the ground with a care that told how great must be the agony it caused him.

"Poor devil," I puffed "He's crazy as a loon. I'm afraid we'll have to use force to get him to go back. It is lucky we overtook him before he reached the island."

"Oh-oh!" gasped the Enigma. "Look!"

Standing in the trail, awaiting Don Innocencio, was an enormously tall and thin Indian. He was naked from the waist up, and stood erect and silent. On his head was a headdress so enormous that, even were it of feathers, it seemed as if the weight must crush him.

It was a dazzling mass of gorgeous colors, and from it two tremendous wings stretched out into the reeds on each side of the trail.

Don Innocencio sighted the Indian. He dropped his pearls and stood still.

Then he limped toward the waiting one with outstretched hands. His attitude was that of prayer. We stood wondering.

The gorgeous head-dress fluttered, every feather seemed to stand on end, a head raised up from out their midst: quick as a flash something flew out and struck Don Innocencio full in the face—just as a centipede swings its tail over its head to strike.

He dropped like a log and the gorgeous thing shook itself, flapped slowly forward, and lighted on his prone body.

"Shoot!" screamed the Enigma.

He began to fire—the thing screeched once—I saw the feathers drop, and then it flapped across the swamp and perched in the palm-tree.

The Indian had disappeared. Not a sign of him anywhere.

When we reached Don Innocencio he lay where he had fallen, the bag of pearls a short distance away.

He looked up, clear-eyed, into our faces, gasping a single word: "Quetzalcoatl!"

Then he was dead and horrible—his face green, his cheeks bloated.

To inter him was our only thought.

We found a place where the swamp was a quicksand and gave him to it, as we had done with the Railroader, fearing to touch him, looking about, shivering, each moment to regard the thing that still sat in the palm.

The Enigma handed me the bag of pearls. "Do you know who Quetzacoatl was?" he asked.

"An Aztec god," I answered dully. "The Aztec Messiah."

"Yes—a god to whom they offered human sacrifice. They used to open victim's breast with a sharp knife and tear out the still beating heart for the god to snatch. And do you know what the name means?"

I shook my head.

"It means the Feathered Serpent."

VI

"You can wait for me or you can go," said the Enigma.

"What are you going to do?"

"I am going to kill it."

"No—no!" I cried, seizing him by the arm "Do not kill it. We have the pearls. Let us go. Let us get away from here."

He shook me off, foaming with fury, threatening me with his gun and eying me fearfully, as if I were as dreadful as the thing itself.

"You may do as you like," he said, "but I am going to kill it, if I have to do so under the eyes of its worshipers, and I will kill you if you meddle with me."

He set off, and I followed him, begging until he threatened me again. After that I still followed, but said nothing and kept at a distance. I knew words were of no use.

He climbed the slope of the island and marched straight up to the head. I could see the thing in the tree shake itself now and then, until finally it disappeared behind the pinnacle of rock.

When we turned the corner of the rocks I was a dozen feet behind the Enigma.

There was the palm-tree, the open space and flat rock below, the lake teeming with crocodiles, and the thing—an immense, shapeless bunch of gorgeous plumage that had neither head nor tail nor wings nor feet. The Enigma leveled his carbine.

He could hardly miss so splendid a mark as that immense and bright thing.

With a hoarse cry, I leaped forward to stop him. Too late!

Once—twice—thrice—he fired right into the center of it.

Feathers dropped, and with a screech it dropped from the tree and flapping its great wings desperately, fell into the lake.

I saw it! Ah, Lord! I saw it—and then the water of the lake was lashed into crimson foam where a horde of hideous jaws were tearing a bright-feathered thing to fragments.

The Enigma and I stared, fascinated, and something caused me to look behind.

I tried to scream, but my tongue hung useless in my jaws.

The next instant a squat deformity of a man with a nose like a parrot's beak had seized the Enigma about the waist and leaped into the lake with him.

I could not save him.

The horrid clamor in the water redoubled, and I found myself staring into the eyes of the tall Indian.

He wore no head-dress this time, and I saw that his head was pointed at the top and quite innocent of hair.

His skin was of a mottled copper-color, he had the tiniest of ears that lay close to his head, and his nose was an atom.

His body was abnormally thin, his neck and cheeks enormous. They seemed to bloat up until they were ready to burst, and then shrank until they were sunken and covered with scaly folds of skin.

He was hideous.

Had it not been for that which I read in the depths of his deep-set eyes, I would have thought that he was going to spit poison at me. You have seen a cobra bloat up its hood when enraged—that was how he did it.

I could not take my eyes from his, and he stepped forward until I could count the scales on his neck and feel his breath upon my face. His slender frame writhed and quivered in mortal agony—like a snake dying upon a hot stove, and his eyes looked into mine with a sad reproachful glance that made my heart ache.

He uttered a single word with a sob that convulsed his whole frame, and my eyes filled with tears.

"Quetzalcoatl!" he exclaimed.

The next instant he had taken the bag of pearls from my unresisting hand, and with a last glance of reproach that cut my heart as with an envenomed and serrated blade, he, too, was gone into the yawning jaws below.

I stepped forward once—twice—and looked down from the very edge.

Then I turned and ran, holding my hand over my ears to drown the clamor and bellowings in the water—lest I, too, follow to those that waited—red-eyed and hungry below, and as I ran I sobbed over and over again: "Quetzalcoatl—Quetzalcoatl!"

THE ALBINO OTTER
Elmer Brown Mason
1915

My friend, Van Dam, had set out for Miami on one of his mysterious quests, so it was there I sent the telegram, announcing that my painting of Hercules, the extraordinary model for which he furnished me, had taken the first gold medal at the National Academy of Artists. I really didn't expect the telegram to reach him; just sent it in the first burst of buoyancy as a written libation to my good fortune. However, an answer came that very same evening:

> You don't say are you going to wear it for a bangle or hang it around your neck at once. Send me here by express ten pounds of round, assorted turquoise blue and light red beads about the size of a small pea and of solid build, and a pound of the purest arsenic railroads toot man felicitations.
>
> Van Dam.

After I had censored the telegraph company's punctuation with an exclamation point after "say," and an interrogation point after "neck," and translated the apparent enthusiasm of the railroads into "*Vraiment, toutes mes félicitations,*" I took up the matter of his commissions.

I never should have been able to get the arsenic had I not happened to mention Van Dam's name in the course of a vehement denial of an intent to poison my neighbors, or at the very least myself. Then, however, the clerk was all interest, and he even

26

directed me to a beadery where I was able to secure the exact articles described. I added of my own volition for good measure some splendidly glittering gold specimens. Despatching the parcel, I returned to the studio and, with the help of three other men, wrote Van Dam the most insulting letter I could compose.

Among other things we asked if the beads were to be his sole costume, and suggested that he swallow the arsenic and feed himself to an innocent alligator for bait. Pretty poor humor, I admit; but I had lost a whole morning of good painting light while making, his absurd purchases, and besides, something I had eaten the night before disagreed with me.

At the end of three months I was getting used to the absence of my eccentric friend, when one afternoon the telephone bell rang.

"Hello!" I said in those dulcet tones reserved exclusively for women, millionaire picture buyers, art dealers, and creditors.

"Glad you have regained your temper, artist-man," drawled Van's voice over the wire. "Come and dine with me this evening," and then I distinctly heard an aside that was plainly not meant for my ears: "Lizzie, stop tickling my neck!"

"All right," I agreed, "but you've got to have something to eat that I have at least heard of before."

Van Dam has a way of concocting mysterious dishes that are delightful until you learn of their derivation from some bird, beast, insect, or reptile, quite unknown to the most cosmopolitan menus.

"And shall I dress?" I added as an afterthought.

"Dress! What for?"

"For Lizzie," I answered with sardonic triumph.

Van Dam laughed. "No, don't bother. She won't mind. We'll have a steak, too. Lizzie likes 'em!"

Van Dam's apartments, or diggings, as he prefers to call them, occupy the entire top story of an immense building, and are really a museum of the natural-history collections he has made in every corner of the globe. There his Jap received my hat and stick as imperturbably as though I called every day, and ushered me to the curtains of the dining-room. I pulled them aside cautiously and peeked in at my host. Never have I seen a man so sunburnt! He wasn't red, or brown, or bronze. He was black, and this color was heightened by contrast with the whiteness of a small animal (little larger than a cat) on his knee, which regarded me with inscrutable, malicious eyes.

"If that darned thing is a skunk I won't come in!" I threatened. My knowledge of natural history is slight, and anyway, I distrust all Van's pets.

"Skunk nothing!" he answered indignantly; "that's Lizzie, and she's a white raccoon—the only case of albinoism I ever heard of in her family," he added proudly.

"Cost you a thousand dollars!" I ventured sarcastically. Van Dam is shamefully rich, and doesn't in the least mind paying for his whims.

"I bought her for two dollars on the edge of the Everglades, and she is as gentle as a kitten."

"Like all of her sex," I commented, entering and sitting down. "Where have you been, Van, and how did you get such an awful sunburn? I can't say I've missed you, because it's the truth—and that's bad form. But I am curious to know how you combined those many bead things and the arsenic, and what resulted therefrom."

"I have been acting as Cupid in the Everglades," he answered; "but let's dine first, and then I will tell you of hate, love, mystery, gold, and great wild places that will make your city-bounded horizon seem as limited as the inside of a teacup."

Van Dam's table is remarkably wonderful. He may, and I have no doubt that he does, live on grass and raw animals during his sojourns in the wilds, but at home his cuisine would quickly make a *bon vivant* out of an ascetic. The steak was a kind of a glorified dish that quite belied its respectable, bourgeois name, and the things that went with it were indescribably good.

During the entire meal the white raccoon climbed impartially over us and the table, varying its acrobatics by filching choice morsels which it held in its curious, tiny, human hands and, before daintily eating them, washed in a glass of water with all the fervor of a religious rite.

"Well," I said, when my pipe was going comfortably and my host had lit a cigarette, "begin at the beginning. What bleached animal started you this time, and what happened?"

"It was an otter," he acknowledged shamelessly. "I met a globe-trotting Englishman at the Old Club who said a Seminole Indian had told him of a white otter in the Everglades that was supposed to have magic powers and charm fish with its ruby eyes. I found out the Indian's name, Osceola, after a former great chief of the Seminoles. With only that to go by, I set out for Miami, which, as you know, is on the edge of the Everglades.

"Speaking of the Everglades, painter man, I suppose you visualize them as an enormous, fertile field, sprouting with corn, watermelons, oranges, and coconut-trees, and cut by neat Dutch canals. You probably owe this conception to someone who was trying to sell you stock in the Drainage Improvement Company Limitless, three hundred per cent profits guaranteed. Your idea is not exactly correct.

"The Everglades are an enormous inland lake, fifty miles broad and a hundred and forty long, with a limestone rim ten feet above mean tide level, and a limestone bottom through which seeps, or sometimes bubbles up, fresh water. This limestone is covered with more or less mud, nearly entirely overgrown with saw-grass, and here and there are islands. The water is fresh and pure, seldom over a few feet deep; the mud is from one to ten feet. There are few mosquitoes since the water moves continually in a northeasterly direction, and is, therefore, unsuited to the development of mosquito larvae. Hence there is no malaria.

"Millions of birds and, I regret to say, an equal number of snakes, some deer, and a few Seminole Indians—the oddest of all the animal dwellers—find a home in this strange place. The Indians live on tiny islands in the midst of the Everglades, or in the impenetrable Great Cypress Swamp to the north. Since their verbal contract with General Worth a century ago they have shown no hostility to white men, in spite of all they have suffered. Time has taught them that in their own protection they must not guide a white man into their fastnesses, though they are always willing to lead out those who get lost in this sea of grass, lured on by legends of islands fabulous in fertility, overgrown with orange and lemon groves, and even harboring pirate gold.

"You can easily imagine that one Indian name gave me little to go on. It is true that there are less than six hundred Seminoles left; but they are seldom seen, and those I did meet could not or would not give me any information in regard to Osceola, and professed to have never heard of such a thing as a white otter. I tried in every conceivable way to get a guide, all without avail; the best I could do was to find an Indian who agreed to take me to a rookery two days' sail down the coast. Quite frankly I hoped to overcome his scruples during this trip, and by a large bribe prevail upon him to lead me into the very heart of the Everglades.

"A rookery, painter-man, is where one species or several species of birds nest together in communities. The one I sought was of both long and short whites, referring to the lesser and snowy egret, the plumes of which during breeding-time were once worth far more than their weight in gold. Now, thank Heaven, their sale is prohibited, largely due to the splendid work of Dr. A. D. Hornaday, and rookeries, no longer shot up as they were in the old days, show an actual increase in all species.

"My guide was addicted to liquor, a weakness that might have been the means of furnishing me with some information had he not confined his remarks entirely to the Seminole tongue after the fifth drink. He proved, however, a competent man.

"I chartered a small sloop with a crew of two 'conches'—so the local coasting sailors are called—and dropped down the coast. Inside a long key the guide and I embarked in a small, light boat I had brought along for the purpose, rowed to the mouth of a small creek, and commenced our real journey.

"This was not in the Everglades proper, painter-man, but a coastal swamp. The tiny creek we followed was of brackish water and quite deep, though narrow. Sea fish had penetrated far up in search of food, and the waters fairly teemed with marine life of every description. Silvery mullet actually jumped into our boat on three occasions, and we grounded on a great drumfish whose hulk all but blocked the channel.

"There were moccasins galore, and birds beyond counting. It was evidently some time since a boat had passed that way, and the quick-growing vegetation had nearly closed our passage. Constant labor alone with ax and knife cleared our path, so it was only at evening we reached the rookery, too tired to even look for a dry place to sleep. From the boat, while the light lasted, we watched the birds returning to their nests in the cypress trees and mangrove bushes, egrets, blue and green herons, snaky-necked water turkeys. When it was too dark to see, we withdrew a short distance and ate our evening meal. One thing struck me as rather odd: The birds did not seem as tame as might have been expected after a long period of non-molestation, and were continually bopping nervously to the end of the branches, and even bursting into a snowflake flight that was like the explosion of silver bombs.

"At daybreak we were suddenly startled from sleep. The birds were all gone, and hardly had we realized that it was the report of a gun that had wakened us when our nerves were shattered by two cries of frightful agony. I yanked away the painter that tied us to a cypress tree, seized one oar, the guide the other, and we pulled toward the sound.

"Beyond the trees of the rookery a small island of scrub palmetto came into view, and lying on the edge of the water was an old Indian, a younger man bending over him and hastily tying a cord around his bared leg. As our boat slid onto the mucky land the trunk of a five-foot diamondback rattler, its head shot away, was thrashing among the palmetto leaves.

"The younger Indian never looked up from his task; he was now cutting deeply across two fang-marks in the elder's calf, and I noticed his own shoulder visibly swelling.

"Science, painter-man, has provided an antidote even against the supposedly deadly venom of the rattlesnake, and I labored over both men with the anti-venomous serum we owe to Calmette of the Pasteur Institute, and with hypodermic injections of strychnin, and washed the opened wounds with the wine-colored precipitate of permanganate of potash crystals. It soon became evident that the younger Indian would survive—the poison of *Crotalus* seldom proves fatal if the victim is carried through the first hour—but the older man's recovery for a time seemed very doubtful.

"I fought for his life as I have never fought before, and finally the tide turned in his favor. We were then confronted with the problem of getting the patients back to the sloop. Our own boat was too small for more than, three men, but we unearthed a rude dugout for the younger and towed it behind. It was something of a task, and once it turned over and I had to splash around in six feet of water in close proximity to a shark while rescuing the Indian boy. On the sloop we were able to make them both comfortable and hoisted sail for Miami.

"During all this time I hadn't said a word to either of the Seminoles and they had been equally reticent. However, when we were well underway I extracted their story in brief form. Father and son, they had been after sharp-nosed alligators, which is the American crocodile, a sinister, slim, gray-green saurian with black blotches. They had penetrated by an inside channel to the rookery, landed on the scrub-palmetto island, and had slept there that night.

"In the morning the elder man had stepped on the snake, whose rattles had been broken off so it could give no warning, and had been struck. The younger shot off the head, tripped, fell on it, and the fangs entered his shoulder—proving for the hundredth time that a rattlesnake head will bite even when separated from the body.

"By a fortunate coincidence the son was no other than the Osceola I sought. Money, I had found, was of no avail in providing a guide for my quest, gratitude might—and it did. They said no word of thanks until we reached Miami, and then the old man spoke:

"My years are many, and it would not have mattered greatly had I died, but my son is young, and life still is sweet to him. You may ask him what you wish; he is your slave till both our debts of life are paid."

"I know savages, painter-man, and I made no pretense of the ha-ha-it-is-nothing attitude with which so-called civilized people meet even real gratitude, but answered simply: 'I shall ask him much.'

"Osceola seemed to have entirely thrown off the effects of the snake-bite, but his father fared badly. There were signs of gangrene in the wound and his vitality was very low. I thought it best to leave him in a hospital, and he was too weak to make any serious objection. Then I had my interview with Osceola.

"'I am a friend of your people,' I said, 'but they do not trust me. I wish to go into the Everglades to the place where the white otter is, and look upon it. I ask you to guide me.'

"The aboriginal savage, Mr. Painter-Man, may have had a stoical control of his features, but this Seminole Indian certainly did not. Surprise, fear, anger and even horror chased themselves across his face, all to be replaced by a look of bitter resignation.

"'The white otter, *hokatee osana*, the white Otter! I wish *chitkolalagochee* (the rattlesnake) had struck my heart,' he answered, 'rather than I should do this—but, alas, my father has spoken for me.'

"I have never felt anything more intense in my whole life than the hate of that tall, young, good-looking Seminole in the days that followed. It simply radiated from him. He made me feel as though I were about to commit some awful desecration, for there was plainly mystery, the secret of which he believed I shared.

"Nevertheless he made his preparations, and even went so far as to suggest, since it was evidently a law of the Seminoles that no white man should penetrate into their fastnesses, that I stain my skin.

"One early morning found me, dyed from head to foot, paddling up the Miami River, and outlet of the Everglades. We soon turned from the open water, and when the saw-grass finally closed over our heads I doubt very much if many men would have envied me. I was going into a land, or rather into a lake, that had never been really explored, in company with a savage who plainly hated and abhorred me from the bottom of his soul.

"It was hot, hot, hot! The edges of the saw-grass cut at the slightest touch—but before me there was always the thought of the white otter!"

Van's eyes glowed fanatically. I could not help thinking that the Indian was not the only savage on that expedition. Surely there is nothing more ruthless than a scientist once he has a definite object to attain!

The white raccoon, to which I was now quite accustomed, curled up between my neck and the back of the chair. Van's low voice took up the tale.

"That day we paddled from early morning until sunset, sometimes along winding channels which were broad and flowing with clear water, but more often through the cruel, cutting saw-grass that parted in the mere shadow of a trail. Often we dragged the dugout along limestone or mud bottoms, and there was never, the long hours through, one word from my companion. At last, as the birds were flying to their roosts, and their evening chorus mingled with the insistent croaking of the frogs, we landed on a small island and pulled up our boat. By a lucky shot I neatly decapitated a Florida wild turkey from a live-oak, and elicited the first sound from my mute Seminole, a guttural 'good.'

"I sha'n't easily forget that night. No sooner were the stars out, and my eyes just closing than there sounded from the shores of our islet the bull-like roar of an alligator, to be answered by another saurian in the distance. All night the limpkins yelled—how birds of their size can make such an awful sound is quite beyond me—and the frogs croaked in seventeen different keys, quite unlike any frogs I had ever heard before.

"I slept little, and toward morning, when my eyes had finally closed in the real rest sleep that every outdoors man knows, I woke suddenly to a frightful, nauseous smell. Turning on my side in the direction of the offensive odor, a luminous mass met my eyes. A huge rattler, its scales shining as though with phosphorus, was piled against the body of the Indian, a raised, triangular head, broad as my two hands, weaving nervously back and forth above its coils. At that very moment the dawn broke, Osceola moved, and the reptile whirred warningly.

"'Keep still,' I whispered sharply, and rolled sidewise from my rubber blanket. A shotgun was beneath my hands and I snatched it up, tempted the snake to strike with a stick, and blew it in two pieces just below the neck. It was fully eight feet long, and it shone with foxfire. Unlike any other member of its family I had ever seen, the stripes ran longitudinally.

"Osceola lay tense and motionless, eyes wide open, staring up into mine as I bent over him. Even when I dashed water in his face he came slowly from his trance. To my insistent demands as to whether he had been struck, he simply shook his head and went dazedly about the preparations for breakfast and departure. I noticed that his eyes followed me continually, however, as I was skinning the snake, and their look of implacable hate had been replaced by a dumb, dog-like wonder.

"That morning our trail led entirely through the saw-grass with no open channel. It was unbearably hot, and we both labored like galley slaves with paddle and pole. Suddenly Osceola broke into feverish talk, and, with his eyes shifting back and forth from mine to the snake skin I had tacked inside the gunwale of the boat to dry, told me the legends of the All-Soul.

"Long, long ago, even before the time of the great chief Osceola, whose name my young Seminole bore, there was but one soul to all the Indians of the Everglades, so no one did wrong, since the punishment must fall on all. *Ollahaw* (the orange), and *shottaw* (the persimmon), were their sole food, and they dwelt in friendship with every bird, beast, and reptile. Came a great wind with darkness, rain, and thunder, and when it had passed, *holwagus* (badness) was among them.

"To one man he said: 'Why do you eat only *ollahaw* and *shottaw* when the flesh of *woodko* (the raccoon) is so much better?

"So the man slew *woodko* and ate his flesh, and so great was the power of *holwagus* for evil that the flesh tasted good to the man, and his descendants ever after ate of *woodko*. And some *holwagus* tempted to eat the flesh of *chofee* (the rabbit), others *foakee* (the quail), others *hilolo* (the curlew), until all the Seminoles were corrupted save one alone, a maiden.

"And the All-Soul left the Seminoles, taking refuge in her as the only good left among them. The beasts, in horror, hid themselves, save *lakosee* (the bear), *kowatgochee* (the wildcat), and *katsa* (the panther), and they grew claws and teeth for defense, or even attack.

"Then the Seminoles spoke among themselves, saying: 'Let us kill this maiden who will not eat flesh, and the All-Soul will be shared among us again and we shall be happy.' But *holwagus* heard them and gave poison fangs to *chitkolalagochee* (the rattlesnake), making him a guardian of the maiden, because he did not wish her to be killed and take the All-Soul out of the world, but to become bad like the rest of the Seminoles. Man, bird, and beast feared his fangs. All except *holwagus*.

"But the maiden hid in the bodies of animals, going from one to another, until *holwagus* gave up looking for her and went away. He warned, however, that he would come again and steal the All-Soul.

"Osceola watched me very sharply during the last part of this recital, and then, lowering his eyes before mine, complained of his shoulder. I stripped away the shirt to find it badly swollen, and, for a moment, feared that the fangs of the striped rattler might, after all, have touched him. There was no new wound, however, and I put the swelling down to auto-suggestion till my own theory so worked on my imagination that I peeled the snake skin from its place and hid it under my rubber blanket.

"The swelling did not increase, but the fever grew on him until, directing me to steer by a cypress that was the only landmark discernible above the sea of saw-grass, he lay down in the bottom of the dugout and promptly lapsed into delirium.

"I pushed steadily on, far from tranquil in mind. The cypress was only visible above the saw-grass when I balanced perilously on the edge of the rude craft. Suppose I should lose sight of it and

Osceola should die? I should be as hopelessly lost as a compassless mariner in the middle of the Atlantic Ocean.

"However, the cypress began to stand out more clearly, and about two o'clock I was suddenly out of the grass. What a picture was spread before my eyes! First came a hundred yards of open water dotted with the brilliantly colored Everglade ducks and ringed by breaking fish. Then, like a green ribbon heavily embossed in silver and gold, a broad band of water-lilies in full bloom girdled an island—an island that fairly smiled with sunlight, happiness, and peace.

"A grove of lemon and orange trees, pollarded so as to rise little above the level of the saw-grass, had shaded out all undergrowth from the clean, gray soil. To the left spread an orderly vegetable garden behind which crouched a low house weather-beaten to silvery gray and surrounded by a multitude of brilliant flowers. Osceola mustered his strength for one look, rose on his elbow, murmured *poyafitsa* (heaven), and fell back unconscious. I paddled to the shore and pulled up the dugout as a very old Indian came from the house to meet me.

"'He is very sick,' I said, pointing to Osceola; 'we must get him out of the sun immediately.'

"The meaning of the words were plainly unintelligible to the old man, but he understood my gesture. Between us we picked up the fever-stricken boy and carried him to the house, where a couch of fragrant rushes received his burning body.

"For two days, painter-man, I listened to the ravings, half in Seminole, half in English, of that savage, and pity grew and grew in my heart as I fought for his life. The old Indian was a quiet and competent assistant. I was vaguely conscious of another presence in the house, that of a woman, but I was far too busy to even glance at her.

"On the third day the fever broke, thanks to a concoction of herbs the old man brought me which I tried in desperation, and my patient sank into a natural sleep. Wearily making sure that he needed no more attention for the present, I twisted into a blanket, shut my eyes, and immediately fell through unlimited space. While the clock went twice round I slept without waking, save when some-one held a cool drink of orange juice to my lips.

"My eyes finally opened to a perfect day. The scent of orange blossoms was in the air and a mocking-bird was trilling from a magnolia outside the window. I looked anxiously over at my patient to find him awake and staring at me.

"'You all right?' I asked.

"'All right;' he grunted morosely.

"'We'll see that white otter soon, then,' I suggested cheerfully.

"For answer he raised his voice and called, 'Ocola! Ocola!' and the old man slipped silently into the room. They spoke rapidly together in the Seminole tongue, and then Ocala disappeared to return in a few moments leading an Indian girl.

"There is Hokatee Osana, the white otter,' said Osceola, turning his face to the wall with a groan.

"In my whole life I have never looked on so proud a creature! She stood poised like a butterfly ready for in flight, her eyes blazing at me, full of hate and fear. She was too small and her features too Seminole to be beautiful, but her hair, showing unmistakable traces of white blood in its brown waviness, was very lovely. Her greatest and most wonderful charm was a birdlike alertness, the lightness of thistle-down, a vitality, quick a sunshine.

"I gazed at her, my mouth wide open, I fear, and her eyes finally tore away from mine and sought the figure on the couch, With the change that came over her face as she looked on Osceola the whole situation became suddenly clear to me. I understood the Indian youth's hate, his bitter sacrifice in guiding me to his treasure, grasped the significance of the legend, and the reason it had been told.

"'Osceola,' I said sternly, 'it is not a woman with a red skin to whom I asked you to guide me; it is to an otter, a real otter, and white. You have deceived me and your father, whose life, as well as your own, belongs to me.'

"'The animal otter is here,' he answered humbly; 'but it is only a shadow; Its soul is in Hokatee Osana, and she is therefore the white otter.'

"'It is not a soul I seek,' I answered angrily; 'it is a skin, a white skin.'

"The old Indian broke in excitedly with a stream of words.

"Osceola translated.

"'He says, "Lord, if you take the skin of the real otter, Hokatee Osana dies. Will nothing else please you?" He offers what all white men desire—for he knows you are a white man.'

"I wanted time to think. Of course I was going to have my white otter, but I have a fundamental objection to offending the religious beliefs of primitive peoples, and, besides, I know there is something in auto-suggestion—the girl *might* die!

"'Show me what gifts you can offer equal to these,' I said scornfully, spilling a pound or two of beads (I received your kindly letter concerning them) on the floor. The girl gave a covetous glance at my offering—she was certainly femininely primitive—the old Indian never even glanced in their direction, but beckoned me to follow him.

"Out in the sunshine we went through the orange-grove toward the sound of running waters, and Osceola, stopping near the signal cypress, drew back and pointed.

"What has been bred in us for centuries, painter-man, cannot be eliminated in a moment, and I was conscious of a thrill of covetousness at what was spread before my eyes. The ground was strewn with scores of small chests, some entirely rotted away, some partially whole, and from every one cascaded a stream of gold pieces that blinked dully in the sun. Doubloons, pieces of eight, English guineas, French pistoles, strange octagonal slabs of gold from India and the Orient lay untouched beneath the cypress-tree since the day when their last buccaneer owner had abandoned them.

"I stepped closer and with my foot stirred a mass of metal to that silky rustling that weaves a spell through the rooms of Monte Carlo's gambling palace, and gradually the lust of desire left my blood.

"'What is this foolishness?' I shouted angrily, unmindful that the old Seminole could not understand; 'I don't want this trash! Show me the real white otter—*hokatee osana*, hokatee *osana!*'

"He included all the scattered chests in a sweep of his arm and then swung his hands, palms upward, to me in a gesture of offering.

"'No, no,' I refused, '*hokatee osana.*'

"Again he went through the dumb ceremony of endowing me with all this strangely stored wealth, and again I shook my head and insistently reiterated my request. Suddenly his expression changed from pleading to fury, and snatching a knife from beneath his garments, he flung himself upon me. An old man, it was an easy matter to send the weapon from his hand to the ground, where it fell with the tinkle of metal against metal.

"Unsubdued, he still defied me with his eyes, and our glances locked. '*Hokatee osana,*' I demanded fiercely again and again, and at last the spirit broke within him. Slowly he turned and I followed his faltering footsteps across a carpet of gold toward the cypress whence came the sound of running water. A stream gushed from the wide-spread roots of the tree, and, as we looked, a white form slipped from beneath and came toward us. It was an otter, painter-man, an otter, white as snow, with two eyes of red fire—an un-earthly, beautiful thing, wonderful— Well, look for yourself!"

Van rose, and, switching on more light, stripped away a sheet from a cabinet in the corner of the room.

In the foreground, posed on a tongue of strange gold coins mixed with sand, stood a creature so wonderfully mounted that it seemed alive.

"Van," I cried reproachfully, "you didn't kill that lovely thing! I can understand the slaughter of gorillas and toucans and—animals; but you *could not* have killed that silver spirit!"

"As a matter of fact, I didn't," he confessed. "Perhaps I shouldn't have killed it, and then again it is quite possible that I should," he added honestly. "You see it is a perfect type of albinoism. The matter was taken out of my hands, however. As it came toward the spot where the old Indian and I stood among the rotted chests, it paused every few steps to gaze at me curiously but entirely without fear from its ruby eyes.

"A spit of heaped gold ran down from us and as its feet touched the first coins something sinuous, deadly, fulvous so as to be nearly indistinguishable from the yellow background, lay in its path. There was a sinister buzz as of some great locust, and I sprang forward shouting. The otter turned quicker than light, but the lash of the rattler's head was a lightning flash—and the beautiful thing was dead when I picked it up."

There was a long silence. Van was gazing musingly into the cabinet.

"Are its eyes genuine rubies?" I asked him.

"Only things I could get to match the real ones," he answered.

"Did the Indian girl die?"

"No."

"What happened to you?"

"I came home."

"See here, Van," I exclaimed angrily, "it's all very well for you to escape alone from places it is impossible to escape from, but you have, in a way, taken me along, and I want to know how you did it? What happened to you next? How did it all end?"

Van's eyes were on the white otter and he murmured absent-mindedly before answering me, "*Lutra canadensis vaga, varietas alba.*

"Where was I?" began Van anew. "Oh, yes!

"Well, I skinned the otter and preserved the pelt with the arsenic you were so glad to send me and began to think of getting home. The situation on the island offered an easy solution for anyone with a grain of imagination. The last rattlesnake incident firmly established my disreputable divine origin, and I simply proclaimed my godhead as a reformed and satisfied *holwagus*, and carried matters off with a high hand. My first decree was that Hokatee Osana—the girl—and Osceola should marry, and I performed the ceremony myself."

"What!" I gasped in astonishment. "How did you do it?"

"Oh, Jabberwocky served my purpose perfectly. The line 'and shun the frumious bandersnatch,' particularly impressed 'em. The rest of my beads I bestowed on the bride and gave the bridegroom my shotgun. Then I asked how I was to get back to Miami.

"It was quite evident that I should have to make the trip by myself, because neither of the men would have dared to trust himself alone with me.

"After a great deal of hesitation Osceola finally confided that by keeping the great cypress in line with a tall, yellow pine barely discernible in the distance, I would strike a deep channel which led, though by twice as long a route as we had come, to the Miami River.

"Next day I found this channel, and only just in time to keep from getting hopelessly lost. They must have begun cutting down the cypress the moment I left, for I saw it fall myself from miles away. No human being save a Seminole can ever again find Poyafitsa Island. The rest of my journey was plain sailing, or rather paddling."

I always make some idiotic remark after hearing Van's latest adventure. It invariably leaves my mind in such a hopeless whirl.

"Didn't you get bitten by rattlesnakes, or frogs, or have to eat curlews or—or raccoons?" I asked.

The animal against my shoulder woke suddenly and bit me severely on the back of the neck.

THE WHITE GORILLA
ELMER BROWN MASON
1915

For eight months no word came from my friend Van Dam.

Those of us in his debt virtuously assured ourselves that we had intended to pay him back at once, and tried to bear up; others who wished to borrow were naturally somewhat resentful at his absence. As usual, he had given no intimation of his flitting, and all who called at his digging—so he designated the enormous top-story apartment where he dwelt among his countless trophies and collections—were met by the always smiling Jap with the information, "Mr. Van Dam, he will be back—oh, quite soon some day."

This same phrase had excused a two years' disappearance of his master in the interior of Borneo. Gradually we ceased to think of him, and each little life traveled around its own restricted orbit as though the absentee had ceased to exist.

My own affairs were going rather well and orders simply poured in. This halcyon state was due to a Hercules, for which Van had provided me with an extraordinary model, and a Pittsburgh millionaire bought because it was the image of a fellow steel worker he had known in his undollared youth.

These orders, however, were entirely for portraits, which I do not like doing—my forte is large allegorical canvases, though Van thinks differently—but never having had any money, I developed an appetite for it and painted all who paid. My most lucrative commission had just come to me, a portrait for a political club, of one of its most prominent—and worst—members, and it was giving me

43

a great deal of trouble. To begin with, the man would not sit more than fifteen minutes at a time, and his face was simply horrible.

I painted it first, nearly from memory, in all its brutal reality of low forehead, eyes set far back, and enormous jaw development—a positively bestial thing. And it looked not the slightest like the original.

Then I conceived the idea that a soul was shining through this fleshy mask and put the light of holiness in the eyes, the curve of renunciation at the corner of the lips. When my man called, his own face made its painted counterpart look like the delineation of some kindly saint. That day I devoted myself solely to the hands—veritable Gargantuan paws they were—and after he had left, very discouraged, started to scrape and turn the face. Just as I had eliminated all but chin and forehead the phone rang.

"Hello!" I said crisply into the transmitter with the intonation I have adopted since I consider myself a successful artist.

"Come to dinner, painter-man," drawled Van's voice over the wire. "I have something to show you."

"I'm very busy," I answered loftily, "but I'll try to manage it if you'll tell me beforehand what we are eating."

Van has one idiosyncrasy that is positively ghastly. He is always cooking the most awful, uncivilized dishes concealed in such delectable sauces that you can't help liking them till you find out what they are. At his table I have eaten a lizard creature tasting exactly like delicate chicken, and a savory dish of what appeared to be roasted oysters and was really the larvae of the black palm weevil.

"What are you busy with?" came over the wire. "If it's a Vulcan, I have a good model for you."

"I'm trying to paint a baboon," I snapped, "and no model will do."

"Surprising," he answered in really animated tones. "I can furnish you with a gorilla, and I have a young cannibal here to go with it."

"Am I to act as a meal for your guests?" I began, but he had hung up.

Van and I dined luxuriously on what I took to be very young lamb and afterward adjourned to the den, on the walls of which are ranged the cases containing his albino collection; the traditional white blackbird, the enormous, glittering, white toucan, the snowy raccoon, the white panther, and that last acquisition in a huge case by itself. There was a roaring wood fire, and before it, partially covered by a snow-leopard's skin, twitched, while he slept, the coffee-colored slim cannibal boy. Once he reached up a long, bare foot and scratched his ear exactly as a dog attends to a flea.

There was a livid, five-inch scar on Van's cheek, and while he talked the blood would pulse to its top, run down underneath the skin, and disappear exactly as an electric advertising sign lights and flashes out.

"Of course you know, painter-man," he began, "that I am in touch with people throughout the world whom I pay to keep their eyes open for the albino phase in animals and birds. The mail daily brings me offers of specimens or word where they may be procured, but, for the most part, they are of species I already have or else out-and-out fakes—I have been offered scores of white elephants. You see, among savages, the abnormal in nature is very often an object of direct worship.

"Contrary to our ideas of religion, the untutored savage has the delicacy not to inflict his beliefs on strangers, and does not, so to speak, wear his god on his sleeve. It is, therefore, hard to get reliable information regarding animals that are white when they normally should be quite a different color.

"It was, as a matter of fact, the very indefinitiveness of the data that sent me on this last expedition. From Libreville, in the French Congo, an Englishman wrote me it was common talk among the Mpangwe, who had recently been driven out of the region at the headquarters of the Gabun River, that their conquerors worshiped and sacrificed to a white woman who walked on her knees and elbows and was covered with long hair. A Dutch trader sent word from Booue that the Fan tribe of cannibals had an old, old man for chief who walked on all fours and was fed entirely on human flesh. A French rubber exploiter in the Sierra de Crystal told one of my agents that there was a large, white monkey in the Ogowé division of the Fan cannibals which was held sacred and accompanied them to war.

"The very meagerness of this information and the improbability of collusion between its widely separated sources gave me something on which to theorize, and I sailed for Libreville. The building of my theory was simplicity itself. The third informant had distinctly stated that the creature was a white monkey. Monkeys are regarded by many tribes in Africa as only slightly modified human beings.

"The final link in my reasoning came from the statement that it walked on its elbows and knees. The gorilla walks, or rather swings itself along, on the backs of its hands—and often turns the toes of its feet under. In short, I hoped for an albino gorilla, and my theory was strengthened by the knowledge that gorillas, when caught young, are docile and easily tamed, in spite of the unquestioned ferocity of the wild, old males. As a matter of fact, we know little more about this largest of all primates than has been vouched us from the fertile imagination of Paul de Chaillu.

"There are current, in Africa, tales of men snatched from the ground to die a horrible death in the tree-tops; of an African tribe that kept a huge, old male for executioner until it was killed by an Englishman about to be sacrificed, who noticed a swelling over its heart and struck it in this vulnerable spot. At any rate, I had never seen a gorilla in the wild state, and the adventure promised many thrills.

"From Libreville I made a short expedition among the Mpangwe whom the more warlike Fans had driven from the interior. Savages, I have found, Mr. Painter-man, belong to two categories; those that are honest, trust-worthy, and truthful, and those that are the exact opposite.

"The Mpangwe belong to the latter class. They were the worst liars I have ever met, and told me only what they thought I wanted to hear. The hairy woman was endowed with wings and made to lay eggs that hatched into serpents, and when they found it was a monkey I was after, they agreed to a man that she always assumed that form at night.

"There was nothing to be learned from these swindling, natives, and I made up my mind to follow rumor to its source and go up the

Gabun River into the gorilla country where dwelt the Ogowé Fans. The local French government, not without a warning against its unsettled state and the absolute lack of positive knowledge of the region into which I proposed to penetrate, finally gave me a permit for a scientific exploring expedition.

"They even went further and provided me with a guard of twenty soldiers—so, you see, I traveled rather *en prince*—and helped to collect the rather large caravan which I required.

"A trip of this nature to one who has been through the same kind of thing before, contrary to the general idea of you city dwellers, is remarkable only for the length of time it takes to reach a given point. There was, of course, the usual revolt of the porters for higher pay, which had to be summarily quelled; the leopard that blundered into my tent-ropes one night, and the killing of a man by a wounded buffalo; also an ill-advised attempt to assassinate me. These are only the incidents one expects in jungle travel, however, and, on the whole, it was rather a dull journey, and a very hot one.

"As we neared our destination the country became rugged with open but shady and damp forests, and there were interminable thickets of scitamines and tree-ferns, on the fruits of which the gorilla feeds. All along the route I made guarded inquiries about my quest, and, from what I could *not* learn, fully made up my mind that a white gorilla, or at least some extraordinary animal, its existence well known to the natives, was in possession of the Fans. I came to this conclusion because every approach to the subject, no matter how indirect, instantly inspired fear, and those interrogated either became dumb or lied wildly.

"One day's journey from our destination I sent ahead runners with gifts to the sorcer (so is designated the local priest) and to the chief. Of course word of my coming had long ago preceded me, and, partially through curiosity, partially through respect for my guard and my large caravan, they sent back friendly messages.

"The next evening, to the monotonous beat of tom-toms, I pitched camp on the edge of the valley in which dwelt the Ogowé

Fans. These savages were quite different from any I had met in Africa. They were not black, but coffee-colored, well made, with thin lips, intelligent faces, and were tall and, according to our standards, excessively slim.

"Best of all, their language was a slight variation of the great Bantu tongue, as spoken by the Zulu Kafirs, and with which I am thoroughly familiar. The women, who were quite handsome, worked in the manioc-fields, while the existence of the men was made up of war and hunting. To a high degree they were both truthful and honorable.

"Savages love ceremony, and our mutual greetings took up all of three days, on the last of which there was a feast with wild dances and much palm-wine. I was not at all sure of the bill of fare, and, in order to be on the safe side, pretexed a vow of fasting, an expiatory rite which they practice, and so understood. My role was that of a sorcer who had come to study their birds and beasts, but most to consort with my brother priests to our mutual advantage, and I was accepted at my own valuation.

"A liberal gift insured me the privilege of dwelling in their country as long as I pleased, and so well did I get on with my hosts that finally, with the chief, I went through that not unpoetic ceremony of mysterious origin which they call blood-brotherhood. This practical adoption into the tribe so reassured me as to my safety that I sent back my guard of soldiers, much to their horror, and in spite of their protestations, and with them the greater part of my porters, retaining only a few in whom I had implicit confidence.

"I've lived with savages before, Mr. Painter-man, and I must say there is no pleasanter or easier life. To a very great extent every man does exactly as he pleases. Food is the only real necessity, and is largely furnished by the labor of the women.

"Moral and ethical considerations are never personal, but the affair of the high priest (better called sorcer), and are left entirely in his hands.

"In spite of ideal conditions for happiness, it was distinctly wanting among the Ogowé Fans. There was an undercurrent of dissatisfaction running through the tribe, and an atmosphere of mental discomfort. Quarrels were frequent, and there were several cases of absolute insanity, the victims of which were promptly put to death, tribal law permitting of no mental or physical deficient.

"In my assumed character it was naturally the sorcer that I saw the most of, and we found much in common. As a matter of fact, the priest among savages represents not only the highest mental, but what we must characterize for want of a better definition, as scientific attainments of the race. My confrere of the Ogowé Fans was a shrewd, middle-aged man, leaning toward asceticism, and a real fanatic in his beliefs.

"He had one daughter, and if one can imagine such a thing as a soft, brown rose glowing in the tropical jungle you will have a fairly accurate picture of her. The Fan faith was a kind of Pan-deism with just a dash of sun worship, interwoven with superstition, its manifestation interpreted by the sorcer from the actions of various sacred animals. There was also an additional and very unusual way of learning the wishes of their deity.

"The priest was master of a crude but nonetheless effective form of hypnotism, which he practiced on members of the tribe, but principally on his daughter. Through her, while she was 'possessed of the spirit,' otherwise in a cataleptic state, he unconsciously impressed his own will on the tribe.

"I give him absolute credit for attributing divine origin to the words that she uttered, which made him only the more determined in his purposes, in the same way that a man with an honest belief is much more likely to be successful than one who must admit in his own heart that he is a faker.

"The girl was so completely under his mental control that a few moments' gazing into a large crystal, which had been roughly rounded and held a thousand lights, made her mind blank and instantly receptive of any impression from him. This crystal was a very sacred thing, and it was the duty of a different warrior each day to rub at the inequalities with fine sand with the purpose of finally bringing it to a perfect roundness.

"The sorcer was enough of a man of the world to appreciate the awe he might inspire by means of a few chemicals I gave him and the—to savages—startling tricks I was able to teach him. As a matter of fact, he ruled these frankly cannibal warriors through fear alone, and so great was his mental dominance that, at times, it seemed to me, he held half the tribe in a semi-hypnotic state. There was a bitter feud between him and the temporal chief.

"The latter wished to move on to new conquests; the priest held firm that they remain where they were for a year until expiation had been made by endless religious ceremonies for the 'blinding of the eyes of piety,' a phrase which meant nothing to me then, but which I now understand.

"I was, of course, more or less affiliated with the chief, since, with him, I had gone through the blood-brotherhood rite, but my closest friend was his son. He was a youth of some twenty summers, and the most marvelous hunter and tracker I have ever known. Ikstu—that is as near as I can Anglicize his name—accompanied me on all my collecting expeditions, and what was of the greatest importance, since I was supposed to know them instinctively, told me the birds and animals that were sacred and not to be molested.

"Chief among those tabu were the gorillas, and they throve and were quite unafraid under such treatment, though naturally retiring beasts. In the manioc-fields, which the women cultivated, toward evening I have literally seen dozens of them. The males would wander out from the jungle with their two or three mates and family, or sometimes I would come upon a solitary old bachelor, grayish-white and, a very dangerous animal to approach.

"Some would run away, screaming with fright, in a tryingly human manner, but there was one old fellow who never gave a step until I myself retired.

"He was fully six feet tall when standing braced against a tree-trunk, his hands hanging below his knees, the hair on his neck and head erect with rage, and the ruff under his chin quivering. Two great canine teeth protruded from each side of his snarling mouth, and beneath their enormous protuberances his little eyes blazed red in his coal-black face. I learned to hate that animal, and, as he hopped away on all fours, his legs swinging out beyond his arms, I longed to turn and put an explosive bullet in him.

"Policy, that was even a question of personal safety, held me in check, however, and I wisely refrained. Ikstu, who feared nothing else in the world, was deadly afraid of these old males, but, even more than he feared them, he hated the sorcer.

"As we became better acquainted and I gained his confidence, the reason for this was apparent. I noticed that on several occasions we found two purple orchids, their stems crossed, lying in the narrow trails through the scitamines thickets, and each time this sign appeared I lost my companion for the rest of the day. The connection was obvious.

"The daughter of the sorcer-priest always wore these orchids in her hair and as a garland—in fact, they formed by far the greater part of her wardrobe.

"Always, however, she was back from these love rambles at her father's hut before sunset, and, after he had made her gaze for a few moments into the sacred crystal, she would hurry off into the jungle with a basket of manioc and fruit of the scitamines on her arm. You may well believe I was curious in regard to these expeditions, but I kept this curiosity to myself. Once I tried to pick up her trail in the morning, and was very nearly impaled in a leopard-trap. That afternoon I received a warning from the sorcer of the presence of a very sacred and awful spirit in the direction I had gone.

"My excuse for lingering in the neighborhood was wearing thin, and the priest was beginning to look on me with unconcealed suspicion. Meantime, there was no hint of what I sought, and the whole tribe was humming with an undercurrent of politics that would have done credit to Tammany Hall during election.

"My time had not been entirely wasted, however, for I had the skin of an albino thrush (it proved new to science), and also a large, white spider of the trap-door variety, the first absolute case of albinoism I had ever found among the *Arachnida*. My camp was ready to be abandoned and my porters to travel, and I made up my mind to start for the coast the moment I had solved the problem of the girl's nightly trip.

The crisis came sooner than I expected. In spite of the objections of the spiritual power, the chief made a raid toward the sea and returned with heavy spoil and ten captives. There was much rejoicing in the tribe, though the sorcer was very angry, and the captives were closely guarded and well fed, so that their ultimate, gruesome disposal was only too obvious. The war party gained in strength, and it was decided the matter of moving on to new conquests be finally decided at the Feast of the Gorillas, when the moon was full.

"My position was now not only very uncomfortable, but positively dangerous, and I kept exclusively to my own camp, my only connection with the Fan village being through Ikstu. Time hanging heavy on my hands, I hit on an expedient that I should have thought of long before.

"Through a pair of powerful field-glasses I spied the girl's route each evening until I finally traced her down to her destination, a rocky amphitheater hardly a mile distant from the village.

"That night darkness came so quickly I could not see what she did, but the next evening the secret of her expeditions and, at the same time, the end of my quest were revealed to me. From the crotch of a great rubber tree I watched her set down her basket and, swaying slightly as people do in the cataleptic state, raised her arms above her orchid-crowned head evidently calling. Twice she did this, and then, from a cleft in the rocks, an unbelievable object swung slowly out to meet her.

"Never have I seen so beautiful and so repulsive an animal. It was an enormous female gorilla with fur long and white as that of an Angora goat. Even in a crouched position, practically on all fours, its jet-black face was above the girl on whom it looked down from eyes that seemed, through my field-glasses, milk white.

"One mighty arm rose and rested on the girl, the other groping in the basket at her feet, and thus the two figures stood while the fruits were crammed into an enormous mouth. Then the girl lifted, with both hands, the great paw from her bare shoulder, and before the quick tropical darkness shut them from my sight, I saw her catch the wreath of purple orchids from her own neck and throw it over the brute's head.

"At camp, with his chest bleeding from a knife wound, I found Ikstu waiting for me. Without giving him time to explain his own errand I told quickly what I had seen. He was in no way astonished, and I doubt even if he heard half I said, so full was he of his own troubles.

"The sorcer had somehow learned of the meetings with his daughter and was keeping her in a continual hypnotic state, so that, quite unconscious of what she was doing or saying, she had actually stabbed him at their last rendezvous and even threatened him with 'the blind eyes of piety.'

"His simple request was that I should take him and the girl away with me after he had killed the sorcer during the coming feast. I consented without the slightest hesitation, bargaining only that he should tell me, in return, all he knew of the white gorilla.

"Gradually, though it was apparent he feared a celestial thunderbolt, I dragged the story from him. The beast, under the care of the sorcer, had been the fetish of the tribe ever since he could remember, and figured in every religious ceremony. At the beginning of the Fans' march toward the coast the gorilla had always gone into battle with them, and, maddened by a great beaker of the potent palm wine, proved a terror to their enemies. Then, to the lasting grief of the sorcer, during a night attack it had lost the sight of both eyes from a firebrand.

"Formerly it had been a docile and friendly animal (when not inflamed by the palm liquor), with the unrestrained freedom of the village, but this accident changed it into a she-devil that dwelt morosely alone and could only be approached by the sorcer's daughter, and that only when under her father's hypnotic influence.

"It's a wild tale, painter-man, and sitting here before the fire one can hardly believe it actually happened. In the jungle, though, with the blackness of the tropical night wrapped around us like velvet ribbons, the squeak of the vampire bats, the far-away roar of a male gorilla, and the cough of a leopard circling the camp, it seemed perfectly natural and fitting for me to be conniving, with a cannibal, at what was nothing but a cold-blooded murder.

"Besides, I wanted the skin of that albino primate, and I was going to have it at any cost. I believed every word of Ikstu's story, even to divine attributes with which he credited the brute and of which I have not told you—you see, I had seen it, and alive."

Van Dam snapped on the electric lights and turned in his chair to face the glass cabinet which contained his latest acquisition. My eyes followed his and I shuddered to the very depths of my city-swaddled soul. The great monkey had been mounted bending slightly forward, its hands swinging between and far below its knees. In its immense paws it held a pear-shaped crystal larger than an ostrich's egg, which caught and imprisoned the light.

Beautiful, long, silky fur, white as silver, clothed the enormously powerful body, and beneath the low forehead, deep in the black face, were set, in lieu of eyes, two round milky-white agates. The mouth was curled back in a fixed grin revealing the broken, yellow, doglike fangs, repulsive beyond belief by contrast with the beauty and power of the rest of the animal.

"Go on, Van," I said, "you couldn't make me disbelieve anything about that thing. For Heaven's sake, out with the lights, though. I don't want to look at it."

The blood showed at the top of the scar on Van Dam's cheek, slithered down its ragged length, and winked out leaving it livid white. He switched off the electric current and we were left again with only the light of the fire.

"I gave Ikstu no advice as to his killing," Van Dam continued, "because I felt that he was quite competent to carry out his private vendetta in his own way. However, since the next evening was to see the beginning of the Feast of the Gorillas, I moved my camp a mile toward the coast and prepared everything for immediate flight. In the afternoon I made Ikstu guide me by a roundabout route, to the very edge of the rocky amphitheater above the beast's den, and ensconced myself, within easy hearing and seeing distance, in the thick top of a scitamines bush.

"Hardly was I comfortably settled when the sorcer and his daughter, both heavily laden with baskets, appeared beneath me.

"I don't think I have ever seen anything more beautiful than the girl. Of actual clothes she wore only a white loin-cloth, but her hair was braided full of the purple orchids and garland on garland of the same flower hung from her neck and covered her lithe, brown body.

"The sorcer was hideously painted in crimson and white and his face was made up to simulate a gorilla, the hair drawn far back and two extra, white eyes daubed on the forehead.

"Immediately the girl, sitting with crossed legs, began to beat a tiny tom-tom, while the sorcer built a, small fire and busied himself with the baskets and three other articles. I recognized them as a leopard skin worn by one of the under chiefs, a mat from a hut, and Ikstu's favorite spear.

"When the fire was going well the girl stood up and called. The third time her voice rose the white gorilla emerged slowly from its den and hesitatingly hopped and swung down to her. Then, before my eyes, took place the most remarkable performance I have witnessed.

"The man cast some herb into the fire and the girl led the animal into the thick, scented smoke. Time and again it broke from her and rushed to its rocky refuge, time and again it came back to her call. Herb after herb, each with a different odor, went into the flames, and gradually the movements of the great beast became slower, lethargic, till it finally stood swaying, its blind agate eyes turned to the sorcer.

"Once the girl faltered and seemed to be awakening from a trance, but her father held the crystal to her eyes till they went blank and she again mechanically did his bidding. Now he transferred the sacred stone to the gorilla's paws and began a chant. The words were not of the Bantu tongue but from some language older than the hills. I don't know what they mean, but I remember the sound, mixed with the beat of the tom-tom, as well as though I were now hearing it.

"Nala (*bong*) Nala (*bong*)
Nala impi (*bong, bong, bong.*)

Nala (*bong*) Nala (*bong*)
Nala impi (*bong, bong, bong.*)
Nala (*bong*) Nala (*bong*)
Nala impi (*bong, bong, bong.*)"

Intoned to the sullen beat of the drum till the world seemed to go to sleep and the brain reach forward for the next repetition.

"The great brute began to move slowly in a swaying dance, keeping time with the rhythm. One by one the girl held the leopard skin, mat and spear against its flat nostrils while, for each separate article, the sorcer pressed a hot coal to the slowly shuffling feet. At every burn the beast reared, and raising the glittering crystal, to which its paws seemed glued, dashed it down on the object before it.

"Extraordinary as was the idea, I recognized at once that, for the usual passes and crystal gazing used in hypnotism, the sorcer had first substituted the scent of herbs and then the chant, and actually held the frightful beast in control by that thin thread of sound.

"Still beating on her tom-tom with measured strokes the voice of the girl took up the mysterious words, and the sorcer grew silent crouched over the fire. Night was coming fast. I slipped from my hiding place as the forest shadows blackened the cliff and silently slid down to the very cleft whence had come the gorilla. There I lay in the darkness peering at the three figures before the fire.

"First one tom-tom, another, a third, till their number seemed countless, awoke in the village. There was a high, shrill scream of agony from far away, then the voice of the whole tribe raised in a great chorus, the words growing distinguishable as they grew nearer.

"In English they would go like this:

"The sun, oh, the sun, from the rising of the sun.
We go through the jungle aisles until the moon is high.
There's blood within our footsteps, and every warrior one
Lifts up a limp, dead body unto the bleeding sky.

"Always before goes the white one.
   (Piety, Piety thou!)
Leads us in the path of the sun.
   (Piety, Piety thou!)
Judge at the feast when the red blood runs free
Leading the Fans to hot, cruel victory,
We come for thy judgment, again come to thee.
   (Piety, Piety thou!)

"Meanwhile, under the roar of voices the girl sang her monotonous strain and beat her tiny drum.

"The whole tribe defiled into the amphitheater, chiefs first with the leopard skins, which they alone are privileged to wear—a custom that links them with the Zulus—then the warriors with the prisoners in their midst, now significantly reduced to nine, and last the women and children.

"These bore fagots which they piled in the center and a large fire was soon blazing. The ceremonies began, to the music of the inevitable tom-toms, with a furious dance by the warriors.

"It was a wild scene, the nearly naked savages brandishing their spears and whirling around the fire; the prisoners conscious of the horrible fate awaiting them, cowering in the background; the crouching figures of the great, white gorilla, the hideously painted sorcer, and the exquisite brown girl intoning her endless chant.

"As a proper stage setting the heavens began to grumble, lightning flashed across the sky, and a few, big, hot drops of rain fell.

"The dance and the tom-toms ceased with such startling suddenness that the voice of the girl cut sharp as a knife through the murmur of the multitude. The priest faced the great white brute and spoke:

"'Piety, against whom the Ogowé Fans have sinned, before we ask thy judgment for the tribe; select from us in expiation. Let the sacred crystal gleam red in thy honor.'

"He raised a close-woven basket full of palm wine to its nostrils, and, while it still held the crystal pendant in its paws, tipped it till it was drained of the last drop.

"For a moment the white gorilla staggered, then hopping forward balanced at its full height before the chief. While the girl's song and the beat of the tiny drum alone broke the silence, it circled to the right, bent with distended nostrils above the chief whose leopard skin was in the sorcer's possession, and, quicker than I can tell it, the great paws rose and the, crystal came crashing down on the doomed man's skull. Resolved to end the scene then and there, cost what it might, I raised my rifle to my shoulder and then lowered it again at what I saw.

"Sinuous as a snake, stealthy as a leopard, Ikstu, a knife in his hand, was creeping up behind the sorcer. Warned by some subtle instinct the priest turned, barely before the spring. One hand shot out, the finger pointing straight at the boy, and their eyes locked with nearly an audible snap. It seemed as though invisible bonds held the would-be murderer. He struggled in vain to raise the knife, to go forward.

"The pointed finger described a slow circle, Ikstu's head followed it. Faster it swung and faster. With a great burst of strength the sorcer snatched the sacred crystal from between the gorilla's paws and held it in the boy's face. For a breath Ikstu swayed away from the glittering lights, then his head went forward, and, eyes glued to the shining thing, he sank with it to the ground.

"The sorcer silently faced the breathless multitude then deliberately picked up Ikstu's own spear and turned toward him. There was a great crash of thunder and the gorilla, still swaying to the girl's music, groped blindly forward. The priest raised the spear. The girl broke off in the middle of a note, and quicker than light, covered her lover's body with her own.

"Released from the spell of the chant, though suddenly animate, the white gorilla tore the priest into his terrible arms and bore him to the ground. A blinding flash of lightning split the heavens as I fired.

"Catching the outline of the gorilla I pulled the trigger again, and sprang down into the arena. Every savage had fled save the chief, who stood, spear poised, between the lovers and the struggling man and brute. With a back-hand sweep of his long arm the gorilla ripped open my cheek at the very moment I sent a final bullet through its forehead.

"The sorcer was quite dead, practically every bone in his body broken by the awful clutch of those hairy arms. The white gorilla still feebly moved though the mushroom bullet had carried, away practically the entire back of its head. The girl, the chief, and I alone were alive and sane and until morning, in the hot rain, we labored to strip the skin from that great carcass.

"Then, the girl, leading Ikstu by the hand, and the skin swinging between us on a pole, we struck out for my camp. The chief, in silence, watched his son depart and did not do anything to hinder us.

"Perhaps he was thinking of the fate of those among the Fans who were found mentally wanting; and, in addition, there was the sacrilege of the attack on the priest."

Van Dam lay back in his chair and carefully, lit a cigarette.

"That isn't all?" I asked after a moment's silence.

"That's all," he answered.

"But what's the end of it? What became of the girl and Ikstu?"

"The girl died on the way out. Ikstu lies there before the fire; his mind never came back to him. I have hopes, however; he has taken to worshiping the beast in the case and bowing down to the crystal. Interest in anything is an encouraging thing."

"You have a pleasant way of entertaining your guests," I said, for want of something better. "Cannibalism, murder, madness, everything, but starvation."

"We had about come to that, too," Van answered carelessly. "On the way back, when we ran into a great migration of spider monkeys. They make very good eating, we just had one for dinner."

BLACK BUTTERFLIES
ELMER BROWN MASON
1916

I
THE MOUNTAIN SPIRIT

It was the obstinacy of Trevor Dillingame, the stark, sheer obstinacy and conceit of the man in his power to handle any situation, solve any jungle secret, that brought us under the shadow.

'Tis a fault of the English. Where a Scotchman is firm, an Englishman is obstinate.

Whereas a Scotchman simply realizes his powers, an Englishman puts no limit to what *he* may accomplish.

Not that I didn't like the man. Losh, who could help it from the mere good looks of him? though I do not put undue faith in male beauties. But he was such a whale of a laddie, six feet tall, four across the shoulders, cold blue eyes, tread as light as *plandok*, the tiny mouse-deer; and big hands, that could crack a cocoanut or hold a butterfly without bruising its wings.

Butterflies were his line, and he knew as much as anyone in the world about them. I'm a cautious man and I'll go no further; he knew as much as anyone in the whole world about butterflies.

'Twas in the low swamp belt of the coast of British Borneo that it all began. We were collecting pretty nearly everything for a lot of stay-at-home scientists who could afford to have the jungle wonders sent to them to be tagged with Latin names at their leisure. It did pay, but it was hard work, dangerous work. The jungle leeches sucked blood from every uncovered inch of our bodies and our flesh

60

was raw from mosquito bites. There were poisonous insects, snakes, and more snakes, and then the heat—moist, deadening; sapping your vitality like the final rounds of a long, long fight.

Shifting uneasily from foot to foot, and tearing away the jungle leeches that would pop onto their bare skins, three little Dyaks stood in the checkered shadows. Trevor Dillingame was bending over a great flower-stalk, around the top of which were symmetrically clustered the red and black caterpillars, with their one creamy segment, of *Cethosia Hypsea*, creating a living, wriggling bloom.

A red thing sailed through the air—a bird, I thought—and settled in a low nipa palm. I saw it was a tree frog at the very moment that a green-and-gold whiplike strand swung down from the treetops and caught it in its narrow jaws.

"*Chalaka, ular Tuan!*" (Very wicked snake, sir), shrieked one of the Dyaks.

From the olive green of a rattan thicket stepped out a woman, covered with wreaths of jasmine, the two wings of a coal-black butterfly pasted on her forehead. Her hands flew to the slender neck of the snake, twisted quickly, and the head with its red prey was left between her fingers.

Dillingame stood stock still, staring at her. Laughing up into his face, she flung away the serpent's head, stripped off a jasmine garland, cast it about his neck—and was gone.

Both Trevor and I knew enough of the mythology of Borneo to realize at once that we had looked upon a *hantus*, one of the spirits that lived on the top of Mount Kina Balu and reappeared as the female priests of the country.

That was all very well; but such things can't be—they *aren't*, whether we had seen one or not; and the woman had been very beautiful.

"Yon's a bonnie lassie who favored you with the flowers," I remarked as Dillingame began to strip off the garland.

"That I leave to your Scotch susceptibility, Andy Freeman," he answered. "But did you get a good look at those butterfly wings she wore, on her forehead? An eight-inch spread to each of them, and black as jet! A new species, a new genus—perhaps even a new family of Lepidoptera. What do you suppose a specimen of that butterfly would bring in Paris or London? A fortune!"

As we talked, we picked our way carefully along the back trail toward where a boat waited us on the water of a sluggish stream that ran to the coast. We did not expect to see the Dyaks again; they had fled in wild panic, but we did hope my Chinaman would still be there and would have enough knowledge of the channel to pilot us to the sea without becoming lost in some backwater. Besides, it was getting dark, and a night in a Borneo swamp jungle is enough to make the most seasoned explorer shudder.

The boat and Chinaman were waiting, as we had hoped; but as for getting out in the darkness, Lee San positively refused to attempt to guide us. Outside of the great probability of being lost he claimed that our craft would arouse countless devils of the night by disturbing the waters.

Strange cuss, that Chinaman! He had been with me for over two years in Sumatra, Sarawak and Dutch Borneo, and never before had pretexed superstition for disobeying an order. He was unusually intelligent, too, and I had given him a large share of my confidence, and gained much interesting inside native information in return. The Chinese are the traders of all that part of the world and know more about the Dyaks, Muruts and other tribes of Borneo than any white man.

We poled the boat out into midstream, and dropped anchor, preparing to make the best of a bad situation. Fortunately there was enough dry wood on board to build a good fire on the dirt hearth so we could boil some water and attend to our countless leech wounds with ammonia. Of course the light lured hordes of bloodthirsty mosquitoes, but we stoked up on quinine (Lee preferred an opium pill) and smoked hard beneath our skeeter nets.

Sleep was impossible. Even if the heat had not put it out of the question the jungle noises would have kept a dead man awake. From a hundred yards away, as regular as the striking of a clock, a bull alligator roared out his love call; *samburs*, the big blue deer of Borneo belled in the distance; great fruit-bats cut the air with a mighty swish of their leathery wings; and underneath all came the chorus of tragedy from the forest floor, the agonized squeak of a small rodent as it was borne off in triumphant jaws, the snarl of some cat animal that had missed its spring, the ceaseless snuffle of the rooting wild hogs.

"Whisky," I said to Trevor—it's bad stuff in the tropics, but the night was unendurable—and he passed the bottle.

"Quinine," he demanded, and we both took ten more grains.

In the bow of the boat Lee San's teeth began to chatter.

"What's the matter, boy?" I sang out.

"No got mo' opium," he answered.

"Come here and drink some whisky," I ordered.

"No can," he objected—the Chinese doesn't often touch it, doesn't seem to like it—but he came down to the stern, just the same, and swallowed the big slug I had ready for him.

Silence for a long time, silence that every one of us wanted to break, but each was waiting for the other. Finally Dillingame's thoughts broke out in a torrent of words.

"Andy, how could that woman be real?—and yet you *know* she was! Hew did she dare grab that deadly tree-snake, that can turn and bite in its own skin, and twist off its head? And why did she do it? Where did those butterfly wings come from? You know no such insect exists in lower Borneo; you know we, or others, would have found it were it here. And if it came from the mountain country, what were its wings doing in a lowland nipa swamp on a girl's forehead? I'd give all we have collected on this trip for one specimen of that black butterfly!"

"So would I," I replied, ignoring his questions, since they were unanswerable. "But I think you are on the right track. It must be a mountain species or we would have found it. Pass the whisky."

We all had another drink. Lee did not demur this time.

"I move, unless we are down with fever in the morning, that we go back, look for the woman, and, if we find her, try to buy those wings—or at least try to discover where they came from. A black butterfly, Andy—"

"Lee savvy black butterfly," chanted the Chinaman. "You want know, you no tell!"

"Sure not," I agreed, and the Englishman grunted an affirmation.

I shan't try to repeat Lee's exact words, for the story filled the entire night; but this is the meat of what he told us. Long before the English took over North Borneo, before Sir James Brooke came to Sarawak, even before the Dutch had seized their portion of the island, the Chinese looked upon all Borneo as their own private treasure-house. From it they exported rattan, teak, precious and semiprecious stones, and gold—quantities of gold—the source of which no Aryan nation has ever been able to discover in after years. And the power, head, moving spirit of the Chinese in those days (as now) was centered in a Tong—a Tong so mighty that it had no name.

The emblem of this Tong was a portion of a butterfly wing, never a whole wing, but just a fragment; and this fragment was always round and always black. Even now the gold that came out of British Borneo passed only through the hands of the Chinese—the Chinese that belonged to the old, old Tong that had the round piece of black butterfly's wings for emblem.

The whisky passed back and forth many times during this recital, a strange one, indeed, to come from an Oriental (they never speak of their secret societies), and Dillingame, leaning toward me, whispered:

"He's lying!"

"'Tis the whisky," I whispered back.

"No lie, no whisky!" vehemently protested Lee San—his ears must have been devilish sharp. "China boy *pantong* (taboo)—mus' die in twenty day for makee Tong mad. No sendum body back to ancestors, jus' scatterum ashes. So no care what come. Tellum tluth!"

"Where do the butterfly emblems come from?" asked Trevor.

"My no savvy. Way off, mebbeso. Seeum only in Blunei town."

A terrible rumpus broke out on the bank of the stream. Gruntings, howls, roars, screams. The light was just breaking, and we could dimly discern vague shapes dancing frantically about. Suddenly the sun shot over the horizon, and we saw a great python lurch into the water, leaving a crowd of big, frantically chattering, long-tailed red monkeys on the bank.

It rained dismally as we retraced our trail of the day before. The *mise en scene* was unchanged. The head of the tree-snake, already half decomposed, lay on the ground, but the red tree-frog was gone from between its jaws. The prickly thicket of rattan whence the *hantus* had come, and into which she had disappeared, was as impenetrable as a solid wall of barbed wire

I lifted up my voice and called. A deer snorted near by, a flight of hornbills sawed the air with their heavy wings. No other sound broke the silence save the drip, drip, drip of the wet jungle.

Morose, and hardly believing what we had seen the day before, heavy from the night's vigil, we retraced our steps to the boat and dropped down stream.

Brunei is built on piles and roofed with thatch, and has all of twenty thousand inhabitants. A globe-trotter once called it "the Venice of the East." There is an English quarter, of course, with a resident who lives in card indexes and considers it low to have anything to do with the natives.

We were not of his favorites. He told us on one occasion that our lack of dignity in mingling with the aborigines lowered the caste of every white man in the East. Dillingame promptly chucked him into the water, and he retaliated by revoking all our collecting permits. It was a nuisance to have to forge others; and then, too, we spelled his name wrong on them. The first real government white man we met in the interior laughed at us, corrected the spelling and passed us on.

It was humiliating, though.

In the Chinese quarter, where all the business was done, they knew us well and, as near as you can gage the feelings of Orientals, liked us. We shipped all our stuff through them, and they cashed our drafts and even lent us money.

Among the Kadyans and Dyaks, in the native quarter, we were rather lords; Dillingame crumpled up all their wrestlers and astounded them with feats of strength. I told them stories in the different vernaculars.

There is absolutely no use in a white man trying to match wits with a yellow one if he wants to find out anything. I went straight to the biggest Chinaman of the lot, told him where and how we had seen the black butterfly wings, and asked him point-blank whence they came. He answered me with apparent frankness that he did not believe such an insect existed today, though it may have in the past. Goods (he did not specify what kind) that came from the mountainous country around Kina Balu often were accompanied by a fetish in the form of a black butterfly's wing, but that wing was made of paper—and to prove it, he gave me one.

This, to my mind, closed the incident.

Dillingame, who had been getting together supplies and packing our stuff for shipment, greeted me cheerfully.

"Hello, dead man," he called, "I have just been informed that anyone who sees a *hantus* is due to cash in the same quarter of the moon. One of our Dyaks ran amuck when the three got back, and was hacked to pieces by his friends; the other two have been gloriously full of arrack ever since. What did you find out about the butterfly?"

I repeated what the Chinaman had told me, taking out the paper wing and laying it before him.

I think I said before that Englishmen are obstinate. Trevor Dillingame absolutely refused to believe a word of it. He pointed out that the paper wing showed an arrangement of veins and a frenulum quite different from that of any known species of butterfly, and stoutly maintained that such a species did exist and the paper counterpart was just a typical oriental plot to throw us off. I tried to show him that there could be no reason why the Chinese would object to us sashaying all over the island after butterflies, since we always attended strictly to our own business; but he wasn't to be budged from his plot theory.

"I'm going to have that butterfly if I rake over all the mountains in Borneo," he announced, "and I'll bet you will have it within a year—or rather that we will; because you are naturally coming along."

"You mean you *may* get it, not *will* get it," I corrected.

"I mean I *shall* get it," he insisted. And yet people say the Scotch don't understand the difference between shall and will!

* * *

Brunel is civilized in that it has one white hell where foregather the captains and mates of the trading ships, globetrotters and men who have made their pile in the black country; in short, every white who has the price. You pay your money and you get what you order. To a certain point you do as you please. Beyond that point a Malay kriss ends the evening's entertainment and the tide takes you out to sea without trouble to your friends.

A Chinaman ran the place, of course. He called it the House of Unending Happiness and Delight. White men called it the Devil's Club.

Neither Dillingame nor I is a saint. We like our bit of fun as well as anyone. 'Twas to the Devil's Club we planned to go that evening; first to talk to one of Rothschild's orchid-collecting agents, then to enjoy whatever happened along. We didn't anticipate much from the agent. He was an evil little rat of a Portuguese who bought low and, in all probability, turned in his purchases at four times what they cost him. Also he was a careful lad with the money, never known to buy a drink could he help it.

Lee San had laid out clean white clothes for us in our nipa-thatched hut, and seemed to be lingering about with something on his mind that he lacked the courage to unload. I gave him a lead, and, explaining that only nineteen days more of existence remained to him according to the sentence of the Tong, he asked for his pay covering the full period.

It's fatal to pay a Chinaman in advance, so I naturally refused and suggested, as a substitute, that he come with us into the interior, thus probably running away from his fate.

The idea of escape had evidently never occurred to him—Tongs even do their thinking for most Chinamen—and I left him to turn it over in his mind.

The entertainment furnished at the Devil's Club is rather unique. Everything starts with a good dinner, of course, and plenty of drinks. Then comes gambling on a rickety roulette wheel; fan tan, or just drinking. If none of these amusements appeals to you, you watch the show. Dyak girls, teeth blackened and ornamented with tiny gold stars let into the enamel, ears bored around the edges with holes from which dangle rings and pendants, wave their long hands, the nails dyed to a crimson, and dance to the slow beat of the native instruments. Chinese girls, always smiling out of their slanting eyes, play toy-like banjos and never cease to wonder at European kisses. Perhaps there are wrestlers, or two sailors from rival ships put on the gloves and fight to a knockout while men from every corner of the earth stand around the ring.

These various kinds of evenings, with their next mornings' headaches, were old stories to us; but this evening furnished something surprisingly new. Gomez, the Portuguese, not only invited us to dinner, but actually paid for it. Then, instead of going into the back room to smoke opium, he sat out with us watching the dancing and talking about everything under the sun. 'Twas plain that the lad wanted something from us, but to save me I couldn't figure out what it was.

Finally, as the crowd thinned out, dropping into or being carried to their boats, he suggested that he accompany us to our own hut, as he had something of importance to take up with us.

Lee San set out the whisky, and as soon as he withdrew, the Portuguese hauled a little package out of his inside pocket.

"Can't handle this alone," he remarked as he began to remove the paper wrapping, "but there should be enough in it for all three of us," and he laid a porcupine quill and a small round object, about the size of a half crown, on the table.

I picked up the transparent quill. The weight together with the color of the contents told me at once that it was filled with gold. Dillingame gave a low whistle over the round article and handed it to me. It was a kind of a locket, holding beneath its thin film of glass a round section cut from the wing of a black butterfly.

"Where did you get these, Gomez?" I demanded.

"What does it matter as long as I know where the gold came from, and we can get more?"

"It matters so much that if you want us in with you, you'll have to tell us."

"I found them on the body of a Murut who had been bitten by a snake," he answered sulkily. "He told me, before he died, that he brought gold down from the mountains each year, that there was plenty of it there."

We hadn't the slightest desire to take Gomez with us, but other considerations besides our personal feelings had to enter into the calculations. It costs like blazes to get to the back country; mainly because one has to carry all the rice for the porters, as well as everything else, and the Portuguese seemed to have lots of cash. Of course we realized the source of at least part of this wealth. Not for a moment did we believe that a single quill of gold was all that had been taken from the dead Murut, any more than we swallowed the story about the poor devil having been bitten by a snake. Gomez had no reputation save that of an excellent shot and being death quick with a knife.

We insisted on one reservation, namely, that all entomological specimens should be our exclusive property—oddly enough it was the black butterfly that appealed to Dillingame's and my imagination even more than the prospect of gold; and then went into the project, each taking a third.

It's devilish hard getting into the interior, but it can be done by determined men who know the jungle. A couple of weeks later found us under the shadow of Kina Balu, its fourteen thousand foot summit. towering high above us. The natives had not bothered us at all; indeed, we hadn't seen much of them, and our supplies were holding out splendidly.

All that day we toiled up the old course of the Tarnpassuk, collecting as we went, and we certainly did well. Everywhere were beautiful green papilios—the Saranak Beauty—and frail, black-spotted *Hestidae*, while lovely, velvety black-and-green male

brookcani went swiftly dancing by. Also the orchids were something unbelievable; *grammatophyllums*, golden-brown spotted
flowers on stout two-yard-long spikes; a greenish-yellow flowered
dendrobium; clusters of tubular *aesclynanthus* like scarlet jewels
beneath the great, leathery, aroid leaves; and the enormous moth
orchids with their hundred snowy flowers.

Already we could easily see a profit on the trip from what we
had gathered if we continued to do even half as well, and were all
as happy as crickets.

That evening we camped on the bank of a half-dry stream, and
while Dillingame and I figured out how much further we could cut
down the loads for the mountain climb, Gomez washed the sands
for gold—his favorite amusement, no matter where we stopped.
Lee San (he had accepted my suggestion to accompany us in defi-
ance of his Tong) was cooking our supper, and the jungle was as
quiet as a high-limit poker game.

Night came quickly, as it does in the East; a black curtain rolled
suddenly across the sky through which the stars would later punch
their twinkling holes, and we gathered around the fire. From far
off in the jungle came the bellowing of wild cattle, a flying lemur
cut a straight line against the horizon across the curves of the circling bats.

Then, in the Ida'an tongue, and with the sudden crash of an
orchestra, came a roaring chorus:

> "Little red flames that flit so fast,
> Through wet, green leaves till day is past—
> Little red flames in the tree-tops shine
> Where the hungry, green-gold serpents twine—
>
> "One and all, great and small,
> We carry you up the mountain tall,
>   Down where the jungle's hot and dim,
>   Under the world's far, farthest rim,
> To HER, to HER
> Where red waters stir,

And the lilies float
O'er the gods demure."

Weapons ready, we stepped out of the circle of the fire and stood in the shadowy edge of the jungle. The moon swept up over the treetops and down its silvery path filed a long procession. They were Ida'ans from the mountains, the taint of them on the breeze, and each of the fifty men was loaded down with a wicker basket whence came a volume of sound like the splashing of countless, tiny waterfalls.

Again crashed out the song:

"Little red flames that feel as cool
To burning hands as the shaded pool—
Little red flames through the jungle fling
The breath of freshness while you sing—

"One and all great and small,
Never cease your piping call,
    Down where the jungle's hot and dim,
    Under the world's far, farthest rim,
While you go to HER
Where the red waters stir
And the lilies float
O'er the gods demure."

"They are going to, not coming from, the mountains," whispered Gomez, "so they haven't any gold. Let's stay hidden."

"Want to know what is in those baskets. They'd see our fires anyway," spoke up Dillingame, and stepped out of the shadow toward the last of the passing men.

It was an idiotic thing to do—I don't believe in hunting trouble—but I followed him, of course. The entire column halted. It was probably the first white man they had ever seen; certainly the first wearing khaki, puttees and an immaculate helmet, and I called for the *orang-kaya* (head man).

A little wizened Chinaman was pushed forward, whom I proceeded to interrogate sternly on the purpose of the expedition just as though I were a government officer.

I got away with it, of course. They were returning from a religious pilgrimage into the lowlands after having washed away their sins in some sacred stream. I said I got away with it, but not with bells on. Indeed, the Chinaman seemed somewhat inclined to interrogate me as to our destination and purpose in that part of the country, a tendency that I promptly suppressed. I also gave him orders to camp well away from our party and not to permit his men to stray in our direction.

During this conversation the fresh sound as though of running water continued to come from the baskets the natives were carrying. Trevor stepped to the nearest one and threw up the lid. It was loosely packed full of green leaves, among which sang hundreds of little red tree frogs.

Back in camp I cussed the Englishman proper for advertising our presence to the natives, and we speculated in regard to the red tree frogs. I knew the Ida'ans considered rats a table delicacy, and the frogs might be in the same category. The strange part was that an expedition should penetrate into the lowlands to collect them—they aren't found far from the coast—and that the expedition should be in charge of a Chinaman.

After all, it did not concern us directly, and gradually, one by one, we dropped off beneath our mosquito nets. The jungle noises blurred from separate sounds into a droning whole, I was drowsily conscious of a pair of large, bright, yellow eyes—a slow loris my brain lethargically telegraphed—and I slept.

I woke, with the first morning light, to the song of birds. The sun popped up over the horizon, and the chorus from the treetops increased to an ecstasy of harmony. In prompt contrast to all this joyousness came a wail of fright from behind our tents, followed by shouts of surprise and fear from the porters.

Jumping into my boots, clad only in pajamas, and an automatic in my hand, I rushed toward the sound of the disturbance. Lee San, surrounded by the Muruts, was raising his voice to high heaven and holding his upper garment away from his body—and from that upper garment fluttered a long piece of paper covered with Chinese characters and signed with a crudely inked butterfly's wing.

"Stop that fool howling," I yelled angrily, tearing away the fluttering strip that was evidently the cause of his anguish, "and tell me what this all means!"

"Lee San only t'lee day to live! That Tong sign. No can get 'way!" and he roared anew.

Grabbing him by the throat I choked the noise back into his gullet.

"Where did that laundry ticket come from?" I demanded.

"Pin to do' when Lee sleep," he moaned.

I was sorry for the little Chinaman, of course; but couldn't let him go on bawling forever. It might stampede my dozen porters any minute. Naturally I surmised that one of them was in Tong employ, and had pinned Lee's sentence to him while he slept. I should have liked mightily to ferret out the guilty one, but didn't dare take the risk of the bunch quitting on me.

Pretending a wrath I was far from feeling and threatening Lee San with immediate death, I sent the men to cooking their breakfasts and then returned to my tent.

We made good progress the next two days, passing several Ida'an villages, the inhabitants of which viewed us with an uninterested stolidity that made me rather nervous, and on the second night camped just below the timberline of Kina Balu.

Gomez claimed that gold came from the western slope, but it was easier to go over the mountain than to try to thread the impenetrable jungle around its base.

We took many rare butterflies, those days, including the *Euthalia magnolia*, known only from Kina Balu; another beautiful local species with a six-inch spread of velvety blackness and a broad band of pea-green across the wings; and then, just before pitching camp, I netted an entirely new species, soft gray with little squares, as though of isinglass, set in its wings, and both venation and frenulum identical with the round fragment of black wing that Gomez had shown us in the little locket.

We had out this talisman and compared the two—after which I slipped the little round thing into my pocket—and it was easy to see that we had a species for an entirely new genus; two species, if we secured the black butterfly. In spite of the rain that began to fall that night Dillingame and I were jubilant, though we could not get Gomez to enthuse—he was after more valuable game.

The altitude and cold rid us of mosquitoes and we turned in early in anticipation of a full night's sleep. Scarcely had I closed my eyes, however, when I was wide awake again and sitting up. Clear as a bell, through the darkness, came the whistle of a kite—and kites don't fly at night—to be answered from the other side of the camp by the drawling snarl of a tiger cat, followed by the unmistakable sound of a girl's laugh.

On my feet in a flash, I stole out beyond the light of the fire and lay down in the shadow, straining my eyes through the blackness. It had stopped raining and not even an insect disturbed the perfect stillness. Suddenly, to my right, a single voice broke into song—a voice so filled with contemptuous raillery that it made me grit my teeth in anger.

> "*Orang, puteh*,* what dost seek
> Toward Kina Balu's lofty peak
> Where the dead troop free
> 'Neath Lugundi's tree
> In the sacred lake
> Whence the spirits flee? . . ."

I raised up on my left elbow and fired twice in the direction of the sound. A mocking laugh came back to me, then silence, save for the waking of the camp. Quieting the men, I told Dillingame and Gomez not to bother me with questions that night, and, turning in, slept till daylight.

*Stranger in our midst.

II

THE TALISMAN

It was deadly cold in the morning and Lee's teeth chattered as he built our fire. I sent him over to wake the porters, only to have him back in a second, hands trembling and face ashy white.

"Come" was all he could say. "Come!"

My twelve porters lay their feet to the dead embers, and on each man's left cheek was stamped in black a butterfly's wing.

There was no holding them, of course, when they awoke and saw the mysterious emblem that had been placed on their very flesh while they slept. Furthermore the marks would not wash off—left an indelible stain that seemed to penetrate the pores of the skin. I threatened, bribed, cajoled, all in vain; and, accepting half what I had promised them for wages, my Muruts fled down the mountain.

Nice fix we were in! All our goods and chattels dumped high on the side of Kina Balu, and no one to carry them! There was only one thing to do: go back to the nearest Ida'an village and hire local carriers—and a villainous lot they proved to be when I finally managed to get ten of them at an exorbitant wage in cloth. Then it was noon before we got started again, and our nerves were on razor edge.

Lee San helped the situation by bewailing the fact that it was the last day on earth allotted to him by the Tong, and stuck so close to me that I finally lost my temper and made him lead the column.

Over the shoulder of Kina Balu the character of the country changed. Jungle grew high up a mountain slope so precipitous that we never should have been able to descend had it not been for a narrow, winding trail. There were no butterflies, the giant trees meeting overhead and shutting out the light, but never have I seen such a riot of orchids, or so many gorgeously colored birds.

My porters balked twice, demanding their wages as having gone far enough; and the second time I was forced to make good my threatenings by knocking one flat. It was beastly hot and sticky, the ground fairly crawled with leeches, and the trail was cut every hundred yards by wild pig runs, along which we three times went astray.

I joined Lee San and we kept well ahead of the column, progressing downward as best we could and clearing the way. The Chinaman had recovered his spirits with the realization that sundown would see the end of his fears—Tong law considers a man dead, no matter whether he is or not, after the date for his execution has passed, and no longer molests him.

The trail became narrower and narrower. I stepped over a liana that stretched across about a foot from the ground, and turned as Lee brought down his jungle knife to sever it. There was a swish overhead and a weighted spear plunged down, entering the man's neck, piercing the length of his body through the thigh, its point going into the ground and holding him upright.

Lee San opened his mouth in an attempt to speak, his head flopped forward, and death claimed him before the words could come.

Dazed for the moment, I stood motionless, my eyes on the spear shaft along which slowly dribbled round drops of blood. A ray of sunlight filtered down from above and played over the dead man. Sable black, two feet from wing tip to wing tip, an enormous butterfly darted straight for the crimsoning spear, poising against it with swiftly fanning wings.

I grabbed with my bare hand, but it dodged, circling about my wrist, to relight on the dead mans bleeding shoulder. Again I lunged for it.

There was a rustle behind me and an arm went around my neck, flinging me flat on the trail. Beautiful as an orchid in her wreaths of fragrant jasmine, a woman caught the sable butterfly between her fingers, jumped lightly over my body, and disappeared into the jungle, while through the great tree trunks came a low, mocking laugh.

Half stunned, I stumbled to my feet, tearing away a great leech that had fastened to my lip, and the first of the porters came down the trail.

It was a trap for wild hogs that Lee San had blundered into, and I sprang two more of them, with a long pole cut for the purpose, within the next mile.

We buried the Chinaman beside the trail—tropical jungles do not admit of delay in such matters—and I certainly did feel cast down over the loss of such a good cook. Also he had been with me over two years and I was very well used to him.

I did not mention the sable butterfly or the woman before Gomez, saving up the incident for Dillingame alone. Perhaps this was because of the rather humiliating role I had played. Anyway, I did not say anything about it at the time to either of them.

Two miles farther down the trail the jungle opened up into a park of enormous teak trees with no underbrush on the forest floor; just a meadow of short grass with a stream running through the middle, on the bank of which we camped. Being completely devoid of confidence in the porters, I had all the waterproof-canvas-wrapped loads piled in a great heap, pitched the two tents, one on each side, and then the three of us matched to see who should cook. Gomez got stuck, much to his disgust; so he had to forego his customary evening's amusement of washing for gold.

Hardly had we finished our supper, and a rotten bad meal it was, when the Ida'ans appeared and asked pay for the full week I had hired them with an additional bonus to the one I had man-handled. As is always the case with natives, and inspired by arrack, they started at the top of the pitch beginning with demands and working down until they reached the pleading stage.

Their argument was based on the fact that we had not climbed Kina Balu as they expected, and as had other white men, but had led them down into the Land of Blood where the spirits stole men's souls. Their spokesman assured me that no one who went into this jungle ever came back, that it was the abode of spirits and devils who, like gigantic leeches, fed on the blood of the living.

In the end I drove them to their fire, and we turned in, agreeing to keep watch, turn by turn, during the night. Dillingame took the first period and I went promptly to sleep.

Then I began to dream. The *hantus* woman stepped out of a rattan thicket and laughed up into Trevor's face. He gathered her into his arms and bent his lips to hers, when a flock of great, black butterflies swept down, forming a cloud about them. I beat at them with my hands to reach the voice calling, "Andy! Andy!"

Someone was shaking me by the shoulder. "Wake up, for God's sake, Andy, wake up!" whispered Dillingame. "This place is enchanted!"

Outside the tent, it was light as day. A luminous mass came hurtling through the air and fell at my feet. I kicked it and a great fungus broke into a thousand pieces, each glowing with fox fire. More fungi were hurled into the open space about the camp. I rolled down several of the canvas-covered loads and we crouched behind them. The Ida'ans, near the dead fire, were standing huddled in a close group whence came no sound.

The shower of luminous fungi ceased. There was a pop like a champagne cork leaving the bottle and one of the porters staggered and fell on his face, a tiny arrow quivering in his forehead.

"Lie down, you fools" I yelled, and pumped a bullet into the edge of the jungle. A shower of tiny arrows rattled among the packs. I picked up one and showed its point, smeared with some pitchy poison, to Trevor.

"No use staying here to be shot down like trapped hogs," he snapped. "Let's make a break for cover. Where is Gomez?"

"Here," came the little man's voice from my elbow. "We're in a tight fix, is it not?"

"We're in all of that," I answered. "Draw their fire, and after the shower of arrows, grab a pack and get into the jungle near them. I'll toss one of those flares we brought for trading where they seem thickest and we'll try to get enough to give them a permanent scare."

One of the Ida'ans rose cautiously to his knees. Came the pop of a blow gun and he went down screaming, his hands to his face. Trevor fired in the general direction whence the arrow came. A storm of the little darts rattled about us, and then we were all running, packs held before us, toward the edge of the jungle.

Safe in its shadow, I touched a match to the flare and flung it whence had come the last volley. There was a yell of fear, and we turned loose a bunch of black outlined figures, long bamboo blow-guns in their hands. Some went down, but about twenty started across the open.

"After them, and get as many as you can," I shouted. "We've got to make this a lesson!"

Under the cover of the trees we ran, shooting as we went, until they crossed the stream and were lost in the blackness beyond.

Something stirred behind us, and Trevor jumped into the underbrush. There was a brief struggle, and then he swore.

"Gimme a light," he demanded. "I've got something queer."

I struck a taper match and held it above my head. Dillingame had two slender wrists grasped in one of his big hands, and as the flame flared higher, my eyes followed his other hand to where it was twisted in a woman's hair—the woman of the nipa swamp, snake and red tree frog, the woman who had snatched the sable butterfly from Lee San's bleeding shoulder!

Gomez switched on an electric torch and we all stood staring at her. Man, but she was beautiful! Short grass skirt, leather sandals bound halfway up her legs, the upper part of her body bare save for wreaths of jasmine. Her skin was as white as the flowers of the great moth-orchid, her lips crimson as red blood, her eyes blazing violet, swimming with flecks of gold, and her hair beneath Trevor's hand was black and soft as silken thread.

Losh, but she was beautiful as she stared back at us, her little hands twisting helplessly in the Englishman's big one, her body tensed.

Then, before we could find words, her form relaxed, her eyes flew to Trevor's face and she laughed up at him. Not a wild, hysterical laugh, just a soft, amused little one with an undercurrent of contempt in it—the sound a woman makes over a child who has done some silly thing.

Out of the corner of my eye I saw Gomez cross himself and shift forward his automatic.

"Laugh, you vixen," said Dillingame, but his eyes were not unkind. "She jabbed a knife into me and fought like a wild cat," he flung us in an aside, then turning back to her, "Do you know I ought to kill you, shoot you down in your tracks?"

Of course the woman did not understand, and again she laughed up at him, her lips curving back over her white teeth, her violet golden eyes half shut.

"*Santa Maria!*" gasped Gomez. "Let me shoot her and then we'll burn her body in the fire. Don't you see she is a *hantus*, a witch? She will enchant us all and the leeches will suck our bodies dry. I am afraid—me!"

"Don't be a fool," I advised gruffly, stepping in front of him, for he was fingering his pistol nervously. "Bring your captive lassie to the tents, Trevor. I'm thinking we won't be troubled with those poisoned darts while she is with us. Gomez, go over and tell the porters to keep down on the ground. If there is one of those blowgun men simply wounded, haul him in and we'll see what we can get out of him."

It had begun to drizzle. I threw wood on the fire and piled the packs in a barricade, the tents for ends. Meanwhile Trevor tied the woman's wrists together, holding the end of the rope in his own hands; nor did she resist. Gomez came back driving a small figure before him and, as it came into the firelight, I nearly yelled.

It wasn't a man, it was a beast, a human ape! There was a sarong around its middle but the rest of the body was naked and evenly covered with a generous growth of reddish hair, arms ending in tiny hands hung below its knees, and its head jerked from side to side with the lightning quickness of an animal while it whimpered over a wounded thigh where a bullet had creased the black skin.

The only human thing about it was its hair, which was elaborately dressed high on the head and through which were stuck several of the tiny poisoned arrows.

Suddenly it caught sight of the woman, and going down in a cringing heap, lay motionless, its face against the ground.

"Five dead," reported Gomez laconically, and took his seat as far as possible from the Englishman and his captive.

I addressed the girl in the Ida'an tongue. "Why did you lead your slaves to kill us? Have we done you harm?"

"You come for gold as do all strangers—our gold is pledged. About that I should not care, but you take the souls of the dead, the butterflies. Not even do you respect the souls of the sacred priests that sail on sable wings!"

"Who are you that talk of souls!"

"Kratas, priestess of the Land of Blood, who knows not death, who lives forever."

"Yon lassie is wrong in her head," I said to Dillingame in English. "Let's try and find out something from the beast-man," and I heaved him to his feet.

What came next happened quicker than word can tell it. Raising her hands to her lips the woman severed the cords that bound her wrists with one snap of her white teeth. Trevor caught her around the shoulders and, whirling, she bit deep into his hand.

"You'll pay for that, my girl," he snarled, gathered her into his arms, bent, and kissed her lips. One second she relaxed, clung to him, then twisted free, caught a tiny poisoned arrow from the savage's hair, drew the point in a long scratch across his back, and leaped over the packs. Trevor sprang after her just in time to slap Gomez's automatic from his hand as he fired.

A taunting laugh floated back out of the darkness.

The beast-man died from the poisoned scratch, toward morning, with many twistings and writhings. With the first light our Ida'ans disappeared up the trail and we could not catch them. They left three dead behind, victims of the poisoned arrows, and we found six beast-men in the jungle and five in the open that had stopped our bullets.

It took some time to dig a pit large enough for all those bodies, and, after we had stamped down the dirt, we sat on the packs and looked dismally at one another.

Gomez broke the silence. "Money I like it much, but if I am dead or crazy it does me no good. Let us go back as quickly as we can with what provisions our shoulders will carry."

"That's all very well for you," spoke up Dillingame, "you have a stake tucked away. Freeman and I have our all in this venture. I move we linger on and try to pick up something else. What do you say, Andy?"

"There is food for a long time," I answered judicially, "and we are more liable to be attacked on the back trail running away than if we stay boldly here. I'll not say it were best to go on, nor will I say it were best to stay, but—"

I. broke off, and dived for my net. A gray butterfly of the new genus was floating just outside the barrier of packs. I caught it in midair. Then I chased another, and another till, with eleven perfect and four damaged specimens, I finally returned to the tents. Dillingame had the real luck, though. He brought in forty of them, all taken over a crimson orchid, and netted an immense *Hestia* besides.

As we removed our catch from the cyanide bottles and folded them, wings back to back, into envelopes before packing them away in our waterproof collecting boxes, we easily calculated with what we already had we'd break better than square on the expedition.

Gomez was not there when we returned, but he drifted in with his gold washing pan shortly afterward, and an I-have-eaten-the-canary expression on his face.

"You found it!" I guessed at once, and could see his under lip stiffen for a lie.

"I have found traces," he answered; "it may be here, though probably in very small quantities. Anyway, I'm brave enough to stay on a little while even if you gentlemen are not."

Dillingame's face went purple, but I spoke before he could explode.

"Sure, we'll stay on. After Trevor and I have done a little more collecting we'll all turn in and pan the stream, and if there is gold we'll find it. Meanwhile let's match to see who cooks today!" And there the matter rested.

I'm a cautious man—being Scotch—and haven't been every place in the world, so I'll not say there are not collecting grounds equal to where we were, but under oath I'll swear these were the best I had ever seen.

We found no further new species of the larger butterflies, but the microlepidoptera would have kept a systematist busy classifying them for an entire year. The unnamed orchids were legion, and we took skins of two new pheasants, not to mention the Argus,

Bullwer and Fireback ones; a rare yellow shrike, gorgeous red and yellow sunbirds, and a cream-white lemur. All day we were off in the jungle so interested in our own work that we paid little attention to Gomez.

Gradually it dawned on us that the Portuguese had developed a virulent grouch, wasn't even civil, and one morning when it was raining torrents, so it was impossible to leave the tents, matters came to a head. It all began by Dillingame detailing our harvest of butterflies, orchids and birds for his benefit, a cataloguing which he terminated by the statement that the next day we would join in the gold search.

Gomez promptly answered with a snarl that he'd attend to his business and it would be healthier for us to keep to ours, that we needn't be afraid he wouldn't make a fair division—even though we had lured him on the trip under false pretenses and made him do all the work. And then, without the slightest warning, he jerked out his gun and barely missed the Englishman. Furious, Dillingame made a jump for him. The Portuguese fired again just as I hauled the tent pole down so the two of them were wrapped in its folds. From the outside I gathered the little man into a neat bundle of canvas. Trevor crawled from beneath, and we undid Gomez with a gun pressed to his stomach, and then tied him hand and foot.

There was no doubt he had intended to kill both of us, and he expected no gentler fate at our hands, especially after we had searched him and found fully a pound of dust in a belt strapped around his waist. There was nothing of the hero about him, and he began to whine for his life, offering the bribe of showing us the exact place he had found the gold.

I'll not deny that the Anglo-Saxon is the greatest of all races, but being one has its disadvantages at times—we talk when we should act. To save a cartridge Gomez should have had a knife stuck into him, and a savage would have applied that practical solution to his problem. White men are civilized beyond logic, however.

I sat down by the trussed-up, treacherous little rat and explained to him carefully that if he appeared at Brunei without us there would be no possibility of any explanation he might offer getting over, that he would have a mighty short time to enjoy his gold before some of our friends got him. Then we turned him loose.

Trevor kicked him once, and, according to the custom of fool Anglo-Saxons, after that we acted as though nothing had happened.

Our combined search for gold was without result. Gomez had taken his from a single pot-hole in the bottom of the creek—he showed us where. There were traces everywhere, but no place worth a second panning. The formation was unusual; the water flowing over a thin bed of sand beneath which was solid rock. The creek itself sprang from a swamp, half a mile up the mountainside, and for the two miles we followed it down, ran between high banks on which grew short grass and mighty teak or cocoanut trees exactly like the place where we were camped.

Since the immediate neighborhood had been thoroughly raked over both for specimens and gold, it seemed best to move on, and the banks of the stream offered open going without the trail danger of being ambushed or speared in a pig trap. We cached nearly everything, including the orchids and bird and animal skins, swinging them high in air by ropes over the limbs of the immense trees, and with our butterflies (which took up little bulk), ammunition, some food, and a small pack of trading stuff, the three of us started down stream.

For three miles the character of the country did not change, and then there was an abrupt dip. The stream broke into rapids and went brawling downwards, both grass and trees disappeared from the banks, their places being taken by immense boulders, stretches of bare rock and sandy beach. Half a mile from the stream, on either side, rose the barrier of the jungle, and it was dry, broiling hot.

We progressed along the sandy beach until well into the afternoon, stopping every now and then to pan the edges of the stream, but getting no color. Before us rose a cloud of vapor that I took at first for smoke and then decided must be mist above some great waterfall.

We camped early. Wood had to be brought from the jungle half a mile away, but the ground was smooth, so we dragged an entire dead tree to the beach without much difficulty. A cool—too cool—wind sprang up at dusk, driving away the mosquitoes, and by the time it was dark we were grateful indeed for the fire.

I suppose it may seem queer to anyone who has not felt the spell of the unexplored wilderness that we should go on and on facing known as well as unknown dangers. Really it was the perfectly logical and natural thing, considering the men we were. Gomez was spurred on by his insatiable lust for gold. Dillingame and I told one another that we must have that sable butterfly; but the real reason lay in that lure, irresistible to men of our race, that Kipling so well expresses:

> Something yet beyond the ranges,
>   Diddle, diddle, diddle come,
> Something calling, something calling,
>   Diddle, diddle, diddle dum.

I don't remember the exact words.

After supper we sat around sleepily watching the bats swoop through the flames and listening to the roar of life from the jungle. A great beetle blundered into the fire and toppled over to the ground at our feet. Dillingame and I bent over it. There was a gasp from Gomez that made us look up.

Sitting on a boulder within the circle of the firelight was Kratas, the priestess; two sable butterfly wings on her forehead; neck and bosom wreathed with jasmine, and an oblong, palmleaf-wrapped bundle between her small hands.

"Welcome, priestess of the *orang utan* (wild men)," I said, shifting my automatic well forward under my fingers. "Many times welcome, wearer of the sable wings."

She did not answer me, just sat motionless, her fearless eyes, filled with curiosity, resting on each of us in turn. Gomez shifted uneasily in his seat, Trevor picked up the floundering beetle and held it between his long nervous fingers, I slipped the strap from the trading pack.

"Do you, then, love to play 'neath the shadow of death that ye linger here, or have ye eaten of the blue root of madness?" she asked.

"Death dare not approach us," I boasted.

She seemed to accept my words as a mere statement of fact.

"And yet there was blood beneath my teeth when they sank into his white flesh," she mused, looking at Dillingame. "My lips were salty with it till his lips ravaged the taste from mine." Then, abruptly changing her tone, "I bring ye the gift that all white men crave," and she tossed the compact palmleaf bundle at my feet. "Let it be *salaamat jelan* (good-by). I bid ye go whence ye came before three suns."

"Tell her we haven't the slightest intention of leaving until we take some of those black butterflies," broke in Trevor obstinately.

"I'll tell her no such thing," was my answer, but the woman had gathered some of the meaning from the tone of his voice.

"Let him remain if he desires it more than life," she said softly, and, gliding to the Englishman, held her lips up to his.

"We, too, offer gifts," I hastened, to attract her attention, tumbling an alarm clock, gross of earrings and bolt of pink calico out of the pack, but she did not even glance at them. Drawing her lips back from his, she laughed up into Trevor's face, and was gone into the night.

"Andy, I don't believe any man but me has ever kissed that woman," he sighed.

"Holy smoke! And who cares if a hundred had?" I demanded.

Gomez tore open the palmleaf bundle and its contents slipped to the ground—twenty hollow porcupine quills filled with gold.

"Fools we were not to keep her once we had her," he cried, gathering up the hollow tubes, avariciously. "There are probably quantities where this came from. A cord around her temples or a little fire. . . . What's that for?" he howled, as Dillingame's boot caught him in the side.

In the morning, we started down stream toward the vapor that hung in the sky.

I listened for the crash of falling water as we approached, but there was no greater sound than the murmur of the stream. After a mile the stream itself switched abruptly to the left while the vapor cloud rose dead ahead and close to the edge of the jungle. We were walking on solid rock that dipped in a series of remarkably symmetrical, spaced steps, so it was like going down a very shallow pyramid.

Nearer, the vapor took definite form, one thick jet going straight up into the air, and touching each side of this central column were two misty, broad, rounded clouds.

"*Santa Maria!*" gasped Gomez. "It looks like one of your cursed butterflies!"

And so it did, the body clearly defined and the wings spread out and moving in the slight breeze.

A hundred yards further on we halted in amazement. At our feet a narrow flight of stone stairs ran down into a valley, or rather an enormous amphitheatre, since it was plainly the work of man. Half a mile broad and three-quarters of a mile long, it was sunk fifty feet deep in the solid rock. Immediately below us three springs boiled up, about a central tank, springs of hot water, judging from the steam that rose and traced the butterfly in the sky. The floor was bare rock, save on the opposite side where a belt of jungle had gained a foot-hold and flourished luxuriantly.

At the end of the amphitheatre, to the left, a hundred-yard flight of easy steps led us to the plain—and, gazing in that direction, I yanked both my companions flat on the ground.

Coming down the steps was a strange procession. In the lead four bearers carried a closed litter, or palanquin, on each side of which marched attendants with long palm fronds in their hands, by means of which they created an artificial breeze for its occupant. Six men brought up the rear, muskets over their shoulders. As they reached the springs immediately beneath us, we saw that all were Chinamen.

The palanquin was placed on the ground, the curtain drawn, and out stepped a mandarin, the largest Chinaman I have ever looked upon. He must have been all of seven feet tall, very broad, and in addition, enormously fat. The attendants pitched a small tent in the stream of the springs and after the tent flap had been respectfully held back for the big man to enter, the last of them joined his fellows in the shade thrown by the litter.

Plainly the mandarin was quite some dog and his preparation for a hot bath a real ceremony.

Before us, the giant amphitheatre for a stage, action developed like the plot on a moving picture screen. From the edge of the jungle directly across trotted out a large bull rhinoceros, its guardian angel, the Buphagus bird, flying ahead. The coolies were squatted behind the palanquin, their master still in his tent, and the great beast approached entirely unobserved.

Twenty yards from the springs, the rhinoceros bird flew back to its charge with a harsh cry of warning. The animal stood stock still for a moment, sampling the breeze; then with a squeal of rage it charged ponderously down on the empty palanquin, behind which the attendant Chinamen were sheltered from the sun.

Howling with fear, the servants fled toward the broad stairway. The horn of the furious pachyderm became entangled in the curtains of the palanquin, and it paused long enough to smash the frame to bits. The tent flap swayed back, revealing a half-naked mandarin who, taking in the situation at a glance, plunged into the tank between the hot springs. Whirling on the tent, the rhinoceros trampled it flat, then stretched its ugly head into the stream through which the figure of the immense Chinaman loomed dimly.

I rose to my feet, our heaviest rifle at my shoulder, drew a bead on the spine at the base of the short neck, and pulled trigger.

A rhinoceros hide may stop an ordinary bullet, but it's no proof against a steel capped projectile, cut to mushroom, and fired from above. The great bulk heaved one step forward and then flattened out, stone dead, while the guardian bird circled around, still uttering its warning cry.

"Come on," I commanded, rising to my feet, "let's go down and get thanked. The Lord knows what we are in for next, the only way to find out is to keep going ahead."

We left our packs where they had dropped and climbed down the narrow stairway. The Chinaman had emerged from his forced plunge, his skin so pink as to indicate the water was slightly too hot for comfort, and, gathering up some garments from the wreck of the tent, stood ready to receive us, the dead rhinoceros at his feet.

As I approached, the size of the yellow man became more apparent. He must have weighed all of four hundred pounds, and there was something queer about his face, something horrible. To begin with a black butterfly was tattooed on his forehead, his eyebrows had been shaved, and each eye was circled by a broad ring of crimson. But it was his mouth that made the shivers run up and down my spine, for the lips had been cut away square in front, showing all his yellow, flat teeth, with two fangs, like those of a dog, at the ends. And he had no ears.

I spoke the Ida'an words of conventional greeting, and the monster mumbled their answer. Gomez and Dillingame came up behind us, and I heard the latter exclaim "My word!" Then there was a silence.

Finally the Chinaman spoke, the words hissing through his teeth.

"Whence came ye?"

I waved my hand in the general direction of the west. To tell the truth, his apparently complete absence of gratitude for preventing a rhinoceros from sharing his bath began to irritate me.

"Why came ye here?" he demanded arrogantly.

Thoroughly angry now, I jammed my hands in my pockets, determined not to answer, even by gestures. My left hand touched something round, and, feeling to see what it was, thin glass shaped beneath my fingers. A sudden inspiration came to me. I drew out the little locket I had taken from Gomez, which held the round section of black butterfly wing, and, shaking off the broken glass, stepped to the dead rhinoceros and held the talisman up to the haughty mandarin standing on the other side.

Have you, perhaps, seen one of those balloons the bairns buy at fairs slowly collapse, the skin loosening, wrinkling, finally sinking into crinkled folds? That is what happened to the man before me. His eyes started from his head, his head sank between his shoulders, and his whole, enormous body seemed to shrink, sinking in on itself. With a groan he spread his hands before his face, salaamed thrice, forehead to the ground, and his voice was a toneless whisper when he said:

"Make known thy bidding! I see the sign and am thy slave."

III
IN THE TEMPLE

Even in after days I never fully understood why Lo Chan (thus did the mandarin name himself) caved in so utterly at the sight of the talisman. I found out before I had been long in the Land of Blood that this same small, round locket accompanied the Murut (never a Chinaman, always a Murut) who brought the tribute of gold dust to the Tong head waiting for it on the coast.

Why, in my hands, it should have such potency, remains an unsolved problem. I evolved the theory, for want of a better, that the breaking of the glass above the section of black butterfly wing had some special meaning in the complicated and mysterious ritual of the Tong.

Such speculations have small significance, however. What really mattered was the fact that the mandarin recognized in the talisman a power that he feared and dared not disobey, and was, in his own words, immediately my slave.

Lo Chan stepped over the dead rhinoceros and blew a blast on a silver whistle, carved in the semblance of a dragon. The coolies reappeared at the top of the broad stairway and came timidly down to the springs. Evidently assuming that we wished to be taken to his headquarters, the Chinaman ordered his servants to pick up our packs, and himself led the way out of the amphitheatre.

It was apparent that walking was not the mandarin's favorite form of exercise, and I was rather sorry for that enormous bulk of a man toiling ahead in the burning sun, sorry as it was possible to be for anyone so utterly repulsive physically.

From the sunken amphitheatre we continued in the direction of the stream, which we struck after two miles of heavy going through sand, and then followed over a road, always sloping downward, paved with large blocks of stone, their surfaces worn as though by innumerable feet. Vegetation reappeared, gradually thickening into jungle, and in the distance rose what I took for a hill of bare rock.

The stream lost itself in wet, swampy ground on either side of the stone causeway; tree tops met overhead, shutting out the light, and we came at last to a long house of bamboo, set upon piles. Ladders admitted us beneath the thatched roof, and we were in Lo Chan's home.

Certainly that fat mandarin did not believe in discomfort. The house was no different in construction from the usual Ida'an dwelling, a single sixty-foot room with no partitions or front; but its contents were of a richness none of us had ever dreamed of. Silk rugs of brilliant colors strewed the floors; on the walls were hung embroideries heavy with gold; there were inlaid tabourets, vases as high as a man's head, and low couches heaped with pillows.

A corner, hidden behind silver-embossed screens, held the complete paraphernalia of the opium smoker, and a great gold-and-red curtain, whence came feminine rustlings and whisperings, barred off one end of the long room.

Behind this curtain Lo Chan retired with a last profound salaam, and we were left alone.

Dillingame began to laugh. They are a feckless people, the English; I could see no joke.

"For a cautious Scotchman as you claim to be," he announced, "it seems to me you are taking big chances. That piece of butterfly's wing is a frail excuse for bossing a mandarin."

"You're a fool," stuttered Gomez, "a reckless fool to run us into this. Do you suppose for one minute that you can trust that mandarin? Do you know what the mutilation of his face means? He has been guilty of the vilest crime a Chinaman can commit; he's a parricide! Had he been a coolie he would have been burned to death. His rank saved him, but not from mutilation that all his race might know and scorn him, and he has plainly been banished to this corner of the world. Give me back that piece of butterfly wing before you get us into more trouble. It's mine, anyway!"

I think I have already said that I am a Scotchman, and therefore firm—not obstinate, firm; and once I have set myself to follow

a certain course I am not to be turned aside. Besides, the Portuguese showed an awful cheek in trying to run matters, considering
his general reputation and what we especially knew of him. I
promptly told him to mind his own business, that I had brought
him to the very source of the gold, and that I'd keep the talisman.

Dillingame backed me up, of course, and together we quickly
silenced the vicious little runt.

With sundown came a meal the like of which we had not tasted
for many a month. Lo Chan did not reappear, and we slept that
night through in absolute comfort.

In the morning there was a council. Gomez urged a direct demand for gold and a quick departure. Trevor had no suggestion to
make except that we do something at once. I proposed to let matters develop along their own lines, trying to pump our host without arousing his suspicions that we really hadn't the slightest idea
what we were doing.

We called the mandarin in and I asked him for a report on his
stewardship. Of course I had no idea what I meant, but it seemed a
safe question. He answered that the coolies had been unable to
wash out the usual quantity of gold, the workings were not half
as rich as formerly, but that the temple tribute came in regularly
every full of the moon.

Not much information in all this. The only thing I could think
of was to take a look at the temple, and I ordered him on.

The wet jungle was cut by numerous stone causeways, between
which I soon decided, had once been rice fields, now grown up save
for occasional patches of paddy, to great trees. Everywhere were
indications of a once flourishing city, stone roads, ruined houses
also often of stone, and the worn surface of the rock on which we
walked.

Finally the jungle opened, revealing what I had taken for an
elevation of naked rock, and we halted in amazement. Built of
blocks of stone, the size of which made it seem impossible they
could have been moved by human hands, rose an immense, pagoda-
like structure of three great stories, the topmost crowned with a
single enormous block of glittering stone.

Strange beasts were carved on the overhanging balconies, and plaques of metal hung down in clusters, tinkling musically in the slight breeze. A small pond, surrounded by a rampart of stone, its edges overgrown with white lilies, spread out in front of the temple, and the water in its centre, bubbling up ceaselessly, was red as blood.

In every cranny where the tropic vegetation could find a foothold it flourished, but not even the great rending power of its growth had been able to move the enormous blocks, and bring to the ground the astonishing edifice. And there was a queer air of emptiness about it, as though it had just been deserted by a multitude that might swarm back at any moment.

Into dim coolness we entered through a lofty square portico. There was absolute silence save for two sounds—the hushed clink of the swaying metallic plaques and a muffled murmur as though of running water. The ground floor was a great bare room of solid rock, with an aperture in the ceiling opening up all the way to the sky through the successive floors, and down which came a thin shaft of light. A strong ladder led up to this aperture, and towards it I pushed the mandarin. But he drew back with an exclamation of horror.

"It is not permitted!"

"Mount," I ordered, and he preceded me, obedient, though trembling.

The next story was full of vague rustlings from a floor knee deep in green foliage. Something moved at my feet, and I bent down. Seven inches long and black as jet, a thick caterpillar was eating ravenously into a camphor tree leaf.

Dillingame picked it up between his long fingers and together we examined it. Never have I looked on anything more repulsive than that twisting, worm-like creature. Unlike any caterpillar I had ever seen, it was furnished with heavy, piercing jaws—it was a flesh-eating, predacious thing that could have bitten through a finger.

"Pretty, isn't it?" commented Trevor, snapping it back disgustedly among the leaves.

At the end of the room were piled great wicker baskets whence came the sound as though of running water. We knew what those baskets held, of course; the red tree frogs from the coast. To make sure I threw back a lid. A crimson cloud floated about me as the little piping things sailed out, to fall among the leaves on the floor.

Then happened something horrible. Like lightning black caterpillars fastened their ugly jaws to the tree frogs, paralyzing them so that in a moment all were silent and still. It was plain that these joyous, crimson travelers were tid-bits indeed to the black larvae—undoubtedly brought from the coast for this purpose.

Rather shaken, I shepherded Lo Chan before us down the ladder and we hurried out into the warm sunshine. The blood-red pond with its border of snow-white water lilies heaved and bubbled as some great body swam across it barely under the water, so as to leave a swirling wake. Half running, half hopping along the causeways, bent figures sped before us. One of them swarmed up the trunk of a tree with all the agility of a monkey. Nearer, we saw that they were those same beast-men whom Kratas, the priestess, had brought down on us in the jungle.

"Let's go back to the house," urged Dillingame, "and kind of orient ourselves before we see any more horrors."

I motioned to La Chan to lead the way, and we retraced our steps. The Chinaman kept glancing back at me, and I knew instinctively that something was wrong—I had blundered in some detail, and he suspected I was not really what he had first taken me for.

Gomez broke out again as soon as we were alone.

"What's the use of all this waiting?" he demanded. "Why not ask the mandarin for all the gold he has, and get out of here? I'm afraid—me! There is magic all around us, black magic. . . . Those frightful worms!"

"Shut up and let me think," I answered crossly. "We have got to make up our minds to some definite plan of action— though I'm hanged if I know what!"

"The first thing to do is to go back and get some of those caterpillars," broke in Trevor. "I'll wager they are the larvae from which the black butterflies develop, even if predacious butterfly larvae had never been heard of before. Also I'll wager we run into Kratas before long."

The Portuguese shivered.

"I'm not going back to that place of evil," he announced decidedly, "especially if there is any chance of meeting the witch."

"Besides, we must look into that red pond and find out what that big thing swimming under water was," continued Dillingame, paying no attention to the interruption.

"Let's have a pow-wow with the Chinee first of all," I suggested, and clapped my hands to summon him.

Lo Chan emerged from behind the red-and-gold curtain, and salaamed. It may have been imagination, but I seemed to detect that there was not quite the same degree of reverence he had shown in the past.

"I desire to look into the matter of the gold," I announced, making my statement as indefinite as possible.

"This afternoon we will go to the diggings," and he salaamed anew.

"What's he saying?" demanded Dillingame, and I translated.

"We're going back to the temple this afternoon," the Englishman insisted obstinately. "Put off the other trip till tomorrow."

"Why not let me go with him," eagerly suggested Gomez, "while you two attend to other matters?"

For a moment I hesitated. The Portuguese was not to be trusted, and I did not know what he might hatch out against us. On the other hand, since he could speak no Ida'an or Chinese, how could be plot with the mandarin? Ashamed of my fears, I gave my consent and advised Lo Chan that only Gomez would accompany him. Again he bowed and withdrew.

Then, since the sun was at its height and it was insufferably hot, we stretched ourselves on the cold *kajang* matting for a noontime siesta.

We were not destined to visit the temple that afternoon, the next day, or the day after; nor did Gomez get to the gold diggings. After an hour's uneasy doze we woke fairly gasping for breath. The heat lay over the world like a heavy blanket, there was not a breath of air, and it was rapidly growing darker. Came a moaning in the treetops, gradually rising to a roar. Coolies clamped heavy shutters over the open front of the house and then scurried for shelter.

The roar increased to thunder, a breath of cool wind slipped in through the loosely woven walls, and then came the rain, a solid sheet of water crashing onto the ground as though hurled from above.

The coolies brought lights and, unable to make ourselves heard in the awful tumult, we settled down to wait for the end of the storm. Gomez began cooking opium pills and was soon lost in oblivion. Trevor found some rice-paper and I tried to teach him more of the Ida'an dialect (he had picked up quite a bit by himself) spelling out the words phonetically.

It rained without ceasing the next day and the next; then at sundown the storm came to an end as quickly as it had begun. The shutters were removed from the front of the house, Gomez emerged from his opium trance, and Trevor and I could hear each other speak. All ground between the stone causeways was under water and every curved leaf was a miniature fountain of silvery spray.

For half an hour we stretched our legs outside and then returned for the rest that had been impossible during the roar of the rain. The sun sank, the birds became silent, and my companions' deep breathing soon told me that they had found sleep.

From the jungle, clear and pure as a silver thread, floated a voice:

> "*Gone is the wind, the rain is past,*
> The moonlit night is here at last.
> I wait, all longing, wait for thee,
> *Come fast, my love, come fast to me.*
>
> "*My skin is pale as the jasmine flower,*
> (Oh, haste you, love, 'tis the sacred hour!)
> My breath is sweet as the areca bloom,
> *Where its purple cups in the darkness loom!*"

Trevor snorted in his sleep and I stirred him with my elbow. "Wake up," I whispered. "You are being serenaded. You or that other handsome laddie, the mandarin."

> "*As the epidendrum holds the anguska tree,*
> Musk-scented, my arms shall twine 'round thee;
> As the teak is held by the clinging vine,
> *Thus shall thy lips be held to mine!*"

"It's Kratas," exclaimed Dillingame, sitting up, "and she isn't serenading that fat Chinaman, either! What did that last verse mean?"

> "Leave this place as quick as you can,
> I much prefer the fat Chinaman,
> Or I'll have to jab a poison dart
> Straight through the middle of your heart."

I translated obligingly—this love affair seemed to me to be verging on the serious.

"You're a liar," he answered promptly, and stepped out boldly into the darkness.

"Come back, you fool," I called after him. "You'll get a knife stuck into you!" But he had disappeared.

Groaning at the stark idiocy of it—Trevor had never shown himself a ladies' man before—I followed down the ladder. Somewhere in the blackness the girl laughed. My foot went off the causeway and I plumped down into the water.

Crawling out again, and cussing beneath my breath, I listened. There was no sound. Disgusted, I climbed back, shed my wet clothes and rolled up in a blanket. Again came the girl's laugh from out of the night. The ladder creaked beneath Trevor's weight and he scratched a match. Around his neck was a jasmine wreath and he held a small palm-leaf package in his hand.

"Did she kiss you?" I asked him disagreeably.

"None of your business, but I couldn't get close enough to her," he growled. "She just chucked the flowers around my neck, gave me this bundle and vanished. I couldn't think of the Ida'an for 'come back,' either."

In the tropics, the morning after a storm is always beautiful. The coolness still lingers, and everything is fresh green and has generally grown about a yard. We woke full of energy; even Gomez seemed to feel no ill effects from his opium debauch, and decided to carry out our original program of visiting the temple while the Portuguese accompanied the Chinaman to the gold diggings.

I was about to clap my hands to summon Lo Chan when he lurched from behind the red-and-gold curtain. Evidently opium had also been his solace for the last two days, and the effects had not worn off. At any rate, he omitted the customary salaam and began a rather heated harangue.

According to the laws of the Tong (so he said) certain privileges were due him, and I had given no intimation that I intended to grant them. For example, even if I had been sent to take his place, I should have told him at once of the manner and time of his death—it was his right. Also where was the acknowledgment of the last tribute of gold sent to the coast, and his written sentence from the Tong?

More and more inflamed by his own words and still swayed by the poppy drug, he began to wave his arms.

How did he know we hadn't stolen the black butterfly talisman? That we weren't impostors? What kept him from calling in his coolies and having us strung up by the thumbs?

This sort of talk couldn't go on, of course. The drugged man was lashing himself into a fury. I gave Dillingame a signal (he always did the fighting for both of us), and the Chinaman went down to an uppercut nicely combined with a trip.

"Dog of a parricide," I thundered, "you shall die a death unnamed, nor shall I tell you when! Who are you, scum of the earth, to question the black butterfly's wing?" and I hauled it out of my pocket.

Lo Chan got slowly to his feet and salaamed, all the fight knocked out of him.

"'Twas a madness," he mumbled. "I do my lord's bidding."

Gomez was scared to death of the big Chinaman after this outburst, but his desire to see the place whence the gold came prevailed over his fears, and away the two then went, surrounded by a guard of coolies.

The very first thing Trevor and I did when we were alone was to open the little package Kratas had given to the Englishman the night before. Inside the palm leaf wrapping was a soft piece of native cloth, which we unrolled, bringing to light two eight-inch-long cocoons, jet black, their fine silk-like threads woven as closely as a piece of line. Dillingame split one open with the sharp blade of his knife and the pupa tumbled out on the floor.

Most pupae of butterflies make you think of angels or souls in transition. This one looked exactly like the devil disguised in the form of a dragon.

"Let's see that butterfly talisman," he demanded, and I laid it before him while he was trying to dissect out the embryonic wing. The pupa was not sufficiently developed to show wing venation, though, so he carefully replaced it in its silk cocoon and did it up with the other.

"Keep the talisman," I suggested, "and try to ask Kratas about it in the intervals of your unholy love-making."

I overhauled our weapons carefully, as became a cautious man, before starting for the temple, and we set out heavily armed. There was water on either side of the causeways and the stones beneath our feet were steaming wet. A little wind fanned the treetops and the whole world seemed to be a waving silver-and-green symphony.

It was not a deserted world, however, as it had been on our previous expedition. The little beast-men were trotting along the stone roads, pressing timorously to the edges while we passed, and all converging in the same direction toward the temple. They lined the rampart around the pond, no longer blood red, in which we had seen the mysterious ripple, and the square in front of the portico was one solid mass of them. There must have been two thousand of the ape-like beings, and from this great multitude came not a sound.

"Go on or hang back?" I interrogated Trevor.

"On, since we started," he answered. "Besides, they haven't even their blowguns."

The crowd opened silently before us as we strode toward the entrance of the temple. Inside, it was as empty as when we had first visited it, save that a single, thin shaft of sunlight came down through the aperture above.

"Come on," called Dillingame, and I followed him upward. The sides being shuttered in, it was quite dark at first as we stood on the top rounds of the ladder and tried to pierce the gloom. The bar of light broadened and I saw the edge of the sun overhead. Dimly we made out that the foliage had been removed from the floor; then as the light increased, we saw the walls hung everywhere with the long, black cocoons, the resting stage into which the black caterpillars had entered.

The sun came square over the hole at the top of the temple, shining down so brightly into our eyes that we were blinded; and at the same moment came a murmur from outside as though each member of the crowd had drawn a single, simultaneous deep breath.

"Next act. Let's see it," I suggested, and we backed down the ladder, shielding our eyes from the glare.

Along a causeway to the left, where were turned all the beast-men's faces, slowly advanced a group of strangely clad figures. Closer, we made out that they were old, old women, wrinkled, bent, tottering, clothed in strips of many-colored cloths that fluttered from their scrawny shoulders. Immediately before the temple they halted and opened out. In their midst appeared one of the beast-men, and bound to his back was the wizened Chinaman we had met leading the Ida'ans whose baskets contained the little red tree frogs.

Suddenly the old women broke into a cackling chorus:

> "*Pale is the pool with the silver rim,*
> Pale should be red,

So we send you to him.
When the sun has painted the world to gold
Pale shall be red as it was of old.

"*Pale is the pool with the silver rim,*
Hungry is he,
So we send you to him.
When the sun has painted the world to gold
Pale shall be red as it was of old."

Straight through the crowd came Kratas till she stood among the shrinking old hags. Catching the beast-man, who bore the Chinaman bound to his back, by the hair, she led him to the edge of the lily-bordered pool.

"*Pale is the pool with the silver rim,*
Waiting is he.
So go to him.
When the sun has painted the world to gold
Pale shall be red as it was of old,"

chanted the cracked voices.

The captive shrieked and struggled on the beast-man's back. With a mighty heave, Kratas sent them over the ramp into the water, their impetus carrying them beyond the border of white lilies.

The center of the pool bubbled as they sank. Up they came, something tipped with pink, something on a thick black stem pushing them half out of the water and fastening to their bodies. For a moment the miserable bound creatures were above the surface; then were drawn slowly under, the water reddening about them.

It all happened so quickly, was done so mechanically, that it was doubly horrible.

"Pretty sweetheart you have," I managed to gasp, "feeding live men to some water monster!"

Dillingame's eyes were popping from his head, but at my words his jaw set.

"Criminals, probably," he stuttered. "She was only seeing justice done—and the pool had to be red."

"Look here," I cried out in horror, "are you defending that—that witch? Have you gone crazy?"

He did not answer; his eyes were on the girl, who was coming through the scattering crowd. I plucked at his sleeve.

"Let's go from here," I begged.

I so hated, and still do hate that woman—indeed, I think she has made me hate all women—that my conscience forces me to do her justice in spite of the wrong she did me. As she stood before us smiling at Dillingame she was beautiful as a dream of Paradise, a goddess of the golden age, Eve, the first woman whence all after drew their charm. I forgot that she was a savage, forgot her beast-men had shot the harmless Ida'an porters, how she had wantonly slain one of them with the poisoned arrow; even forgot the tragedy of the two bound wretches cast to a horrible death in the water-lily-bordered pool. All I could see was that she was beautiful, desirable beyond the whole world.

Paying no attention to me, she halted not a hand's breadth from Trevor, and spoke:

"I am Kratas, priestess of the Land of Blood, who knows not death, who lives forever. The lives of all men—your life—are between my hands.

"I am Kratas, the priestess, guardian of the souls of the dead. Even the sable butterflies are beneath my law.

"I am Kratas, who guards the yellow dust all strangers desire.

"I am Kratas, all-powerful, and I come at set of sun to take you to my house as my slave and mate."

"I don't get that last part," complained Dillingame, turning to me.

"Merely a proposal that will not take 'no' for an answer," I explained. "Shall I tell the lassie you'll think it over?"

"She's very beautiful," he sighed, letting his eyes stray to her.

"The Great Lord from Afar has already a wife whom he loves," I explained hastily in Ida'an, "and *orang putehs* have but one mate."

Her arms were around his shoulders now, and she gave me one venomous backward glance.

"Her blood shall fatten hungry leeches," she hissed, "and he will forget . . ." Her lips found his.

IV
THE PRICE OF MY FREEDOM

Dillingame and I quarreled bitterly when we got back to Lo Chan's house. The man was mad, bewitched, and in his stark obstinacy defended himself. Hadn't he a perfect right to kiss a pretty girl if he wanted to? Hadn't she spared us when she might have wiped us out any minute? Wasn't it through her that we hoped to get the black butterfly—and gold?

There was no arguing with such a maniac, and I told him so.

Gomez came back alone, around four o'clock, and in a most disconsolate state of mind. It seems that the gold diggings were in the bottom of a dry creek and the rain had brought down an entire bluff on top of them. The little man was in despair, whined and bemoaned his fate that he had ever come with us, and declared himself ruined.

To tell the truth, we paid little attention to him. Dillingame was stretched out on one of the *kajang* mats looking exasperatingly comfortable and complacent. I was sulkily packing up our belongings at the other end of the house—and it was to me that Gomez gravitated.

The trouble with villains is that they are apt to consider the rest of the world as bad as they are, especially when it is a question of gold. Gomez proceeded to tell me that as soon as he had found out Lo Chan understood Portuguese he had pretended to conspire with him, to discover what he could. He suggested to the Chinaman that Dillingame and I be murdered, and the piece of black butterfly wing in their possession, they grab all the gold in sight and flee to Dutch Borneo.

Lo Chan had been delighted with the murdering idea when he learned that the talisman was Gomez's property—"had to tell him that, you know"—explained the little man ingenuously—and confided to him that, without it, he would be unable to collect the tribute from the temple.

As to fleeing to Dutch Borneo, however, he did not want to because of the difficulty of transporting his three wives.

"My plan now is," the little villain continued, "to pretend to be
hand-in-glove with Lo Chan, and through the black butterfly
locket—which seems to be the key to the situation—hold him in
check. I will let him have the talisman to collect the tribute, then
we'll kill him and return to Brunei."

Fine arrangement, wasn't it? All Gomez wanted was to get the
little round locket in his hands and then it would be good-by to us.
I lost no time in passing all this up to Dillingame, and he lost no
time in kicking the Portuguese down the ladder. It was not a dip-
lomatic thing to do, but I couldn't altogether blame him.

We paid for it later, as you will see.

Gomez did not return, and Trevor and I picked up our quarrel
where we had left off. I argued for an immediate return to Brunei;
what we had already collected would show a good profit on the
expedition. Further intercourse with the Portuguese was all but
impossible. Dillingame obstinately stood out for waiting till we had
secured a specimen of the black butterfly—in other words, until
the pupae had developed in the cocoons and emerged; and added
that he might trade for some more gold from Kratas—that she
seemed to like him.

Seemed to like him! I should say she did! That was my main
anxiety, combined with the fact that *he* "seemed to like" *her*.

We argued, if facts being presented by him can be called arguing, till nearly dark, and then we ceased speaking to each other.

Behind the gold-and-red curtain at the end of the house a
woman screamed, and the sound was cut off short as though someone had grabbed her by the windpipe. Instinctively we jumped for
our weapons. Without the slightest warning the curtain went down,
unmasking a huddled crowd of coolies armed with muskets. I
yanked Dillingame to the floor just as the house was filled with
the roar and smoke of a volley.

"Got me through the shoulder," he gasped, and rolling over,
turned loose with his automatic. I pumped my rifle into the thick
of the smoke, and then they were upon us.

The first Chinese face that loomed up before me changed to a blur of blood beneath the butt of my gun. With my foot I slid a couch in front of us and then hauled the Englishman to his feet.

In a yellow avalanche the coolies piled over our frail barricade. Dillingame swinging a heavy tabouret, cleared the floor in front of him. I literally blew men from the mouth of my pistol. The smoke rose. I tried to slip in new shells, but there was no time. Over the motionless or squirming bodies of their companions they were upon us again. The Englishman went down, dragging a halt a dozen of his assailants with him. Forced against the wall, my arms were twisted upward, a cord slipped around my wrists, binding me helpless, and my knees were pinioned.

The fight had been voiceless, just a silent striving punctuated by the firearms, till this moment, when there was a scream of deadly fear from a coolie. In the open front of the house stood Kratas, her face a mask of rage. From beneath the jasmine wreaths that clothed the upper part of her body she snatched a long knife, and, light as a butterfly, sprang over the couch to where Dillingame lay.

Three times the knife fell, dripping red after each stroke, and she rolled three dead Chinamen from the body of the unconscious Englishman. Then, with one sweep of her round arms she swung him to her shoulders, spat out some words I did not understand to the cowering coolies, and heedless of my frantic yell for help, went swiftly down the ladder with her limp burden.

The house was a shambles. There were no less than a dozen dead and wounded men lying about, not counting the three Kratas had knifed. Floor, walls, couches and overturned screens were splotched with blood, and the air was heavy with gunpowder and the smell of death.

Gently enough, though I cursed them, I was bound to a bamboo couch, a cushion even being slipped under my head to ease it. The gold-and-red curtain at the end of the room was replaced, dead and wounded were carried away, and I was left in the darkening twilight.

Not for long, however. I heard Gomez speaking in Portuguese at the bottom of the ladder.

"I hope thy are both dead, damn 'em. You may take the talisman from Freeman and keep it, for all I care. Just give me a load of gold and I'll find my way down into Dutch Borneo somehow."

"True friend," purred Lo Chan, "it shall be as you desire," and they both came up the ladder.

"You turn me loose, Gomez," I roared, "or I'll beat you to death later."

"I'm going to kill you slowly as soon as I have taken away that talisman," he snarled, "you all-virtuous, heavy-handed fool!" and he began to investigate my pockets.

I shut my jaws tight and let them search me. Finally they stripped off most of my clothes and literally tore them to pieces.

"Where's that butterfly thing?" demanded the Portuguese furiously.

"I gave it to Dillingame," I answered in Portuguese so both would understand.

"Dillingame is dead, thanks to me," said Gomez, also in Portuguese. "We'll take a look at his body, Lo Chan."

"He's not dead, as you will soon find out," I interrupted. "Kratas carried him off and the talisman is with him."

"*Santa Maria!* That witch again!" and the little man crossed himself.

His perturbation was nothing to the terror that convulsed the mandarin's frightfully mutilated face, making it doubly hideous.

"If Kratas gets that talisman, I shall die the unknown death," he wailed to me. "Go, go at once to Dillingame Tuan and beg it of him for me! I will send you from here unharmed, I swear it by the sacred black butterfly, and with all the gold three strong men can carry!"

"What of this swine?" I asked, jerking my head toward Gomez. "Speak Ida'an so he may not understand."

"He shall be burnt over slow fire for your imperial pleasure, or thrown into the silver-rimmed pond. You may see him torn with hot pincers or fed living to the fire ants of the jungle. . . ."

"Enough," I commanded, and translated carefully into English for the Portuguese's benefit.

"Get the sable butterfly's wing and we will kill the Chinaman," he whined, back at me. "You wouldn't have a fellow Christian done to death by a yellow heathen, a companion murdered in cold blood!"

"Nothing I'd enjoy more," I answered heartily. "Now, turn me loose."

On my feet, freed of bonds, I restrained myself, though with difficulty, from kicking the little man—it had brought us bad luck before. Food appeared, and with it two iron-bound chests that were humbly laid at my feet. Raising the covers I saw they were filled to the brim with raw gold-dust.

Again, his eyes on the yellow metal, Gomez began to plead that I join him in murdering the mandarin and make away with his fortune. I had but finished translating this for Lo Chan's benefit, just so everything would be nice and friendly, when Kratas stepped in from the darkness.

Without as much as a glance at the other two men she beckoned to me, and I followed her down the ladder. Catching my hand she guided me through the shadows along the causeway. Before the red pond she stopped for a breath, and pointed.

"If he dies—you go there," she hissed.

Past the temple we went and into the black jungle. Ahead of us a voice began to sing, and the words were in English.

> *"They stuck him full of pins to remind him of his sins,*
> And still he swilled down beer and rum together.
> So they cut off his fool head and filled him full of lead—
> *And a boy's best friend is his mother."*

"He prays to his gods," sighed Kratas, dragging me on faster.

I sprang up the ladder into a torch-lit house and hurried to Trevor's side. He was tossing on a broad bamboo couch, a bandage of crushed leaves against his wounded shoulder, and his eyes hot and wild with fever. For a moment he recognized me.

"Hello, Andy, old top! Come to preserve the proprieties, hey? You're a hell of a chaperon.

> *"Oh, Andy married Margaret,*
> Oh, Andy married Jane:

He gave his name to Mary
Eloped then with Elaine. . . ."

and he was in the clutch of the fever-devils again.

Thirty long anxious days Kratas and I nursed the Englishman, nursed him with the care and tenderness that a man receives only from his best friend and the woman who loves him.

Each morning Gomez appeared before the house and begged for the butterfly talisman, and each morning I cursed him and bade him be gone.

Kratas, beautiful as a dream of bliss and tender as a mother, never left the sick man's side save twice, and both times I heard the cackling chorus from the direction of the lily-bordered crimson pond.

> *"Pale is the pool with the silver rim.*
> Waiting is he,
> So go to him.
> When the sun has painted the world to gold
> *Pale shall be red as it was of old."*

The thirty-first day, Dillingame's fever broke, and he knew me, reaching out his hand with a little unsteady smile. Kratas knelt beside him and her lips brushed his as lightly as a passing butterfly. Then he slept.

Once Trevor was on the road to recovery, his progress was rapid. In a week he was up and could walk about, though still woefully thin and white. Kratas was unceasing in her devotion and had a retinue of old women—the priestesses clad in the strange garments of strips of colored cloths—waiting on and cooking for him.

Our traps had been brought from Lo Chan's house, and I found time to do quite a bit of collecting, always in the opposite direction from the temple. I couldn't even think of that place without a shudder.

Conditions would have been ideal for a man who loved the jungle and found happiness in solving its secrets had it not been for one thing; Kratas was jealous of every word I spoke to the Englishman. He had made marvelous progress in the Ida'an tongue, and they held long conversations together, part of which Dillingame retailed to me, throwing some light on our situation.

Kratas's story of her own life was extremely simple. She calmly asserted that she was the first woman that had been put on earth, and that she would live forever.

Years ago there were many brothers of Lo Chan in the wilderness, who had built the temple and washed out great stores of gold, which were buried beneath it. Then they had all died, and for a long time there were no Chinaman. Finally Lo Chan and his coolies appeared with the black butterfly talisman to vouch for them, and had started to wash for gold.

Each full of the moon, according to the age-long custom, he was given as many quills of the precious metal as he could hold in both hands; but while in past years the dust had been collected by the beast-men, it was now drawn from the horde beneath the temple. This tribute was then sent to the coast by a Murut, who carried the round piece of butterfly's wing as a passport.

The messenger had not returned from his last trip (Gomez could have told why), but he was expected any moment, since the time of tribute was but two days off.

In regard to the lily-bordered pool, the information was extremely sketchy. It was there dwelt the God of Blood, father of the black butterflies; but what exactly that god was, Kratas did not make clear.

"You see, Andy," Trevor explained to me a dozen times, "what we consider cruel bloodthirstiness in the girl is nothing but custom—a heritage from her ancestors. Since she has always been supreme, the life of a miserable beast-man means nothing to her. Consider for a moment how frightful it must seem to her that we catch and kill butterflies—the souls of the dead!"

He was teaching her to speak English, too; though I hardly saw the necessity of beginning with "darling" for the first noun, and "love" for the verb.

Gomez had not appeared for several days, but that morning he came to the foot of our ladder with an entirely new plan. Lo Chan had promised to send out the gold by him if the Murut did not return—"As I know well he will not," he interjected—if he could secure the black butterfly talisman, which, once recovered, Lo Chan had sworn should never again leave his hands. Instead of going to Brunei we could simply steer for Dutch Borneo, the Portuguese explained, and make away with the gold. He begged and pleaded for the talisman, but I only cursed him while Trevor laughed and tantalized him by holding it up so he might see it.

A pretty pair they made, Gomez and Lo Chan, cold-blooded murderers, both of them, and each continually plotting to destroy the other. Lo Chan's plot, in this instance was perfectly plain to us. Gomez and his gold would never leave the Land of Blood without the black butterfly wing talisman.

That evening the three of us were sitting in the dusk, and Trevor and I were engaged in a long argument regarding the possible food plants of some new species of butterflies. Twice Kratas had spoken to the Englishman and, absorbed in what we were discussing, he had not answered her.

Without the slightest warning she was on her feet with a snarl of rage.

"Offspring of the wild hog, killer of the souls of the dead," she shrieked at me, "You have dared too much! You would steal my Lord Trevor from me. Now you shall die. I have spoken who cannot unsay my words!"

Quick as a snake, she sprang at me, and I caught the bare blade of her knife in my left hand so it cut deep into the fingers. Dillingame threw himself upon her and I wisely retreated down the ladder. For a long time he tried to soothe her, but quite in vain. She was absolutely determined on my death—she had spoken who could not unsay her words.

Finally he got her calmed and willing to let me live for the present—and he won this concession with kisses.

My hand bled freely, the blood even soaking through a bandage, and I lay down on my bamboo couch near Dillingame with the pleasant feeling that I should probably be murdered in my sleep.

I woke at dawn to a pang of agony from my wounded hand. There was a great hole in the mosquito net and a soft black thing brushed my face.

Wide awake, as the pain increased, I looked down on a sable butterfly, a foot from wing tip to wing tip, poised above my head, its powerful jaws tearing and biting through the bloody bandage until they reached the live flesh beneath. Light as air it evaded me; then I smothered it beneath folds of the netting, giving it that pinch every butterfly collector knows and it went limp. Marveling at the wonder of those sloe-black wings and fierce jaws, the like of which had never before been known among butterflies, I pinned it, finally, in the cyanide poison box. And it was borne in on me that this winged creature was a cannibal thing that came to human blood.

At intervals all through the next day Gomez came to our house and pleaded desperately for the talisman.

Kratas would not speak to me that day, only glared; and Trevor was plainly disturbed. At last she set out toward the temple and twice we heard the chorus that indicated another wretch had gone to the horrible unknown death in the blood-red pool. It was an anxious twelve hours, and in the evening Kratas simply sent me out of the house while she talked with Trevor.

It rained that night as it rains in the tropics, the drops coming down so that the world held no other sound but their crashing fall. I could not sleep, more than alarmed since I had not been able to get one single word alone with Trevor. Even now Kratas, awake and motionless, crouched in the dark between our beds.

Hours slipped by and suddenly I was conscious of a spot of shadow against the darkness moving silently nearer and nearer to where Dillingame slept. On my feet, I touched the girl's bare shoulder and she sprang forward as though shot from a bow.

The rain drowned all sound of the struggle and I struck a light. Gomez, his hands twisted behind his back, lay on his face, a broad-bladed knife by his side. Dillingame moaned in his sleep and the girl hastily dragged her captive within the house.

"Lo Chan sent him to murder Trevor," I shouted to her above the noise.

She nodded, her face black with fury, and quicker than a wild-cat twisted the Portuguese onto his back, burying her knife in his throat. An imperative hand bade me be gone, and as the match flickered out I saw her slip an earthen vase beneath the couch to catch the blood dripping from the dead man's severed jugular vein. When morning came she was still crouched by Dillingame's couch, and all our weapons had disappeared.

Not a word would Kratas let us exchange, her knife at my throat whenever I turned to the Englishman, and the sun was just rising when she led me down the ladder.

"This looks like the end of Andy Freeman," I shouted back to him.

"Kratas, if harm befalls my friend, I too, die," called Dillingame. "Here, take this, Trevor," and he flung at my feet the chamois skin bag that held the black butterfly talisman.

The same painfully silent crowd of beast-men was before the temple. Inside, the ladder to the second story had been removed and a thin shaft of sunlight came down through the hole in the ceiling, gilding a pile of porcupine quills, through whose transparent sides winked the glint of gold. The old hags with their garments of multi-colored strips of cloth filed in, the leader carrying a covered earthenware vase, which she laid at Kratas's feet. The ray of sunlight from above broadened and the priestess began to sing:

> "*Fill up thy hands with the golden thing.*
> Both hands cram-full of the dust we bring
> From the secret horde alone we know,
> *Stored up by thy brothers long ago.*"

Lo Chan, his horrible features dead white, entered the temple alone and stood before the pile of porcupine quills.

> "*The moon is full, thy people pay,*
> Lord of the Pool, on this thy day,
> Tribute to those who long did raise
> *This temple to thy glorious praise.*"

Through the aperture above came a solid shaft of sunlight, filling it to the edges. A sable butterfly sped down this golden stream of light; another, and then another, until the air was black with their wings. Lo Chan bent down, burying his hands among the heavy quills; and at that very moment Kratas poured the contents of the earthenware vase over his back and shoulders, soaking him from head to foot with red blood. The Chinaman straightened up with a startled cry. First one and then a swarm of black butterflies darted upon him till his body was all but concealed beneath their quivering wings. He staggered toward the door, beating with shrieks of anguish at the monstrous flying things that fastened to his wrists, his lips, his face. The hole above vomited out a solid column of the horrible insects, and Lo Chan was smothered beneath them.

The mass of quivering wings rose from the ground, hurtled out into the sunlight. Once the man broke free and rushed toward the lily-bordered pool. Then they were on him again, whirled him in their midst above the water.

The surface broke and a pink thing protruded out into the light, a gaping pink mouth a foot broad attached to seven feet of flat, inky body that now lay on the surface—a loathsome, gigantic leech.

The butterflies raised their victim ten feet in air, then slowly sank down with him toward the water. The pink head of the leech went blindly groping among the sable wings; then man and butterflies together disappeared beneath the bubbling water that soon had changed to a livid pink.

For a moment they reappeared, then sank once more, and only the ripples rocking the big white lilies disturbed the calm of the blood-red pool.

"Let us go back," I begged Kratas, a great nausea coming over me.

"*You* go back to the land whence you came," she answered, "living only through my infinite mercy."

Before the bamboo house were waiting five of the beast-men loaded with my baggage. I attempted to mount the ladder, but Kratas jerked me back, and herself ascended.

"It's no use, Andy," said Trevor from above. "You have to go or die. I can not move the girl, and our weapons are gone."

"But aren't you coming?" I whispered, a great horror over me.

"No," he said. "No. It is only by staying that I bought your life. The talisman will protect you on your way out."

Behind him Kratas leaned against his shoulder and snuggled her cheek to his.

"Come back—some time," he said, looking down at me. "I sha'nt be unhappy here, but—come back—some time."

The jasmine-clad girl slipped one beautiful, warm arm around his neck and raised her face to his. Their lips met. . . .

LOST—ONE MYLODON
Elmer Brown Mason
1916

The fact of the matter is that, for a man who makes a profession of exploring expeditions, Pete Wells (which is me) had been in civilization too long. I was ripe to go any place where there were no waiters to be tipped. Certainly Bones' physical charms didn't lure me from my happy table in Old Swartz's Café, Jacksonville, Florida, U.S.A. The top of his head looked like an ostrich's egg, his face was a jungle of straw-colored beard, stiff as the spines of a hedge-hog, out of which peeped two innocent blue eyes, and the rest of him was completely globular. In height he was six feet, all but nine inches, and his name was Nicholas Vladmir Versch-and-all-the-rest-of-the-alphabet-well scrambled.

But, law me, how that miracle of rotundity could talk! That evening, from the time I laid down his letter of introduction until next morning, I simply listened spellbound.

His specialty was bones, the bones of extinct animals, and he wanted me to go with him to a place called Ultima Speranza in southern Patagonia, where there was a famous cave full of bones, and then up along the Chilean Andes prospecting after the remains of beasts that had been dead so long that no one really knew how they had looked.

The proposition in itself did not appeal to me—I had tried it once before in a salt marsh on the Brazilian coast, and. the 'skeeters had nearly eaten me alive—not until after the second drink, any-way, when he really began to talk. Then I started in seeing things. From a bunch of drawings of prehistoric and modern bones, he sorted the same kinds together, and explained how he correlated them. First, he compared the thigh of a common or garden guinea pig to a busted up, secondhand-looking relic of what he called a toxodon, and before I realized it, so vividly reconstructed a nine-foot rodent, with tremendous, chisel-like teeth, that I reached under my armpit to see if my automatic was loose in its scabbard.

Then came pterodactyls, flying reptiles with long, beak-like jaws and an eighteen-foot spread of leathery wings; a cute little atlantosaurus with a thigh bone larger than an elephant's; eighty-foot-long diplodocuses. . . . Honest, I was glad when the morning light filtered in, and only half of my quart of Scotch was gone, too, though the Russian had gotten away with two full bottles of white, blockade liquor—so like his native vodka, he apologized.

Of course I agreed to go with him, just couldn't help myself, and in less than a week we were on board a steamer for Valdiva, Chile.

It was a long trip, and I had plenty of time to size up my companion, and that fat little Russian seemed so simple that I just couldn't believe in him. Apparently his one object in life was the collecting of bones, and his present direct purpose to controvert some German scientist against whom he nursed a royal grouch because of the assertion that mylodons had sat on their haunches while pulling down the tops of trees to feed on, instead of standing up like human beings.

I don't mean by all this that Bones was a freak and didn't know anything else. Quite the contrary. I don't think there was anything he didn't know something about, only nothing but prehistoric animals really interested him. He sang in the ship's concerts like a tuneful mockingbird, if you can imagine a bewhiskered mockingbird in a dinner coat that would have fitted a hogshead, never laid down two pair to a one-card draw, and took the masculine normal, or perhaps twice the normal, amount of alcohol.

He hadn't any use for the señoritas, though. A flock of them fluttered around him, but he let 'em flutter. I suppose they were attracted to him because he was so darned ugly. Women are often taken that way—no better proof than that I have had two romances in my own life, both ending happily.

Valdiva is some little city. We put up at a hotel that even a commercial traveler couldn't have criticized. Bones slid out to look for the consul and a lot of people to whom he had letters, while I spread myself all over the waterfront trying to pick up a craft for the rest of our journey down the coast.

Gosh, but that was a punk lot of shipping! There was enough paint spread over rotten wood and rust-honeycombed iron to decorate several battleships, but not one thing I'd care to trust myself in off a lee shore. Had to give it up finally, it was getting so dark. Besides, a kind of a crowd had collected after I handed one to a skipper who demanded a hundred pesos from me for jabbing a knife into his schooner below the water-line—claimed I'd ruined it, which was probably true.

Back at the hotel, I found Bones down in the lobby, surrounded by a group of what it took no finesse to identify as reporters. They were asking him the usual fool questions: how he liked the country, how it compared with Russia, and so on, and they were calling him Count. He introduced me to the bunch, but, being only a plain American, I didn't make any big hit with them, so I bought a drink just to show how much I cared, and went up in the elevator.

"Can't stay in this town long, Pete," the Russian announced as he came into our apartments, "or we'll be done to death socially. I was simply forced to accept a dinner invitation for us."

"All right, Count," I agreed amiably; "I'll go downstairs and rob a waiter of his glad rags. Never be it said I deserted the aristocracy in their need."

It went at that. Somehow, he never was much stuck on my horsing; didn't seem to get it.

Annexing clothes proved no trouble, and when I came back the little man had hung medals all over himself.

"Gosh!" I cried in admiration. "You certainly look the part! Sure you are only a count, not one of those grand dukes?"

He answered rather shortly that his family had always been respectable, which kind of had me guessing exactly how he meant it, and then we were whisked away in a large touring car to a club.

It was a men's dinner. If I had known that in advance, I should have worn my own clothes—and felt like a fool in them, too, since everyone else wore evening dress, mostly with some decoration. The food was fine, the drink better, and Bones was sure the whole cheese. One old chap, with more medals than a baking-powder advertisement, made a long speech about how honored they were at having the great scientist, Count Vladmir, in their midst, and the count got up and said in a few well-chosen words he was darned glad to be there. Then we ate some more and drank a lot more, while the orchestra played "There'll Be a Hot Time in the Old Town To-night," which seemed to have just struck that burg and struck it hard.

To be perfectly truthful, I didn't have a roaring good time. The man on my left did nothing but eat. The man on my right would only converse in English, and all he knew was "You tak' li'l drink wis me?" which I did, until he couldn't talk at all. The feast finally ended, however, and we motored back to the hotel, only hitting one lamp-post on the way.

The next morning I was off to the wharves again, and with no better result. Finally, though I hadn't the slightest hope of securing it, just on a chance, I had myself rowed out to a dandy little steam yacht in the offing. Who should come to the rail but my right-hand neighbor of the night before with his "You tak' li'l drink?" I did, and then, since he consented to talk Spanish, I explained my predicament to him.

Easiest thing in the world! His yacht was quite at our service. It really would be a favor to him to use it, since he was forced to visit his *hacienda* in the interior for several months. He was tickled to death to be able to serve Count Vladmir. The crew was on board, the yacht provisioned.

He really meant it, too, and, congratulating myself on a piece of pure luck, we had another "li'l drink," and I beat it back to the hotel.

It was a long steam down the roughest coast I have ever seen until we swung it back of Desolation Island, and we simply never should have arrived at Ultima Speranza fiord had it not been for the luck of finding that perfectly appointed yacht with its pilots who knew the channels. As it was, within those land-locked waters we had to nose cautiously further and further inland, to the anxi-

ety of a nervous captain and with a crew harassed by endless sound-
ings and perpetual lookouts until, somewhat below 50°, Bones was
contented to go ashore; The yacht was dismissed with orders to
return in two months, and, hiring two sturdy white men from the
little settlement to pack our supplies, we began forthwith our hunt
for the cave.

It was an extraordinary country and, from my point of view,
not a pleasant one. For a long way back from the sea, the land was
arctic, bare, and very rough; then came forests of enormous trees,
above which rose the mountains, with silvery glaciers twisting from
their sides like ribbons of burnished steel. We froze at night and
boiled during the day, while the humidity was so great that mists
were always rising from hidden valleys or streams, like the smoke
of volcanoes.

Somehow, it all depressed me—gave me a feeling as though
there was no going forward, no looking back—as though there was
an inertia in all things.

I lost that feeling after we found the cave, though.

It isn't quite correct for me to say we found the cave. What we
really did was to stumble on a little farm where dwelt an old, old
white man, who directed us where to look. He claimed that within
his time an immense piece of skin covered with greenish hair unlike that of any known animal, had been brought from there and,
together with several barrels of bones, sold to men who came in
ships. Then there had been some trouble with a wandering tribe of
the big Patagonian Indians, and the cave had been gradually forgotten.

It was a terrifically hot and muggy day when we reached the
place. From the outside, it did not look like much; merely a symmetrical black half moon set in the green of the hillside. Inside,
however, it opened up into a hundred-foot chamber, with walls fully
thirty feet high, and the dry, sandy floor showed signs of having
been disturbed in the center. It appealed to me principally as a
place to get out of the sun, but the count went straight up in the
air as soon as he was within.

Exactly as it had been described by Dr. Nordenskjöld! Humid atmosphere, but not too humid to reduce everything to peat. Cave dry—might find anything there!

He grabbed one of the two pointed shovels which, with a couple of mattocks, were our only collecting impedimenta, and, dashed it into the undisturbed sand close to the wall. And promptly he did find something, the skeleton of a man about seven feet tall.

I didn't like it. It's all very well to dig up prehistoric animals, but I don't approve of meddling with graveyards, and a graveyard it proved to be. All along the edge of the cave, hardly two feet beneath the sand, were the skeletons of men and women, not one measuring less than six feet.

"Look here, Bones," I said. "Cover up those giants and let's get out of here. I absolutely refuse to dig up dead men, even in the interest of science."

"I don't understand," he answered, more to himself than to me. "Skeletons of comparatively modern savages, Patagonians according to the cranium. They have no business here. We'll try the middle of the cave, Pete."

I shoveled back the sand along the edges while he dug in the center, cussing quite fluently the while. It became evident that all the middle of the cave had been worked over, and his labors were rewarded only by the rib of a guanaco and a pointed sliver he claimed had been fashioned into an eating utensil from a dog's leg bone. Disgusted, we sat down, and realized for the first time that both our white bearers had disappeared, leaving their packs behind them.

After hallooing outside for a time, we saw night was falling and went back into the cave to escape the heavy dew. There was no wood for a fire, and as we sat in the darkness munching hard tack, I for one heartily wished myself back at Old Swartz's.

"It's been cleaned out," finally sighed my companion. "Our only hope is that, farther in, it may be untouched. Are you afraid to explore the entire cave to-night, Pete?"

Darned if I wouldn't have refused if he had put it in any other way. The skeletons were on my nerves, but I didn't propose to be bluffed by any foreigner, not if he had so many medals he had to wear them on the tails of his coat.

"After you, my dear Count!" I answered, fishing our electric torches out of the packs, together with a half-dozen balls of twine.

Beyond the faint moonlight from the mouth of the cave it was black dark—not the darkness of out of doors when there are neither moon nor stars, but the enclosed blackness of the inside of a camera before the cap is taken off. I tied one end of a ball of twine tightly to a shovel driven in the sand, and followed the rotund form of my companion.

Around the walls we went, and then, bending our heads, dived under a shallow arch, walking on living rock. One ball, two balls, three balls of twine unwound as we explored a narrow passage which opened up finally into a small chamber with sandy floor.

"Here's something!" exclaimed the Russian, dragging a bone from the soil. "Another guanaco," he finished disgustedly, and went on. To the left the darkness became opaque, and there was the sound of slowly dripping water. A broad passage opened before us, and suddenly above our heads, through an aperture high, high in the rock, appeared a luminous body, the moon. We swept the place with our torches and nearly at our feet a tiny spring seeped up through the sand, flowing down an incline of white, luminous slime into the darkness. Bones took one step forward, lost his footing, fell, and, dropping his torch at my feet, rolled swiftly out of sight down the sloping way, his round body picking up the clay like a snowball adds to its bulk as it hurtles down a hillside.

To save my soul I couldn't help it—I roared. There was a crash in the distance like the breaking of dry branches before a fleeing deer, and then the count's voice:

"Laugh, you damned hyena," came cheerily up to me; "I've fallen into a boneyard. Wrap my torch in your shirt and throw it down to me."

"Hadn't I better come down?"

"Don't! don't!" he yelled. "It's slippery as ice! You'll have to get a rope to haul me out!"

I raised my own light high above my head and, putting his torch into a bundle with my shirt, threw to where I could dimly discern his figure, a glittering white globe below me. The bundle fell short. In vain he tried to climb up the slippery incline to it, while I howled with laughter; then, abandoning his attempts, he began to dig steps in the slime with a large, pointed bone. In half an hour he had progressed to where my shirt lay, and then, as the easiest mode of locomotion, rolled back to the bottom again.

The snapping on of his light showed the walls clearly. It was nothing more than a shoot down which he had fallen, a shoot paved with luminous, white phosphorescent clay all the way to the bottom, where it ended in a chamber twenty feet in circumference and literally filled with bones. They were banked up the sides, protruding from the ground. The little fat man was standing on them.

As he pulled the gruesome relics about the Russian growled out short sentences, "Damned guanacos again! Rabbit! A jaguar femur—what should that be doing here? Pete! Pete! I've found it, and part of the skin on it! A mylodon! A mylodon without question!"

"Hurrah for the mylodon!" I shouted enthusiastically. "I'll go back now and get a rope, and meanwhile, you work as far up the slide as you can. Tomorrow, we'll arrange some kind of a light in here and dig the whole thing up."

"All right!" he yelled. "Hurry back, though! It isn't pleasant, being left alone in the bowels of the earth!"

I tied the cord to a projecting piece of rock and turned back, letting the twine run through my fingers as I walked. Not twenty feet around the next corner, my torch suddenly went out, the battery exhausted. Great God, but it was dark! The sweat poured from my bare shoulders in spite of the fact that it would only mean leaving Bones alone in the darkness if I took his torch, and there were other batteries to recharge the lights in our packs.

Slowly, both hands cramped to the cord, I went forward. It seemed as though I had been groping on for centuries. Once the string snapped out of my hands, and I threw myself on the ground panting with fear until I found it again. At last, after I felt I had been long enough in the cave to be classed as a prehistoric animal myself, the cord slackened, light showed ahead, the flickering illumination of a fire, and I instantly decided our white bearers had returned. With a shout, I dropped the limp cord and ducked into the main cave.

I had only time to see seven tall figures facing me around a fire, when strong hands grasped me on either side. Furiously, I struck out, then tried to drag my automatic from under my left arm. Down I went with two big men on top of me, and in less time than it takes to tell I was trussed up like a fowl and dragged to the fire.

There were nine great Patagonians, seven men and two women, grouped about me, dressed in mantles fashioned from guanaco skins and armed with knives, old muskets and bolas.

Beside the fire, nearly at my feet, lay a tenth savage, an immense man, but thin to the point of extreme emaciation—dead.

The younger woman (she was a right good-looking savage for all her six feet of height) whispered excitedly to the elder. The men regarded me silently.

"What the devil does this mean?" I sputtered in Spanish. "Turn me loose at once!"

"You'll have to get your devil to turn you loose," a man sneered at me in the same tongue. "We shall not. You have come into the cave of the Sacred Moon and disturbed those who were sleeping. To-morrow you die in honor of the one who lies before you."

Nice, wasn't it? End of Pete Wells, Esq., sacrificed to the glory of a Patagonian stiff with no clothes on, and buried in a cave haunted by the ghosts of prehistoric animals! I lost my temper.

"You don't say?" I remarked sarcastically. "Well, my devil *will* be here, and he'll make you turn somersaults under the 'Sacred Moon'."

"Aren't you afraid?" curiously asked the man nearest me.

"Not of you," I answered furiously, and, twisting one leg free, applied my foot forcibly to the pit of his stomach.

It was a fool thing to do, and he was on me in a second with raised knife. I thought my last moment had come, but the others pulled him away.

"No blood must be shed in the cave of the Sacred Moon," said the elder woman sternly. "To-morrow we will see to him. Now let us bury our dead."

Muttering evilly, my assailant stepped aside. Raising the dead man, the others carried him to a shallow depression near the wall and unceremoniously scratched sand over him. Then, while the men stood in a circle and swayed before the dying fire, the girl began to sing in. the corrupted Spanish that seems to have taken the place of the Patagonian tongue, if there ever was one:

> "*Night has come that ends not,*
> Night has come to thee,
> With the Great One quickly
> Thy spirit wanders free.
> Body lies in sacred ground,
> Spirit will fly soon
> Where the light is softest,
> *Up to, the bright, round moon.*
>
> "*Where the light is softest,*
> *Up to the bright, round moon.*"

The other savages crooned in unison, swaying back and forth and then settling to the ground.

There was a long silence, and the girl's voice again rose:

> "*Night has come that ends not,*
> Thou wilt go on high
> Where the light gleams always
> In the darkest sky.
> Earth will hold thy body,
> Ever and for ay;
> Spirit goes a floating
> *Where the moonbeams play.*
>
> "*Spirit goes a floating*
> *Where the moonbeams play.*"

I shifted my position painfully, and felt something hard beneath my elbow. It was the shovel to which I had tied the guiding cord for our expedition into the cave, and, rolling further over, I sawed the rope that bound my arms against its point. The edge of the moon came down over the top of the entrance to the cave, and again the girl began to sing:

"*Night has come that ends not,*
But she comes, her light,
Silver sparkling pathway,
Guides thy steps aright.
Sacred, O most sacred!
Shines on sea and dune,
Sacred, O most sacred,
Bright and shining moon.

"*Sacred, O most sacred!*
Bright and shining moon."

The silvery disk outside lowered, filling the foreground of the cave with light. The ceremony evidently over, the Patagonians rose to their feet, and two of them stepped across the dead fire towards me.

The rope about my right arm was sawed through. With numbed fingers, I tried to draw my automatic from under my left armpit. The shovel slid from beneath me, began to progress into the darkness at the end of its cord.

With a flash of inspiration I pointed my free arm towards it.

"Look!" I howled. "Look! I send the senseless wood and iron for my devil! Tremble, fools, he is coming, the devil, the devil . . . from the moon!" I added as a happy afterthought.

Came a roar of fury from the blackness behind us.

"What in hell do you mean by leaving me this way, Pete Wells? What is all this row?"

There was the glare of an electric torch, and from its light emerged Bones. Great Caesar's ghost, but he nearly scared me!

His whiskers were plastered with mud and blood running from his freely bleeding nose; his great round body was one luminous mass of shiny white clay, and he lurched forward like a Bacchanalian moon, spitting curses at every step.

With a simultaneous yell of terror the savages dived for the entrance of the cave. I jerked out my automatic and fired at the rock above, them, bringing down a piece in their midst. The mouth of the cave cleared like magic, and Bones stood over me, throwing his light on the motionless figure of the girl, who lay stunned by the fragment of rock that my bullet had brought down.

We revived our captive with a dash of water in her face, none the worse save for a lump on the side of her head, and decided to hold her as hostage for the present in case any of her friends returned. As a matter of fact, she showed no inclination to escape— just sat still, watching Bones with awe-filled eyes. Even when he had exchanged his glittering, clay-coated garments for prosaic khaki, it was evident she still looked on him as some kind of a god—or devil.

We slept across the entrance of the cave, guns beneath our hands, and save that the Russian conversed steadily about mylodons in his sleep, it was a perfectly quiet night.

Morning found us penetrating into the cave, the Patagonian maid walking ahead with both of the packs which our bearers had abandoned. She picked them up unbidden, and didn't seem to consider their weight at all. Also the darkness evidently caused her no fear, since she kept on the very edge of the illumination thrown by our torches.

The top of the slippery clay chute where I had left Bones the night before presented an entirely different appearance in the daytime. The sunlight streamed down through the aperture in the rock above, and even lit the cell-like chamber at the bottom of the incline. The rude steps by which Bones had escaped were now overrun by the slimy clay, but we found it a simple matter to dig with our shovels a somewhat slippery but practical stairway to the bottom.

Then we really began to work. Not a bone was missing from the skeleton of the mylodon, and, furthermore, there were six square feet of skin, vivid and green, and studded on the inside with small bosses of bone, showing, the count said, that the animal had a rudimentary protecting shell beneath its fur, something after the fashion of an armadillo.

It was a happy fat man that collected this fifteen-foot skeleton, the bones in perfect preservation, even with pieces of sinew attached.

By relays, the girl silently doing more than her part, we transported the pieces into the main cave, and then it was noon. Lunch quickly gobbled, we went back to our excavating, and not another thing rewarded us. The rest of the bones, down to solid rock, proved to be of guanacos, jaguars, dogs and rabbits, not one single remnant dating back even a few thousand years.

"Don't understand it at all, Pete," complained the count. "Why should a mylodon's bones be mixed with those of modern animals? I can understand their being well preserved, because of the extraordinary conditions in the cave, but why mixed with modern animals, when all authorities claim mylodons have been extinct for a thousand years?"

"Simple enough," I answered. "Why couldn't one of your little pets have survived until recently, and then have been driven to suicide through loneliness, and jumped down that hole?"

"Why isn't the moon made of green cheese, as you English say?" disgustedly asked Bones.

"In the first; place, I am an American, *not* an Englishman," I flared up, on my ear at once, "and, in the second place how are you going to prove the moon isn't made of green cheese or bacon rinds, as far as that goes?"

"It simply isn't," he snarled.

"How are you going to prove it? How are you going to prove that there isn't a mylodon sitting outside the cave this minute? You've got to *show* me."

The Lord knows it was silly, but we were both red hot by that time and shouting at the top of our voices. Glaring at one another, we both opened our mouths again at exactly the same time, thought better of it and snapped them shut. Then we went back into the main cave, where the count began to wrap his treasures in yards of thin, oiled silk, and staked the piece of skin out flat on the ground to dry. I built a fire from wood the girl collected and started to cook our evening meal.

All day long that Patagonian woman had toiled with us, carrying enormous burdens, collecting fuel, and had never once opened her lips to speak. So noiseless and unobtrusive had she been, in spite of her great height and splendid proportions, that we really hardly noticed her.

Subconsciously I had been aware that she seldom took her eyes from the little fat man, and when we had hauled out that piece of green fur I felt, rather than saw, her start. Now that the skin was pegged out flat and Bones had come to the fire, I could dimly discern her in the darkness kneeling by it, her arms stretched up to the roof of the cave.

We had finished our meal and lit our pipes, when there came from behind us a soft crooning:

> *"Ou-ou, ou-ou, ou-u-u,*
> *Ou-ou, ou-ou, ou-u-u."*

Then, very softly at first, growing in volume with every note, the savage girl began to sing:

> *"Moon, moon; moon, moon,*
> Bright with fire and white with snow.
> Moon, moon; moon, moon,
> Look down here below.
> By thy sacred sheep I kneel,
> Lest some wicked one should steal
> What is thine— Heed my appeal!
> *Moon, moon; moon, moon."*

Bones started to rise, but I pulled him back. A beam of moonlight showed the kneeling figure, face bowed to the green skin. Once more she raised her hands above her head, and again her lips opened:

> "*Messenger to earth thou sends,*
> Moon, moon, O sacred moon.
> Lowly to him my heart bends,
> Moon, moon, O sacred moon.
> I, thy daughter; soon will go
> Through the cold, and ice, and snow,
> Where the molten streamlets glow,
> Where thy sheep are grazing slow,
> *Sacred flocks to tend.*"

Her voice sank at the end. Came the softly crooned "*Ou-ou, ou-ou, ou-u-u,*" then silence.

"Let me talk to her. I have an idea," I whispered to Bones, a wild suspicion growing in my mind, and I called out in Spanish.

She came at once and stood before us. Straight as a mountain pine, six feet tall, head high, and great eyes fixed on my face, the woman was without fear, without servility, and yet was dominated, in the grip of a power she could not understand. Her apparent mental attitude might perhaps be paralleled with that of a child who obeys willingly, though it knows not why. She was really beautiful, too, that dark, splendidly strong girl, beautiful like a heroic statue.

"Do you want to go back to your people?" I asked.

"My lords servant knows I cannot, since I have looked on him," she answered, turning her great eyes towards Bones.

"What will you do when we leave here?"

"Tend the sheep of the Sacred Moon with those so old they are no longer of the tribe."

"Where are these sheep?"

"Beyond the snow, and ice, and fire."

"We will go with you in the morning. Sleep now."

"As my lord wills," and she drew back into the darkness of the cave.

"What do you make of that?" I demanded excitedly of the Russian.

"Well, I don't know. The tribe has sheep some place that the very old people tend. I suppose the girl is kind of taboo through associating with us. Don't see why we should waste time running after the sheep, though."

"What kind of sheep do you suppose the sheep of the Sacred Moon are?"

"I don't know. You can't mean. . . . Oh, you're crazy Pete!"

"Crazy or not, I'm going to find out," I answered. "What was she singing about, if not that Irish-colored fur? I'm going to see those sheep. Can't prove the moon isn't made of green cheese, but I can and will run this down."

The silk-wrapped bones and piece of skin were left at the little farm with the old, old man, who when he heard we were going down the coast with the girl announced that they would come in handy for fertilizer—said we wouldn't return to claim them. Even the Patagonians who went that way, were never seen again. With this cheerful prophecy as a send-off, packs stripped down to the bare necessities, but still with our shovels and mattocks, we set out.

I have been on many a hike in my life, but never one to touch that. Our guide first led us several miles back from the sea, and then turned due north. All day, we followed a trail along the barren rocks of the coast zone—rather a line than a trail, since it was but three inches wide. The Patagonian easily covered the ground, walking, as do most savages, with a swing to her hips that enabled her to put one foot almost directly in front of the other. To us, following that narrow path was like walking a tight rope. How the fat man did it I really don't know; it must have been an agony of effort for him. Nevertheless, from sun up till dark his great round body progressed steadily on before me.

That night we slept in a cave where bubbled up a spring of sulphur-laden, boiling water, and we slept hard.

At dawn, our trail wound up through the forest from which we emerged; at noon the mountains towered high above us. Crossing a swampy tundra, we descended a gentle dip, and stood on the edge of an immense glacier, smooth, straight, reaching down in steep incline to where sparkled, miles and miles away, the waters of the Pacific.

Here the girl paused and, pointing out a peak across the ice, indicated that a path must be cut towards it. Our mattocks and shovels came into play, and while the woman and I hewed a way in the ice, the Russian shoveled out the fragments behind us, tossing them on the smooth surface, along which they slid towards the sea, their tinkle growing fainter and fainter until swallowed up in the distance. Darkness caught us still laboring, and we were forced to spend the night on the edge of the glacier, doubly cold through comparison with the glowing reflection of a volcano on the night sky.

As soon as it was light enough to see, we were at it again. A great wall of vapor or steam rose on the opposite side of the glacier, ending abruptly at the point where our path was aimed. By two o'clock we were safely across, and paused in awe at the panorama spread before us.

The glacier was held by a thin ridge of rock, on the other side of which ran a broad stream of boiling water gushing out from a cavern beneath our feet. Above hung a cloud of vaporous steam, spreading out over a valley and completely hiding it, while on every side towered snowcapped mountains. The whole place looked like a great pit filled to the top with snow.

"How long do you suppose the rock will hold the ice back from the valley?" I asked Bones in a whisper. Somehow, it didn't seem right to speak aloud in the immensity of all things.

"Don't know," he answered. "The ice has been grinding at one side, the stream wearing at the other, probably for thousands of years. This place seems like the beginning of the world."

We crossed above where the boiling spring gushed out from the cavern, and found grass growing luxuriantly not ten feet from the glacier. Along the bank of the stream the girl led, with us following, the land sloping gently downward, the precipice rising higher and higher on the opposite bank. Once, the count touched my shoulder and pointed to a great fissure in the rocky wall fully a yard-wide, seemingly created that very moment, ice squeezing through it at the top and melting, drop by drop, to fall hissing on the seething water below.

The grass rose to our thighs, to our shoulders; trees appeared, then dense thickets, tangled, lush, green. Our leader turned at right angles and plunged into the vegetation. The cloud of vapor seemed to be resting on the treetops. It shut off the sky, and, condensing, fell steadily in an infinitesimally fine rain.

We walked in a humid, breathlessly hot mist. The trail opened into a broad, hard-beaten road, flat as though crushed down with a roller. On either side rose enormous trees hung with lianas and orchids, beneath them a nearly impenetrable tangle of underbrush thirty feet high, sappy, living green, save for splashes of the white, crimson or gold orchids.

"Here pasture the sheep of the Sacred Moon, here shall I dwell forever," spoke the girl.

"Where are the sheep?" I demanded.

As if in answer came a crash close to the road, and the underbrush swayed. Breathless, I glanced at Bones, but his staring eyes were riveted on something above my head.

"Wheet-wheet, wheet-wheet," came a tiny voice from the tree-tops, and I looked up straight into a face peering down at me. And what a face! The round, yellow, foolish eyes were set well up in the narrow, greenish forehead; two flat, sniffing nostrils expanded and closed above a thick-lipped, vacuous mouth, from which protruded a long, slender, blue tongue, like a piece of satin ribbon. Never have I seen anything that portrayed such complete imbecility as that face!

"The utter damned fool!" I heard myself say aloud.

"Wheet-wheet," came the ridiculously tiny voice, the underbrush parted, and an immense bulk moved out into the open.

If you could have forgotten the idiot face (which you couldn't), I suppose the mere size of the animal would have made it impressive. It was as big as an elephant, as an elephant sitting on its haunches. The hind legs were enormous, doubled under it, and ending in great, flat paws; the back was curved, nearly humped; the forelegs were short, powerful, and armed with stupendous claws; the neck was long, a cord dangling from it, and topped by that fool head, maddeningly out of proportion to the bulk of the rest of the animal; while the entire body was covered with short, very green fur.

"Heavenly saints!" breathed the Russian. "It's a mylodon come back from the birth of time—utterly different from what we have conceived, but a mylodon; yes, a mylodon; a mylodon; yes, a mylodon. . . ."

He kept repeating "A mylodon; yes, a mylodon," till my nerves snapped like cotton thread.

"Nobody said it was a teakettle!" I roared. "Supposing it is a mylodon, what in hell are you going to do with it?"

"We'll go on further," the little man answered, as though talking in his sleep, and paying not the slightest attention to my words; "perhaps we'll find something else."

"Heaven forbid!" I piously ejaculated. "This is enough for me!"

The creature let itself down on all fours, and with a final silly "Wheet-wheet" half hopped, half walked into the jungle, while we continued down the road in the dripping mist.

The ground rose and the trees became more scattered. A great cave opened in the mountainside and, pausing before it, the girl called out.

From within came eight Patagonians, seven men and one woman, or rather eight relics of the past. They were the oldest human beings I have ever looked upon—bent, gnarled, wrinkled, not one could have been less than a hundred years old. Peering out from age-bleared eyes, they blinked at us like an assembly of galvanized mummies.

"I come to watch the sheep," the girl said tonelessly, "and he"— pointing at Bones—"is a messenger from the Sacred Moon who would see how we tend our charges."

"You are over-young to leave the tribe never to return," the withered hag mumbled.

"My lord brought me here," the girl answered simply.

Within the cavern it was dark as pitch and dripping wet. Another pleasant discovery we made was that nothing would burn.

Tree and shrub were too full of sap; there was no dead dry wood, just wet decay. The Patagonians evidently lived entirely on fruits, and it was on fruits that we dined.

Dusk was approaching, indicated by an evener opaqueness in the midst and less condensation into rain. The nine Patagonians, our guide included, moved off down the road. The count busied himself putting his camera to rights, grumbling aloud meanwhile about the difficulty of taking pictures in that perpetually cloudy atmosphere and cursing the fates that he had but one flashlight powder. I pressed the moisture out of my clothes between two flat stones.

Suddenly a perfect chorus of "Wheet-wheets" broke on our ears, and the most extraordinary procession man has ever looked upon defiled up the road.

Each of the old, old Patagonians was leading—yes, *leading*—a mylodon by a rope around its slim neck, the girl bringing up the rear with a cunning little one, evidently very young and merely some six or seven feet tall. The other eight colossal green beasts ran in size from fifteen to twenty feet, the largest, the only male in the bunch, having a kind of a crest of upright bristles along its back. Past us they wheeled into the cavern—round, yellow eyes gazing aimlessly in every direction, blue, ribbony tongues hanging from vacuous mouths.

"Hea-venly days!" I ejaculated, and sat down in a puddle. The count's eyes were popping from his head, and he began to repeat something in Russian that may have been a prayer, but sounded like the sputtering of a dynamite fuse. I recovered my senses first.

"Come on!" I commanded. "Let's see the little dears tucked into their beddies and then drink the bottle of brandy we brought along for medicine. I know I'm sick—symptoms, a strange belief in things I *do* see but that *can't* be true."

We followed the procession into the blackness, electric torches in hand, and came to a further cave that was nearly dry. Here the Indians were slipping the ropes loosely about stakes in the ground. The great beasts loomed up under our lights like green mountains, and the glare of the electricity brought forth a disturbed chorus of the ridiculous, tiny cries. Their guardians angrily motioned us back, and we retreated outside.

"This, Pete, Is the greatest thing that has happened in science for five hundred years!" exclaimed Bones. "Let's bend every thought and energy to getting the most out of it. We'll find out all we can from the girl, and then, when the savages are asleep, steal in and take a flashlight of that sleeping flock of prehistoric survivors."

As we talked, a change came over the sky. The cloud of vapor caught the rays of the setting sun and reflected them through in countless rainbows of every color in the spectrum. Out into the beautiful illumination came the Patagonians and, grouping in a circle, with the old hag in the middle, sang a kind of an evening hymn:

> "O sacred moon now rising,
> (Alas, we cannot see!)
> All day we faithful tended
> Thy holy flocks for thee.
> Now night comes in its glory,
> Forget us not below,
> Remember thy great promise
> That death we shall not know."

After this lyric rendering, we called the girl to us and put her through a long interrogation. It was rather difficult to get things straightened out, because she assumed we knew so many things of which we were ignorant. Finally, however, a chain of information was evolved.

When first she knew of the vapor-hidden valley there were only two mylodons. The other seven sprang from the original pair. The legend was that as long as there were mylodons so long would those who tended them live, and the Patagonian race as a whole survive. Their ever present anxiety was that something would happen to the old male, the only representative of his sex, all his progeny having been females.

Of course, Patagonians died outside the valley and were buried in the cave of the Sacred Moon, the girl conceded, and sometimes those within the valley, through their infirmities, became tired of living and slipped quietly into the boiling stream, but no one there was obliged to die. Within the records of the tribe the old woman had been there a hundred and then forty snows. Once a year all the Patagonians came to the valley to count the moon sheep. They were due very soon now, she concluded, and would worship the messenger of the Sacred Moon with song and dance.

After the girl had retired, we sat outside the cave steaming in the hot, wet darkness, and talked things over. Without an argument we agreed that it was too great a risk to trust to Bones' clay-created godhead for our safety and await the arrival of the able-bodied Patagonians. What we had to do must be done quickly. That very night we would take the flashlight photograph within the cave, and the next day use the balance of our films in the forest.

For two hours, in order that the savages might all be asleep, we waited, and then, slipping off our shoes, stole within the cave. The way was easy to find even without a light, our feet feeling the solid path beaten by the weight of the monsters, and we knew at once, when we were inside the second cavern, by a roaring like the sea, the snoring of the great beasts. Then I snapped on my torch so Bones could set up his camera. With the flood of light, first one then another of the mylodons awoke and rose to its feet, looming up monstrous shadows whence came weird twitterings. I stepped back of Bones and spread the flashlight dust inside my tobacco pouch, the only dry thing I had. Match after match refused to light, then one flickered and blazed up, and I dropped it into the powder.

There was a puffing blind of light showing the terror-stricken eyes of the immense animals turned toward us, the click of the camera shutter, then darkness shaken by a mighty tread. I pressed the button of my torch and jerked Bones, the camera in his arms, against the wall of the cave. The mylodons were thundering down on us like an avalanche, and the air was full of their shrill calls, while from the distance came the frightened cries of the Patagonians.

Hours we leaned motionless against the rock, scarce daring to breathe, then stole silently to the entrance of the cave and, rolling in our wet blankets, waited for dawn.

No matter how great the excitement sleep will not be denied to tired, healthy men, and we both dropped off just as the vapor outside began to whiten. The next I knew, I woke to a wailing as though of lost souls, sat up to find it broad daylight, and Bones bending over me.

"Something terrible has happened, from the sound those savages are making," he whispered. "Keep your gun ready and let's go see."

I followed him out into the fine drizzle, and we turned down the broad road. The old, old Patagonians were rolling on the ground and raising their hands to heaven in frantic sorrow. Before them lay the male mylodon dead, its neck broken where it had collided with a giant forest tree in the darkness.

The mourners paid no attention to us; just kept up their horrible wailing interjected with broken plaints:

"The father of the sheep of the Sacred Moon is gone, is gone, and soon we, too, shall be no more. . . . We, who hoped to live forever, must die. . . ."

Leaving the frantic savages, we went back and got the camera, passed down the road unmolested, and plunged into the jungle. It was easy to locate where the monsters were feeding from the crash of breaking trees and the swaying of the underbrush, but quite another matter to photograph them. In the first place their color blended so perfectly with the lush green of the forest that, in spite of their bulk, it was very hard to see them; then again, we could never get all of a mylodon at once because of the thickness of the vegetation.

Finally, when we reached the spot where the first monster had been seen on our entrance into the valley, we decided that the only practical plan was to lead one out into the road and snap it there. Plunging into the underbrush, we fought our way through to where the treetops were waving, and I took hold of the rope that hung from a mylodon's neck, not without inward quakings. It followed me like a lamb. When we were nearly out of the underbrush, Bones raised his hand.

"Wait," he whispered; "I hear something."

So did I. From the direction of the glacier came the sound of many voices singing. Nearer it came, till we could distinguish the words:

> "*Children of moon are we,*
> Fear not the darkest shade,
> Trusting, O moon, to thee,
> *Of darkness unafraid.*
>
> "*Come to thy cloudland*
> Where thy flocks be,
> There, hand in hand,
> *To worship thee.*"

Peeking out through the tree trunks, we saw an entire tribe of splendid Patagonians file by—warriors, women and children, and not an adult under six feet.

We lay still in the woods until the mylodon began to graze and nearly pulled a tree down on top of us.

"Oh, hell," I broke the silence; "we're in for it now, Count. There isn't a chance of getting away if that bunch gets after us. All we can do is to shoot as many of 'em as we are able before going under. Let's lead Irene, here, to the road. You snap her till you're tired, and then we'll beat it."

Out in the open, I tied the cord to a tree, and standing behind Bones, whistled so the beast would turn its idiotic face toward us. The count took picture after picture from every angle, and while he was doing it a mad plan had occurred to me.

"Look here, Bones," I stuttered; "let's take this prehistoric silly with us. She'll serve as a breastwork to get behind if we have to fight. I know it's like stealing a whole church, but I'll try anything once."

The Russian gave a whoop of joy.

"Pete, I never thought of it! It we get your Irene to the coast we'll be the most famous men on two continents."

Down that road we went, Bones leading, through the brush and out by the flow of boiling water, the mylodon following docilely at the end of the rope. Across the hot stream, the crack in the side of the precipice was now twenty feet wide, and great masses of ice were pushing through. I saw Bones glance at it apprehensively and shake his head. Over the rock, whence gushed the water, we climbed, and out on to the path we had cut in the glacial ice. And here we had to go more slowly. The beast's great pads kept slipping on the smooth surface, and her foolish face was contracted with fear at the cold beneath her feet.

"Stop a minute," I suggested, "and let Irene rest."

"All right. I'll take a snap of you leading her, with the glacier for background."

I felt the ice tremble under my feet as the camera clicked.

"Get up, old girl," I clucked, jerking at the cord.

The mylodon did not move. She lifted from the ice first one enormous cold foot, then another, swinging her foolish head from side to side, and uttering her inadequate, plaintive cry. Then she started to lie down.

"For God's sake, don't do that," I yelled, jerking at the rope; "you'll slide clear to the coast."

Paying no attention to my frantic yanks, down she went on her side, lifted her feet in the air and turned on to her great, round back, then rolled ponderously over and tried to scramble to her feet. She slipped, the rope pulling through my hands; recovered herself, slid, whirled about and went swiftly down the steep incline, gathering impetus with every second.

There was a mad chorus of yells behind us. The Patagonians were climbing on to the ice. I felt the glacier heave. With a terrific crash the barrier of rock on the shore gave way. Half the glacier, splitting from the main body, went over into the boiling stream, carrying our pursuers with it.

The mylodon was a speck in the distance, growing rapidly smaller against the sparkle of the Pacific.

How the count and I reached solid ground, I do not clearly remember. I have some vague recollection of hitting him on the point of the jaw to keep him from following the mylodon, and then running across the ice, his hand in mine. Anyway, when we were up on the bank, the glacier splitting into fragments below us, he was crying like a child. And cry he did for two whole days, his mind seemingly quite gone.

I lost the trail we had followed coming in, and had to strike for the coast by compass. The rest was one long agony of going forward, always forward, through the forest, across another glacier, over a bleak, boulder-strewn land, and then coming to a little white settlement on the seashore. There a British tramp steamer picked us up and landed us at Valparaiso, where for two months I nursed Bones through a raging brain fever.

An end comes to everything if you wait long enough. Time found us on a passenger steamer for San Francisco, but we were not the same men. At least the Russian wasn't the same. Every recollection of what had happened to us had been wiped from his mind. He knew who he was, who I was, and was rational in every other respect, but he didn't know where he had been or why.

When I called him rational in every respect, I told a lie. He had gone plumb dippy over women. Before we landed I found out that he was engaged to all three of the unmarried girls on the boat.

At San Francisco I took the train across the continent to Jacksonville. Bones hated to have me go; begged me to come to Russia with him at any salary I cared to name; said he was going to get married and settle down. I told him that, with his fund of feminine appreciation, Russia would never do for him; he'd end up in Turkey, and I'd never be able to live happily in a land where the women wore trousers.

At parting he presented me with a magnificent watch, and I never saw him again.

Jacksonville certainly looked good to me. The second evening I sat in Swartz's Café, with the old Dutchman himself across from me, and started to tell him of my adventures. As a preliminary I passed over the flashlight of the mylodons Bones had taken in the cave. Swartz looked at it a moment, and then asked:

"A new kind of mice, *nicht wahr?*"

I picked up the photograph and examined it. There stood the mylodons, just as I had seen them when the powder flashed, but, unless you had known it, there was no means of gauging their size, nothing in the picture with which to compare them. I opened my mouth to explain, and then shut it again.

"Yes, a new kind of mouse," I agreed. The story of my wanderings, I improved.

Up in my room that night, I gazed for a long time at the snapshot of me leading Irene, the lady mylodon, across the glacier. Then, with a sigh, I hid it in the very bottom of my trunk.

What was the use?

THE WHIMPUS
Tod Robbins
1919

I

The Box on the Beach

"There's things out there, Miss Bessie, that you never heard tell of. I know, you're school-learned and all, but the old sea's got more secrets hid away than there are shells on this beach."

Elizabeth Wilkinson smiled down on the garrulous, old fisherman, who sat cross-legged on the sand patiently mending the broken strands of a net. He had been in her father's employ since she could first remember and had always had that quality, so endearing to the very young, of being able to lie prodigiously and convincingly. Even now she enjoyed his wild tales. The savor of the sea was in them. While listening to them, she felt very childlike and very frightened. It was just as though she were swept off her feet and carried away in a heavy surf.

"Now, own up, Captain Ben," she said, attempting to make his watery blue eyes drop before her steady brown ones, "you just thought of that on the spur of the moment. There never was such a creature as a whimpus."

The old man's under-lip shot out as it always did when his word was doubted. He assumed a grieved and disgusted expression. His thick, blunt fingers once more busied themselves with their task.

"What's the use of tellin' you anythin', Miss Bessie?" he mumbled. "You're gettin' to be just like your pop, with no belief in nothin' but what you sees with your own eyes. If all folks was like you there wouldn't be no religion, even. It ain't what we see what

142

makes life interestin', it's what's just around the corner. There's things happenin' right now that ain't never been writ up in books, and there's creatures crawlin' about what would make Ringling Brothers' head animal-trainer take to his heels if he ever suddenly happened to catch sight of 'em."

"But a whimpus, Captain Ben! You say it has a tail and fins like a fish?"

"It has so, Miss Bessie; and big blue eyes, most like a gal's. Leastwise, so Dick Jamieson told me—him who was wrecked in the China Sea. And Dick was a truthful man when not in liquor."

"How long are they, Captain Ben?"

"About the length of my arm, missy, with pointed teeth which can give a man a cruel bite if they catched him in the calf of the leg."

"And hair, Captain Ben? I believe you said they had long, curly hair?"

"So Dick told me, missy. With a flash to it like gold in the sunlight. He leaned down and put his hand on one of 'em, thinkin' he had found a treasure or somethin'. It was nothin' more or less than a whimpus sleepin', her hair slung over her like a net; and she wakes up, fightin'-mad, and bites a piece off his little finger for his boldness. Then she gives a flip to her tail and away she sails as saucy as you please—leavin' Dick on the bank, jumpin' with pain."

For a long moment there was silence. The girl had half turned away from the old fisherman and was looking out to sea. It was a day in late August. Above the gray tumbling waste of waters, a pale opalescent curtain of fog was slowly descending. The *Adventurer*—Mr. Wilkinson's yacht—rode at anchor barely to hundred yards from shore. Already she was swathed in drifting tides of vapor. Like a phantom ship, she appeared and disappeared. At one moment she seemed to be scarcely a stone's throw from the beach; at the next, a mile or so offshore. It had been blowing hard on the preceding night. The waves were like an army coming home with victory on their shields. They thundered out their deep-throated war song on the beach. Far out in the impenetrable mist, like a voice from another world, the melancholy call of a seagull rose for a moment above the tumult of tumbling waters.

"No, Miss Bessie," Captain Ben continued with a shake of his head, "there's more things hid away in the sea than ever man heard tell of. But the fog's gettin' precious thick. I think you'd best be off to the house or you'll get wet to the skin."

But Elizabeth had caught sight of something in the surf which held her undivided attention. It was a large box which, at that moment, was riding the snowy crest of a wave. On it came smoothly, like a miniature ship, sinking at last into a milky chasm as the billow tripped on the beach with its treasure and fell sprawling. For an instant the box was left high and dry.

Moved by a sudden impulse which she was soon to regret, Elizabeth ran forward across the wet, quivering sand and bent over the box.

"Come back, missy!" Captain Ben called in a shrill, quavering voice. "What ever are ye thinkin' of? Come back this instant afore one of them big waves catches yer!"

Elizabeth raised the box. Holding it tight to her breast, she hurried back just as another huge wave charged down on her with a threatening roar. Lowering her prize to the sand beyond the reach of its many long arms, she surveyed Captain Ben triumphantly.

"This belongs to me now, doesn't it?" she asked, indicating the box with a slender, moist finger.

"Aye, aye, missy," Captain Ben said solemnly. "What a man fishes out of the sea, belongs to him, no matter who it belonged to afore. The King of England's crown jewels might be in this here box and they wouldn't be no more his now than Mike Rafferty's pig." He paused and scratched his grizzled chin. "But I guess these ain't crown jewels," he added rather sorrowfully. "They're more like to be lemons."

"Why lemons?"

"Cause a tramp steamer run aground in the fog last night off Wishbone Point. They had to lighten her cargo afore they got her off; and they do say she was loaded down with crates of lemons. Some of the boys in the village was fishin' for 'em all mornin'."

"I don't believe it is a crate of lemons," Elizabeth said with a shake of her head. Once more she bent down and turned the box over on its side. At the next moment, with a stifled cry, she stepped back so hurriedly that she nearly tripped over the old man's outstretched legs.

"Why, what's the matter, missy?" Captain Ben asked, looking up from the net in surprise. "You looks as if somethin' had bit yer!"

"There's something alive in that box," she said in a rather unsteady voice. "I heard it move. Do you suppose it could be a baby, Captain Ben?"

The old fisherman's mouth extended from ear to ear. A glimpse of his gums could be seen, with here and there a single discolored tooth rising from them like so many weather-beaten tombstones. He was laughing silently.

"Don't laugh at me!" Elizabeth cried angrily. "I tell you there *is* something alive in that box! I heard it rattling about when I moved it!"

Captain Ben rose stiffly to his feet and bent over the box. "I misdoubt it's a baby, Miss Bessie," he mumbled. "A baby wouldn't have much chance of weatherin' through such a sea in this old craft. Mebbe the lemons ain't packed very tight. Let's see."

He put one of his gnarled hands on the box and turned it over. On the instant a strange flapping sound could be heard issuing from the interior, followed almost immediately by a loud scratching as though long, sharp nails were at work.

Captain Ben uttered an ejaculation of amazement. "That's mighty strange!" he muttered. "There must be fish and crabs in this box. But who ever heard tell of—" He paused and scratched the top of his weather-beaten hat. "Shall I open it?"

"No," Elizabeth murmured. "I don't want to see what's in it. There's something horrible, I know. I wish I hadn't taken that box out of the water."

"Why, what's the matter, missy? You look all upset. It's only fish and crabs thrown in higgledy-piggedly in an old chest. It ain't like you to get worked up over nothin'."

Elizabeth hit her lip. What made her feel this way about a harmless old box? It was ridiculous! And yet, try as she would, she could not even look at it now. When she had bent over it and put her hand on its cold, wet surface, when she had heard those strange flapping and scratching sounds within, a wave of intense, if unaccountable, fear and repulsion had passed through her. Now trembling little patches of gooseflesh stood out on her brown arms. This was absurd. She must have caught cold. Or perhaps she just had a touch of malaria.

"I think I'll go back to the house, Captain Ben," she said at last. "I feel cold."

"You don't look very hearty today, missy, and that's a fact. You'd better change yer shoes and stockin's, I reckon. But what will I do with the box?"

"Bring it up to the house, Captain Ben. You can leave it on the back stoop."

"Aye aye, missy. I'll tote it up in a wheelbarrow. Mebbe there's some likely-sized fish in this here chest. They seem lively enough. And a good crab ain't to be sneezed at, neither, if it's cooked proper."

II

A Claimant for the Chest

Mr. Wilkinson greeted his daughter as she mounted the veranda. He was a stout, middle-aged man with a sallow complexion, dull, prominent eyes and a predilection for a quiet, uneventful life. The one excitement which he allowed himself was an occasional flyer in Wall Street. He was proverbially lucky in such speculations. The considerable fortune, which his father had left him, had never taken wings—on the contrary, like a snowball rolling down-hill, it had gathered to itself many lesser fortunes. But this success without effort had given him no flicker of joy.

Each year his complexion had grown sallower, his eyes duller, his muscles flabbier. The boredom which must necessarily attend a smooth existence, was smothering the manhood in the financier. Beneath a mountain of down, he was snoring his life away.

Now he rose ponderously, and laid a plump, moist hand on his daughter's shoulder. "I've got a surprise for you, Bessie," he said in a slow, heavy voice.

"A surprise, dad? What is it?"

Mr. Wilkinson smiled sleepily. He had intended teasing her, but now lacked the vitality. "The surprise is upstairs, shaving," he said, sinking back into the easy-chair like a large stuffed doll.

Elizabeth flushed. In an instant she forgot all about the wooden box and her dread of its flapping, scratching contents. "You don't mean that the surprise is Jay, dad, do you?"

Mr. Wilkinson nodded and smiled, "Yes," he murmured. "Dropped into my office just after he got off the boat. Didn't wire— wanted to make it a surprise. But here he is to tell you about it himself."

At this moment a tall, athletic young man opened the screened door, and, seeing Elizabeth, hurried forward and took her in a bearlike hug. Jay had never been a gentle lover, but she liked him all the better for that.

"Well, old girl," he said at last, holding her off at arm's length and regarding her attentively with his steady gray eyes, "you're looking pretty fit. You didn't expect me home so soon, eh?"

"No, I didn't," she murmured. "You wrote me that you intended doing Europe with the rest of the team."

He smiled a trifle shamefacedly. "I intended to," he said. "I thought that you'd think all the more of me if I stayed away a little longer. After we beat the Englishmen that deciding game, the team broke up. Larry and Martin dropped in on Paris; Henry and I were going to do Scotland and Ireland, but at the last moment I quit. I had to do some explaining. Henry was as sore as a boil." He paused and stroked the cleft in his prominent chin meditatively. "Well, here I am," he finished, "and willing to step up to the altar most any time."

"Wait till somebody asks you, sir," she said with a sudden flash of color. "Do you still think that polo is the most important thing in life?"

The young man shook his head. "No, but it's exciting; and I crave excitement."

Elizabeth experienced the disquieting sensation at her fiancé's words which is common enough to most girls when they are brought face to face with their great enemy—that priestess of adventure which beckons the swift and the strong. It is the instinct of feminine love to be everything, and it must content itself with so little.

After a moment she said a trifle bitterly: "At one moment, Jay, you talk of settling down, of becoming thoroughly domesticated; at the next, you sigh for speed and thrills. Which side of you am I to believe? I like excitement, but I don't put it above everything else in the world."

"You're a girl," her fiancé answered calmly, "and with a girl it's different. But a fellow has to be doing strenuous things or else—" He paused and shrugged.

"Haskin' pardon, lady and gentlemen," said a strange, husky voice which sounded like the scraping together of two rusty iron bars, "a chap down at the beach says as 'ow you 'ad picked up a old chest."

All three turned their heads in surprise. There, standing on the lower step of the veranda, swinging a mildewed, canvas cap between finger and thumb, was one of the strangest figures Elizabeth had ever seen.

Above medium height, but so bent that his back rounded out like a drawn bow; his long legs wide apart as though balancing himself against the shock of the sea; his head, with its great bulbous nose and close-set black eyes, cocked on one side shrewdly like a bird about to take flight—he resembled some scarecrow posturing in a cornfield. And yet, on the second glance, one felt the humanness of the man. It was in his crafty, thin-lipped mouth, in the swing of his lantern jaws, in the twitching of his corded, brown fists, which resembled two sea-spiders. All in all, from his tangle of straw-colored hair to his shining boots, he looked as out of place on Mr. Wilkinson's broad, sun-swept veranda as one of the pirates in *Treasure Island*.

"The chap as I spoke to," the man continued, "said as 'ow 'e 'ad brought the chest up 'ere a few minutes back. Now could I once lay my eyes on it, lady and gentlemen, I'd know it fast enough by some 'oles I drilled in its side."

"I think he must mean the box I picked out of the surf," Elizabeth said, turning toward her father. "There was some holes in that, I remember."

"Was there, lady, was there?" cried the man in evident excitement. "The Lord love yer, lady! That's news to warm a poor sailor's soul! Now did these 'oles form a kind of a 'eart, lady—a 'eart like yer see on this 'ere arm of mine?"

He rolled up his sleeve, disclosing a sunburnt arm on which was tattooed in gay coloring a three-masted schooner; two lovers sitting under a dark blue tree; a queen of spades; and, lastly, a mermaid reclining on a cliff and pulling up, hand over hand, a large scarlet heart, on which was inscribed in minute lettering, "Caught again! September 15, 1935."

"You're well decorated, my man," said Mr. Wilkinson with a flicker of an eyelash in Jay's direction. "Who was the artist?"

"It's a tasty bit of work, ain't it?" said the sailor in evident pleasure. "That's what I halways says—*tasty!* Black Tom did 'em hall— 'im who was my shipmate aboard the *Sea King*. Lord, 'e was a hartist-born, was Tom! Liked nothin' better than to get a poor chap in front of 'im like a bloody blackboard to draw purty pictures on. 'E did this 'ere when we was shipwrecked together on a coral island in the China Seas. 'E never got off that island neither, did Black Tom."

"Never got off it!" Elizabeth cried. "Did he die there?"

"Now I wouldn't say so much as that, gal. Leastwise, I ain't. 'E went off and left me sudden one mornin' and 'e never showed up no more. They catched 'im, I guess."

"*Who* caught him?" Jay broke in.

The sailor half-closed his eyes till they were mere pin-points. "*They*," he muttered. "Them things what live on coral islands in the China Seas."

"He means *whimpus*," said Captain Ben, who had at that moment hobbled up.

"Right you are, matey," said the man. "The whimpus got Black Tom, soul and body. 'E was uncommon fond of gals, was Tom."

At this point Mr. Wilkinson rose impatiently to his feet. "Now what can we do for you?" he said rather sharply. "If you've come up here to tell us lies about mermaids you're wasting your time. We've got a first-class liar here as it is." He gave Captain Ben a significant stare.

"There's more things afloat, Mr. Wilkinson, than you ever heard tell of," Captain Ben began in a plaintive, asthmatic whine. "This man here is right when he speaks of whimpus. I heard tell of 'em afore."

But the sailor cut him short. "Look here, lady and gentlemen," he said, stepping forward, "I come peaceful enough for my property, and I'm bound I'll 'ave it!"

"My daughter picked the box out of the water. Well, according to law, it now belongs to her. If you want it back, you'll have to pay salvage," said Mr. Wilkinson.

Now the sailor turned toward Elizabeth. "I'll pay salvage, lady," he whined. "Now would a ten-pound note be agreeable? Say the word, lady." He began to fumble in his pocket.

"Don't take it, Bessie," Mr. Wilkinson advised, enjoying the affair as a child enjoys a new kind of game. "Take an old business man's advice. He offers fifty dollars—well, it must be worth a good deal more."

"Lord love yer, no, lady! There ain't nothin' in that old chest but a few keepsakes and trinkets. Pictures of gals and the likes of that. I wouldn't give no ten pounds if my 'eart wasn't kinder set on 'em."

Elizabeth bit her lip to repress a laugh. The sailor was lying so poorly that a child would not have been deceived. But what could be in the chest? Something alive—she had heard it move—something which this man considered to be worth more than fifty dollars. It was worth finding out.

"It couldn't be your box I found," she said at last.

"And why ain't it, lady? Ain't there no 'eart cut in it?"

"Yes, I believe there is a heart."

"Well, ain't that proof enough, lady, that it's Bill Farley's chest right enough?"

"Is your name Bill Farley?"

"Aye, aye, ma'am. And you'll find a *B* and a *F* on the tother end, burnt there with a red-hot poker—rough, I grant you; but plain to see in the sunlight."

"That's all very well, Mr. Farley," said Elizabeth very sweetly. "You seem to know what the outside of the box looks like. But that isn't enough. I believe you said that there were a few trinkets inside?"

"Yes, ma'am."

"Well, that isn't so, Mr. Farley. There's something alive in that box."

For a moment there was a disconcerting silence. The sailor's crafty eyes wandered here, there, and everywhere: Mr. Wilkinson's round face indicated surprise; Jay began stroking his amber-colored mustache thoughtfully. At last Captain Ben spoke up.

"It's no use, Bill Farley, or whatever your name may be," he said. "You've gone and steered yourself into a fog. None of us here will rest easy till we've had a peep into that chest of yourn. You've lied yourself into a heap more trouble than ten pounds will buy yer out of."

Suddenly Elizabeth uttered a little cry of horror. "Have you a baby in that box?" she asked excitedly.

"Perhaps he's a kidnaper," Jay suggested. "They're quite common."

"He's got a bad face," Captain Ben muttered, casting a suspicious look at the cowering Bill Farley. "When a Britisher is bad, he's most uncommon bad."

Mr. Wilkinson took a step forward with the air of a stern judge. "What *have* you got in the box?" he demanded harshly.

The sailor looked from right to left, as though contemplating escape, and then into the faces of his persecutors. Tiny beads of perspiration had gathered on his forehead; his eyes looked like those of a trapped animal.

"I got—" He paused for breath and swallowed several times.

"What?" they demanded almost in unison.

"I got a whimpus in that there chest," Bill Farley said a trifle wearily.

III

A Chinese Mermaid

For several moments there was a dead silence. All regarded the sailor with open-eyed amazement. Mr. Wilkinson was the first to speak.

"You've got a *what?*" he asked.

"I got a whimpus," Bill Farley repeated stubbornly. "It's a Chinese mermaid fish, common enough on that coral island where me and Tom was cast away."

Jay allowed himself an incredulous smile. "Where did you put that box, Captain Ben?" he asked.

"It's on the back porch, sir. Will I get it?"

"Yes," Mr. Wilkinson broke in, "get it. This man must be drunk or mad. A whimpus—a mermaid—whoever heard of such nonsense?"

Captain Ben turned away with a shake of his head. "I told you more times than once, sir, that there be strange creatures in the sea what you never heard tell of," he mumbled.

Bill Farley stared sullenly at his boots with the air of an abused man. "What's the odds whether a chap lies or tells the Gospel truth?" he muttered. "'E ain't believed neither way."

"A whimpus!" Mr. Wilkinson continued irritably. "And perhaps you'll be kind enough to tell us how you happened to catch your mermaid?"

"I will that," said Bill Farley. "It 'appened this way: I rigged up a kind of dragnet while I was on that there coral island, and put it out each mornin' to catch gay-colored fish of which there was aplenty. One mornin' I pulls the net in and finds 'er lyin' there as snug as a bug in a rug. She give me a start, lookin' at me most like a gal with 'er big blue eyes kinder smilin' in 'er 'ead, 'Lord, Bill,' I says to myself, 'you've 'ad a touch of sun, my poor lad!'"

"Here comes Captain Ben with the box, dad," Elizabeth broke in.

As she spoke her eyes were fixed on the chest which the old fisherman carried; and once again that wave of incomprehensible fear passed through her.

"Why open it, dad?" she murmured. "Let the man have it."

It is doubtful if Mr. Wilkinson heard her. At that moment he and Jay were bending over the box. Captain Ben had placed it on the veranda in a stream of sunshine. In this bright light the small, drilled holes, so arranged that they formed the outline of a human heart and the blurred *B* and *F* were plainly to be seen. Several knotted cords encircled the chest.

Jay, with the impatience of a small boy on Christmas morning, pulled out a penknife and severed them. Mr. Wilkinson began to lift the lid.

"'Ave a care!" Bill Farley warned him. "She's got a most uncommon nasty temper with strangers. You're like to lose a finger if you don't watch your 'and!"

Mr. Wilkinson, in spite of his incredulous smile, raised the lid slowly and cautiously. A shaft of sunlight stole into the chest. At the next moment he uttered an ejaculation of amazement, which was echoed by Jay. Captain Ben hobbled up and bent forward in his turn.

"It's a whimpus, sure enough!" he cried, a shrill note of triumph ringing through his voice like the clanging of an old, cracked bell. "What did I tell you, Mr. Wilkinson? Do yer see that fish's tail, and them claws, and them long, pointed teeth? And she has yaller hair, too, same as that feller said what had his finger bit off by one of 'em. But look at them gal's eyes! Ain't they purty, though—blue as seashells, yet with a sparkle to 'em! Aye, aye, Mr. Wilkinson, this sure is a whimpus."

"Well, I'm hanged if I ever saw anything like it before!" Jay muttered under his breath.

Even the financier's rather irritating common sense was shattered for the moment. He stared down at the contents of the sailor's chest in blank amazement. His pursed lips seemed on the point of emitting a long-drawn "Oh!" of astonishment.

"Well, now that you 'ave taken a squint at my whimpus," Bill Farley said sullenly, "perhaps you'll be so kind as to return a poor man's property and let 'im be off about his business."

The sailor's words seemed to restore a measure of Mr. Wilkinson's presence of mind. "Not so fast," said he, straightening his back. "You've got a most peculiar freak of nature here; I'll grant you that. The only one in existence, I imagine."

"There's 'undreds and 'undreds of 'em on Whimpus Island," Bill Farley said composedly.

Once more an incredulous smile flitted across Mr. Wilkinson's face. "I doubt that very much," said he. "However, let's come to terms. You've got a freak in the fish world here—something which will cause considerable comment. What did you intend doing with it?"

A sly, secretive smile played for a moment beneath the sailor's bulbous nose, creasing his face till it resembled a walnut-shell. "This 'ere whimpus is worth money," he muttered. "I was thinkin' of sellin' 'er to a zoo."

"That won't be necessary. I'll buy it myself. How would a hundred dollars strike you?"

"A 'undred dollars—twenty pounds! Gawd, governor!" Bill Farley's face took on an expression of lively disgust. "This whimpus is worth 'er weight in diamonds. I wouldn't take a thousand pounds for 'er, and that's a fact."

Mr. Wilkinson nodded briskly. "Very well, my man. I'm afraid we can't do business. Good afternoon."

The sailor seemed greatly relieved. Passing the back of his hand across his forehead, he bent down awkwardly and laid hold of the chest. "Come on 'ome with Bill, Lizzie," he muttered. "We've 'ad a mighty tough day of it, old gal."

"Hold on, there!" Mr. Wilkinson called sharply. "What are you about? You can't have that fish until you pay salvage. You said it was worth its weight in diamonds, that you wouldn't take a thousand pounds for it—well, that should make the salvage pretty high."

"Gawd! Ain't you 'ard on a poor chap, gove'nor?" Bill Fancy released his hold on the chest and straightened himself. His face drew up into knots of anxiety and grief. "I cawn't pay no 'igh salvage 'cause I ain't got no more than thirty pounds in all the world! This here whimpus is mighty nigh my entire fortune!"

"Now, why not tell us the truth, Farley?" the financier said in a kindlier tone. "It's no use lying—you've got something up your sleeve. Why do you think this fish is worth so much? Tell us the whole story, and I give you my word we'll deal squarely by you."

Bill Farley hesitated and shifted uneasily on his feet. "You 'ave me, gove'nor," he said with a new note of respect in his tone. "Whichever way I turn, you 'ave me. A poor seafarin' chap ain't got a Dutchman's chance with a far-seein' gentleman like you. But I got a question to ask afore I spins my yarn. Is that craft, lyin' so snug in the cove, your yacht, gove'nor?"

"The *Adventurer?* Yes, she belongs to me."

"That's good news, gove'nor. Now, 'as the young lady 'ere a bit of a ring, a bracelet, or somethin' kinder shiny which she would lend a poor sealarin' chap for the sake of a test?"

Elizabeth nodded. Drawing a thin band of gold from her finger, she presented it to the sailor.

"Thank yer kindly, ma'am," said he. "Now, gove'nor, lady, and gentlemen, will yer take a little walk down to that pier yonder, and I'll show you what Lizzie 'ere can do once she's sot her mind on it."

"What are you driving at?" Mr. Wilkinson asked with some asperity.

"Never you mind, gove'nor. Just you step along with old Bill, and 'e'll show you what's what. You ain't afeared, gove'nor?"

Jay burst out into a laugh. "What do you know about that?" he said. "He thinks we're afraid of his mermaid. Let's see what he's got to show us down on the pier."

"Very well," said Mr. Wilkinson, with an uneasy look at the water-soaked box. "Are you coming with us, Bessie?"

Elizabeth shook her head. "Not if you're going to take that creature with you."

"Surely you're not afraid of a fish, Bessie?" Jay broke in. "Why, you haven't even looked at it yet!"

"It isn't fear exactly. I don't know how to explain it. It's the same feeling I have for a mouse—only a thousand times worse. I've had a horror of it from the very first. If I looked at it, I know I'd scream."

"Poor old Lizzie!" Bill Farley muttered, picking the box up in his arms. "You ain't very popular with the gals, are yer, Lizzie? Well, gove'nor, lead the way."

The four men descended the steps of the veranda and started across the lawn toward the pier which stretched out like a wooden arm over the sea. Mr. Wilkinson and Jay led, Captain Ben and Bill Farley brought up the rear.

Elizabeth watched them receding in the distance with a wildly beating heart. Her natural curiosity was battling with that strange repulsion for which she was unable to account. At one moment she wished she had accompanied them; at the next, she was glad that she had remained where she was.

The pier was several hundred yards from the house. Elizabeth, although she strained her eyes, was unable to ascertain what the men were about. By this time they had reached their destination. Looking very small and toylike, they were bending forward as though examining something.

An involuntary shudder passed through the girl's frame. They were now opening the box and examining that horrible creature which Captain Ben had described as having long yellow hair and eyes like a girl's—that must be what they were about. How could they do it? Men were callous. Perhaps they would even touch it. Perhaps Jay, her Jay, might fondle it, might run his fingers through its hair, might—

Something very near akin to jealous rage made Elizabeth rise and hurry toward them. But before she had traversed more than a quarter of the distance, she encountered Captain Ben, who had detached himself from the group on the pier and was hobbling across the front lawn.

"I was comin' up to tell yer all about it, missy," he said, smothering a yawn with a huge fist. "You missed it. It's too late now—they've put the whimpus back in her box."

"What happened, Captain Ben?" she asked breathlessly.

The old man once more paused to open his mouth in a cavernous yawn before he answered. "Funny how sleepy I feel!" he muttered.

"What happened?" Elizabeth repeated impatiently.

"Why, when we got down to the pier, that there sailor opened the box, grabbed the whimpus quick by the neck, and jerked her out. She begin to scratch at him with her claws and gnash her teeth—but it weren't no use, for Farley had her safe by the neck all the time. Well, missy, he had a piece of fishin' line in his trouser-pocket. No sooner did she stop her antics than he made it fast about her. It was curious the easy way he handled the critter."

"What did he do then?" Elizabeth asked.

"Why, then he took that ring that you give him and chucked it into the sea. That made me howlin' mad, I can tell yer. I never expected to see it no more. 'Have yer taken leave of yer senses?' I says, steppin' forward with the thought of layin' my fist on that ugly jaw of his. But he just kinder smiles superior and throws his whimpus overboard, not forgettin' to hold on to the other end of the line. 'Watch my Lizzie,' he says, very proud. 'She's no end of a gal when it comes to findin' valuables.'"

"And then what happened, Captain Ben?"

"Why, we all watched that there fishin' line goin' out farther and farther. Then, all of a sudden, it stopped dead; and Farley begun to pull it in, hand over hand. Pretty soon that whimpus pops out of the water. And what do you think, missy— there was your ring, gripped tight in her claws."

"It picked my ring up?"

"Yes, missy. And Farley let her keep it for a while, sayin' them bright things made the poor gal happy. She's got it along with her now in her box, and she's hummin' like a thousand tops goin' at once."

"Humming?"

"Aye, aye, missy. She hums when she's content, Farley says. And it's a soothin' sound—a most soothin' sound." The old man broke off, and once more displayed his gums in a prodigious yawn.

IV

MOONSHINE AND MADNESS

"Well, now, as I 'ave showed yer what my Lizzie could do, let us talk business, gove'nor."

It was Bill Farley who spoke. Leaning back comfortably in one of Mr. Wilkinson's easy chairs, a corpulent Havana cigar between his yellow teeth, he surveyed the others with a strange air of mingled civility and triumph. The financier, his face still mirroring astonishment and a measure of expectancy, crossed his plump legs and lit a match. Elizabeth and Jay interchanged glances, but remained silent. Captain Ben had taken up a trowel, and was making a pretense at weeding the flower-bed in the shadow of the veranda; while, in reality, he was straining his old ears to catch any scattered fragments of the conversation.

"I don't see how your fish's accomplishments alter the case," Mr. Wilkinson said finally. "It recovered my daughter's ring, certainly: but my daughter recovered *it*. In a word, the more valuable you make your fish appear, Farley, the higher salvage may be demanded."

"But you ain't got me right, gove'nor," the sailor cried. "Lizzie is a valuable possession—not because she ain't known in these parts, not because she can pick up a gold ring occasional, but because she 'as a fortune of all 'er own. She's a capitalist, that's what my Lizzie is."

"I'm sure I don't know what you're driving at," Mr. Wilkinson broke in.

"Look 'ere, gove'nor—I'll explain." Bill Farley leaned forward and knocked the ash of his cigar off on the toe of his boot. "There's a coral island in the China Seas where there's 'undreds and 'undreds of Lizzies. Them mermaid fish is all alike. They're the same as gals— a diamond or a gold ring, anythin' kinder dazzlin', tickles 'em to death. Now, down on the bottom of the sea there's loads and loads of such things lyin' kinder careless about. Think of the ships what's foundered off the China coast, gove'nor, in them ragin' typhoons; ships loaded down with gold and precious stones, and the like of that. What do yer think them whimpus 'as been doin' these thousands of years? Get my drift, gove' nor?"

"You mean that they've been storing up treasure-trove from wrecked vessels?" Mr. Wilkinson asked, sitting up very straight in his chair.

Jay drew his breath in through his teeth with a hissing sound. "Oh-ho, what an idea!" he muttered.

"That's what I'm a tellin' yer," Bill Farley continued patiently. "Them whimpus 'ave been stealin' from foundered ships since the world was new. There's undreamed-of wealth for the chap what finds their cave, gove'nor. Captain Kidd's treasure wouldn't be a ante in that game. Now, suppose I knowed the whereabouts of that island, gove'nor, and suppose Lizzie 'ere could do the rest?"

Mr. Wilkinson rose and began to pace the veranda. "Of course, all this is just foolishness," he muttered. "And yet—"

"You 'ave a tidy little yacht in the 'arbor," Bill Farley said hopefully. "Just you say the word, gove'nor, and I'll pilot yer to Whimpus Island. We'll split the pot—all 'ands what sails. There'll be enough treasure to spare, or sink me for a Dutchman!"

Mr. Wilkinson came to a sudden halt in front of the sailor. "I want to hear all about this," he said querulously. "How did you happen to get hold of this fish? It'll pay you to stick to the truth."

"Gawd blast me if I lie, gove'nor! It 'appened this way: I was aboard the *Sea King* what went down in a tornado just off the China coast. Me and Black Tom rigged up a raft. Two days and two nights we drifted, and then we touched ground on one of them coral islands, which is as thick as fleas on a mangy dog in them parts. Lucky for us there was a big, 'ollowed-out place in the center of the island which 'ad caught a deal of rain-water. For food we 'ad the fish, which was all colors of the rainbow, and sweet-tastin' enough."

"Was that Whimpus Island?"

"Aye, aye, gove'nor. We didn't see 'ide nor 'air of 'em for the first few days. Only we 'eard a low 'ummin' sometimes which would put Black Tom and me to sleep like we was kids. One day Black Tom catches one sunnin' 'erself. 'E come runnin' to me, 'oldin' 'er in a bit of fish-net.

"'Just look 'ere, Bill!' 'e says, swallowin' 'ard. 'Look what this gal 'as in 'er fist!'

"Well, I gives 'er a stare; and she stares back at me, as bold as you please, through the 'oles in the net. Pretty soon I see somethin' shinin' in 'er claws. Gawd! I give my eyes a rub, but it weren't no use! That there shinin' stone in 'er fist was a diamond as big as a robin's egg.

"'We're rich men, Tom,' I says joyful.

"But 'e gives a shake of 'is 'ead, bein' a gloomy, sorrowful chap mostly. 'We might be bloody millionaires, Bill,' says 'e; 'but what good would it do us on this blawsted gridiron?'

"Well, for all that, Black Tom took the diamond out of the whimpus's fist—though 'e 'ad to treat 'er a bit rough first, she bein' havaricious, as are most females. Then 'e made a pet of 'er, feedin' 'er bits of fish, and now and then givin' 'er a swim on the end of a cord. And it was a most unnatural thing to see, that there fish and Black Tom sleepin' alongside one another each night—she with 'er 'ead on 'is breast, 'er golden 'air brushin' 'is cheek. Lord, it give me the creeps—the way she 'ad of lookin' at 'im like a lovesick gal on 'er 'oneymoon! And it made me feel kinder lonesome, too. I began to wish I 'ad a whimpus of my own.

"One day I was all alone, sunnin' myself on a bit of rock. Black Tom was out walkin' with 'is whimpus—though 'e did all the walkin', wadin' about the island while she swum alongside. Pretty soon I 'ears a great 'ullabaloo; and 'ere comes Black Tom, runnin' fit to bust, 'is lady friend under 'is arm.

"'What's the row?' says I. 'Row?' says 'e. 'We're the richest men in the world, Bill! And it's all because of this little gal 'ere.' Then 'e gives 'is whimpus a squeeze which makes 'er cock one blue eye at me kinder coy.

"''Ave you found another diamond?' I asked.

"'A diamond, Bill!' says 'e kinder scornful. 'Where I just come from they're as thick as pebbles on the beach.'

"Then 'e went on to tell me as 'ow the whimpus 'ad took 'im into a cave while they was walkin', and pretty soon they come to a strip of sand where there was a pile of rubies and diamonds and gold pieces. And there was bones, too—human bones, white as chalk—and bits of junk which weren't no use to nobody.

"'You come away in a hurry,' says I.

"'I did that,' says 'e, blinkin' 'is eyes at me solemn. 'There was some skulls sittin' on them piles of precious stones, and they give me the creeps. 'Owsomever, I'm goin' back now and take another squint.'

"'I'll go with yer,' says I.

"'No, yer won't,' says 'e, givin' me a nasty look. 'Two's company, three's a crowd.' 'E give a little 'itch to 'is knife which I knew meant trouble. 'Dolly and me 'll treat yer square, Bill,' 'e says, 'but we don't want yer nosin' around in there.'

"With that 'e starts back again with a ugly grin at me over 'is shoulder and 'is 'and on the 'aft of 'is knife. Now, bein' a peaceful man myself, 'avin' sung in the church choir in my youth, I let 'im 'ave 'is way—more especial as 'e was a wicked chap to cross and as tall as a steeple. Pretty soon I lost sight of 'im and 'is whimpus behind a bit of rock. And. I never laid eyes on either of 'em since that day, gove'nor."

Bill Farley paused to light his cigar, which had gone out. Elizabeth glanced at Jay, and saw that his eyes were flashing brightly, and that there was a hectic splash of color in each cheek. She glanced at her father, and saw that he, also, showed marked signs of excitement. The sailor's box stood near the railing. A low, intermittent buzzing sound came from it.

"How is it that you never saw him again?" Mr. Wilkinson asked.

"I dunno, gove'nor. That there cave 'e told me about must 'ave swallowed 'im like the whale swallowed Jonah. 'E never come out alive—nor dead neither, I reckon."

"Did you discover the entrance of the cave?" Jay asked suddenly.

"Not me, sir," Bill Farley answered with a weak smile. "Black Tom would 'ave skinned me alive 'ad I followed 'im. 'E was a mean man when crossed. But Lizzie, she knows where that cave is, right enough."

"How did you happen to catch your whimpus?" Mr. Wilkinson asked.

"I catched 'er with a bit of net when I was fishin' off the rocks. But I wasn't takin' no chances at explorin' caves with no one 'andy in case of trouble. I put Lizzie in my old sea-chest, and a day or so later I got picked up by a tramp steamer bound for New York.

Natural enough, I didn't tell them what I knowed. There was too many 'ands aboard. 'When I gets to New York,' I says to myself, 'I'll find some skipper I can trust, and then—'"

"But how did the chest happen to be in the water?" Jay broke in.

Bill Farley moved his feet uneasily, and a guilty flush spread over his face. "That tramp steamer went aground off Wishbone Point," he muttered. "Them custom officers might 'ave made things 'ot for Lizzie and me, so I took French leave in one of the life-boats when none of the crew was lookin'. Pretty soon a squall comes up, and the boat capsizes. Lizzie come aground 'ere, but I swam to shore half a mile farther up. Gawd, I was near out of my 'ead till that old chap told me 'e 'ad seen my chest."

"That's a very strange tale," said Mr. Wilkinson, chewing savagely on his cigar. "If you're lying, you do it very well."

Bill Farley's heavily wrinkled face took on a grieved expression. "So 'elp me, I ain't spinnin' a yarn, gove'nor! This 'ere is Gospel truth. You've a sizable yacht in the cove. What do yer say if we go treasure-'untin'?"

"This is all moonshine and madness." Mr. Wilkinson muttered. "Still, I was thinking of taking a cruise; and it might as well be the China Seas as anywhere else."

"I'm all for it!" Jay cried enthusiastically. "This is the kind of thing which makes life worth while."

Suddenly a long, solemn face appeared over the railing of the veranda. It was Captain Ben's. "What have I always told yer, Mr. Wilkinson?" he said. "There's more strange critters and strange adventures out there"—he pointed unsteadily toward the surging stretch of sea—"than you ever heard tell of. Can't I go along, sir? I ain't so spry as I was, but I'm a deep thinker and all."

"You can go, Captain Ben!" cried Mr. Wilkinson with a strange note of boyish enthusiasm in his voice. "How about you, Bessie?"

Elizabeth nodded her head. "I'll go, too, dad," she murmured. "Perhaps I might be able to help some way. There might be something that—"

Suddenly she broke off. A dozen feet from her, from the interior of the sailor's chest, a strange flapping, scratching sound could be heard.

"Never you mind 'er, ma'am," said Bill Farley, with an embarrassed smile. "Lizzie 'as tantrums when she ain't fed regular. Poor gal, she's 'ad a 'ard day."

V

ANCHORS AWEIGH

For the next few days Maple Ridge, as Mr. Wilkinson's country place was called, was humming with activity. The preparations for the extended voyage went on apace, and the obese financier attended to the work with unusual animation.

Captain Ben and Farley slept together in the fisherman's cottage. They kept the sailor's chest in the same room with them. Often, and especially while the moon was full, the whimpus would emit that strange humming sound so peculiar to it, and at these times the men's snores would grow in volume till the tiny apartment seemed the interior of some huge beehive.

But Elizabeth, unlike the others, did not view the contemplated cruise for treasure with sparkling eyes and flushed cheeks. No; on the contrary, an involuntary tremor passed through her when she thought of it. During these days a shadow dogged her footsteps. And because this shadow was so vague in outline, so incomprehensible, it was doubly terrifying.

"What am I afraid of?" she would ask herself; "Am I afraid of a trip by sea to the China coast?"

"No," an inner voice would answer. "You are afraid of arriving safely at an island where there will be hundreds and hundreds of creatures like that creature, which is now in the sailor's box."

"Perhaps. But why should I fear these creatures. I did not even see the one in the box."

"Very true," the voice would answer with terrifying calmness; "but you have a feminine intuition which tells you that there are worse things than death—an intuition which has shown you the meaning of such creatures in your dreams. Beware the whimpus! Was it not chanted over your cradle by another woman who, in her turn, heard it almost at dawn of thought? The whimpus, that intangible something which robs women of husbands and homes—

the whimpus, that destroyer of our faith in those we hold close to our breasts, that breaker of men's destinies, that flapping, scratching creature of guile—beware the whimpus!"

And Elizabeth could not rid herself of that shadow. She saw it reflected in her father's kindling eyes and flushed cheeks; she saw it written in the curve of Jay's prominent chin; and she noted that even the aged Captain Ben, bore its dread echo in his shrill voice as the rusted antique bugle holds the echo of war somewhere in its dry throat. Like a relentless Medusa, it was turning to stone all those kindlier, gentler traits of man. Somewhere in the distance— on a coral island in the China Seas—strange, flapping, scratching creatures were beckoning to them. The men heard their call. They were going, even as Bill Farley had gone, even as all men had gone through all centuries. It was destiny—destiny sad for women to look upon. She was alone, and they were many; she went unprotected, and they were armed with all the hidden guile of the infinite. What was waiting for her on Whimpus Island?

At last came that never-to-be-forgotten day when the *Adventurer*, who had not earned her name till then, weighed anchor and swept majestically out of the harbor into the open sea. Elizabeth, from the upper deck, watched the shore slip past and finally disappear like a cloud of smoke. Several gulls followed the yacht, emitting shrill, plaintive cries. The wind had freshened, and a sprinkling of spray was borne against her face. The waves, in a long slanting procession, marched gaily forward against the prow of the *Adventurer*, only to be disemboweled and cast aside. They seemed an army seeking suicide. Each perished with a little gasp. A few somber clouds rode the heavens. They looked down on the bright tumult beneath like elderly, corpulent generals who watch the battle from afar.

"Well, ma'am, 'ow's it feel to go sailin' arter treasure?"

It was Bill Farley who spoke. He and Captain Ben had sauntered over to the rail, within arm's reach of Elizabeth's chair. They both wore a grin, now that they were safe at sea.

"Of course, I feel very excited," Elizabeth murmured. "What have you done with your fish, Mr. Farley?"

"Who? Lizzie, ma'am? She's as safe as a bug in a rug. I 'ave 'er alongside my 'ammock. I wouldn't take 'alf a chance with Lizzie."

"I'll miss the sound of her to-night, Bill," Captain Ben broke in. "That there whimpus has a soothin' sound when a feller's sleepy—a most soothin' sound."

"So I 'ave took notice, matey," Bill Farley muttered reflectively. "She's different than most gals there—beggin' your pardon, ma'am. I 'ad a wife in Singapore once. Gawd, that gal wouldn't lull yer off to sleep none, not 'er! She was hall for talk. She 'ad a tongue like a tin knife beatin' on a fryin'-pan. Give me Lizzie in a 'urricane to 'er."

The yacht had weighed anchor in the late afternoon. Now night began to settle down over the waste of tossing waters. The lips of foam, which rode each wave, seemed encrusted with tiny sparks of living fire. The wake was a flaming phosphorescent streak. Very gradually, very timidly, the stars appeared and looked down vacantly on the sea. The moon rose grinning from a patch of clouds far ahead. It had an air of jovial hospitality about it. "I'm glad you've come," it seemed to be saying through its wide, toothless mouth. "Step this way, won't you? I've got a surprise for you on the other side of the world."

Elizabeth rose with a little shiver. Night had suddenly reached out and gripped the *Adventurer* in her huge shadowy palm. Mystery and adventure were all about in those charging waves, in that somber sky, in that surge and sweep, in that power and passion of the sea.

VI

AN IRON WHIRLWIND

It was a calm day. Not a breath of air ruffled the placid surface of the sea which stretched out like some solid, luminous substance. The *Adventurer* plowed her way forward unconcernedly, casting a foam-capped furrow on either side.

"Aye, aye, governor," Bill Farley said in reply to a question of Mr. Wilkinson's, "we should sight Whimpus Island to-morrow night. And a very fine cruise we 'ad of it, weather as though served to order and no sea to speak of."

"We ain't there yet," Captain Ben broke in with a pessimistic shake of his grizzled head. "It's a treacherous sea at this time of the year. Them iron whirlwinds pops up as sudden as a devil, out of bell!"

"An iron whirlwind?" Jay asked.

"'E means a typhoon, gov'nor," Bill Farley explained. "They calls 'em iron whirlwinds 'ereabouts."

At that moment Elizabeth mounted the companionway and joined the four men. "Isn't it warm?" she murmured.

"Aye, aye, it's 'ot," Bill Farley replied.

"It is," said Captain Ben. "I recollect that it was on a day like this that—"

"Hello!" Mr. Wilkinson broke in. "Here comes the skipper! I wonder what he wants?"

The tall, lean figure of the captain of the *Adventurer* came striding toward them. His usually placid countenance wore a lugubrious expression.

"Well, what is it, Masters?" Mr. Wilkinson asked.

"The barometer has been falling for the last hour, sir. I think we're due a bit of rough weather."

Bill Farley drew in his breath sharply. "That looks bad 'ereabouts," he muttered.

"Bad signs both," said Captain Ben. "Take an old sailor's advice and don't let a iron whirlwind sneak up behind yer when you're not lookin'. Listen! What's that I hear?"

Far away across the calm expanse of water to the east a faint moaning could be heard. It was as though a grieving human soul were wandering in that vast amphitheater between sea and sky. Now other voices joined it in a melancholy chorus. The pack was coming from all sides—that pack of wind-wolves which would soon be down on them with a rush and a roar.

"What is it?" Mr. Wilkinson asked in a bewildered tone.

"There's a typhoon comin' up, gov'nor," said Bill Fancy, tightening his leather belt. "There'll be 'ell presently. Take a squint at the sky, gov'nor."

Even as he spoke great black clouds, like knights fully capa-risoned for the lists, rode swiftly into the pale-blue sky. They had appeared with startling suddenness as though they had been cre-ated in an instant by some malevolent magician of the infinite; and, with their coming, the whole face of the heavens was altered A soft glow suffused the heights above. The sky glowed ruby red in spots as though it were a glass door against which gigantic tongues of flame were pushing forward. At any moment one expected to see it come crashing down in red-hot fragments.

Suddenly the mournful wailing ceased. It was followed by a silence so profound that the ticking of Captain Ben's large silver watch was distinctly audible to all. There was something awe-inspiring in this silence. One felt that all about in that sullen sky, in that motionless sea now shot with fiery corrugations, in those swiftly gathering clouds, a relentless force was creeping forward noiselessly on hands and knees.

A solid white wall had risen up from the sea a mile or so away. For an instant it hovered there, a mound of snow against a murky background, and then it swept toward them with a sullen roar.

"Hurry, missy, hurry!" cried Captain Ben in a high falsetto.

Seizing Elizabeth's hand, he half led and half dragged her to-ward her cabin. Scarcely had they stumbled down to comparative safety before a huge wave tossed the *Adventurer* up on her beam-ends as though she were a toy; and a frantic, tearing wind, like a mad old woman, screaming, chuckling, roaring, circled about over-head, raking the yacht from stem to stern.

The sudden wild bound of the *Adventurer* skyward threw Eliza-beth on the floor of her cabin, and Captain Ben, head first, against the wall. Both were stunned. For a long time they lay there, un-conscious of the progress of the typhoon.

When Elizabeth opened her eye again, night had fallen. But what a strange night it was!—a luminous night which enveloped the raging sea with a pall of fire. Through the doorway she caught a glimpse of a blood-red heaven. Indeed the sea and the sky had apparently become as one—a fiery brotherhood, inseparable on the horizon's edge.

The typhoon had not abated in fury since those first few blinding moments.

On the contrary, the ocean had been so lashed by that terrific and luminous wind that it had risen up in wild revolt, threatening the very sky. Great billows, with fiery locks, charged down on the *Adventurer* and tossed her heavenward in derision. Each instant it seemed that she must perish in those glowing chasms ahead; but she fought her way through them somehow and rose up gamely on the other side, salt incrusted from her keel to her smoke-stacks.

Elizabeth was too weak to move. She lay there, a blinding pain creasing her forehead, staring about her like a terror-stricken child. There was no light in the cabin except those strange, vivid flashes which stole in through the doorway and which served to illumine objects in a fragmentary fashion. Now Captain Ben's face could be seen. He lay within arm's reach of Elizabeth, huddled up against the wall. She wondered if he were dead.

But now something happened which made her forget Captain Ben entirely. Suddenly the roaring of the wind died down as though by magic—it was as though nature were holding her breath—and she heard strange flapping, scratching sounds in the cabin where the steps led up to the main deck. Whatever it was, it was coming closer.

A great, numbing fear enveloped Elizabeth like a coverlet of snow. Only too well she knew those flapping, scratching sounds. She tried to scream, but her voice was frozen in her throat; she tried to rise, but her limbs refused their office. And now even the luminous light from the sea failed her. An inky blackness succeeded it which draped all things in impenetrable shadow.

But the flapping, scratching sounds continued. They were not more than two feet away—now less than a foot—now— Suddenly she felt something cold and sharp touch her outstretched palm.

"Lizzie!" a hoarse voice shouted. "Lizzie! Where 'ave yer got to, Lizzie?"

Bill Parley's dark figure blocked the cabin door. Striking a match, he peered about him anxiously. At this moment Captain Ben sat up and rubbed his head.

"Who's that?" he called weakly.

"It's Bill Farley, matey. 'Ave yer seen my Lizzy 'ereabouts? That there iron whirlwind smashed my chest ag'in' the wall; and Lizzie took it into 'er 'ead to skedaddle."

Captain Ben drew an electric flash-light from his pocket and touched the button. As the cabin became illumined, Bill Farley uttered a cry of joy.

"There she is!" he shouted jubilantly. "Lizzie, old gal, don't you go for to desert Bill. Come out from under that bed afore I go arter yer. Bli'me, if this ain't luck!"

Before dawn the typhoon wore itself out. All night the *Adventurer* had been running before the hurricane like a chip in a mill-race; now she was able to pursue her course unmolested. The wind had died down to a gentle breeze; and, although the waves still rode mountain high, their crests were no longer flecked with foam. Soon the sun rose and looked down reassuringly on a wind-scarred sea.

The passengers of the yacht, looking much the worse for the night's rough usage, gathered under the awning on the afterdeck.

"Here comes Captain Masters," said Elizabeth suddenly. "He seems to be rather excited."

"Perhaps the old tub's sprung a leak," Bill Farley suggested. "These pleasure-boats ain't built for seas like we was ridin' all of last night."

By now, Captain Masters had drawn up alongside the owner of the *Adventurer*. "There's land off our port bow," he said, raising his hat. "A coral island, I believe, sir."

"You don't say so!" Mr. Wilkinson began to fumble with his case of binoculars. "I think I'll take a look at it, Masters."

Bill Farley silently went aft, reappearing a moment later with a long, brass telescope. "I can see it now," Jay said, shielding his eyes with the palm of his hand. "There was a curtain of mist hiding it, but it's rising."

Bill Fancy raised the telescope to his eye and gazed long and attentively. Suddenly it began to shake oddly. "Gawd!" he muttered, "if it ain't Whimpus Island!"

"There must be some mistake!" Mr. Wilkinson cried. "We couldn't have run into it by accident like this!"

"Nary a mistake, gov'nor. There she is just as I seen her last, shaped like a 'orseshoe and all. And there's that bit of flag-pole what me and my mate rigged up with Black Tom's red flannel drawers still flappin' there, or what's left of 'em."

Jay took the telescope from his hand. "He's right, Mr. Wilkinson," he said at length. "At least I can see the pole and something red flying from it."

"Run in closer, Masters," Mr. Wilkinson ordered.

The *Adventurer* ran slowly forward. It came to a halt along the coral shores which glowed like molten metal in the sun. A great splash of foam told that the anchor had been lowered.

"What's that?" Jay cried suddenly. "I thought I saw something dive off that ledge of coral into the water."

"It was a whimpus, gove'nor," said Bill Fancy composedly. "I saw 'er myself. There's 'undreds 'ere—'undreds."

"When shall we begin searchin' for the treasure?" Captain Ben asked, moving his nutcracker jaws as though he were chewing a delectable morsel. "I'm most too tired to go skinnin' my shins on diamonds till I've had a few winks of sleep."

"And me too, matey," Bill Farley agreed. "My 'ead's swimmin' around, I'm that wore out. Let's us 'ave our beauty sleep, governor, afore we tackle treasure-'untin'."

"I'd like to start right now," Jay cried impatiently. "We've got all the rest of our lives to sleep."

But Mr. Wilkinson shook his head. "No, no Jay. Captain Ben and Fancy are right. We want to start at this thing when we can do our best. Let's turn in now, and in the afternoon we can land and look over the ground."

"Right you are, gove'nor!" Bill Farley cried with alacrity. "I'm off to my 'ammock this minute. Sweet dreams to one and all." With a smile which was half a grimace and a bow which bent him double, the sailor turned and made off toward his quarters.

"I don't fancy that fellow's manners," Jay said with a flush. "He's entirely too free and easy. What he needs is a strenuous toe-application on the right spot."

"Never mind, Jay," Mr. Wilkinson said. "We can teach him his place after he's found the treasure for us. But speaking about place, mine should be in a downy couch this minute. How about you, Bessie?"

"I'm awfully tired, dad. I'm going to turn in."

"Every one is goin' to take a snooze," Captain Ben said. "Even the crew. Captain Masters has give orders to that effect. Well they deserve it, the poor lads." Smothering a yawn, he turned and hobbled off.

Fifteen minutes later Elizabeth lay on her berth in the cabin sound asleep.

Almost immediately she heard the muffled sound of oars working smoothly in well-oiled oarlocks.

When the girl awoke the red rays of the setting sun streamed through the porthole.

Conscious that some one was pounding on the door, she sat up and rubbed her eyes.

"Who is it?" she called softly.

"It's Jay," said a voice which shook with anger. "I came to wake you. What do you think happened while we were all asleep?"

"I haven't an idea. What?" the girl asked.

"Why, that Cockney sailor sneaked off to Whimpus Island in one of our life-boats and he hasn't come back."

"What of it? Probably he's taking a little row. He'll be back for supper," she said.

A bitter, incredulous laugh rasped through the keyhole. "I fancy not," Jay said calmly. "He's taken his whimpus with him."

VII
"Aye, Aye, Sir—Just Fish"

Elizabeth dressed quickly and hurried on deck. In spite of Jay's disappointment, she felt relieved at the disappearance of the sailor and his whimpus. She had great difficulty in hiding her real feelings from the group of excited, angry men whom she encountered near the empty davits where the missing life-boat had reposed.

"This is a pretty kettle of fish, missy!" Captain Ben cried in his high treble. "But I never liked that Britisher from the first."

"I can't see his game," Mr. Wilkinson said irritably. "How can he double-cross us? We've got the yacht; and, without that, all the treasure in the world wouldn't do him any good."

"He's got something up his sleeve," Jay muttered.

"Funny we can't see him on the island," Mr. Wilkinson said thoughtfully. "He's probably hiding on the other side of that mound."

"Or in the treasure-cave," Captain Ben suggested. "That's where he's at—fillin' his pockets with diamonds, I wouldn't wonder."

Elizabeth shaded her eyes and gazed over the now calm stretch of water toward Whimpus Island. To the west, a red sullen sun swam on the horizon. It colored the coral with a last faint glow before it sank beneath the surface of the sea. The wind had died away. Not a breath of air ruffled the placid surface; and the red rags, which had once served as a part of Black Tom's wardrobe, hung disconsolately from the flagpole.

Suddenly the girl uttered a shrill cry. "Why, there's the boat now!" she said. "No, two of them—one right behind the other!"

Mr. Wilkinson raised the binoculars to his eyes in some excitement. After a moment he lowered them with an exclamation of disgust. "It's only Masters," he told his daughter. "We sent him to look for Farley in the other life-boat."

"Yes, but there are two boats coming this way."

"Masters has Farley's boat in tow. He probably found it on the island."

"Well, the man can't dodge us!" Jay cried. "He'll stay on the island till we say the word. I think we've got him where we want him."

"Perhaps he drownded," Captain Ben suggested. "A lot of them sailors can't swim. I recollect one time off Gibraltar there was just such another feller—"

But Mr. Wilkinson interrupted the old fisherman with scant ceremony. Raising his voice to a bellow, he hailed Captain Masters who was not more than a stone's throw from the *Adventurer*.

"Is Farley on the island?"

"He must be there, sir," Captain Masters answered through his speaking-trumpet. "We found his boat pulled up on the shore."

"Hiding in the cave," Mr. Wilkinson muttered. "Well, we'll starve him out. But I don't see his little game."

"Nor I," Jay agreed. "He stands to win nothing by acting this way. But don't you think we could find the cave without him or his whimpus?"

"Not me," said Captain Ben. "It's like lookin' for a needle in a haystack. That there island is hollowed out with caves, thousands and thousands of 'em. We ain't got no chance without a whimpus."

For the next few days a cloud of despondency hung over the *Adventurer*. In vain the coral island was kept under strict surveillance, not a vestige of Bill Farley was to be seen; in vain exploring parties ransacked it from end to end, no cave in any way resembling Black Tom's description was to be found. At the end of the week, even Jay had given up hope. Undoubtedly Bill Farley and his secret had died together.

On the following Monday Mr. Wilkinson made known his intention of quitting the island and starting home. "We're just wasting our time here," he told Jay. "If Bill Farley were still alive, we'd have heard from him before this."

"I suppose so," the young man muttered. "He must have fallen into some hole and broken his neck. But it seems a shame to turn back without getting a glimpse of the treasure."

Mr. Wilkinson nodded solemnly. "I know. But what's to be done? I've told Masters to weigh anchor to-morrow."

At this moment Captain Ben's decrepit figure was seen approaching across the deck at a strange ambling trot. He was waving his arms about like a windmill; his long white hair was flying in the wind.

"Well, what is it?" Mr. Wilkinson asked.

The old man moistened his lips and launched out into speech. "I've been fishin' for the last few days while you all have been searchin' this island. There's some most curious fish in these parts—gay-colored, with tails most like a lady's fan and pop eyes like a frog. But they're tasty, too, when cooked with plenty of butter."

"Is that all you've got to tell us about—*fish?*" Jay cried impatiently. "I thought that perhaps you'd discovered something. So it's just fish, eh?"

"Aye, aye, sir—just fish," said Captain Ben, a sly smile creeping under his nose.

"Well?"

"Well, Mr. Wilkinson, this mornin' I lost my sinker; and, havin' nothin' handy but a gold goat which my sister's son give me for a watch-charm, I hitched it on my line till I could find somethin' better and threw it overboard. Now I didn't get a bite for nearly ten minutes; then, all of a sudden, somethin' gives that line a awful jerk. 'What's this?' I says to myself, for the coral fish don't pull near so hard. 'Perhaps a young shark has laid hold.' Well. I pulled that fish up on deck, although I had a sweatin' time of it, and what do you think it was gentlemen?"

"I'm sure I don't know," said Jay.

"Was it a shark?" Mr. Wilkinson asked.

Captain Ben surveyed his employer with an air of triumph. "Not so you could notice!" said he. "That there fish was nothin' more nor less than a whimpus."

"A whimpus!" cried Mr. Wilkinson.

"Yes, sir. As like to Bill's Lizzie as two peas. Just as ugly natured, too. She had laid hold of that gold goat; and, when I tried to pry it free, she begins bubblin' like a tea-pot and gnashin' her teeth. Well, I tied her up in a net and give her the goat to play with for a spell."

"Where is she now?" Mr. Wilkinson asked.

"Down in my quarters, sir. She's safe enough."

"If this is true," Jay cried with flashing eyes, "if Captain Ben has actually caught another whimpus, we don't need Bill Farley at all. We can take that whimpus on shore and let it lead us to its cave. We'll tie a string to its claw, eh?"

"Let's land on the island the first thing to-morrow morning," Mr. Wilkinson said.

"Not one or two of us, but every man on board. And we'll go armed. Whatever is in that cave must have finished Bill Farley off."

"Probably," Jay agreed. "But lead us to your whimpus, Captain Ben."

The life-boat was lowered carefully into the sea. One by one the men, each armed with a revolver, climbed down the rope ladder and seated themselves. Captain Ben, Jay, and Mr. Wilkinson were the last to leave the deck. They all turned to Elizabeth for a final word of leave-taking.

"We'll be home in time for lunch," Jay said. "Do you see this, Bessie?" He held a large canvas bag aloft. "I brought it along so that I could bring back the diamonds and gold."

"Don't look so downhearted, Bessie," Mr. Wilkinson said good-humoredly. "I'd take you along if we didn't have a lot of climbing and wading in front of us. Too rough work for a girl, eh, Captain Ben?"

"True enough, sir."

"Have you got the whimpus safely aboard?"

"That I have, sir. I got her in a birdcage one of the men had. These whimpus can cut up rough."

"What will I do if anything should happen to you, dad?" Elizabeth asked.

"What could happen to *us?*" Mr. Wilkinson said reassuringly. "We're eight strong and all armed to the teeth. Don't worry, Bessie—we'll be back for lunch."

"All aboard!" cried Jay. "The sooner we start the sooner we'll be back with the booty."

But Captain Ben lingered for an instant after the other two had clambered down into the boat. "Don't you fret, missy," he said, giving her shoulder a furtive pat. "We'll make out all right. I've got a wise head on my shoulders."

But in spite of these reassuring words, Elizabeth felt a lump rising in her throat when she saw the life-boat push off and the oars flash in the early sunlight. Ever since the preceding afternoon, when the second whimpus had been caught and she had learned of the intended expedition, the girl had been the prey of wild fancies. All night, dark forebodings of she knew not what had haunted her pillow. And now a settled despondency enveloped her optimism like a wet blanket.

For some time she stood at the rail, watching the progress of the life-boat. Finally, after it had disappeared around one of the curving arms of Whimpus Island, she turned away with a sigh and entered her cabin.

Elizabeth glanced about in search of some refuge from herself. She saw a book lying on the table within arm's reach. Picking it up hurriedly, she opened it at random and began to read. Unfortunately for her peace of mind, the book happened to be a volume of Poe's verses. The particular poem she turned to was *The Bells* and those lines which run:

> They are neither man nor woman—
> They are neither brute nor human—
> They are Ghouls—

She dropped the volume with a cry of disgust and hurried up to the main deck. It was well past noon. A blazing sun rode the sky, casting its rays on Whimpus Island which seemed to be wavering in the intense heat. Elizabeth gazed long in that direction, but she could see no vestige of humanity on the shimmering shore.

"It's nearly one o'clock," the girl murmured. "I've half a mind to go and see what's happened to them."

There was a small skiff on the after-deck which she had often used when at home. To-day the sea was so calm that a canoe could have ridden it with perfect safety. Acting on a sudden impulse, she lowered the skiff into the water and, in a moment more, was seated in the stern, paddling swiftly toward Whimpus Island.

In less than fifteen minutes the skiff grounded on the shore and Elizabeth began her search.

Whimpus Island extended for nearly three miles. In breadth, however, it rarely exceeded two hundred yards. The walking was very rough. There were all manner of hummocks, which rose up like bumps on a bald head, and fissures in the coral which had to be taken into account.

Elizabeth was a strong, active girl, but she was nearly worn-out before she had circled the island. Every now and then she stopped to rest. At these times she called aloud, whereupon her voice would be caught up by every cave and echoed back hollowly. But no human voice answered hers; no human figure met her eye in all that weary tramp. Indeed, a blight seemed to rest on the island. Unlike any other which she had ever seen, no sea-gulls whined about its cliff and no grasses grew even where there was a stretch of solid soil.

"They must still be in the cave," Elizabeth murmured in a vain effort to fight off growing depression. "It won't do any good hunting for them. I'll go back to the boat and wait there."

When she came to this decision, she was standing on the hummock from which Black Tom's gaudy nether garments fluttered brazenly in the wind. The girl, tired in both body and mind, seated herself for an instant beneath this barbaric emblem and rested her chin in her hands. Several paces from her, a long red fissure in the coral seemed to grin at her as though it were a human mouth.

Suddenly she heard a strange sound which made her start and look up. It was a dull droning like the humming of innumerable bees, not unmusical and rather soothing except for an occasional loud snort which broke into it like a peremptory command. These sounds evidently issued from the fissure already alluded to.

"What can it be?" Elizabeth wondered. She walked over to the fissure and tried to peer down.

Now the dull buzzing sounds grew louder. Suddenly there came such a loud snort from the shadowy depths that Elizabeth involuntarily recoiled.

"Sea-lions!" she murmured. "I've heard them snort just like that in the zoo. The buzzing sound must be water running into some cave. No doubt the tide rises and falls."

At last she retraced her steps to where she had left the skiff, and, with a heavy heart, paddled back to the *Adventurer*. As she neared the yacht, hope rose up in her. Perhaps they had returned while she had been out of sight on the other side of the island; perhaps they were safe on board, laughing at her fears.

Making the skiff fast, she clambered aboard the *Adventurer* and was greeted by silence and shadows. A glance at the empty davits where the life-boat usually reposed, blighted her hopes. She experienced a moment, of complete weakness. Sinking down on the hard deck, she began to sob.

Night was slowly falling. A gray mist stole up silently from the water, enveloping Whimpus Island in an impenetrable curtain of mystery. The sun sank with startling suddenness as though its fiery light had been extinguished by the touch of that calm, luminous sea. A legion of languid shadows stole about the hysterical girl on noiseless feet. They bent backward and forward like flowers fondled by the breeze; they pointed at Whimpus Island with ghostly fingers; they were like embodied dreams which seek release.

But Elizabeth wept on, quite unheeding their silent supplications; wept on, while the stars opened timidly like frightened eyes; wept on, while the moon, grinning, rose up triumphantly as though to say: "Well, what did I tell you? Here we are on the other side of the world. Look where I am looking, and you will see something very strange. Come, this is a surprise!"

VIII

A Woman and a Whimpus

The hours which followed the disappearance of the treasure-hunters, seemed like so many years to Elizabeth.

All alone on the *Adventurer*, a prisoner in a floating prison, she experienced a thousand and one terrors which threatened her very reason.

At one moment, she would abandon herself to despair; at the next, a sudden sound—the swishing of water against the ship's side, the creaking of an overtaxed beam—would make her leap to her feet in a frenzy of hope.

A hundred times during that first terrible night, she thought she heard the squeaking of oar-locks. Then she would hurry up on deck, her heart beating wildly, expecting to see the life-boat pull up alongside. At each disappointment, her spirits would sink again into the darkest depths of despondency.

The next morning she paddled her skiff to shore and searched the island from end to end. She returned sadly to the ship.

On the third day all hope deserted her. Straining her eyes across the silver-shod sea, she saw the island like a sinister red question-mark standing out against a pale blue page. Not a vestige of life was stirring there. Black Tom's tattered garments—how dear, how human a symbol after all!—waved in melancholy triumph over a hot, blistering waste of coral.

Perhaps it was this still vivid remnant of a brave man who had gone to his everlasting rest, perhaps it was a fine frenzy of despair, but certain it is that Elizabeth took her courage in both hands and went out alone to battle against the whimpus.

Very calmly, though with a wildly beating heart, she went down to Captain Ben's quarters, ransacked his belongings and returned on deck with a strong fishing-line. Her next problem was to bait the hook properly. She examined her trinkets, one by one, and finally decided on the ring which Jay had given her on the day of their engagement. Why did she choose this ring among all the others? Was it because she loved it best; or, perhaps, because it symbolized her love which was as keen and brave as a sword?

Elizabeth lowered her bait carefully over the side. Bending forward, she saw it slip into the water, which was as clear as crystal; saw it sink down lowly into the depths, saw a host of flaming darts shooting this way and that—coral fish, which were all colors of the rainbow—and finally saw it resting on a strip of snow-white sand. For several minutes she stood there, immovable, staring down; and then she uttered a low exultant cry.

Several dark gliding shapes began to approach the glittering bait. They formed about it in a solemn circle as though deciding. Elizabeth caught a glimpse of slowly moving tails, beneath a long, silky substance which trailed out behind and which glimmered dully. Surely these were whimpus. She even caught a glimpse of an outstretched, avaricious claw. What was in that held them back? Why didn't they bite?

She leaned forward further still and saw the answer to her question mirrored on the placid water. Her own face looked back at

her. Yes, evidently the whimpus had seen her. Now they were pointing upward with their clawlike fingers, now they were stealing off
in a stately procession. Soon they had disappeared.

"Perhaps they are as afraid of me as I was afraid of them," Elizabeth told herself.

This thought gave her a new confidence and a new idea. Pulling the line up, hand over hand, she hurried into her cabin, and,
opening one of the port-holes wide, threw her bait out into the sea.
Then she seated herself and waited.

In her present position she could not be seen from the water.
If they had not gone too far away, perhaps they would return and
nibble, now that she had disappeared. At any rate, it was just possible.

For five minutes, ten minutes, Elizabeth sat as silent as a statue,
with a white face and flashing eyes; and then, just as she was about
to pull the line in and cast again, she felt a violent jerk which nearly
pulled her to her feet. The line had suddenly grown taut and it took
all her strength to hold it.

And then the struggle began. Elizabeth was an athletic girl. Her
muscles served her well that day. Little by little, with gasping
breath and straining arms, she fought it out. Often she gained a
yard, only to lose it again. But now her fighting blood was up; she
knew no weakness or fear.

Gradually, inch by inch, the girl drew the whimpus to the surface of the water and then above it. Now it was dangling in the air;
now it shot through the porthole like an arrow and fell, flapping
and scratching, to the floor.

Then, at last, the whimpus relinquished its frenzied hold on
the glittering bait. Moving its small, round head from side to side,
it clawed its tangle of golden hair from its face and stared at Elizabeth. Slowly the large blue eyes became dilated with fear, the large
loose-lipped mouth fell open, disclosing sharp yellow fangs, the
tail flapped wildly, and both claws were raised on high like terror-
stricken hands.

And Elizabeth looked at this monster concocted in the laboratories of the sea—at this creature, half fish and half vampire; at

this composition of scales and flesh—with horror, it is true, but without fear. Her imagination had long ago pictured it. She had seen it so often in her dreams, that now the reality was not so difficult to view.

And thus it was that a woman and a whimpus faced each other for the first time since the world began—while the clock in the cabin ticked on contentedly; while the chairs presented their stolid wicker backs like disinterested strangers; while the sea, as though amused at what it saw, tickled the yacht's sides, and, laughing merrily, sped by.

IX

Treasure Trove

Elizabeth was the first to act. A colossal calmness had descended upon her which had crystallized her every thought, her every sensation, into a well-formulated plan. She must not fail now. She realized with a perfect clarity of vision that all her hopes of ultimate happiness, her life and the lives of her dear ones, depended on an immediate exertion of her mental and physical powers. She loathed this abysmal monster on the floor with both a fleshly and spiritual loathing, but she must not falter in her self-appointed task.

There was a large wicker lunch-basket on the chair beside her. Picking it up, she raised the lid and took a step forward.

And the whimpus, which, up to this, had been in an attitude of frozen horror, its clawlike hands raised above its head—now seemed to read its adversary's intent. Hissing faintly, its fishy eyes covered by a gray film of fear, it squirmed backward as Elizabeth advanced till finally its flapping tail touched the wall. There it paused and, with gnashing teeth and extended nails, awaited the attack.

But the girl did not hesitate. Stepping bravely forward, she bent down and attempted to force the creature into the lunch-basket. Hissing, it squirmed to one side and escaped. Once more she essayed her task; and this time the whimpus' sharp teeth were embedded for a moment in her arm.

Now a blind fury drove Elizabeth on. As she felt the sudden pain, her left hand found the monster's throat and tightened there till it relinquished its hold to gasp for breath, till its tongue protruded like a scarlet streamer, till its eyes were nearly popping from its head. And then she lifted it from the floor; lifted it and held it at arm's length. Her fingers, like steel rings, still encircled its slender throat.

But as the whimpus' pale, leprous face turned scarlet, as its blood-shot eyes rolled upward till nothing was visible of them but their crimson-threaded whites, she relaxed her hold. It would never do to kill it outright. It must serve her first; it must guide her to her loved ones.

The whimpus squirmed only very feebly now. Elizabeth had no difficulty in placing it in the lunch-basket, where it lay flapping faintly. Her next task was to tie the fishing-line securely about its waist, where the fish's tail joined the woman's body. Now it could not escape, but its swimming powers would remain unimpeded.

She then closed the lid on her prisoner, secured it, and carried the lunch-basket up on deck.

She tied a handkerchief about the wound, and climbed down the ladder, still holding the lunch-basket, and into the skiff. Slipping the oars into place, she bent her strong, supple back to the task and was soon propelling the boat swiftly toward the island.

When the skiff was finally grounded on the shore, she sprang out with all the eagerness of one who goes willingly to battle.

Elizabeth opened the lunch-basket and drew out the whimpus. The monster by this time had regained some of its strength. As she held it suspended in mid air on the end of the fishing-line, it squirmed frantically, gnashed its teeth, and emitted a strange hissing sound.

For a moment she swung it back and forth to see that the line held; then she threw it from her into the sea.

At first the whimpus swam straight out with incredible swiftness—so fast, indeed, that she was put to it to give it free play—but after it had traversed a hundred yards or so, it turned and began to creep back further down the shore. Fortunately the fishing-line was very long; but, at that, she was soon forced to follow it along the beach.

In this way Elizabeth half circled the island. At last she came to a tangle of salt grass which grew in profusion against one of the coral cliffs. To her amazement the fishing-line passed through this tangle as if the creature on the other end had clambered back on shore. And yet this seemed impossible, for the shoulder of the island at this point was precipitous.

As she paused before the green, swaying door of salt grass, there came another tug on the line which showed her that the whimpus was still in active flight. Pushing the nodding sea-foliage aside with her left hand, she uttered an ejaculation of surprise.

There, in the coral wall, was a cave hollowed out as though by human hands. Undoubtedly this subterranean passageway led into the very heart of the island. Perhaps the whimpus was leading her into the treasure-chamber where, dead or alive, she might find the missing passengers of the *Adventurer*.

Elizabeth, with a wild beating heart, stepped through the dark portal and was immediately swallowed up in. the gloom. Not a light glimmered; soon the opening in the cave was lost to view. Walking in pitch blackness, a stream of running water above her ankles, the taut line leading her forward as a blind man is guided by holding to the leash of some intelligent dog, she stumbled on for a hundred yards or more. Suddenly a strange sound came to her out of the darkness far ahead.

Elizabeth paused and listened, in spite of a sudden angry tug on her-wrist. There it was again—only louder now. A drowsy, humming sound it was, followed almost immediately by a loud snort.

It is no telling whether Elizabeth could have mustered up enough courage to go further had not the whimpus at that moment given the line such a frenzied jerk that she was carried forward a step in spite of herself. This step was the deciding one. There was no use turning back now. Behind her lay loneliness, starvation, death; before her? Well, that might be quicker, at any rate.

The frightened girl waded onward through the blackness, while the strange sounds grew louder and louder. Now a gray shaft of

light stole around a bend in the passage. She reached it; she turned
an abrupt shoulder of rock and uttered a cry which echoed through
the vault. She was destined never to forget the sight which met her
eyes.

The passageway here terminated in a spacious hall. Through a
fissure in the ceiling, javelins of flaming sunlight poured down on
a strip of shimmering sand which barely raised its head above the
shallow water. And on this sand, piled up in a glittering heap and
indiscriminately mingled, were precious stones, pieces of colored
glass, yellow bars of gold, brass door-knobs, a child's toy sword,
several helmets which the soldiers of Cesar might have worn, rattles
with colored beads, a crown set with gigantic emeralds which might
have adorned some fair Egyptian's brow. But one and all caught
the shafts of sunlight and reflected them, casting a luminous light
on the dark, dripping walls and on the pale sheet of water.

It was not the sight of these precious stones and glittering gew-
gaws which wrung the cry from Elizabeth. No, it was the group
which sat about this treasure in a solemn circle—these men, with
their chins resting on their breasts; these skeletons from whom
hung in tatters the clothing of an earlier age; these gleaming skulls
and moldy thigh-bones, more aged relics still, which time had
crumbled into little powdery heaps beneath the weight of its relentless hand. And also it was that outer ring of custodians which
guarded both—that swimming ring of whimpus, whirling round
and round in a magic circle and emitting that strange, unearthly
humming sound as they went—those singular creatures that were
neither brute nor human, their large blue eyes fixed with a glassy
stare on what rested on that strip of sand, their long, golden hair
floating behind them in a filmy gauze.

Scarcely had Elizabeth's cry echoed through the chamber than
a change took place. The humming died away as though by magic.
Now a hundred pairs of terror-stricken eyes were turned on her, a
hundred pairs of terror-stricken clawlike hands were raised on
high, a hundred scaly tails churned the water into foam. Once,
twice, the whimpus sped around the strip of sand and then straight
toward her and the passageway.

She floundered to one side; the fishing-line dropped from her nerveless hand. The next instant they were past her, gliding by swiftly and out into the passageway. Leaving a trail of foam, they vanished in the gloom. She was left entirely alone with the dead.

But, ah, no, they were not all dead! What was that? Surely it was a human snore—a snore so awe-inspiring, so sonorous, that from a distance it had seemed the snorting of an animal in pain.

Elizabeth stepped cautiously forward. The light reflected from the heap of treasure was blinding. She shaded her eyes with her hand.

Could it be? Yes, it was. There was no doubt about it. The snorer was Captain Ben! There he sat, his cavernous mouth gaping, his hairy fists doubled on his knees. And next to him, his head resting on his shoulder, a strange expression of physical loathing on his face, sat—Jay! Surely there was her father on his right, sleeping soundly, his chin resting on his breast! And the other sleepers were the crew of the *Adventurer*. None were dead as yet—thank God!—not one.

Elizabeth put her hand on Captain Ben's shoulder and shook him. "Wake up!" she cried. "Wake up!"

The old man's stentorian snore ceased on the instant. He raised his face and Elizabeth saw that it was bedewed with perspiration. "Don't you touch me!" he muttered. "Can't you see I'm an old man? I—I—"

"It's Bessie!" the girl cried. "Don't you know me?"

Suddenly the light of recognition flared up in the old fisherman's eyes. "Oh, missy," he said feebly, like a frightened child, "take me out of here. I want to go home, missy."

But Elizabeth was shaking Jay. "Wake up! Wake up!"

The young man opened his gray eyes. "Oh!" he cried. "Get me out of here! Oh, Bessie, dearest girl, it's you! You don't know what a horrible dream I've had!"

But Elizabeth had turned to her father. "Wake up, dad!" she cried.

"What do you want?" the financier muttered. "Oh, Dolly, Dolly, shameful Dolly!"

"Wake up, dad!"

And then Mr. Wilkinson opened his eyes and stared solemnly at his daughter. "I've had a nightmare, Bessie," he said. "Get me out of here if you can. I'm about all in!"

But Elizabeth woke the others first. Captain Masters and his crew. Last of all, she came to Bill Farley. He was sitting beside a skeleton which still wore a tattered sailor suit. The cockney had a sentimental smile playing beneath his bulbous nose. One of his arms were buried to the elbow in a heap of precious stones; the other clasped the body of a dead whimpus to his breast. His eyes were swallowed in cavernous hollows; his lips were a chalky white.

"Wake up!" Elizabeth cried bravely, although the man's face frightened her. "Wake up!"

Bill Farley was silent. But his smile broadened and twitched his upper lip above two yellow fangs.

"Wake up!" she cried again, shaking him violently.

The sailor did not move, but his eyes flickered open for an instant. "I 'ears you, ma'am," he said very faintly. "Call louder, ma'am. A girl such as you can pull a chap outer 'ell, if she tries real 'ard. Call louder, ma'am."

Once more Elizabeth's voice echoed through the chamber. "Wake up!" she cried. "It's time we went home!"

Again Bill Farley's white lips moved. "It ain't a bit of use, ma'am. I'm goin' 'ome, but not with you. Black Tom 'ere is more my kind. 'E and me—them whimpus 'as got us, soul and body. Lizzie, 'ere, she kept on singin' to me on the *Adventurer*. It weren't me that double-crossed yer, ma'am, it was 'er. Gawd! What was a poor sailor-man to do? She 'ad a 'old on me most as strong as a gal; and she was all for gettin' 'ome. I guess I—"

The muffled voice died away; the long, lean head rolled over on one shoulder; a frozen, sentimental smile was still stamped on the chalky lips.

"It ain't no use, missy," Captain Ben said, touching her on the arm. "That feller's dead. Let us clear outer here afore them things come back. I had a horrid dream, missy!"

X

THREE WEEKS LATER

The *Adventurer*, her engine beating rhythmically like a human heart, plowed through the shadowy sea. To the west a last faint, crimson streak in the sky showed where the sun had struggled for the mastery and died. Now night ruled the world.

Elizabeth, Captain Ben, Mr. Wilkinson, and Jay, sat on the after deck. A silence had fallen between them which was broken only by the faint gurgling of the fisherman's ancient pipe as he inhaled silver threads of smoke into his lungs. The girl was the first to speak.

"You haven't told me how you happened to fall asleep there," she said with some asperity. "That would be the last thing I'd do after finding all those precious stones."

Captain Ben cleared his throat; Mr. Wilkinson rose and walked to the rail; Jay seemed engrossed in a silent contemplation of the stars.

"Well, aren't any of you going to tell me?"

Captain Ben took the pipe out of his mouth and yawned. "Yes, missy," he said, "I'll spin you the yarn. But remember you're a gal, and there's lots of things gals can't seem to get into their heads."

"I wouldn't be so sure of that, Captain Ben."

"Well, it's as true as gospel, missy. Just you take them whimpus for instance. They couldn't do you no harm 'cause you're a gal and they ain't got no power over gals. You was stronger than they was, and they know'd it. There ain't a whimpus livin' what can hold her own against a decent gal like you, missy. They're common critters, mostly."

"But I want to know how you happened to fall asleep in that cave."

"Aye, aye, missy, I'll tell yer. The whimpus what had its in tow led us into that cave as pretty as you please. When we seen all them diamonds and things, we didn't stop for nothin'—just waded through them swimmin' whimpus and climbed up on the sand and begin to play with the jewels like we was babies. Even the skeletons didn't scare us none—though Bill Farley give me kind of a start when I seen that silly grin on his mug. Well, you know the sound them whimpus made while they was swimmin'?"

"Yes," said Elizabeth. "It got on my nerves. It was a most unpleasant sound."

Captain Ben shook his aged head. "It might have sounded unpleasant to you, missy, 'cause you're a gal; but it didn't to us. Lord, no! It was a soothin' sound—a most soothin' sound! Well, pretty soon I give up countin' diamonds and take a look about me. What do you think I saw, missy? Why, there was your pop, Mr. Jay, and them sailors, all fast asleep! They had kinder silly grins on their faces—leastwise, so I thought."

"You old liar!" cried Jay with some heat. "I heard that snore of yours before I even closed my eyes."

"And I, too," Mr. Wilkinson muttered. "He was asleep before any of us."

But Captain Ben went on as though he had not heard them. "Well, I kinder wondered why they should all go off to sleep like that. But pretty soon that hummin' sound grew louder and crept into my head—the same as gas does when some dentist feller goes to yank yer tooth. I tried to fight it, missy, but it weren't possible. Pretty soon, before I realized it, I slipped off into a dream."

"A dream? What kind of a dream? That's what I want to find out. When you woke up, you all said that you had had such horrible dreams."

The three men exchanged covert glances. Captain Ben rose and knocked the ashes out of his pipe. "You ask your pop, missy," he said. "He's a whole lot better at tellin' things than me."

Mr. Wilkinson frowned. "I don't remember anything about it," he muttered, "not a thing. But I think I'll go up and ask Masters where we are. He said we might sight Fire Island Light before the moon rose."

"I'll go with yer, sir," said Captain Ben, hobbling after his employer. "It takes the young fellers to remember them dreams right. Mr. Jay, I reckon, can tell about his'n like it was a story outer one of them books you're always readin', missy."

"What *was* your dream, Jay?" Elizabeth asked after the two elder men had gone.

The young man's eyes avoided hers.

"I can't tell you, Bessie," he said. "That dream was too much a part of myself to share it with another. There come such dreams in a man's life—dreams, distorted and terrible, which one must keep always in the dark closet of one's mind. Women should be satisfied with realities—a man's dreams must always be his own."

"I suppose you're right. But it must have been horrible dreams which drove you all out of the cave without the treasure."

"They *were* horrible dreams, Bessie—at least, mine was." Jay paused and stroked his chin meditatively. "But it cured me, Bessie"

"Cured you?" the girl asked in surprise. "What did it cure you of?"

"It cured me of that wild craving for adventure which used to drag me from place to place as a kitten drags a mouse. This time I've absorbed enough excitement for the rest of my life. You'll find that when I get my feet on dry ground I'll turn out to be the most thoroughly domesticated husband in the world."

"I'll be so glad of that," Elizabeth said earnestly. "If that happens, I will never ask you about your dream; if that happens, I shall know that I have really conquered the whimpus."

There was a moment's silence; and then, from the bow of the *Adventurer*, came a hail which brought them to their feet. It was Captain Ben shouting through Masters's speaking-trumpet.

"Land, ho!" the old man cried in a shrill falsetto. "Land ho, missy!"

THE TERRORS OF THE UPPER AIR
Frank Orndorff
1928

Pemberton, the Great Detective, renowned as never having failed to get his man, spoke to the Secretary of the President of the State Fair, and passed on to the President's office door marked "Private." He entered without knocking.

"Well! What happening is responsible for this visit?" The President sprang up and grasped Pemberton's hand and pulled a chair out for him. "You are not in the habit of calling on me lately except on business. Who are the unlucky people at the Fair that you want? For my guess is that you are after some poor birds."

Pemberton sat down and placed his hat on the President's desk. "You are right to call them birds. I am after your human birds, and they can't particularly be called 'poor'—not now, anyhow."

"What!" exclaimed the President, as he half rose in his seat, "surely you are not after Kidwell and Dexter, the aviators who are flying for the Fair."

"The very two men I am after."

"But what have they done? It must be something serious."

"It is serious. You remember the Windsor Bank Robbery of over a week ago, where the cashier was killed and nearly a half a million dollars, mostly in large bills was stolen? The two men who did the job escaped in an auto. They were chased to a large wooded tract just about nightfall. When the pursuers closed in, they found the car but the men and the money were gone."

"I remember that and also the mystery of their escape from the hundreds of men that surrounded the woods."

"They did not escape *through* this fence of men, but *over* them. As soon as I had gone over the ground, I found tracks of where an aeroplane had made a short run in a break in the woods and could easily have shot upwards above the trees and away. The place was far enough from the edge of the woods, to enable the roar of the motor to go unheard as the two men fled away in the night.

"The run to the woods and the flight in the aeroplane was most likely planned ahead by the two men and would have remained undiscovered had it not been for a mark made in the soft ground by two small cuts in one of the aeroplane tires. It was one chance in a thousand that we ever found the aeroplane tracks and one in a million that it left the print of these two small cuts in the tire's tread. Hundreds of aeroplanes are being driven across that part of the country each day and it would have been practically impossible to find the one that made the track if it had not been for the two small cuts. My men have informed me that the aeroplane of Kidwell and Dexter has a tire on it with two small cuts the same size and distance apart as the two marks left in the woods. I have just arrived and we expect to arrest the two aviators within the next few minutes. I thought I would notify you first, as I realize it will stop your exhibition flight for the Fair."

"If these two men are murderers and robbers, as you state, I want you to arrest them at once—exhibition flight or no exhibition flight. You will have to hurry or wait until—listen—" The President broke off and turned his head to one side to hear better.

A roar of a multitude cheering came to the two listening men— the huge crowd at the Grand Stand were splitting the air with deafening cheers for something. "They are up and off." The President continued after listening awhile. "You will have to wait until they come down. They are up to beat the world's highest altitude record. Here is one of our advertisements for today. Read it." Pemberton took the paper that was handed him and read the following:

"WILL TRY TO BEAT THE WORLD'S
HIGHEST ALTITUDE RECORD"
State Fair—August 25, 19—

Kidwell and Dexter—the world's most daredevil aviators will try to beat the world's highest altitude
record for an aeroplane. They will use the latest type
of aeroplane with new wing devices for climbing and
flying in the rarefied air of miles above the earth.
They will carry an extra supply of oxygen. They will
have the latest thing in wireless telephone instruments and will be in constant communication with
the receiving station established in front of the
Grand Stand. To the receiving instrument will be
attached a sound magnifier and those within a radius
of several hundred feet can listen to the account from
the aviators' own lips as they circle up—up—up.

Don't Forget the Place and Date

Pemberton handed the paper back and inquired, "How long will
it take them to make the flight?"

"About two or three hours is all they figured they would need,"
he answered.

Pemberton decided to go to the receiving station to listen, and
the President went with him.

The two men made their way across the crowded Fair Grounds
until they came in front of the large Grand Stand. Here a crowd of
several thousand people were jammed around a platform on which
were a few men, and a table of instruments, the largest part of
which were four huge phonograph-like horns that faced in four
directions. They made their way through the crowd and had just
climbed to the platform, when a voice issued from the horns. The
words were:

"Have just reached three thousand feet."

Looking upwards, Pemberton could see a speck circling above
and rapidly growing smaller. It was the aeroplane winging its way
ever higher and higher. He leaned over to the President, "How is it
we can hear their voices and can not hear the roar of the motor?
On the ground it was impossible to hear a voice because of the deafening roar of an aeroplane motor."

The President leaned over and tapped one of the men on the shoulder, who was tinkering with the instrument, and said, "Billy, tell Mr. Pemberton here about the wireless telephone—tell him why one can hear a voice from above and yet not hear the roar of the motors."

Billy dropped into a chair next to Pemberton and keeping one eye on the instrument, explained:

"Kidwell and Dexter are using the same kind of wireless telephone instruments that our aviators in France had begun to use when the war ended, to communicate with each other and with headquarters. You know sound is vibration of the air and travels in waves and in a straight line unless turned aside by something. The aviator's instrument is like a helmet and covers most o his head. The receivers are flat and lie over his ears. The outside sound is deadened by the padding in the helmet and it was found that it would be necessary for the padding to cover most of the lower jaw to kill the outside sound. The mouth-piece, the part they talk into, is fastened directly in front of the mouth. It is padded to stop the outside sound. Only a tube-like opening directly even with the person's mouth is left unpadded. There are three or four small holes in the tube and when the person talks, his voice is thrown straight through the small openings and makes the instrument work while other sounds pass by as the waves do not get a straight entrance to the diaphragm."

"Both the receivers and the mouth-piece have wires running to a plug in the side of the aeroplane which connects with the batteries and instrument that send the wireless waves in all directions and reach us; they also catch any that we should send and transfer it to speech when it reaches the ears. Instead of the usual receiving instrument, we have hooked on a sound magnifier here, so that everybody can hear directly. Now the very—"

"One mile up and everything is running fine."

The voice of one of the men from the speck above spoke from the horns. A cheer greeted the announcement.

"Who is doing the talking?" Pemberton asked.

"Kidwell will do all the talking because it is he who is equipped with the long distance sending and receiving apparatus. Dexter can talk with Kidwell and Kidwell can talk with Dexter by changing the plug at the side of the machine, so he is directly connected with Dexter. Dexter is the pilot in the rear seat and will drive unless something happens. If something should happen, Kidwell can drive as they have double controls."

"Hey, below! We are having fun up here chasing toy balloons. Those that have been let loose on the Fair Grounds have reached this far up. There are twenty or thirty in sight. We have run down three or four. One was thrown back by the propeller's draft and hit Old Dex on the head and busted. He would have jumped out of his seat if he were not tied down with a safety belt. Thought part of the machinery had hit him, I guess. We are climbing in circles and staying over the Fair Grounds as nearly as we can. The hand on our instrument is gradually crawling near two miles and we can begin to tell it is getting very cold. We feel sorry for you poor land mortals below sweating in that 100 degrees in the shade. But say, 'you don't have to stay in the shade'—Ha, Ha!"

The sound of Kidwell's laughter from two miles above roared through the horns. It ceased and no other sound came from above for several minutes.

"Got another balloon; caught it alive this time; going to tie my pipe to it and drop it overboard. The pipe will pull it down. Tell the kids down there I will give five dollars to the one who gets it and I will wring their necks if any of them busts my pipe. Here she goes—"

Cheers and laughter greeted this last announcement and many small boys jammed in the crowd began to crowd and squirm frantically to get out into the center field where they could watch for Kidwell's pipe pulling a toy balloon down.

"You below! We are going to have trouble in just a minute. Saw several balloons above us snatched and rushed east at a speed that makes us look like a snail. It's one of those terrific wind currents that different persons have discovered two or three miles up. We will be O. K. when we get in it, but going from slow to fast air is going to give us some rough riding. We are starting; I can feel our old machine beginning to pitch. Here we go!—God, we are pitching and spinning like a leaf. We are on our tail—now we are upside down. Over we go sideways—now we are level—whew, we just made a complete flip-flop. It's a wonder we hold together—we are rocking and pitching like a row boat on a stormy ocean.

"We are getting up in the main current and don't pitch so much. It is all I can do to hold my dinner down. I'm sea-sick—we are heading west, but I think we are losing several miles a minute as this terrific air current drifts us east."

A deadly hush fell on the crowd below as they pictured the aeroplane being tossed and pitched about in one of the mighty air currents that are found miles above the earth. They could see the two men fighting to keep their machine right side up, as they fought through the eddies and whirls at the edge of the current and into the steady but fast moving air of the center. When Kidwell announced that they had made it, a mighty cheer went up. Several minutes passed and no sound came from the men miles above—then—

"Hurrah for the Liberty Motor—we just had another fight to get out of the big current and are now in still air above it. We were pitched and flung about, upside down and every which way, just as when we entered it. Our motor did not miss a lick. Old Dex got sick. I saw him gulping and raise his helmet and lean over, but nothing happened. Now we are riding smoothly. We are heading straight west instead of circling so as to gain the distance we were carried backwards in the big air current. It is getting cold. We are using oxygen from our tanks as the air is mighty thin here—Dex has just called my attention to our instrument—what do you reckon she reads?—whoop—she has touched it. She's reached thirty thousand feet. We'll make it. We'll break that old world's altitude record."

A roar that shook the Grand Stand went up from the listening crowd below. For ten minutes they cheered and flung things in the air in their excitement. A few more minutes and the world's highest altitude record would belong to America once more. The cheering died down and then broke out afresh.

"What is the world's record?" Pemberton leaned over and shouted above the din into the president's ear.

"A little less than thirty-five thousand feet," the President answered in one of the partly quiet spells of the crowd.

"Thirty-one thousand" came from the horns,—only those right
against them could hear, but they began to relay the news. "Thirty-
one thousand." Another deafening cheer rang out. The crowd became silent as the President raised his hand for silence and pointed
to the horns.

"Thirty-two thousand and Old Dex grinning like a frog."

This time only a laugh from the crowd greeted the announcement. They would hold their cheers for the last as they wanted to
hear all now.

"It's just about there—now its closer—just a little more—near—
nearer—Gee, it moves slowly—just ready to touch—now it touches—
whoopee—it's over—we have reached the world's altitude record—
now we have passed it."

The Grand Stand roared and shook as the crowd below let loose.
Hats flew high in the air, men thumped each other like boys. Once
more the world's altitude record belonged to America—to the
United States—brought to it by the two dauntless aviators, far out
of sight in the vast space above. Those in the Grand Stand began
to stamp and shout in unison and stopped only when the stand
threatened to break under the strains of the thousands of thump-
ing feet. At the rear of the mass of people, a boy with a toy balloon
struggled to get through to the platform.

"Hey, kid, look out or you'll get hurt crowding in like that," a
man addressed him.

"I caught the pipe," the boy cried as he held aloft a pipe tied to
the balloon string.

"Kidwell's pipe—Kidwell's pipe"—the man shouted as he gathered the boy up and held him above the crowd's head. From hand
to hand they passed the boy to the platform, where the President
of the Fair met him and led him to the front of the platform where
the boy held up the toy balloon with the pipe tied to it. The boy
was still panting, for he had caught the pipe nearly a quarter of a
mile away and had run all the way back to the crowd, while other
boys chased him. The President took a five dollar bill from his

pocket and gave it to the boy and took possession of the pipe. The boy struck through the crowd, headed for the refreshment stands, while the President returned to his seat.

"Forty thousand feet up and cold as fifty North Poles."

The people became quiet with awe. Not satisfied with breaking the world's altitude record, these two daredevils were steadily climbing higher and higher. Forty thousand feet—miles high—how far would they go?

"We have just noticed a queer color of the air just a short way to our west, although we can hardly call it color. It might be just our imagination; anyway Dex has headed the machine in that direction—yes we notice the difference more as we get closer—turn her Dex—turn her—My God it's a whirlwind—loop her back, Dex—turn—"

The last, regarding turning the machine, came from the horns in a shout and must have been meant for Dexter. It broke off suddenly as Kidwell must have changed the plug from below to connect with Dexter.

Thousands of eyes unconsciously looked upward, although all knew that it was impossible to see to the great height the aeroplane had attained. But all realized that something serious was happening miles above. What had happened? Would the aeroplane come flying down from above and land a shattered wreck?

Minutes passed and no voice was heard through the horn. The suspense became unbearable. Several more minutes passed and at last came—

"Hello, below,—we thought we were gone that time. We ran into a whirling draft of air of cyclone speed. Our machine was caught in it and we were pitched over and over like a feather, whirling, tossing, and tumbling. We were flung up—up—and up. We don't know how far up we are now, because we were carried upward for many minutes at many miles a minute. Our instrument only registers sixty thousand feet and the hand reached that mark long before we were pitched out of the whirling mass and into still air. The current seems to come up and then turn east and we were flung to the top side. We must be fifteen or twenty miles high—way above any height we dreamed a person could fly. Our motor does not run as smoothly as it did below, but it is doing fairly well. We still have to use our own supply of oxygen. The movements of the machine are rather slow and sluggish. It might be that we are flying in air hurled up in that mighty up-rushing funnel of air from below. We cannot understand it. We are circling about, getting our nerve back to make a dive for the earth. If we get through the high eastward current of air and miss the upward whirlwind, we will be O. K. If we hit the upward whirlwind, we will be flung back like a leaf. We can feel the intense cold through all our furs. It must be fifty degrees below zero. Nothing but space, space, space, as far as you can see and in every direction. You feel like loosening your belt, stepping on the edge of the machine and stepping off into—nothing—you feel as though there were no world—no God—No—"

The voice broke off and then continued with a note of excitement in it.

"We have made a discovery; there are clouds up here—Dex just pointed several out to me and we are headed for them. They seem very dense as we get nearer."

For several minutes the voice stopped and those below talked in suppressed excitement. They were past the cheering stage now. What had happened miles above the earth had made them curious and started them thinking. Then the voice came, quivering with a tone of excitement.

"People, below! I am going to make a statement to you that will seem unbelievable, a statement that will upset all past theories of the upper air. If I were not sure of bringing down proofs of my statements, I would not make it and I don't even ask you to believe it, until we come back.

"People, below—there is vegetable and animal life here. We are now flying above a floating island of vegetable substance while around us and above are hundreds of other floating islands of the same substance. I have managed to catch a small handful of the substance as it floated in the air between the larger bodies of the same thing.

"It is nearly transparent, but has a pale greenish color. It is spongy and tough, being made up of a rubber-like material full of thousands of small gas pockets. It must be this gas that keeps it afloat at this great height. It grows on long rope-like branches like sea-kelp or some kind of moss. What we took for clouds were great masses of this plant matted together and floating about. I believe we could walk on these islands, but it would be impossible to land our aeroplane for it would sink too deep to get it out again.

"We have seen a small bat-like animal fly from one island to another. Another of the same kind of creatures is flying alongside us and keeps turning its head to watch us as though it wonders what we are. I believe it is as much surprised to see us as we are to see it. Dex has just notified me that he will try to run it down and wants me to catch or kill it. We must bring down proofs or we would never dare tell of such things as are up here. Here we go—we are after the bat-like animal. Zip!—the blamed little thing is gone; it was just fooling along with us and when we whirled to reach it, it shot away like a bullet. They are too speedy for us to run down. I was close enough to see that it was nearly the size and shape of a bat, except that it had a head like a bird with large owl-like eyes, and had a beak instead of a mouth with teeth. It was of the same pale sickly green like the plants we have found.

"Dex has spied something else ahead and is pointing for me to see but I fail to make it out. Now I see it. It is something long twisting through the air. It is turning and coming this way. It is another animal, or a reptile for it is more like a snake. No, not like a snake either, for it is about ten feet long and flat as can be. Its head is also formed with a beak. It looks like a huge ribbon floating through the air. It has turned and is flying above and to one side of us, looking down at us while it winds its way along. If we can get within striking distance, I will take a swipe at it with a wrench. I would like to bring it down—Look out, Dex—now—hold her steady."

The last came in a shouted command and must have been meant for Dexter, then—

"That queer snake-like thing turned and in a flash had straightened out in a line and shot down on us like a bullet. It hit the top of our right wing and went through as though the wing were a spider web. Then it struck one of our stay wires and was split long ways for a foot or more. It clung to the wire, thrashing about, a

blood of that pale greenish color oozing out. When I was ready to
go out on the wing and try to get it, it fell on the lower plane and
was blown off. It fell below to the plant island over which we are
flying now. If it had struck either of us, it would have been death.
A short distance more and we will make the dive for earth as our
oxygen supply is getting low. I have been catching stray pieces of
the plants of which the islands are made and have a bunch packed
in the bottom of my cockpit. There is also a large bunch caught in
the wires of our left wing and several small bunches caught in other
places. These might hold fast until we get down. I have been wondering if the change of pressure on the plant and animals—if we
can catch any animals to bring down—will cause them to contract.
The effect on them should be just the opposite of the effect on the
fish that have been brought up from two miles or more under the
sea; when they came up, the pressure was so much less that some
swelled up and exploded. I believe these animals would be pressed
together more if brought to the denser air of the earth's surface.
This plant up here might be made good use of below at some future time and if—of all the sights—what monsters! What fierce
fighting monsters. Look at the great gashes they are tearing in each
other. They can't last.

"Oh, I forgot, you below—we just turned a half circle around
the end of a medium-sized floating island and have come upon one
of the most awful battles between two of the biggest and fiercest of
monsters. One is like a large flying alligator, except that it has a
huge beak and large bat-like wings. The other is shaped like an
octopus, but has flat arms and two large balloon-like appendages
on its back. It has a hellish beak. They are closed in one biting,
clawing and choking mass. We are circling them and watching. The
flying alligator just laid open one of the devil-fish of the air's balloons. It shrank as though it were full of gas. Now they are whirling on the air so fast you can hardly tell what is happening. The
alligator has lost the use of one of its wings. The octopus has
wrapped several of its arms around it. They are starting to sink.
They're dropping, two of the arms, bitten off. Everything up
here is that sickly green, both monsters are that color and they are

bleeding the green blood—if it is blood. They are now covered with gashes all over their bodies. They can't last much longer. There goes the other balloon. It shrinks—now they are falling.

"They don't stop fighting. We are following them down and still circling around them. The two fighting air demons have fallen on the big island below us. They are hardly able to move. The alligator devil is now on top and rending the octopus to shreds. Its days are over. The flying alligator—for I don't know what else to call it—is victor, but it will never be able to fly again. One wing is completely torn in shreds and the other is not much better. Its body is full of big wounds. The din of their screams and clashing of their beaks must have been awful. Where they came from or what they were fighting about, we do not know. It was one of the most terrific and most awe-inspiring sights, man ever witnessed.

"The flying alligator has risen on its hind legs and is trying to lunge itself into the air, but it can only flutter like a broken-winged bird. It is giving out its cry, as we can see by the motion of its beak.

"Dex shut off the motor for an instant and drifted over its head. It uttered a piercing scream like a thousand wild cat whistles, and lunged up for us. I hate to think what would have happened if it had been able to fly. I believe it would have rent us in pieces in a second. We are leaving here right now, for Dex has pointed out another flying alligator about a mile away, which is coming this way. It must be answering the wounded one's cries. It is traveling fast and coming from the north. We can see its giant, bat-like wings beating the air and it rises and falls at each stroke. We are speeding westward and as soon as we reach the edge of this extra large floating island over which we are flying, we will dive for the earth. We cannot see the edge, but it cannot be over a mile or so. We have left the wounded flying alligator about a half mile back, and the other monster has already reached it and has circled above it once.

"God, it has turned and is headed after us, its huge wings beating faster than before. We must reach the edge and dive, for it travels twice as fast as our sluggish-acting machine. I am not scared, for I can see the edge about two miles ahead and we will reach it before the demon can overtake us. Another has dropped from above where the wounded alligator is and it, also, is now headed after us. Miles above the earth and being chased by two hideous monsters. Have you ever noticed birds flying? When they beat their wings downwards, they not only go forward, but partly upward as well, and when they raise their wings for another stroke, they sink a little instead of keeping a straight course ahead. That is the way these demons fly. Dex is giving our machine all it will take.

"The two demons are going fast, but we will reach the edge before they can catch us. God help us, another monster and straight ahead. We cannot go that way and must turn south or north. No, not north for I see two coming from that direction. We are nearly surrounded and our only hope is south. I see the edge south, but it is a mile farther away than west. But we will make it. I don't see any of the demons coming from that direction. Our machine is roaring at full speed, but we are not making over fifty or sixty miles in this rarefied sir. The demons of this upper air are flying twice as fast and now there are nearly a dozen close on our trail and swiftly gaining. . . . We are near the edge and our danger is over. A minute more and we would have been lost, for now there are two monsters in front of us. We are surrounded, but we will reach the edge and will head down like a bullet before they can get near enough to head us off. Their screams are bringing other monsters from all directions.

"Just passed one of those hideous flying devil-fish and see another ahead and above us. We are just at the edge and are tipping down for our long dive. Will be with you in a few—Dex, Dex, look out for the devilfish. For God's sake, look, Dex— Oh, God, too late— We are done. Our propeller is shattered, we are falling. Look out below— No, we have fallen on the edge of the island. We are tearing through. No we have stopped. God, we are in a fix. The devilfish flung itself at us and into our propeller and wrecked it and blocked the controls and we fell straight down. . . . We are within a few hundred feet of the edge, the weight of the machine has sunk us until we rest in a sloping crater about fifty feet deep. The monsters are arriving and flying in circles above us. Our motor is quiet and when we raise our receivers, the screams and snapping of their giant beaks almost deafen us. Our only hope now is to reach the edge and trust ourselves to our safety parachutes."

For several minutes the horns were quiet and the people jammed around them listening for further word from the two men in the void above. They whispered together in low undertones and every minute or so their eyes traveled upward in an attempt to pierce the blind of the miles distance. But in vain. At last—it seemed hours, though it was only a few minutes—the voice came again.

"We took our parachutes from their holders on the side of the machine and started up to the top of the sink-hole we are in. The monsters began to come closer as we neared the top and one made a dive for us, so we retreated to the machine. They seem to be afraid to come into this pit we are in. We found a place on one side of the pit where the vegetable has been pulled until it has pulled apart and we can see below. We are going to this hole now and enlarge it sufficiently to enable us to drop through—all is clear below—so goodbye, but watch for us to come sailing down soon. We are carrying oxygen tanks with us to breathe."

The voice ceased and the crowd began to watch above for any specks that might turn out to be the two men and their parachutes. Many minutes passed, then the voice came, a voice filled with a tone of despair and terror.

"They got poor Dexter. He went first, after we had enlarged the hole, and before he had dropped five hundred feet a dozen of the monsters were after him. Helpless in the parachute, they dived on him and dragged him up to the top of the island and tore him to shreds. Now they are screaming and snapping their beaks above this pit and are swooping nearer and nearer. Their taste of blood seems to have made them wilder. I will fight them from the cockpit and if I can hold out until night, I might crop through the hole and escape in the darkness. I have broken a spar loose for a club. They are coming closer. I struck at that one. It just missed my head. They are gathering in a bunch. They are diving for me in one mass. I'm lost—Goodbye."

A shriek of a man in mortal agony and terror rang out in the air, followed by a shriek from the crowd. Then all was still. The people knew all was over in the far upper air. Men stood gazing upward, ghastly white, while women buried their faces in their hands and wept.

A dull thud was heard at the far side of the infield and people began to gather there on a run. A hole showed where something had fallen with enough force to bury itself. Hurriedly digging, they unearthed an oxygen tank, one of the tanks that Kidwell and Dexter had taken up with them. A cry from some people as they pointed aloft drew thousands of eyes in that direction. Fluttering and falling, something was coming down. Several hands grabbed it as soon as it came within reach. One uttered a cry and let go. He held up his hands in horror. They were wet with fresh blood.

A broken and torn part of an aeroplane wing, spattered with red blood, fell. Kidwell and the aeroplane must have been torn to pieces by the demons of the far upper air, and the tank and pieces of the plane scattered over the edge of the floating vegetable island, must have fallen to earth.

Another shout and once more all looked aloft. The air was full in all directions with thousands of fluttering pieces that looked like paper. When they fell among the crowd a shout of surprise went up.

"Money—Money—One dollar bills."

Over the ground for miles around the Fair Grounds there fell a shower of one dollar bills. This was the last thing ever heard or seen of the two men and the aeroplane.

A few weeks later Pemberton and the President of the State Fair were talking in the President's office. The President spoke:

"I have had two different planes up since Kidwell and Dexter were lost. The men went armed with shotguns and prepared for trouble. They were unable to find any upward current of air and they cruised all around in search of it. I am informed, though, that such a current would not necessarily always be in the same place, else it might stop altogether, just like winds near the earth. I have given up hope of anybody reaching the scene of the awful tragedy above."

"If there ever was an awful tragedy above," Pemberton added. The President looked at him in blank surprise.

"What?"

"I say if there ever was an awful tragedy above—if Kidwell and Dexter ever did get over two or three miles high."

"What? Don't you think that Kidwell and Dexter were killed by the monsters many miles above the earth, as they described? Why do you think they weren't?"

Pemberton slowly answered:

"I don't know what to think. There is no reason for my doubting the truth of their death miles above the earth. I have gone over it all hundreds of times, yet I cannot make up my mind whether far above float the remains of two of the bravest men, or whether far away on the earth's surface are two of the slickest rascals that ever lived. Did what Dexter described really happen or did they fly above out of our sight and concoct the story? Did they cast down an oxygen tank, smear blood on a piece of plane that they might have taken with them for the purpose, and cast it down to fool us? A small cut on a finger might have furnished the blood, and they might have cast down part of the stolen money. Why did only one-dollar bills come down? Where are the half-million dollars of large bills? They *could* be floating far above with the wrecked plane. Where is the upward whirlwind? Still, it might have moved or died out. We might have listened to one of the most awful death struggles, or we might have been the victims of one of the cleverest jokes ever played on the public. And the men escaped with half a million dollars. Who knows?"

DANGER
Irvin Lester and Fletcher Pratt
1929

The wind rose in the night and by dawn the sky was streaming with
torn and ragged masses of cloud moving from south to north like
an army in flight. There was a shiver of cold in the air and the seas
ran so high that effective work was impossible, so we gathered in
Professor Hartford's cabin to help the old man brave out his discomfort by getting him to talk. The way in which he kept up his
spirit, if not his body, through all the miseries of seasickness on
that trip, was one of the finest exhibitions of courage I have seen
anywhere.

As the senior member of the Museum's staff he was, in a sense,
in charge of the expedition, though like the rest of us, he was inclined to let things run themselves while he pursued his specialty.
Perhaps it was fortunate for him that the protozoa can be studied
as well on a constantly moving steamer as on dry land; for the work
kept his mind off his troubles. At all events, every day that was
calm enough for him to be out of bed, found him poring over his
microscope in search of hitherto undescribed forms in this remote
corner of the Pacific.

On days such as this he lay in his bunk, and between uneasy
heavings of the *mal-de-mer* that plagued him, lectured our crowd
of assorted scientific experts on the importance of unicellular life.
Very interesting lectures they must have been to the other chaps;
even I was sometimes caught by the spell of the professor's keen
and philosophical observation, and as a mere artist I always felt
more or less a misfit among all those -ologies and -isms.

I remember this day in particular, partly because the evening brought us to our first view of Easter Island and partly because the conversation turned to those scientific generalizations; which are both easier to understand and more interesting to the non-scientific hearer. But even then, I probably would have recalled it only as one of a number of similar talks, had not after events given it a peculiar, almost a sinister significance.

Burgess, our entomologist, had been trying to draw the professor out by descanting on the rising tide of insect life. "Sooner or later," he declared, "we will have to fight for our lives with them. Science always plods along behind their attacks. They have taken the chestnut, the boll-weevil and corn-borer are taking two more of our economically important plants. Who knows but that nature is working in its slow way to send us after the dinosaurs?"

Slap, slap, went the waves against the cabin wall.

"Perhaps, perhaps," mused Professor Hertford, "though I incline to think that the insects will never drive man from the planet. Evolution allows a group only one opportunity—the insects had their chance to rule the world in the Carboniferous, and failed.

". . . No," he went on, "there are many lines of evolution untried, but none of them lead through existing forms. When a more capable type than man appears, it will be in a wholly new form of animal life—perhaps even a direct evolution from the protozoa. So far as we know, evolution along that line has never taken place to any great extent. The division between the one-celled and many-celled animals is sharper than that between an insect and an elephant. Think of a one-celled animal, practically immortal as they are and possessed of intelligence. No matter what work we do, no matter what records we leave, the greater portion of human knowledge perishes with the minds that give it birth. Think what it would mean if one person could go on gathering knowledge through the centuries."

"But," objected Burgess, "a paramecium hasn't any brain tissue. You can't have that without some nervous organization."

"But, my dear Burgess," said the professor, urbanely, "is brain tissue necessary to thought? You might as well say fins are necessary to swimming. Neither the polar bear nor the octopus have them, yet both can swim very well. Nature has a queer way of accomplishing similar results by all sorts of different means. Suppose thought is what Osborn hints it is—a matter of chemical reaction, and interaction—is there any need for brain tissue in which the thought must take place?"

"All true enough," said Burgess, "but you must admit that without proprioceptors there can be no sensation, and with a cortex—"

The conversation became so technical that I was perforce eliminated from it, and wandered down the iron stairway to watch the engines. For a time I sat there, vainly trying to put on paper the flicker of those bright moving parts—so beautifully ordered, so Roman in their efficient performance of their task, whatever else was happening. But it was no use; a job for a Nevinson, and I clambered back to the deck.

There I found the weather had moderated. The whole southwest was streaked with the orange presage of a fairer day and, right in the center of the illumination, grey and ominous, a huge cone rose steeply from the water.

"That's Puakatina," said Bronson the mate, pausing beside me. "There's an anchorage right beneath it, but we'll have to work round to the west of Cook's Bay to get shelter from the wind. I was here on a guano ship ten years ago. Damnedest place you ever saw—no water, no fish, no nothing."

Morning found us at anchor in the bay and already scattering to our several pursuits. For me, Easter Island was a fairyland. Never, among primitive work, have I seen such sculpture. It far surpassed the best Egyptian work, for every one of those cyclopean heads was a portrait, and almost a perfect one. I cannot better express my feeling for them than by saying that now, as I am writing this account with the memory sharp in my mind, of she strange and terrible events that took place later, I must still turn aside to pay tribute to those statues.

After all they are not so far from my story. Indeed, it was the statues that gave me what should have been a clue—a queer idea that all was not quite as it should be on this island—an idea that I would dismiss as an afterview, were it not that I find on the margin of one of my sketches, made at the time, a note to the effect that something very curious must have happened on the island. Those stones were carved by nothing less than a race of conquerors, with stern high faces, utterly different from the easy-going Polynesians of today. What became of them?

The same impression, of some weird catastrophe, was confirmed by other members of the expedition. There were almost no fish, very little life for the botanists to chew on, and Hertford announced at one of our cabin conferences that the waters, as Agassiz had reported, were quite devoid of plankton. He pooh-poohed the idea of the subsidence of a large land put forth by De Salza, our geologist. "Subsidence," he said, "would leave the plankton and fish untouched. It is more as though some destructive organism had swept every trace of life from the locality. All the birds and the few fish are obviously recent immigrants, like the people."

Despite my entreaties for more time to make sketches, the scientists had done about all they could with this barren land in a week or so, and we hauled up anchor for Sala-y-Gomez, three hundred miles further east, taking a couple of the islanders with us. In spite of its atmosphere of ruin and gloom I was sorry to leave Easter Island, but there was the possibility that Sala-y-Gomez might contain some traces of the Easter script or carvings, and I felt it necessary to refuse Hertford's offer to leave me and stop on the way back.

Upon Sala-y-Gomez too, we came just at evening, marking it by the white line of foam along its low-lying shores as we felt our way slowly among the reefs, and here occurred another of those trivial incidents which are straws pointing in the direction of hidden things.

I was standing by the rail with Howard, the ichthyological man, idly watching the wires of the dredge where they interrupted the slow curls of water turned back by our bow when there was a heavy muffled clang, and we saw the lines of the dredge tighten to tensity. Howard signaled for it to be drawn in, and together we watched the big scoop, eager to see what it had encountered. To our surprise it held only a little seaweed.

"Now that's odd," said Howard, searching the seaweed, with a small hand glass. "I could have sworn that dredge caught something heavy."

"It did," I answered, pointing. There was a long scratch of bright metal along one side.

"Corals possibly," he remarked. "Hey, Bronson, any reefs charted here?"

The mate strolled up. "Not on the charts," he said, "but you never can tell. These Chilean charts aren't very good, you know."

"M—m—m," murmured Howard, continuing his examination. "There ought to be fragments of coralline formation here, but there aren't. Wonder what is could have been? Almost as though we'd caught something and it got away."

The thought of Hertford's comment about a destructive organism slipped into my mind, to be dismissed as not worth mentioning. Rock, shark, almost anything would have made that mark on the dredge.

There were no specimens ready to be sketched in the morning, and I went ashore with the first boat to wander about the island with my drawing materials. It must have been nearly noon when I rounded a jutting outcrop of rock to see before me a little sandy cove, placid and unresponsive in the heat, without a sign of life. Far ahead, a dark blob of rock was the only mark on the perfect line of the beach. It was so suavé a scene that I sat down to make a sketch. After I had penciled it in and was mixing the brown color for the cliffs, I noted that the rock seemed to have moved, but I attributed it to imagination and went on with my coloring. It must have been quite ten minutes when I looked up again. This time there could be no doubt—neither the outline nor the position of the rock were at all as I had recorded them.

In some excitement, I started to climb down the cliff toward this singular rock that changed place and form, but the distance was considerable, and while I was still a quarter of a mile away, it moved again, visibly this time, sliding down to the water's edge, where it disappeared beneath the gentle surge. The most peculiar thing about it was that there seemed to be no sensible method of progress; it flowed, like a huge, irregular drop of liquid.

I hurried back to the camp with my sketch and my tale, but found the rest in no condition to listen. Old Makoi Toa, one of the Easter Islanders we had brought along with us, had been killed, apparently by a snake. "He was fishing down the beach ahead of the rest," said Howard, "just out of sight beyond that rock. We all heard him scream, and hurried to the spot. When we got there he was already dead, with a round hole in his chest, and shortly after he turned that hideous blue black that people turn to who die of snake-bite. It might have been one of those sea-snakes but for the size of the wound."

"I'm sure I saw something sliding away into the water," added Greaves, the botanist, "but it didn't look in the least like a snake."

The shadow of the old man's death lay on our little cabin conference that night, inhibiting speech, though the means of it remained a mystery. It was not until I told my tale that there was any conversation at all. As I finished there was a little moment of silence, during which each one made the obvious parallel between the occurrence and the death of Makoi Toa, and then Professor Hertford asked to see my sketch. He looked at it closely for a moment.

"Unless I am mistaken, gentlemen," he said, "we are facing an unknown organism of serious potentialities. May I ask that you do not go ashore to-morrow unless you are well armed and in pairs?"

"What is it, professor?" asked de Salza.

"I would prefer not to hazard a guess just yet. I may be in error." And that was the last word on the subject that we could draw from him, although de Salza laughed at the idea of anything sinister in connection with this little spot of land.

The next day was bright and clear, and after attending the burial service for Makoi Toa, I sought Greaves and together we made for the spot where I had seen the moving rock. I admit we were culpable in not going armed as the professor advised, but who would then have thought . . . ?

We reached the place about the same time I had been there the previous day, climbed down the cliffs with each other's help, and walked across the white sand of the cove, to where I had seen the moving rock. It was not more than ten yards from the edge of a place where the receding tide of years had left a number of little arched caves. Just where I had sketched the rock was a ridge of sand pulled aside by the weight of whatever had been there, and in the center of it, a round, bard ball, perhaps three or four inches in diameter. Greaves picked it up, turning it over curiously.

"Why, it's feathers and bones," he said, extending if to me, "just as though it had been regurgitated by a pelican or an eagle after a meal."

I reached my hand for it, and just then, by the grace of Providence, caught a flicker of motion out of the tail of my eye. I turned to meet it; my foot gave on the soft sand, and I fell prone. It was the fall that saved me for something sharp whistled not an inch past my shoulder as I went down. The next instant I heard Greaves shout, and felt him tug my arm, and in the same moment something cold and clammy and hard grated and gripped against my foot. A horrible fear, the fear of imminent death, turned me to ice; I seemed incapable of movement, but somehow got to one knee, and between my own efforts and Greaves' pull, the grip on my foot relaxed. I half stumbled, half-rolled down the sand, and as I did so, there was another whistling flash and something struck the pocket of my coat, going right through the cloth and the sketch pad beneath it, to fall short of my skin by the narrowest of margins. Greaves was pulling me to my feet, and in a moment we were running.

In the interests of science I regret that we stood not on the order of our going. Neither of us spoke till we turned and paused at the top of the cliff, after a breathless climb. The cove was as empty as it had been before.

"My God—What was it?" I gasped.

"I don't *know*, I don't *know*." Greaves was half sobbing with excitement. "Something big and sort of—all soft—threw those things at us—half a dozen of the them—My God."

We were both so much shaken that the journey back to the camp seemed interminable, and it was some time after our arrival before a consecutive story could be gotten out of Greaves. When he did tell his tale, it appeared that he had noticed the thing almost as soon as I—a great, dead brown object of uncertain form which had slid up softly from the water and shot out the darts I had seen without warning or sound, "as a cuttlefish does when you touch it," said Greaves, with a shudder. "The horrible part about it was that the thing had no eyes but seemed to see perfectly and know just where to move to head us off. I thought I'd never get you pulled loose. . . . All the time I was dodging those darts I kept thinking about Makoi Toa. . . ."

"I think you will agree," said Professor Hertford, when he had finished his rather incoherent account, "that my anticipations have been realized. Everything points to the presence in these waters of an efficient and destructive organism, capable not only of dominating the whole animal environment, but possibly even of depopulating Easter Island. From your description which is very rough and inaccurate, I should not be surprised to find it a giant new species of infusorian of jellyfish. Both types have those stinging tentacles. I am in favor of remaining until we obtain more data about this animal, but as some—er—danger may attend such a course, I should prefer to leave it to the majority."

What could we do in the face of such an appeal? Personally, I had felt the grip on my foot and had no desire to feel it again. I could understand the flame of scientific interest driving the others, but it was rather with foreboding than enthusiasm that I listened to the eager plans they made for entrapping one of the animals which had attacked us.

I doubt whether anybody except de Salza (who was a human fish, intolerant of anything but the record of the rocks) was absent from the group which gathered behind the top of the cliffs the next morning to watch the fluttering antics of a chicken pegged out on the sand where we had met our adventure. Howard and Grimm (the conchologist) were armed with the only two rifles the expedition afforded, it having been agreed that it was better to examine a dead specimen before trying to take a live one.

The sun grew unconscionably hot as it swung across the sky. We conversed in low tones and were wondering whether we had come on a wild goose chase when I saw Howard beside me, stiffen to attention. I looked around—there was a break in the ripple, and through it slowly emerged the shape of the monster, dull brown in hue. I felt a quiver of excitement; the chicken was straining to the limit of its rope. There was a crack! that made all of us jump, as someone fired. "No, not yet," cried the professor, but the dark form took no notice, only moved on, formless and flowing, with half a score of short tentacles waving before it. Then it appeared to notice the chicken, paused, waved a tentacle or two at it, and there was a flicking motion as one of the darts shot out. The chicken went limp and the monster flowed gently over it. When it had passed, chicken, rope, and even the stake, were gone.

Both men were now firing, but they might as well have been throwing peas. The fantastic mound of jelly rolled back into the water in the same leisurely fashion it had come out, and disappeared.

Everybody began to talk at once, "The thing must be bullet proof!" "Invertebrate, but what an invertebrate!" "So that's what cleaned up Easter Island!" "Did you notice the ossicles?" "It's a hydroid!" "More like a medusid." "What do you think, Dr. Hertford?"

On one thing the conference that followed was agreed: that the animal, whatever it was, must be captured and examined. Various wild suggestions about dynamite and chemicals came up to be laughed down, and it was Dr. Hertford, as usual, who supplied the determining factor.

"It seems to me," said he, "that it would be worth while to postpone our trip to the continent and attempt to take one of these animals in one of the mammal cages. I believe the one you shot at was at least seriously injured; it seems incredible that it could be altogether bullet proof. We may, therefore, have a wall before another appears. What do you say?"

De Salza's was the only dissenting voice. I kept silence. I wish I had not, for though my protest might have done little good, it would at least have taken a load from my conscience that can never be quite clear now. However, I made no protest. The cage was rigged up on the shore with another chicken inside and a trick arrangement to slam the door shut on the invader and we sat down at the cove to wait.

It was the afternoon of the third day from the installation of the cage, and I was in my tent at the camp, trying to capture the color pattern of a small and very wiggly fish when the excited voice of Howard hailed us to announce that the cage held a prisoner. At once everything else was forgotten and we all hurried off, pell-mell, Dr. Hertford for all his years, well in the lead.

Sure enough the little mammal cage was filled to overflowing with the brown jelly-like mass of the monster, a tentacle or two waving in a friendly manner from the edges of the mass where it bulged between the bars. I admit it gave me a gone feeling in the pit of the stomach to watch it; it was like nothing I had ever seen or heard of, but among the scientists it produced only the liveliest interest.

Warned by previous experience, they approached it with some caution, Howard carrying a piece of sheet iron from the ship before the professor like a shield-bearer in the days of the Iliad, while Greaves and Grimm came behind at a respectable distance, bearing rifles at the ready.

As they drew near, I heard the professor cry out in excitement, "Why, it's a protozoan! Look, the nucleus, and those cilia! And the triocysts! A single celled animal, by all that's holy! Related to *Loxodes* unless I am mistaken." Simultaneously, Greaves and Grimm, attracted by his words, drew a step nearer, and even Howard lowered the sheet iron to peer at the animal. And in that moment it happened.

With an indescribable swaying motion, the jelly-like mass in the cage seemed to surge through the narrow opening in the cage, and as it surged, the air about it was filled with the flash of those deadly darts. I heard Howard cry out, I saw Grimm leap; a gun was discharged, and the sheet iron clanged on the sand. Then there was silence and the brown mass in the cage oozed slowly across the sand to the four dead men, who writhed for a moment and lay still.

I think I must have gone a little mad in the next moments. I can never recall quite accurately what happened. I remember only a paralyzing mist of horror, and the walls of my cabin. They tell me that the cove was found utterly empty save for the cage with its door shut tight . . . I do not know . . . I do not know. A round ball, like the ball of feathers and bones found by Greaves was picked up later on the beach. It held shattered human bones, a fragment of blue cloth and a brass key, nothing more. I did not see it.

Even today, the memory of the horror of that moment gives me sleepless nights and days of shuddering. All too clearly I recall the words of that brave and gentle man who went to his death on the beach of Sala-y-Gomez, "When a type to replace man appears, it will be a direct evolution from the protozoa. . . ." All too clearly, I remember his last words, and the desolation wrought by these animals on Easter Island and through that great stretch of the Eastern Pacific known as the Agassiz triangle, and I wonder how long it will be before they invade the continents.

It will be long, of that I am certain. The length of the time makes me wish to forget it and leave the future to care for itself. But I feel it a duty to the memory of Dr. Hertford to lay aside my own feeling. and place this story before the public, especially since de Salza, the only surviving member of that disastrous expedition, has cast doubt upon his conclusions and has disparaged his memory. If, in the face of a de Salza's reputation, I have succeeded in convincing even a few that humanity is on the verge of a battle to the death with a perhaps superior form of life, I am content; I have accomplished my purpose.

FROM AN AMBER BLOCK
Tom Curry
1930

"These should prove especially valuable and interesting without a doubt, Marable," said the tall, slightly stooped man. He waved a long hand toward the masses of yellow brown which filled the floor of the spacious workrooms, towering almost to the skylights, high above their heads.

"Is that coal in the biggest one with the dark center?" asked an attractive young woman who stood beside the elder of the men.

"I am inclined to believe it will prove to be some sort of black liquid," said Marable, a big man of thirty-five.

There were other people about the immense rooms, the laboratories of the famous Museum of Natural History. Light streamed in from the skylights and windows; fossils of all kinds, some immense in size, were distributed about. Skilled specialists were chipping away at matrices other artists were reconstructing, doing a thousand things necessary to the work.

A hum of low talking, accompanied by the irregular tapping of chisels on stone, came to their ears, though they took no heed of this, since they worked here day after day, and it was but the usual sound of the paleontologists' laboratory.

Marable threw back his blond head. He glanced again toward the dark-haired, blue-eyed young woman, but when he caught her eye, he looked away and spoke to her father, Professor Young.

"I think that big one will turn out to be the largest single piece of amber ever mined," he said. "There were many difficulties in getting it out, for the workmen seemed afraid of it, did not want to handle it for some silly reason or other."

217

Professor Young, curator, was an expert in his line, but young Marable had charge of these particular fossil blocks, the amber being pure because it was mixed with lignite. The particular block which held the interest of the three was a huge yellow brown mass of irregular shape. Vaguely, through the outer shell of impure amber, could be seen the heart of ink. The chunk weighed many tons, and its crate had just been removed by some workmen and was being taken away, piece by piece.

The three gazed at the immense mass, which filled the greater part of one end of the laboratory and towered almost to the skylights. It was a small mountain, compared to the size of the room, and in this case the mountain had come to man.

"Miss Betty, I think we had better begin by drawing a rough sketch of the block," said Marable.

Betty Young, daughter of the curator, nodded. She was working as assistant and secretary to Marable.

"Well—what do you think of them?"

The voice behind them caused them to turn, and they looked into the face of Andrew Leffler, the millionaire paleontologist, whose wealth and interest in the museum had made it possible for the institution to acquire the amber.

Leffler, a keen, quick moving little man, whose chin was decorated with a white Van Dyke beard, was very proud of the new acquisition.

"Everybody is talking about the big one," he continued, putting his hand on Marable's shoulder. "Orling is coming to see, and many others. As I told you, the workmen who handled it feared the big one. There were rumors about some unknown devil which lay hidden in the inklike substance, caught there like the proverbial fly in the amber. Well, let us hope there is something good in there, something that will make worth while all our effort."

Leffler wandered away, to speak to others who inspected the amber blocks.

"Superstition is curious, isn't it?" said Marable. "How can anyone think that a fossil creature, penned in such a cell for thousands and thousands of years, could do any harm?"

Professor Young shrugged. "It is just as you say. Superstition is not reasonable. These amber blocks were mined in the Manchurian lignite deposits by Chinese coolies under Japanese masters. They believe anything, the coolies. I remember working once with a crew of them that thought—"

The professor stopped suddenly, for his daughter had uttered a little cry of alarm. He felt her hand upon his arm, and turned toward her.

"What is it, dear?" he asked.

She was pointing toward the biggest amber block, and her eyes were wide open and showed she had seen something, or imagined that she had seen something, that frightened her.

Professor Young followed the direction of her finger. He saw that she was staring at the black heart of the amber block; but when he looked he could see nothing but the vague, irregular outline of the inky substance.

"What is it, dear?" asked Young again.

"I—I thought I saw it looking out, eyes that stared at us—"

The girl broke off, laughed shortly, and added, "I suppose it was Mr. Leffler's talking. There's nothing there now."

"Probably the Manchurian devil shows itself only to you," said her father jokingly. "Well, be careful, dear. If it takes a notion to jump out at you, call me and I'll exorcise it for you."

Betty blushed and laughed again. She looked at Marable, expecting to see a smile of derision on the young man's face, but his expression was grave.

The light from above was diminishing; outside sounded the roar of home-going traffic.

"Well, we must go home," said Professor Young. "There's a hard and interesting day ahead of us to-morrow, and I want to read Orling's new work on matrices before we begin chipping at the amber."

Young turned on his heel and strode toward the locker at the end of the room where he kept his coat and hat. Betty, about to follow him, was aware of a hand on her arm, and she turned to find Marable staring at her.

"I saw them, too," he whispered. "Could it have been just imagination? Was it some refraction of the light?"

The girl paled. "I—I don't know," she replied, in a low voice. "I thought I saw two terrible eyes glaring at me from the inky heart. But when father laughed at me, I was ashamed of myself and thought it was just my fancy."

"The center is liquid, I'm sure," said Marable. "We will find that out soon enough, when we get started."

"Anyway, you must be careful, and so must father," declared the girl.

She looked at the block again, as it towered there above them, as though she expected it to open and the monster of the coolies' imagination leap out.

"Come along, Betty," called her father.

She realized then that Marable was holding her hand. She pulled away and went to join her father.

It was slow work, chipping away the matrix. Only a bit at a time could be cut into, for they came upon many insects imbedded in the amber. These small creatures proved intensely interesting to the paleontologists, for some were new to science and had to be carefully preserved for study later on.

Marable and her father labored all day. Betty, aiding them, was obviously nervous. She kept begging her father to take care, and finally, when he stopped work and asked her what ailed her, she could not tell him.

"Be careful," she said, again and again.

Her father realized that she was afraid of the amber block, and he poked fun at her ceaselessly. Marable said nothing.

"It's getting much softer, now the outside shell is pierced," said Young, late in the day.

"Yes," said Marable, pausing in his work of chipping away a portion of matrix. "Soon we will strike the heart, and then we will find out whether we are right about it being liquid. We must make some preparations for catching it, if it proves to be so."

The light was fading. Outside, it was cold, but the laboratories were well heated by steam. Close by where they worked was a radiator, so that they had been kept warm all day.

Most of the workers in the room were making ready to leave. Young and Marable, loath to leave such interesting material, put down their chisels last of all. Throughout the day various scientific visitors had interrupted them to inspect the immense amber block, and hear the history of it.

All day, Betty Young had stared fascinatedly at the inky center.

"I think it must have been imagination," she whispered to Marable, when Young had gone to don his coat and hat. "I saw nothing to-day."

"Nor did I," confessed Marable. "But I thought I heard dull scrapings inside the block. My brain tells me I'm an imaginative fool, that nothing could be alive inside there, but just the same, I keep thinking about those eyes we thought we saw. It shows how far the imagination will take one."

"It's getting dark, Betty," said her father. "Better not stay here in the shadows or the devil will get you. I wonder if it will be Chinese or up-to-date American!"

The girl laughed, said good night to Marable, and followed her father from the laboratory. As they crossed the threshold a stout, red-faced man in a gray uniform, a watchman's clock hanging at his side, raised his hat and smiled at the young woman and her father.

"Hello, Rooney," cried Betty.

"How d'ye do, Miss Young! Stayin' late this evenin'?"

"No, we're leaving now, Rooney. Good night."

"G' night, Miss Young. Sleep happy."

"Thanks, Rooney."

The old night watchman was a jolly fellow, and everybody liked him. He was very fond of Betty, and the young woman always passed a pleasant word with him.

Rooney entered the room where the amber blocks were. The girl walked with her father down the long corridor. She heard Marable's step behind them.

"Wait for me a moment, father," she said.

She went back, smiling at Marable as she passed him, and entered the door, but remained in the portal and called to Rooney, who was down the laboratory.

He came hurrying to her side at her nervous hail.

"What is it, ma'am?" asked Rooney.

"You'll be careful, won't you, Rooney?" she asked in a low voice.

"Oh, yes, ma'am. I'm always careful. Nobody can get in to harm anything while Rooney's about."

"I don't mean that. I want you to be careful yourself, when you're in this room to-night."

"Why, miss, what is there to be wary of? Nothin' but some funny lookin' stones, far as I can see."

The young woman was embarrassed by her own impalpable fears, and she took leave of Rooney and rejoined her father, determined to overcome them and dismiss them from her mind.

All the way home and during their evening meal and afterwards, Professor Young poked fun at Betty. She took it good-naturedly, and laughed to see her father in such fine humor. Professor Young was a widower, and Betty was housekeeper in their flat; though a maid did the cooking for them and cleaned the rooms, the young woman planned the meals and saw to it that everything was home-like for them.

After a pleasant evening together, reading, and discussing the new additions to the collection, they went to bed.

Betty Young slept fitfully. She was harassed by dreams, dreams of huge eyes that came closer and closer to her, that at last seemed to engulf her.

She awakened finally from a nap, and started up in her bed. The sun was up, but the clock on the bureau said it was only seven o'clock, too early to arise for the day's work. But then the sound of the telephone bell ringing in the hall caused her to get up and don her slippers and dressing gown and hurry out into the living room.

Before she reached the phone, however, she heard her father's voice answering.

"Hello. . . . Yes, speaking. Good morning, Smythe."

Smythe was the janitor of the museum. Betty, standing behind her father, wondered what he could want that he should phone so early in the morning. Her father's next words sent a thrill of fright through her heart.

"My God! I—I can't believe it!" cried Young. "Is he dead?"

There was a pause; Betty caught the sound of the excited Smythe's tones through the receiver.

"Who—who is it?" she whispered, clasping her parent's arm.

"I'll be right down, yes."

Young hung up, turned to his daughter. His face was sad, heavily lined with shadows of sorrow.

"Dear, there's been a tragedy at the museum during the night. Poor Rooney has been murdered—at least so they believe—and Smythe, who found him, wants me to come down and see if anything has been stolen. I must go at once. The body is in our laboratory."

"Rooney? Ah, poor fellow."

The girl wept a little, but braced herself to assist her father.

"I'm going with you," she said.

"No, no. You'd better remain here: you can come along later," said Young. "I don't like to have you see such sights, dear. It wouldn't be good for you."

"I'll be all right. I promise you I will."

She insisted and he was forced to let her accompany him to the museum. They hailed a cab and were soon at the door. The elevator took them to the top floor, and swiftly they passed along the corridors and came to the portal which led into the rooms where the amber blocks were.

Smythe greeted them, a worried look on his seamed face. "I've sent for an ambulance, Professor," he said.

Young nodded, brushed past him, and entered the laboratory. In the morning light the amber blocks had taken on a reddish tinge. Now, they seemed to oppress the young woman, who had bravely remained at her father's side as he walked quickly to the base of the biggest block.

A vague shape lay in the shadows between the wall and the largest amber mass. Professor Young bent over the body of Rooney, and felt the pulse.

"He's been dead some time," he said.

She nodded, stricken to the heart by this terrible end of her old friend Rooney.

"There's nothing we can do for him, now," went on her father soberly. "It looks as though he had been set upon and stabbed time after time by his assailant or assailants, whoever they were."

"How—how pale he is," said Betty. "Poor Rooney was so jolly and red-faced, but his skin is like chalk."

"And he's shrunken, too. It seems there's no blood left in his veins," said her father.

Marable, who had been called also, came in then and aided in the examination. He said good morning to Betty and her father, and then went to bend over Rooney's body.

"See the look of abject terror on his face," Betty heard Marable say to her father as the two examined the corpse. "He must have been very much afraid of whoever killed him."

"They beat him up frightfully," said Young. "There must have been several of the assassins; it would take more than one man to do such damage."

"Yes. His ribs are crushed in—see, this gash, Professor, would be enough to cause death without any of the other wounds."

Betty Young could not take her eyes from the ghastly sight. She steeled herself to bear it, and prayed for strength that she should not faint and cause her father trouble. She could see the two men examining a large blistered area under the corpse's armpit, in the center of which was a sharp vertical slit which had without doubt punctured the artery near the surface of the axilla. Perhaps it had pierced even to the heart.

"Bloodless," exclaimed Marable, noticing the same thing as her father had spoken of. "It is as if the blood had been pumped out of his body!"

"Yes, I think it has drained out."

"There is not much of a pool here where he lies, though," said Marable, in a low voice. "See, there are only splotches about, from various cuts he received."

"Maybe he was dragged here from another room," said Young. "When the others come, we will soon know if anything is missing. It seems that men desperate enough to commit such a murder would not leave without trying to get what they came after. Unless, of course, the killing of Rooney frightened them away before they could get their booty."

Smythe approached the group, with a physician in tow. The latter confirmed the facts which Marable and Young had found: that Rooney had been killed by the deep gash near the heart and that most of the blood was drained from the body.

"They seem like the slashes from an extremely sharp and large razor," said the medical man.

Others were coming in to look at Rooney, and the museum was buzzing with activity as various curators, alarmed about the safety of their valuable collections, feverishly examined their charges.

"He punched his clock in here at two A.M.," said Smythe. "I seen that. It's the last time he'll ever do his duty, poor feller."

"Curious odor," said the doctor, sniffing. "It smells like musk, but is fetid. I suppose it's some chemical you use."

"I noticed that, too," said Professor Young. "I don't recognize it, myself."

Marable, who had been looking at the floor between the great block of amber and the body, uttered an exclamation which caused the two men to look up.

"There are wavy lines leading around back of the block," said Marable, in answer to their questions.

The young man disappeared behind the block, and then he called to them excitedly to join him. Betty Young pressed closer, and finally slipped past the corpse and stood by her father.

Before her, she saw a large pool of black liquid. It had been hidden by the corner of the block, so that they had not noticed it, so busy were they looking at Rooney.

And there was a great cavity in the heart of the amber block. Pieces of the yellow brown mass lay about, as though they had fallen off and allowed the inky substance to escape.

"It's hardened or dried out in the air," said Young.

"It looks like black lacquer," said Betty.

The musky smell was stronger here. The great amber block seemed to stifle them with its size.

"Our chipping and hammering and the heat of the radiator caus-ing it to expand must have forced out the sepia, or whatever it is," said Young. There was a disappointed note in his voice "I had hoped that inside the liquid we would discover a fossil of value," he went on.

Marable looked at Betty Young. They stared at one another for some seconds, and both knew that the same thought had occurred to the other. The frightful eyes—had they then been but figments of the imagination?

Marable began looking around carefully, here and there. Betty realized what he was doing, and she was frightened. She went to his side. "Oh, be careful," she whispered.

"The giant block has been moved a little," he replied, looking into her pretty face. "Have you noticed that?"

Now that she was told to look, she could see the extremely heavy amber block was no longer in the position it had been in. Marks on the floor showed where it had been dragged or shifted from its original resting place.

Betty Young gasped. What force could be so powerful that it could even budge so many tons? A derrick had been used, and roll-ers placed under the block when men had moved it.

Reason tried to assert itself. "It—it must have exploded. That would cause it to shift," she said faintly.

Marable shrugged. His examination was interrupted by the arrival of the museum's chemist, sent for by Young. The chemist took a sample of the black liquid for analysis. Reports were coming in from all over the museum, different departments declaring, one after another, that nothing had been disturbed or stolen from their sections.

Betty Young went again to Marable's side. She followed the direction of his eyes, and saw long, clawlike marks on the floor, radiating from the sepia.

"Doctor Marable," she said, "please don't—don't look any longer. Leave this terrible place for the day, anyway, until we see what happens in the next twenty-four hours."

He smiled and shook his head. "I must make a search," he re-plied. "My brain calls me a fool, but just the same, I'm worried."

"Do you really think . . .?"

He nodded, divining her thought. The girl shivered. She felt terror mounting to her heart, and the matter-of-fact attitudes of the others in the great laboratory did not allay her fears.

Rooney's body was removed. The place was cleaned up by workmen, and Marable's search—if that was what his constant roving about the laboratory could be called—ceased for a time. The chemist's report came in. The black liquid was some sort of animal secretion, melonotic probably.

In spite of the fact that they had learned so many facts about the murder, they as yet had not solved the mystery. Who had murdered Rooney, and why? And where had his blood gone to? In no other rooms could be found any traces of a struggle.

"If you won't do anything else, please carry a gun," begged Betty of Marable. "I'm going to try to take father home, right after lunch, if he'll go. He's so stubborn. I can't make him take care. I've got to watch him and stay beside him."

"Very well," replied Marable. "I'll get a revolver. Not that I think it would be of much use, if I did find—" He broke off, and shrugged his broad shoulders.

Leffler came storming into the room. "What's this I hear?" he cried, approaching Marable. "A watchman killed in the night? Carelessness, man, carelessness! The authorities here are absurd! They hold priceless treasures and allow thieves to enter and wreak their will. You, Marable, what's all this mean?"

Leffler was angry. Marable looked into his red face coolly. "We do the best we can, Mr. Leffler," he said. "It is unlikely that anyone would wish to steal such a thing as that block of amber."

He waved toward the giant mass.

Leffler made a gesture of impatience. "It cost me many thousands of dollars," he cried.

"It is time for lunch, Professor," said Betty.

Marable bowed to Leffler and left the millionaire sputtering away, inspecting the various specimens he had contributed.

The one o'clock gong had struck, and all the workers and investigators were leaving in paleontological laboratories for a bite to eat.

Marable, with Betty, went out last. Leffler was over in one corner of the room, hidden from their sight by a corner of an amber block. They could hear Leffler still uttering complaints about the carelessness of the men in charge of that section of the museum, and Marable smiled at Betty sadly.

"Poor Rooney," he said. "Betty, I feel more or less responsible, in a way."

"No, no," cried the girl. "How could you have foreseen such a thing?"

Marable shook his head. "Those eyes, you know. I should have taken precautions. But I had no idea it could burst from its prison so."

For the first time Marable had definitely mentioned his idea of what had occurred. The girl had understood it all along, from their broken conversation and from the look in the young scientist's eyes.

She sighed deeply. "You will get a revolver before you search further?" she said. "I'm going to. Smythe has one, and I know he'll lend it to me."

"I will," he promised. "You know, Leffler has the same idea we have, I think. That's why he keeps talking about it being our fault. I believe he has seen something, too. His talk about the devil inside the block was half in earnest. I suppose he put it down to imagination, or perhaps he did not think this fossil to be dangerous."

They went out together, and walked toward the restaurant they frequented. Her father was there, lunching with one of the superintendents of the museum. He smiled and waved to Betty.

Everyone, of course, was discussing the killing of Rooney.

After an hour, during which the two young people spoke little, Marable and Betty Young left the restaurant and started back toward the museum. Her father was still at his table.

They walked up the driveway entrance, and then Marable uttered an exclamation. "Something's wrong," he said.

There was a small crowd of people collected on the steps. The outer doors, instead of being open as usual, were closed and guards stood peering out.

Marable and Betty were admitted, after they had pushed their way to the doors.

"Museum's closed to the public, sir," replied a guard to Marable's question.

"Why?" asked Marable.

"Somethin's happened up in the paleontological laboratories," answered the guard. "Dunno just what, but orders come to clear the rooms and not let anybody in but members of the staff, sir."

Marable hurried forward. Betty was at his heels. "Please get yourself a gun," she said, clutching his arm and holding him back.

"All right. I'll borrow one from a guard."

He returned to the front doors, and came back, slipping a large pistol into his side pocket.

"I want you to wait here," he said.

"No. I'm going with you."

"Please," he said. "As your superior, I order you to remain downstairs."

The girl shrugged. She allowed him to climb the stairs to the first floor, and then she hurried back in search of Smythe.

Smythe obtained a gun for her, and as she did not wish to wait for the slow elevator, she ran up the steps. Smythe could not tell her definitely what had occurred in the upper laboratory that had caused the museum to be closed for the day.

Her heart beating swiftly, Betty Young hurried up the second flight of stairs to the third floor. A workman, whom the girl recognized as a manual laborer in the paleontological rooms, came running down, passing her in full flight, a look of abject terror on his face.

"What is it?" she cried.

He was so frightened he could not talk logically. "There was a black fog—I saw a red snake with legs—"

She waited for no more. A pang of fear for the safety of Marable shot through her heart, and she forced herself on to the top floor.

Up there was a haze, faintly black, which filled the corridors. As Betty Young drew closer to the door of the paleontological laboratories, the mist grew more opaque. It was as though a sooty fog permeated the air, and the girl could see it was pouring from the door of the laboratory in heavy coils. And her nostrils caught the strange odor of fetid musk.

She was greatly frightened; but she gripped the gun and pushed on.

Then to her ears came the sound of a scream, the terrible scream of a mortally wounded man. Instinctively she knew it was not Marable, but she feared for the young professor, and with an answering cry she rushed into the smoky atmosphere of the outer laboratories.

"Walter!" she called.

But evidently he did not hear her, for no reply came. Or was it that something had happened to him?

She paused on the threshold of the big room where were the amber blocks.

About the vast floor space stood the numerous masses of stone and amber, some covered with immense canvas shrouds which made them look like ghost hillocks in the dimness. Betty Young stood, gasping in fright, clutching the pistol in her hand, trying to catch the sounds of men in that chamber of horror.

She heard, then, a faint whimpering, and then noises which she identified in her mind as something being dragged along the marble flooring. A muffled scream, weak, reached her ears, and as she took a step forward, silence came.

She listened longer, but now the sunlight coming through the window to make murky patches in the opaque black fog was her chief sensation.

"Walter!" she called.

"Go back, Betty, go back!"

The mist seemed to muffle voices as well as obscure the vision. She advanced farther into the laboratory, trying to locate Marable. Bravely the girl pushed toward the biggest amber block. It was here that she felt instinctively that she would find the source of danger.

"Leffler!" she heard Marable say, almost at her elbow, and the young man groaned. The girl came upon him, bending over something on the floor.

She knelt beside him, gripping his arm. Now she could see the outline of Leffler's body at her feet. The wealthy collector was doubled up on the ground, shrivelled as had been Rooney. His feet, moving as though by reflex action, patted the floor from time to time, making a curious clicking sound as the buttons of his gray spats struck the marble.

But it was obvious, even in the murky light, that Leffler was dead, that he had been sucked dry of blood.

Betty Young screamed. She could not help it. The black fog choked her and she gasped for breath. Leaving Marable, she ran toward the windows to throw them open.

The first one she tried was heavy, and she smashed the glass with the butt of the gun. She broke several panes in two of the windows, and the mist rolled out from the laboratory.

She started to return to the side of Marable. He uttered a sudden shout, and she hurried back to where she had left him, stumbling over Leffler's body, recoiling at this touch of death.

Marable was not there, but she could hear him nearby.

Cool air was rushing in from the windows, and gradually the fog was disappearing. Betty Young saw Marable now, standing nearby, staring at the bulk of an amber block which was still covered by its canvas shroud. Though not as large as the prize exhibit, this block of amber was large and filled many yards of space.

"Betty, please go outside and call some of the men," begged Marable.

But he did not look at her, and she caught his fascinated stare. Following the direction of his gaze, the girl saw that a whisp of smoky mist was curling up from under the edge of the canvas cover.

"It is there," whispered Betty.

Marable had a knife which he had picked up from a bench, and with this he began quietly to cut the canvas case of the block, keeping several feet to each side of the spot where the fog showed from beneath the shroud.

Marable cut swiftly and efficiently, though the cloth was heavy and he was forced to climb up several feet on the block to make his work effective. The girl watched, fascinated with horror and curiosity.

To their ears came a curious, sucking sound, and once a vague tentacle form showed from the bottom of the canvas.

At last Marable seized the edge of the cut he had made and, with a violent heave, sent the canvas flap flying over the big block.

Betty Young screamed. At last she had a sight of the terrible creature which her imagination had painted in loathing and horror. A flash of brilliant scarlet, dabbed with black patches, was her impression of the beast. A head flat and reptilian, long, tubular, with movable nostrils and antennae at the end, framed two eyes which were familiar enough to her, for they were the orbs which had stared from the inside of the amber block. She had dreamed of those eyes.

But the reptile moved like a flash of red light, though she knew its bulk was great; it sprayed forth black mist from the appendages at the end of its nose, and the crumpling of canvas reached her ears as the beast endeavored to conceal itself on the opposite side of the block.

Marable had run to the other side of the mass. The air, rushing in from the windows, had cleared the mist, in spite of the new clouds the creature had emitted, and Betty could see for some feet in either direction now.

She walked, with stiff, frozen muscles, around to join Marable. As she came near to him, she saw him jerking off the entire canvas cover of the block to expose the horrible reptile to the light of day.

And now the two stood staring at the awful sight. The creature had flattened itself into the crevices and irregular surfaces of the block, but it was too large to hide in anything but a huge space. They saw before them its great bulk, bright red skin blotched with black, which rose and fell with the breathing of the reptile. Its long, powerful tail, tapering off from the fat, loathsome body, was curled around the bottom of the block.

"That's where it's been hidden, under the shroud. We've been within a few feet of it every moment we've been at work," said Marable, his voice dry. "There were many hiding places for it, but it chose the best. It came out only when there was comparative quiet, to get its food. . . ."

"We—we must kill it," stammered the girl.

But she could not move. She was looking at the immense, cruel, lidless eyes, which balefully held her as a serpent paralyzes a bird. The tubular nostrils and antennae seemed to be sniffing at them, waving to and fro.

"See the white expanse of cornea, how large it is," whispered Marable. "The pupils are nothing but black slits now." The interest excited by this living fossil was almost enough to stifle the dread of the creature in the man.

But the girl saw the huge flat head and the crinkled tissue of the frilled mouth with its sucker disks.

Suddenly, from the central portion of the sucker-cup mouth issued a long, straight red fang.

The two drew back as the living fossil raised a short clawed leg.

"It has the thick body of an immense python and the clawed legs of a dinosaur," said Marable, speaking as though he were delivering a lecture. The sight, without doubt, fascinated him as a scientist. He almost forgot the danger.

"Oh, it's horrible," whispered the girl.

She clung to his arm. He went on talking. "It is some sort of terrestrial octopus. . . ."

To the girl, it seemed that the living fossil was endless in length. Coil after coil showed as the ripples passed along its body and the straight fang threatened them with destruction.

"See, it is armored," said Marable. "Betty, no one has ever had such an experience as this, seen such a sight, and lived to tell of it. It must be ravenous with hunger, shut up in its amber cell inside the black fluid. I—"

A sharp, whistling hiss interrupted his speech. The reptile was puffing and swelling, and as it grew in bulk with the intake of the air, its enamel-like scales stood out like bosses on the great body. It spat forth a cloud of black, oily mist, and Marable came to himself at last.

He raised his revolver and fired at the creature, sending shot after shot from the heavy revolver into the head.

Betty Young screamed as the reptile reared up and made a movement toward them. Marable and the girl retreated swiftly, as the beast thumped to the floor with a thud and started at them, advancing with a queer, crawling movement.

It was between them and the door. Betty thrust her gun into Marable's hands, for his own was empty and he had hurled it at the monster.

"Hurry! Run for your life!" ordered Marable, placing himself between Betty and the reptile.

She would not leave him till he swerved to one side, going dangerously close to the beast and firing into its head. The rush of the flowing body stopped; it turned and pursued him, leaving the girl safe for the moment, but separated from Marable.

Luckily, on the smooth marble it could not get an efficient grip with its clawlike arms. It was clumsy in its gait, and for a time the man eluded it.

Betty Young, looking about for a weapon, calling for help at the top of her lungs, caught sight of a fireman's ax in a glass case on the wall. She ran over, smashed the glass with the small hammer, and took out the heavy ax.

Shot after shot reverberated through the big laboratory as Marable tried to stop the monster. Betty, bravely closing in from the rear, saw Marable leaping from side to side as the brute struck viciously at him time and again.

The creature had been emitting cloud after cloud of black fog, and the atmosphere, in spite of the open windows, was dim in its vicinity. Vaguely Betty heard shouts from the far hall, but all she could do was to call out in return and run toward the horror.

Marable, out of breath, had climbed to the top of an amber block. Betty, close by, saw the reptile rear its bulk up into the air, until it was high enough to strike the man.

Before it could send forth its death-dealing fang to pin Marable to the block, however, Betty Young brought the ax down on its back with all her strength.

There was a sickening thud as the sharp weapon sunk deep into the fleshy back. She struck again, and the creature fell in folds, like a collapsing spring. It lashed back at her, but she leaped clear as it slashed in agony, thrashing about so that the whole room seemed to rock.

Marable came scrambling down the side of the block to help her. He was breathing hard, and she turned toward him; as Betty looked away, a portion of the scarlet tail hit her in the body and she fell, striking her head on the floor.

Marable reached down, seized the ax, and in a desperate frenzy hacked at the reptile's awful head. He leaped in and out like a terrier, sinking the ax deep into the neck and head of the beast. He gave the impression of slashing at heavy rubber, and Betty Young, trying to drag herself away from that dangerous body, heard his whistling breath.

They were almost hidden from one another now, in the mist which came from the thing's nostrils.

"Help, help!" screamed the girl, mustering her last strength in the despairing cry.

She saw Marable go down, then, as the reptile hit him a glancing blow with its body. When the powerful young fellow did not rise, the girl thought it was all over. The air really became black to her; she fainted and lay still.

When Betty Young opened her eyes, the air had cleared greatly, and she could see the familiar outlines of the paleontological laboratory and the bulks of the amber blocks. Her father was holding her head in his lap, and was bathing her temples with water.

"Darling," he said, "are you badly hurt?"

"No," she murmured faintly. "I'm—I'm all right. But—but Walter—did it—"

"He's all right," said her father. "The reptile was dying, and could do him no damage. We finished it off."

Then, Marable, covered with blood, which he was trying to wipe from his hands and clothes, came and smiled down at her.

"Well," said Professor Young, "you two have mutilated a marvelous and unique specimen between you."

There were several men examining something nearby. Turning her eyes in their direction, Betty saw they were viewing the remains of the reptile.

Marable helped her to her feet, and stood with one arm about her. Professor Orling, the famous specialist on fossil reptiles, was speaking now, and the others listened.

"I think we will find it to be some sort of missing link between the dinosaurs and mososaurs. It is surely unbelievable that such a creature should be found alive; but perhaps it can be explained. It is related to the amphibians and was able to live in or out of the water. Now, we have many instances of reptiles such as lizards and toads penned up in solid rock but surviving for hundreds of years. Evidently this great reptile went through the same sort of experience. I would say that there has been some great upheaval of nature, that the reptile was caught in its prison of amber thousands and thousands of years ago. Through hibernation and perhaps a preservative drug it emitted in the black fluid, this creature has been able to survive its long imprisonment. Naturally, when it was released by the cutting away of part of the amber which penned it in, it burst its cell, ravenous with hunger. The fanglike tooth we see was its main weapon of attack, and it set upon the unfortunate watchman. After knocking him unconscious, its sucker-like fringe glued the mouth near the heart while the fang shot into the arteries and drew forth the body fluids. There is a great deal to be done with this valuable find, gentlemen. I would suggest that—"

Marable grunted. "Oh, hell," he murmured in Betty Young's ear. "To the devil with paleontology, Betty. You saved my life. Come out and let's get married. I love you."

The girl smiled up into his eyes. The scientists close by were listening fascinatedly to Orling's words, and had no time to watch the two young people, for they stared at the reptile's body as the great man went from section to section, lecturing upon one point after another.

"You've forgotten paleontology for a moment, thank goodness," said Betty. "I'm glad."

"Yes, Betty dear. This terrible experience has shaken me, and I realized how much I love you when I saw you in danger. What an awful few minutes! If I had to live them over again, I don't think I could face them."

"Never mind," she murmured. "We are safe, Walter. After all, it's not every woman who is helped by a living fossil to make the man she loves realize he loves her!"

OUT OF THE DREADFUL DEPTHS
C. D. WILLARD
1930

Robert Thorpe reached languidly for a cigarette and, with lazy fingers, extracted a lighter from his pocket.

"Be a sport," he repeated to the gray haired man across the table. "Be a sport, Admiral, and send me across on a destroyer. Never been on a destroyer except in port. It . . . would be a new experience . . . enjoy it a lot. . . ."

In the palm-shaded veranda of this club-house in Manila, Admiral Struthers, U. S. N., regarded with undisguised disfavor the young man in the wicker chair. He looked at the deep chest and the broad shoulders which even a loose white coat could not conceal, at the short, wavy brown hair and the slow, friendly smile on the face below.

A likable chap, this Thorpe, but lazy—just an idler—he had concluded. Been playing around Manila for the last two months—resting up, he had said. And from what? the Admiral had questioned disdainfully. Admiral Struthers did not like indolent young men, but it would have saved him money if he had really got an answer to his question and had learned just why and how Robert Thorpe had earned a vacation.

"You on a destroyer!" he said, and the lips beneath the close-cut gray mustache twisted into a smile. "That would be too rough an experience for you, I am afraid, Thorpe. Destroyers pitch about quite a bit, you know."

He included in his smile the destroyer captain and the young lady who completed their party. The young lady had a charming and saucy smile and knew it; she used it in reply to the Admiral's remark.

"I have asked Mr. Thorpe to go on the *Adelaide*," she said. "We shall be leaving in another month—but Robert tells me he has other plans."

"Worse and worse," was the Admiral's comment. "Your father's yacht is not even as steady as a destroyer. Now I would suggest a nice comfortable liner. . . ."

Robert Thorpe did not miss the official glances of amusement, but his calm complacence was unruffled. "No," he said, "I don't just fancy liners. Fact is, I have been thinking of sailing across to the States alone."

The Admiral's smile increased to a short laugh. "I would make a bet you wouldn't get fifty miles from Manila harbor."

The younger man crushed his cigarette slowly into the tray. "How much of a bet?" he asked. "What will you bet that I don't sail alone from here to—where are you stationed?—San Diego?—from here to San Diego?"

"Humph!" was the snorted reply. "I would bet a thousand dollars on that and take your money for Miss Allaire's pet charity."

"Now that's an idea," said Thorpe. He reached for a check book in his inner pocket and began to write.

"In case I lose," he explained, "I might be hard to find, so I will just ask Miss Allaire to hold this check for me. You can do the same." He handed the check to the girl.

"Winner gets his thousand back, Ruth; loser's money goes to any little orphans you happen to fancy."

"You're not serious," protested the Admiral.

"Sure! The bank will take that check seriously, I promise you. And I saw just the sloop I want for the trip . . . had my eye on her for the past month."

"But, Robert," began Ruth Allaire, "you don't mean to risk your life on a foolish bet?"

Thorpe reached over to pat tenderly the hand that held his check. "I'm glad if you care," he said, and there was an undertone of seriousness beneath his raillery, "but save your sympathy for the Admiral. The U. S. Navy can't bluff me." He rose more briskly from his chair.

"Thorpe. . . ." said Admiral Struthers. He was thinking deeply, trying to recollect. "Robert Thorpe. . . . I have a book by someone of that name—travel and adventure and knocking about the world. Young man, are you *the* Robert Thorpe?"

"Why, yes, if you wish to put it that way," agreed the other. He waved lightly to the girl as he moved away.

"I must be running along," he said, "and get that boat. See you all in San Diego!"

The first rays of the sun touched with golden fingers the tops of the lazy swells of the Pacific. Here and there a wave broke to spray under the steady wind and became a shower of molten metal. And in the boat, whose sails caught now and then the touch of morning, Robert Thorpe stirred himself and rose sleepily to his feet.

Out of the snug cabin at this first hint of day, he looked first at the compass and checked his course, then made sure of the lashing about the helm. The steady trade-winds had borne him on through the night, and he nodded with satisfaction as he prepared to lower his lights. He was reaching for a line as the little craft hung for an instant on the top of a wave. And in that instant his eyes caught a marking of white on the dim waters ahead.

"Breakers!" he shouted aloud and leaped for the lashed wheel. He swung off to leeward and eased a bit on the main-sheet, then lashed the wheel again to hold on the new course.

Again from a wave-crest he stared from under a sheltering hand. The breakers were there—the smooth swells were foaming— breaking in mid-ocean where his chart, he knew, showed water a mile deep. Beyond the white line was a three-master, her sails shivering in the breeze.

The big sailing ship swung off on a new tack as he watched. Was she dodging those breakers? he wondered. Then he stared in amazement through the growing light at the unbroken swells where the white line had been.

He rubbed his sleepy eyes with a savage hand and stared again. There were no breakers—the sea was an even expanse of heaving water.

"I could swear I saw them!" he told himself, but forgot this perplexing occurrence in the still more perplexing maneuvers of the sailing ship.

This steady wind—for smooth handling—was all that such a craft could ask, yet here was this old-timer of the sea with a full spread of canvas booming and cracking as the ship jibed. She rolled far over as he watched, recovered, and tore off on a long, sweeping circle.

The one man crew of the little sloop should have been preparing breakfast, as he had for many mornings past, but, instead he swung his little craft into the wind and watched for near an hour the erratic rushes and shivering haltings of the larger ship. But long before this time had passed Thorpe knew he was observing the aimless maneuvers of an unmanned vessel.

And he watched his chance for a closer inspection.

The three-master *Minnie R.*, from the dingy painting of the stern, hung quivering in the wind when he boarded her. There was a broken log-line that swept down from the stern, and he caught this and made his own boat fast. Then, watching his chance, he drew close and went overboard, the line in his hand.

"Like a blooming native after cocoanuts," he told himself as he went up the side. But he made it and pulled himself over the rail as the ship drew off on another tack.

Thorpe looked quickly about the deserted deck. "Ahoy, there!" he shouted, but the straining of rope and spars was his only answer. Canvas was whipping to ribbons, sheets cracked their frayed ends like lashes as the booms swung wildly, but a few sails still held and caught the air.

He was on the after deck, and he leaped first for the wheel that was kicking and whirling with the swing of the rudder. A glance at the canvas that still drew, and he set her on a course with a few steadying pulls. There was rope lying about, and he lashed the wheel with a quick turn or two and watched the ship steady down to a smooth slicing of the waves from the west.

And only then did the man take time to quiet his panting breath and look about him in the unnatural quiet of this strangely deserted deck. He shouted again and walked to a companionway to repeat the hail. Only an echo, sounding hollowly from below, replied to break the vast silence.

It was puzzling—inconceivable. Thorpe looked about him to note the lifeboats snug and undisturbed in their places. No sign there of an abandonment of the boat, but abandoned she was, as the silence told only too plainly. And Thorpe, as he went below, had an uncanny feeling of the crew's presence—as if they had been there, walked where he walked, shouted and laughed a matter of a brief hour or two before.

The door of the captain's cabin was burst in, hanging drunkenly from one hinge. The log-book was open; there were papers on a rude desk. The bunk was empty where the blankets had been thrown hurriedly aside. Thorpe could almost see the skipper of this mystery ship leaping frantically from his bed at some sudden call or commotion. A chair was smashed and broken, and the man who examined it curiously wiped from his hands a disgusting slime that was smeared stickily on the splintered fragments. There was a fetid stench within his nostrils, and he passed up further examination of this room.

Forward in the fo'c'sle he felt again irresistibly the recent presence of the crew. And again he found silence and emptiness and a disorder that told of a fear-stricken flight. The odor that sickened and nauseated the exploring man was everywhere. He was glad to gain the freedom of the wind-swept deck and rid his lungs of the vile breath within the vessel.

He stood silent and bewildered. There was not a living soul aboard the ship—no sign of life. He started suddenly. A moaning, whimpering cry came from forward on the deck!

Thorpe leaped across a disorder of tangled rope to race toward the bow. He stopped short at sight of a battered cage. Again the moaning came to him—there was something that still lived on board the ill-fated ship.

He drew closer to see a great, huddled, furry mass that crouched and cowered in a corner of the cage. A huge ape, Thorpe concluded, and it moaned and whimpered absurdly like a human in abject fear.

Had this been the terror that drove the men into the sea? Had this ape escaped and menaced the officers and crew? Thorpe dismissed the thought he well knew was absurd. The stout wood bars of the cage were broken. It had been partially crushed, and the chain that held it to the deck was extended to its full length.

"Too much for me," the man said slowly, aloud; "entirely too much for me! But I can't sail this old hooker alone; I'll have to get out and let her drift."

He removed completely one of the splintered bars from the broken cage. "I've got to leave you, old fellow," he told the cowering animal, "but I'll give you the run of the ship."

He went below once more and came quickly back with the log-book and papers from the captain's room. He tied these in a tight wrapping of oilcloth from the galley and hung them at his belt. He took the wheel again and brought the cumbersome craft slowly into the wind. The bare mast of his own sloop was bobbing alongside as he went down the line and swam over to her.

Fending off from the wallowing hulk, he cut the line, and his small craft slipped slowly astern as the big vessel fell off in the wind and drew lumberingly away on its unguided course.

She vanished into the clear-cut horizon before the watching man ceased his staring and pricked a point upon his chart that he estimated was his position.

And he watched vainly for some sign of life on the heaving waters as he set his sloop back on her easterly course.

It was a sun-tanned young man who walked with brisk strides into the office of Admiral Struthers. The gold-striped arm of the uniformed man was extended in quick greeting.

"Made it, did you?" he exclaimed. "Congratulations!"

"All O.K.," Thorpe agreed. "Ship and log are ready for your verification."

"Talk sense," said the officer. "Have any trouble or excitement? Or perhaps you are more interested in collecting a certain bet than you are in discussing the trip."

"Damn the bet!" said the young man fervently. "And that's just what I am here for—to talk about the trip. There were some little incidents that may interest you."

He painted for the Admiral in brief, terse sentences the picture of that daybreak on the Pacific, the line of breakers, white in the vanishing night, the abandoned ship beyond, cracking her canvas to tatters in the freshening breeze. And he told of his boarding her and of what he had found.

"Where was this?" asked the officer, and Thorpe gave his position as he had checked it.

"I reported the derelict to a passing steamer that same day," he added, but the Admiral was calling for a chart. He spread it on the desk before him and placed the tip of a pencil in the center of an unbroken expanse.

"Breakers, you said?" he questioned. "Why, there are hundreds of fathoms here, Mr. Thorpe."

"I know it," Thorpe agreed, "but I saw them—a stretch of white water for an eighth of a mile. I know it's impossible, but true. But forget that item for a time, Admiral. Look at this." He opened a brief case and took out a log-book and some other papers.

"The log of the *Minnie R.*," he explained briefly. "Nothing in it but routine entries up to that morning and then nothing at all."

"Abandoned," mused the Admiral, "and they did not take to the boats. There have been other instances—never explained."

"See if this helps any," suggested Thorpe and handed the other two sheets of paper. "They were in the captain's cabin," he added.

Admiral Struthers glanced at them, then settled back in his chair.

"Dated September fourth," he said. "That would have been the day previous to the time you found her." The writing was plain, in a careful, well-formed hand. He cleared his throat and read aloud:

"Written by Jeremiah Wilkens of Salem, Mass., master of the *Minnie R.*, bound from Shanghai to San Pedro. I have sailed the seas for forty years, and for the first time I am afraid. I hope I may destroy this paper when the lights of San Pedro are safe in sight, but I am writing here what it would shame me to set down in the ship's log, though I know there are stranger happenings on the face of the waters than man has ever seen—or has lived to tell.

"All this day I have been filled with fear. I have been watched—I have felt it as surely as if a devil out of hell stood beside me with his eyes fastened on mine. The men have felt it, too. They have been frightened at nothing and have tried to conceal it as I have done.—And the animals. . . .

"A shark has followed us for days—it is gone to-day. The cats—we have three on board—have howled horribly and have hidden themselves in the cargo down below. The mate is bringing a big monkey to be sold in Los Angeles. An orang-outang, he calls it. It has been an ugly brute, shaking at the bars of its cage and showing its ugly teeth ever since we left port. But to-day it is crouched in a corner of its cage and will not stir even for food. The poor beast is in mortal terror.

"All this is more like the wandering talk of an old woman muttering in a corner by the fireside of witches and the like than it is like a truthful account set down by Jeremiah Wilkins. And now that I have written it I see there is nothing to tell. Nothing but the shameful account of my fear of some horror beyond my knowing. And now that it is written I am tempted to destroy—No, I will wait—"

"And now what is this?" Admiral Struthers interrupted his reading to ask. He turned the paper to read a coarse, slanting scrawl at the bottom of the page.

"The eyes—the eyes—they are everywhere above us—God help—" The writing trailed off in a straggling line.

The lips beneath the trim gray mustache drew themselves into a hard line. It was a moment before Admiral Struthers raised his eyes to meet those of Robert Thorpe.

"You found this in the captain's cabin?" he asked.

"Yes."

"And the captain was—"

"Gone."

"Blood stains?"

"No, but the door had been burst off its hinges. There had been a struggle without a doubt."

The officer mused for a minute or two.

"Did they go aboard another vessel?" he pondered. "Abandon ship—open the sea-cocks—sink it for the insurance?" He was trying vainly to find some answer to the problem, some explanation that would not impose too great a strain upon his own reason.

"I have reported to the owners," said Thorpe. "The *Minnie R.* was not heavily insured."

The Admiral ruffled some papers on his desk to find a report.

"There has been another," he told Thorpe. "A tramp freighter is listed as missing. She was last reported due east of the position you give. She was coming this way—must have come through about the same water—" He caught himself up abruptly. Thorpe sensed that an Admiral of the Navy must not lend too credulous an ear to impossible stories.

"You've had an interesting experience, Mr. Thorpe," he said. "Most interesting. Probably a derelict is the answer, some hull just afloat. We will send out a general warning."

He handed the loose papers and the log book to the younger man. "This stuff is rubbish," he stated with emphasis. "Captain Wilkins held his command a year or so too long."

"You will do nothing about it?" Thorpe asked in astonishment.

"I said I would warn all shipping; there is nothing more to be done."

"I think there is." Thorpe's gray eye were steady as he regarded the man at the desk. "I intend to run it down. There have been other such instances, as you said—never explained. I mean to find the answer."

Admiral Struthers smiled indulgently. "Always after excitement," he said. "You'll be writing another book, I expect. I shall look forward to reading it . . . but just what are you going to do?"

"I am going to the Islands," said Thorpe quietly. "I am going to charter a small ship of some sort, and I am going out there and camp on that spot in the hope of seeing those eyes and what is behind them. I am leaving to-night."

Admiral Struthers leaned back to indulge in a hearty laugh. "I refused you a passage on a destroyer once," he said, "and it was an expensive mistake. I don't make the same mistake twice. Now I am going to offer you a trip. . . .

"The *Bennington* is leaving to-day on a cruise to Manila. I'll hold her an extra hour or two if you would like to go. She can drop you at Honolulu or wherever you say. Lieutenant Commander Brent is in command—you remember him in Manila, of course."

"Fine," Thorpe responded. "I'll be there."

"And," he added, as he took the Admiral's hand, "if I didn't object to betting on a sure thing I would make you a little proposition. I would bet any money that you would give your shirt to go along."

"I never bet, either," said Admiral Struthers, "on a sure loss. Now get out of here, you young trouble-shooter, and let the Navy get to work." His eyes were twinkling as he waved the young man out.

Thorpe found himself comfortably fixed on the *Bennington*. Brent, her commander, was a fine example of the aggressive young chaps that the destroyer fleet breeds. And he liked to play cribbage, Thorpe found. They were pegging away industriously the sixth night out when the first S.O.S. reached them. A message was placed before the commander. He read it and tossed it to Thorpe as he rose from his chair.

"S.O.S.," said the radio sheet, "*Nagasaki Maru*, twenty-four thirty-five N., one five eight West. Struck something unknown. Down at the bow. May need help. Please stand by."

Captain Brent had left the room. A moment later, and the quiver and tremble of the *Bennington* told Thorpe they were running full speed for the position of the stricken ship.

But: "Twenty-four thirty-five North," he mused, "and less than two degrees west of where the poor old *Minnie R.* got hers. I wonder . . . I wonder. . . ."

"We will be there in four hours," said Captain Brent on his return. "Hope she lasts. But what have they struck out there? Derelict probably, though she should have had Admiral Struthers' warning."

Robert Thorpe made no reply other than: "Wait here a minute, Brent. I have something to show you."

He had not told the officer of his mission nor of his experience, but he did so now. And he placed before him the wildly improbable statement of the late Captain Wilkins.

"Something is there," surmised Captain Brent, "just awash, probably—no superstructure visible. Your *Minnie R.* hit the same thing."

"Something is there," Thorpe agreed. "I wish I knew what."

"This stuff has got to you, has it?" asked Brent as he returned the papers of Captain Wilkins. He was quite evidently amused at the thought.

"You weren't on the ship," said Thorpe, simply. "There was nothing to see—nothing to tell. But I know. . . ."

He followed Brent to the wireless room.

"Can you get the *Nagasaki*?" Brent asked.

"They know we are coming, sir," said the operator. "We seem to be the only one anywhere near."

He handed the captain another message. "Something odd about that," he said.

"*U. S. S. Bennington*," the captain read aloud. "We are still afloat. On even keel now, but low in water. No water coming in. Engines full speed ahead, but we make no headway. Apparently aground. *Nagasaki Maru*."

"Why, that's impossible," Brent exclaimed impatiently. "What kind of foolishness—" He left the question uncompleted. The radio man was writing rapidly. Some message was coming at top speed. Both Brent and Thorpe leaned over the man's shoulder to read as he wrote.

"*Bennington* help," the pencil was writing, "sinking fast—decks almost awash—we are being—"

In breathless silence they watched the pencil, poised above the paper while the operator listened tensely to the silent night.

Again his ear received the wild jumble of dots and dashes sent by a frenzied hand in that far-off room. His pencil automatically set down the words. "Help—help—" it wrote before Thorpe's spellbound gaze, "the eyes—the eyes—it is attack—"

And again the black night held only the rush and roar of torn waters where the destroyer raced quivering through the darkness. The message, as the waiting men well knew, would never be completed.

"A derelict!" Robert Thorpe exclaimed with unconscious scorn. But Captain Brent was already at a communication tube.

"Chief? Captain Brent. Give her everything you've got. Drive the *Bennington* faster than she ever went before."

The slim ship was a quivering lance of steel that threw itself through foaming waters, that shot with an endless, roaring surge of speed toward that distant point in the heaving waste of the Pacific, and that seemed, to the two silent men on the bridge, to put the dragging miles behind them so slowly—so slowly.

"Let me see those papers," said Captain Brent, finally.

He read them in silence.

Then: "The eyes!" he said. "The eyes! That is what this other poor devil said. My God, Thorpe, what is it? What can it be? We're not all insane."

"I don't know what I expected to find," said Thorpe slowly. "I had thought of many things, each wilder than the next. This Captain Wilkins said the eyes were above him. I had visions of some sky monster . . . I had even thought of some strange aircraft from out in space, perhaps, with round lights like eyes. I have pictured impossibilities! But now—"

"Yes," the other questioned, "now?"

"There were tales in olden times of the Kraken," suggested Thorpe.

"The Kraken!" the captain scoffed. "A mythical monster of the sea. Why, that was just a fable."

"True," was the quiet reply, "that was just a fable. And one of the things I have learned is how frequently there is a basis of fact underlying a fable. And, for that matter, how can we know there is no such monster, some relic of a Mesozoic species supposed to be extinct?"

He stood motionless, staring far out ahead into the dark. And Brent, too, was silent. They seemed to try with unaided eyes to penetrate the dark miles ahead and see what their sane minds refused to accept.

It was still dark when the search-light's sweeping beam picked up the black hull and broad, red-striped funnels of the *Nagasaki Maru*. She was riding high in the water, and her big bulk rolled and wallowed in the trough of the great swells.

The *Bennington* swept in a swift circle about the helpless hulk while the lights played incessantly upon her decks. And the watching eyes strained vainly for some signal to betoken life, for some sign that their mad race had not been quite vain. Her engines had been shut down; there was no steerage-way for the *Nagasaki Maru*, and, from all they could see, there were no human hands to drag at the levers of her waiting engines nor to twirl with sure touch the deserted helm. The *Nagasaki Maru* was abandoned.

The lights held steadily upon her as the *Bennington* came alongside and a boat was swung out smartly in its davits. But Thorpe knew he was not alone in his wild surmise as to the cause of the catastrophe.

"Throw your lights around the water occasionally," Brent ordered. "Let me know if you see anything."

"Yes sir," said the man at the search-light. "I will report if I spot any survivors or boats."

"Report anything you see," said Commander Brent curtly.

"You go aboard if you want to," he suggested to Thorpe. "I will stay here and be ready if you need help."

Thorpe nodded with approval as the small boat pulled away in the dark, for there was activity apparent on the destroyer not warranted by a mere rescue at sea. Gun-crews rushed to their stations; the tarpaulin covers were off of the guns, and their slender lengths gleamed where they covered the course of the boat.

"Brent is ready," Thorpe admitted, "for anything."

They found the iron ladder against the ship's side, and a sailor sprang for it and made his way aboard. Thorpe was not the last to set foot on deck, and he shuddered involuntarily at the eerie silence he knew awaited them.

It was the *Minnie R.* over again, as he expected, but with a difference. The sailing vessel, before he boarded it, had been for some time exposed to the sun, while the *Nagasaki Maru* had not. And here there were slimy trails still wet on the decks.

He went first to the wireless room. He must know the final answer to that interrupted message, and he found it in emptiness. No radio man was waiting him there, nor even a body to show the loser of an unequal battle. But there was blood on the door-jamb where a body—the man's body, Thorpe was sure—had been smashed against the wood. A wisp of black hair in the blood gave its mute evidence of the hopeless fight. And the slime, like the trails on the deck, smeared with odorous vileness the whole room.

Thorpe went again to the deck, and, as on the other ship, he breathed deeply to rid his lungs and nostrils of the abhorrent stench. The ensign in charge of the boarding party approached.

"What kind of a rotten mess is this?" he demanded. "The ship is filthy and not a soul on board. Not a man of them, officers or crew, and the boats are all here. It's absolutely amazing, isn't it?"

"No," Thorpe told him, "about what we expected. What do you make of this?" He touched with his foot a broad trail that shone wet in the *Bennington's* lights.

"The Lord knows," said the ensign in wonder. "It's all over and it smells like a rotten dead fish. Well, we will be going back, sir." He called to a petty officer to round up the men, and the boat was brought alongside.

Their return to the *Bennington* again through a pathway of light that Thorpe knew was safe under the black muzzles of the destroyer's guns.

Or was it, he asked himself. Safe! Was anything safe from this devilish mystery that could pluck each cowering human from the lowest depths of this steel freighter, that could drag her down in the water till the radio man sent his cry: "We are sinking! . . ."

He told Brent quietly, after the ensign had reported, of the struggles in the wireless room and its few remaining traces. And he watched with the commander through the hour of darkness while the *Bennington* steamed in slow circles about the abandoned hulk, while her search-lights played endlessly over the empty waters and the men at the guns cast wondering glances at their skipper who ordered such strange procedure when no danger was there.

With daylight the scene lost its sense of mysterious threat, and Thorpe was eager to return to the abandoned ship.

"I might find something," he said, "some trace or indication of what we have to fight."

"I must leave," said Commander Brent. "Oh, I'm coming back, never fear," he added, at the look of dismay on Thorpe's face. The thought of leaving this mystery unsolved was more than that young seeker after adventure could accept.

"I'm coming back," Brent repeated. "I've been in communication with the Admiral—Honolulu has relayed the messages through. All code, of course; we mustn't alarm the whole Pacific with our nightmares. The old man says to stick around and get the low-down on this damn thing."

"Then why leave?" objected Thorpe.

"Because I am coming around to your way of thinking, Thorpe. Because I am as certain as can be that we have a monster of some sort to deal with . . . and because I haven't any depth charges. I want to run up to the supply station at Honolulu and get a couple of ash-cans of TNT to lay on top of the brute if we sight him."

"Glory be!" said Thorpe fervently. "That sounds like business. Go and get your eggs and perhaps we can feed them to this devil— raw. . . . And I think I'll stay here, if you will be back by dark."

"Better not," the other objected; but Thorpe overruled him.

"This thing attacks in the dark," he said. "I will lay a little bet on that. It left the orang-outang on the *Minnie R.*—quit at the first sign of daylight. I will be safe through the day, and besides, the beast has gutted this ship. It won't return, I imagine. And if I stay there for the day—live as they lived, the men who manned that ship—I may have some information that will be of help when you get back. But for Heaven's sake, Brent, don't stop to pick any flowers on the way."

"It's your funeral," said Brent not too cheerfully. "The old man said to give you every assistance, and perhaps that includes helping you commit suicide."

But Robert Thorpe only laughed as Commander Brent gave his orders for a small boat to be lowered. A ship's lantern and rockets for night signals were taken at the officer's orders. "We'll be back before dark," he said, "but take these as a precaution."

One favor Thorpe asked—that the ship's carpenter go over with him and help him to make a strong-barred retreat of the wireless cabin.

"And I'll talk to you occasionally," he told Brent. "I tried the key while I was aboard; the wireless is working on its batteries."

He waved a cheery good-by as the small boat pulled away. "And hurry back," he called. The destroyer commander nodded an emphatic assent.

On board the *Nagasaki Maru*, Thorpe directed the carpenter and his helpers in the work he wanted done. The man seemed to know instinctively where to put his hands on needed supplies, and the result was a virtual cage of strong oak bars enclosing the wireless room, and braces of oak to bar the single door. Thorpe was not assuming any bravado in his feeling of safety, but he was doing what he had done in many other tight corners, and he prepared his defences in advance.

These included weapons of offense as well. As the boat with the destroyer's men pulled back to the *Bennington*, he placed in easy reach in a corner of the room a heavy calibered rifle he had taken from his belongings.

And, still, with all his feeling of security, there was a strange depression fell upon him when the *Bennington's* narrow hull was small upon the horizon, and then that, too, was gone and only the heaving swells and the wallowing hulk were his companions.

Only these? He shivered slightly as he thought of that unseen watcher with the devil-eyes whose presence Captain Wilkins had felt—and his men, and the poor terrified ape! He deliberately put from his mind the thought of this; no use to start the day with morbid fears. He went below to examine the cabins. But he carried the heavy elephant gun with him wherever he went.

Below decks the signs of the marauder were everywhere, yet there was little to be learned. The slimy trails dried quickly and vanished, but not before Thorpe had traced them to the uttermost depths of the ship.

There was not a nook or corner that had gone unsearched in the horrible quest for human food. And one thing impressed itself forcibly upon the man's mind. He found a lantern, and he used it of necessity in his explorations, but this thing had gone through the dark and with unerring certainty had found its way to every victim.

"Can it see in the dark?" Thorpe questioned. "Or. . . ." He visioned dimly some denizen of the vast depths, living beyond the limits of the sun's penetration, far in the abysmal darkness where its only light must be self-made. But his mind failed in the attempt to picture what manner of horror this thing might be.

Even in the hold its evil traces were found. There were tiers of metal drums that still shone wet in his lantern's light. Calcium carbide—for making acetylene, he supposed—marked "Made in U.S.A." The *Nagasaki* must have been westward bound.

He went, after an hour or so, to the wireless room, and only when he relaxed in the safety of his improvised fortress did he realize how tense had been every nerve and muscle through his long search. He tried the wireless and got an instant response from the destroyer.

"Don't shoot it too fast," he spelled out slowly to the distant operator: "I am only a dub. Just wanted to say hello and report all O.K."

"Fine," was the steady, careful response. "We have had a little trouble with our condensers—" There was a short pause, then the message continued, this portion dictated by the commander. "Delay not important. We will be back as agreed. Have picked up *S. S. Adelaide* bound east in your latitude. Warned her to take northerly course account derelict. See you later. Signed, Brent, commanding *U. S. S. Bennington*."

The man in the barred room tapped off his acknowledgement and closed the key. He suddenly realized he had had no breakfast, and the hours had been slipping past. He took his gun again and went down to the galley to prepare some coffee. It was not the time or place for an enjoyable meal, but he would have relished it more had he not pictured the *Adelaide* and her lovely owner steaming across these threatening seas.

He knew the captain of the *Adelaide*. "Obstinate pigheaded old Scotchman!" "Hope he takes Brent's advice. Of course Brent couldn't tell him the truth. We can't blat this wild yarn all over the air or the passenger lines would have our scalps. But I wish the *Adelaide* was safe in Manila."

His explorations in the afternoon were half-hearted and perfunctory. There was nothing more to be learned. But he had seen in his mind some vague outline of what they must meet. He saw a something, mammoth, huge, that could grasp and hold an ocean freighter—against whose great body he had seen the waves dash in a line of white spray. Yet a something that could force its way down narrow passages, could press with terrific strength on bolted doors and crush them inward, wrecked and splintered. Some serpentine thing that felt and saw its way and crawled so surely through the dark—found its prey—seized it—and carried off a man as easily as it might a mouse.

No octopus, no matter what proportions, filled the description. He gave up trying to see too clearly the awful thing. And he kept away from the ship's rail when once he had ventured near. For there had come to him a feeling of fear that had sent the waves of cold trickling and prickling up his spine. Was there something really there? . . . A waiting lurking horror in the depths?

"The eyes," he thought, "the eyes! . . ." And he went more quickly than he knew to his barred retreat where again he might breathe quietly.

The position of the deserted ship was south of the regular steamer lanes on the Trans-Pacific run. Only a trace of smoke on the northern horizon marked through the afternoon the passage of other craft. It was a long and lonely vigil for the waiting man. But the *Bennington* would return, and he listened in at intervals hoping to hear her friendly signal.

The batteries operating the *Nagasaki's* wireless were none too strong; Thorpe saved their strength, though he tried at times to raise the *Bennington* somewhere beyond his reach.

The sun was touching the horizon when he got his first response. "Keep up the old nerve," admonished the slow, careful sending of the *Bennington's* operator. "We have been delayed but we are on our way. Signed, Brent."

The man in the wireless room placed the oak bars across the door, and tried to believe he was nonchalant and unafraid as he laid out extra clips of cartridges. But his eyes persisted in following the sinking sun, and he watched from within his cage the coming of the quick dark.

The protecting glare of day must be unbearable to this monster from the lightless depths, and daylight was vanishing. Thorpe's mind was searching for additional means of defense. He found it in the cargo he had seen. The drums of carbide! He could scatter it on the deck—it reacted with water, and those slimy arms, if they came and touched it, could find the contact hot. He took his lantern and went hastily below to stagger back with a drum upon his shoulder.

In the half-light that was left him he forced the cover and then rolled the drum about the swaying deck. The gray, earthly lumps of carbide formed erratic lines. Useless perhaps, he admitted, but the threatening dark forced the man to use every means at his command.

He was scattering the contents of a second drum when he stiffened abruptly to rigid attention.

The ship, thrown broadside to the wide-spaced swells, had rolled endlessly with a monotonous motion. But now the deck beneath him was steadying. It assumed an abnormal levelness. The boat rose and fell with the waves, but it no longer rolled. There was something beneath holding, drawing on it.

Thorpe knew in that frozen second what it meant. The drum clattered to the rail as he dashed for his room. Gun in hand, he watched with staring eyes where the deserted deck showed dim and vague in the light of the stars and the bow of the ship was lost in the uncertain dark of night.

Wide-eyed he watched into the blackness, and he listened with desperate attention for some slightest sound beyond the splashing of waves and the creaking of spars.

Far in the west a light appeared, to glow and vanish and glow again in the tumbling waters. The *Bennington!* His heart leaped at the thought, then sank as he knew the destroyer's lights would not appear from that direction.

Through a slow hour that seemed an eternity the oncoming ship drew near, and he knew with a sudden, startling certainty that it was the *Adelaide*—and Ruth Allaire—coming on, through into the horror awaiting.

He leaned forward tensely as a sound reached his ears. A ghostly echo of a sound, like the softest of smooth, slipping fabric upon hard steel. And as he listened, before his staring eyes, a something came between him and the lighted yacht.

It wavered and swung in the darkness. It was formless, uncertain of outline, and it swung in the night out beyond the ship's rail till it suddenly neared, waved high overhead, and the cold light of the stars shone in pale reflection from an enormous, staring eye.

It surmounted a serpentine form that took shape in the dim radiance without and came lower in undulating folds to crash heavily upon the deck.

Thorpe's hand was upon the wireless key. He had wanted to warn off the yacht, but not till the thud of the creature on the bare deck proved its reality could he force his cold fingers to press the key.

Then, fast as his inexperience allowed, he called frantically for the *Adelaide*. He spelled her name, over and over. . . . Would the sleepy operator never answer?

The *Bennington* broke in one. "Is that you, Thorpe? What is up?" they demanded.

But Thorpe kept up his slow spelling of the yacht's name. He must get a warning to them! Then he realized that the *Bennington* could do it better.

"*Bennington*," he called, "*Adelaide* approaching. I am attacked. Warn them off. Warn them—" His frantic, hissing dots and dashes died immediately. Beneath his feet the *Nagasaki Maru* was rolling again, swinging free to the lift and thrust of the swells beneath.

"Good God!" he shouted aloud in his lonely cabin. "It's gone for the yacht. *Adelaide*—turn north—full speed—" he clicked off on a slow, stuttering key. "Head north. You are being attacked!" He groaned again as he saw the *Adelaide's* shining ports swing away from the safety of the north; the ship broached broadside to the waves and came slowly to a stop.

"*Bennington*," he radioed. "Brent—it has got the *Adelaide*. Help—hurry! I am going over."

He tore wildly at the barred door, and he made a dash across the deck to slip sprawling in a heap against the rail where the slimy traces of the recent visitor stretched glistening on the deck.

How he lowered the boat Thorpe never knew. But he knew there was one that the men from the *Bennington* had swung over the side, and tore madly at the tackle to let the boat crash miraculously upright into the sea. He slung the rifle about his neck with a rope end—there were cartridges in his pocket—and he went down the dangling lines and cast off in a frenzy of haste.

What could he do? He hardly dared form the question. Only this stood clear and unanswerable in his mind: The yacht was in the monster's grip, and Ruth Allaire was there on board. Ruth Allaire, so smiling, so friendly, so lovable! Food for that horror from the depths. . . . He rowed with super-human strength to drive the heavy boat across the wave-swept distance that separated them.

Between gasping breaths he turned at times to glance over his shoulder and correct his course. And now, as he drew near, he saw though indistinct the unmistakable, snakelike weaving of horrible tenuous fingers, rolling and groping about the yacht.

They were plain as he drew alongside. The trim ship rose and fell with the water, while over her side where Thorpe approached swung a long, white monstrous rope of flesh. It retreated like the lash of a whip, and the horrified watcher saw as it went the struggling figure of a man in the grasp of flabby lips. And above them a single eye glared wickedly.

Another vile, twisting arm rose from the afterdeck with a screaming figure in its grasp and vanished into the water beyond the yacht. There were others writhing about the decks. Thorpe saw them as he made his boat fast and clambered aboard.

A wave of reeking air enveloped him as he reached the deck; the nauseous stench from the monster's tentacles was horrible beyond endurance. He gagged and choked as the stifling breath entered his lungs.

A huge rope of slippery, throbbing flesh stretched its twisted length toward the stern. It contracted as he watched into bulging muscular rings and withdrew from the afterdeck. The deadly end of it stopped in mid-air not twenty feet from where he stood. The jawlike pincers on it held the limp form of an officer in its sucking grip, while above, in a protuberance like a gnarled horn, a great eye glared into Thorpe's with devilish hatred.

The beak opened sharply to drop its unconscious burden upon the deck, and the watching man, petrified with horror, saw within the gaping maw great sucking discs and beyond them a brilliant glow. The whole cavernous pit was aflame with phosphorescent light. Dimly he knew that this light explained the ability of the beastly arms to grope so surely in the dark.

The eye narrowed as the gaping, fleshy jaws distended, and Robert Thorpe, in a flash that galvanized him to action, was aware that his fight for life was on. He fired blindly from the hip, and the recoil of the heavy gun almost tore it from his hands. But he knew he had aimed true, and the toothless, seeking jaws whipped in agony back into the sea.

There were other arms whose eyes were searching the stern of the yacht. Thorpe plunged frenziedly down a companionway for the cabin he knew was Ruth Allaire's. Was he in time? Could he save her if he found her? His mind was in a turmoil of half-formed plans as he rushed madly down the corridor to find the body of the girl a limp huddle across the threshold of her cabin.

She was alive; he knew it as he swung her soft body across one shoulder and staggered with his burden up the stairs. If he could only breathe! His throat was tight and strangling with the reeking putrescence in the air. And before his eyes was a picture of the strong oak bars of his own retreat. Somehow, some way, he must get back to the abandoned ship.

An eye detected him as he came on deck, and he dropped the limp body of the girl at his feet as he swung his rifle toward the glowing light within the opening jaws. The sucking discs cupped and wrinkled in dread readiness in the fleshy, toothless opening. He emptied the magazine into the head, though he knew this was only a feeler and a feeder for a still more horrible mouth in the monstrous body that rose and fell tremendously in the dark waters beyond. But it was typical of Robert Thorpe that even in the horror and frenzy of the moment he rammed another clip of cartridges into his rifle before he stooped to again raise the prostrate figure of Ruth Allaire.

The forward deck for the moment was clear; it rose high with the weight of the writhing, twisting arms that weighed down the stern of the yacht where the crew had taken refuge.

To think of helping them was worse than folly—he dismissed the thought as another great eye came over the rail. Once more he used the gun, then lowered the girl to the waiting boat, and cast off and rowed with the stealthiest of strokes into the dark.

Behind him were whipping points of light above the white brilliance of the yacht *Adelaide*. The boat was tossing in great waves that came from beyond, where a body, incredibly huge, was tearing the waters to foam. There were ghostly arms that shone in slimy wetness, that lashed searchingly in all directions, as the monster gave vent to its fury at Thorpe's attack. There were screaming human figures grasped in many of the jaws, and the man was glad with a great thankfulness that the girl's stupor could save her from the frightful sight.

He dared to row now, and his breath was coming in great choking sobs of sheer exhaustion when at last he pulled the senseless form of Ruth Allaire to the deck of the *Nagasaki* and drew her within the frail shelter of the wireless room.

Stout had the oaken bars appeared, and safe his refuge in the barricaded room, but that was before he had seen in horrible reality the fearful fury of this monster from the deep. He placed the braces against the door and turned with hopeless haste to seize the wireless key.

"*Bennington*," he called, and the answer came strong and clear. "Where are you. . . . Help—" His fingers froze upon the key and the answering message in his ears was unheeded as he watched across the water the destruction of the yacht.

This craft that had dared to resist the onset of the brute, to fight against it, to wound it, was feeling the full fury of the monster's rage. The gleaming lights of the doomed ship were waving lines that swept to and fro in the grip of those monstrous arms. The boat beneath Thorpe's feet was tossing in the waves that told of the titanic struggle. He had meant to look south for some sign of the oncoming destroyer, but in fearful fascination he stared spellbound where the masts of the trim yacht swept downward into the waves, where the green of her starboard lantern glowed faintly for an instant, then vanished, to leave only the darkness and the starlit sea.

A voice aroused him from his stupefaction. "Where am I . . . where am I?" Ruth Allaire was asking in a frightened whisper. "That terrible thing—" She shuddered violently as memory returned to show again the horror she had witnessed. "Where are we, Robert? And the *Adelaide*—where is it?"

Thorpe turned slowly. The insane turmoil of the past hour had numbed his brain, stunned him.

"The *Adelaide*—" he mumbled, and groped fumblingly for coherent thoughts. He stared at the girl. She was half-risen from the floor where he had laid her, and the sight of her quivering face brought reason again to his mind. He knelt tenderly beside her and raised her in his arms.

"Where is the yacht?" she repeated. "The *Adelaide*?"

"Gone," Thorpe told her. "Lost!" A thought struck him.

"Was your father on board, Ruth?"

Ruth was dazed.

"Lost," she repeated. "The *Adelaide*—lost! . . . No," she added in belated response to Thorpe's question. "Daddy was not there. But the men—Captain MacPherson . . . that horrible monster. . . ." She buried her face in her hands as she realized what Thorpe's silence meant.

He held the trembling figure close as the girl whispered: "Where are we, Robert? Are we safe?"

"We may win through yet," he told her through grim, set lips. He realized abruptly that he was seeing the face of Ruth Allaire in the light. He had left a lantern burning! He withdrew his arms from about her and sprang quickly to his feet to put out the tell-tale light. In darkness and quiet was their only safety. And he knew as he sprang that he had waited too long. A soft body crashed heavily on the deck outside.

The girl's voice was shrill with terror as she began a question. Thorpe's hand pressed upon her lips in the dark where he stood waiting—waiting.

A luminous something was glowing outside the cabin. It searched and prodded about the deserted deck to whip upward at the audible hiss of wet carbide. Another appeared; the rifle came slowly to the man's shoulder as a pair of jaws gaped glowingly beyond the windows and an eye stared unblinkingly from its horn-like sheath. It crashed madly against the walls of the wireless room to shatter the glass and make kindling of the woodwork of the sash. Thorpe fired once and again before the specter vanished, and he knew with sickening certainty that the wounds were only messages to some central brain that would send other ravening tentacles against them. But the oak bars had held.

He reached in the brief interval for the key, and he sent out one final call for help. He strained his ears against the head-set for some friendly human word of hope.

"—rocket," the wireless man was saying. "Fire rockets. We can't find—" A swift, writhing arm wrapped crushingly about the cabin as the message ceased.

Thorpe seized his rifle and fired into the gray mass that bulged with terrible muscular contractions through the window. He fired again to aim lengthways of the arm and inflict as damaging a wound as his weapon would permit.

The arm relaxed, but a score of others took up the attack. Again the sickening stench was about them as gaping jaws gleamed fiery beneath the hateful eyes and tore at the flimsy structure. Thorpe jammed more cartridges into the gun and fired again and again, then dropped the weapon to fumble for the rockets that Brent had given him.

He lighted one with trembling fingers; the first ball shot straight into a waiting mouth. Another ignited a searing flame of acetylene gas where a wet arm writhed in the hot carbide trail. The man leaned far out through the broken window.

No time to look around. He let the red flares stream upward high into the air, then dropped the rocket hissing on the deck to seize once more the rifle.

A mass of muscle crashed against the door; it went to splinters under the impact, and only the two oak bars remained to hold in check the horrible tentacles and the darting heads. One mouth closed to a pointed end that forced its way between the bars. The oak gave under the strain as Robert Thorpe pulled vainly at an empty gun. Beside him rose shrieks of terror as the monstrous thing came on, and Thorpe beat with frantic fury with his clubbed rifle at the fleshy snout.

He knew as he swung the weapon that the shrieks had ceased, then smiled grimly in the numbing horror as he realized that Ruth Allaire was beside him. A piece of oak was in her hands, and she was striking with desperate and silent fury at the slimy flesh.

It was the end, Thorpe knew, and suddenly he was glad. The nightmare was over, and the end was coming with this girl beside him. But Robert Thorpe was fighting on to the last, and he tried to make his blows reach outward to the hateful devilish eye.

He saw it plainly now, for the deck was a glare of white light. He saw the eye and the thick arm behind it and the score of others that made a heaving, knotted mass were brilliant and wetly shining. He could see now how best to strike, and he turned his gun to thrust with the barrel at the eye.

It withdrew before his stroke—the jaws slid backward to the deck. There were sounds that hammered at his ears. "The guns! The guns!" a girl was screaming. Across the deck, where a search-light played, huge arms were lashing backward toward the sea. The waves beyond had vanished where a monstrous body shone wetly black in a blinding glare.

And the man hung panting, helpless, on the one remaining bar across the doorway to look where, beyond, her forward guns a spit-ting stream of staccato flashes, the *Bennington* tore the waves to high-thrown spray. Her four clean funnels swung far over as the slim ship, with her stabbing, crashing guns, swung in a sweeping circle to bear down upon the black bulk slowly sinking in the search-light's glare.

The vast body had vanished as the destroyer shot like one of her own projectiles over the spot where the beast had lain. And then, where she had passed, the sea arose in a heaving mound. The big ship beneath the watching man shuddered again as an-other depth charge grumbled its challenge to the master of the deeps.

The warship went careening on an arc to return and throw the full glare of her search-lights on the scene. They lighted a vast sea, strangely stilled. An oily smoothness leveled waves and ironed them out to show more clearly the convulsions of a torn mass that rose slowly into sight.

Thorpe in some way found himself outside the cabin. And he knew that the girl was again beside him as he stared and stared at what the waters held. A bloated serpent form beyond believing was struggling in the greasy swell. Its waving tentacles again were flung aloft in impotent fury, and, beneath them, where their thick ends jointed the body, a head with one horrible eye rose into the air. A thick-lipped mouth gaped open, and the gleam of molars shone white in the blinding glare.

The twisting body shuddered throughout its vast bulk, and the waving arms and futile staring eyes dropped helpless into the splashing sea. Again the revolting head was raised as the destroyer sent a rain of shells into its fearful mass. Once more the oily seas were calm. They closed over the whirling vortex where a denizen of the lightless depths was returning to those distant, subterranean caverns—returning as food for what other voracious monsters might still exist.

The man's arm was about the figure of the girl, trembling anew in a fresh reaction from the horror they had escaped, when a small boat drew alongside.

"They're safe," a hoarse voice bellowed back to the destroyer, and a man came monkeywise up a rope where Thorpe had launched his boat.

And now, as one in a dream, Thorpe allowed the girl to be taken from him, to be lowered to the waiting boat. He clambered down himself and in silence was rowed across to the destroyer.

"Thank God!" said Brent, as he met them at the rail. "You're safe, old man . . . and Miss Allaire . . . both of you! You let off that rocket just in time; we couldn't pick you up with our light—

"And now," he added, "we're going back; back to San Diego. The Admiral wants a word of mouth report."

Thorpe stilled him with a heavy gesture. "Give Ruth an opiate," he said dully. "Let her forget . . . forget! . . . Good God, can we ever forget—" He stumbled forward, heedless of Brent's arm across his shoulders as the surgeon took the girl in charge.

Admiral Struthers, U.S.N., leaned back from his desk and blew a cloud of smoke thoughtfully toward the ceiling. He looked silently from Thorpe to Commander Brent.

"If either one of you had come to me with such a report," he said finally, "I would have found it incredible; I would have thought you were entirely insane, or trying some wild hoax."

"I wish it were a damn lie," said Thorpe quietly. "I wish I didn't have to believe it." There were new lines about the young-old eyes, lines that spoke what the lips would not confess of sleepless nights and the impress of a picture he could not erase.

"Well, we have kept it out of the papers," said the Admiral. "Said it was a derelict, and the wild messages floating about were from an inexperienced man, frightened and irresponsible. Bad advertising—very—for the passenger lines."

"Quite," Commander Brent agreed, "but of course Mr. Thorpe may want to use this in his next book of travel. He has earned the right without doubt."

"No," said Thorpe emphatically. "No! I told you, Brent, there was often a factual basis for fables—remember? Well, we have proved that. But sometimes it is best to leave the fables just fables. I think you will agree." A light step sounded in the corridor beyond. "Nothing of this to Miss Allaire," he said sharply.

The men rose as Ruth Allaire entered the room. "We were just speaking," said the Admiral with an engaging smile beneath his close-cut mustache, "of the matter of a bet. Mr. Thorpe has won handily, and he has taught me a lesson."

He took a check book from his desk. "What charity would you like to name, Miss Allaire? That was left to you, you remember."

"Some seamen's home," said Ruth Allaire gravely. "You will know best, if you two are really serious about that silly bet."

"That bet, my dear," said Robert Thorpe with smiling eyes, "was very serious . . . and it has had most serious consequences." He turned to the waiting men and extended a hand in farewell.

"We are going to Europe, Ruth and I," he told them. "Just rambling around a bit. Our honeymoon, you know. Look us up if you're cruising out that way."

THE CAVE OF HORROR
Captain S. P. Meek
1930

Dr. Bird looked up impatiently as the door of his private laboratory in the Bureau of Standards swung open, but the frown on his
face changed to a smile as he saw the form of Operative Carnes of
the United States Secret Service framed in the doorway.

"Hello, Carnes," he called cheerfully. "Take a seat and make
yourself at home for a few minutes. I'll be with you as soon as I
finish getting this weight."

Carnes sat on the edge of a bench and watched with admiration the long nervous hands and the slim tapering fingers of the
famous scientist. Dr. Bird stood well over six feet and weighed two
hundred and six pounds stripped: his massive shoulders and heavy
shock of unruly black hair combined to give him the appearance of
a prize-fighter—until one looked at his hands. Acid stains and scars
could not hide the beauty of those mobile hands, the hands of an
artist and a dreamer. An artist Dr. Bird was, albeit his artistry ex-
pressed itself in the most delicate and complicated experiments in
the realms of pure and applied science that the world has ever seen,
rather than in the commoner forms of art.

The doctor finished his task of weighing a porcelain crucible,
set it carefully into a dessicator, and turned to his friend.

"What's on your mind, Carnes?" he asked. "You look worried.
Is there another counterfeit on the market?"

The operative shook his head.

"Have you been reading those stories that the papers have been
carrying about Mammoth Cave?" he asked.

Dr. Bird emitted a snort of disgust.

"I read the first one of them part way through on the strength of its being an Associated Press dispatch," he replied, "but that was enough. It didn't exactly impress me with its veracity, and, from a viewpoint of literature, the thing was impossible. I have no time to pore over the lucubrations of an inspired press agent."

"So you dismissed them as mere press agent work?"

"Certainly. What else could they be? Things like that don't happen fortuitously just as the tourist season is about to open. I suppose that those yarns will bring flocks of the curious to Kentucky though: the public always responds well to sea serpent yarns."

"Mammoth Cave has been closed to visitors for the season," said Carnes quietly.

"What?" cried the doctor in surprise. "Was there really something to those wild yarns?"

"There was, and what is more to the point, there still is. At least there is enough to it that I am leaving for Kentucky this evening, and I came here for the express purpose of asking you whether you wanted to come along. Bolton suggested that I ask you: he said that the whole thing sounded to him like magic and that magic was more in your line than in ours. He made out a request for your services and I have it in my pocket now. Are you interested?"

"How does the secret service cut in on it?" asked the doctor. "It seems to me that it is a state matter. Mammoth Cave isn't a National Park."

"Apparently you haven't followed the papers. It *was* a state matter until the Governor asked for federal troops. Whenever the regulars get into trouble, the federal government is rather apt to take a hand."

"I didn't know that regulars had been sent there. Tell me about the case."

"Will you come along?"

Dr. Bird shook his head slowly.

"I really don't see how I can spare the time, Carnes," he said. "I am in the midst of some work of the utmost importance and it hasn't reached the stage where I can turn it over to an assistant."

"Then I won't bother you with the details," replied Carnes as he rose.

"Sit down, confound you!" cried the doctor. "You know better than to try to pull that on me. Tell me your case, and then I'll tell you whether I'll go or not. I can't spare the time, but, on the other hand, if it sounds interesting enough. . . ."

Carnes laughed.

"All right, Doctor," he said, "I'll take enough time to tell you about it even if you can't go. Do you know anything about it?"

"No. I read the first story half way through and then stopped. Start at the beginning and tell me the whole thing."

"Have you ever been to Mammoth Cave?"

"No."

"It, or rather they, for while it is called Mammoth Cave it is really a series of caves, are located in Edmonson County in Central Kentucky, on a spur railroad from Glasgow Junction on the Louisville and Nashville Railroad. They are natural limestone caverns with the customary stalactite and stalagmite formation, but are unusually large and very beautiful. The caves are quite extensive and they are on different levels, so that a guide is necessary if one wants to enter them and be at all sure of finding the way out. Visitors are taken over a regular route and are seldom allowed to visit portions of the cave off these routes. Large parts of the cave have never been thoroughly explored or mapped. So much for the scene.

"About a month ago a party from Philadelphia who were motoring through Kentucky, entered the cave with a regular guide. The party consisted of a man and his wife and their two children, a boy of fourteen and a girl of twelve. They went quite a distance back into the caves and then, as the mother was feeling tired, she and her husband sat down, intending to wait until the guide showed the children some sights which lay just ahead and then return to them. The guide and the children never returned."

"What happened?"

"No one knows. All that is known is the bare fact that they have not been seen since."

"A kidnapping case?"

"Apparently not, in the light of later happenings, although that was at first thought to be the explanation. The parents waited for some time. The mother says that she heard faint screams in the distance some ten minutes after the guide and the children left, but they were very far away and she isn't sure that she heard them at all. At any rate, they didn't impress her at the time.

"When half an hour had passed they began to feel anxious, and the father took a torch and started out to hunt for them. The usual thing happened; he got lost. When *he* failed to return, the mother, now thoroughly alarmed, made her way, by some uncanny sense of direction, to the entrance and gave the alarm. In half an hour a dozen search parties were on their way into the cave. The father was soon located, not far from the beaten trail, but despite three days of constant search, the children were not located. The only trace of them that was found was a bracelet which the mother identified. It was found in the cavern some distance from the beaten path and was broken, as though by violence. There were no other signs of a struggle.

"When the bracelet was found, the kidnapping theory gained vogue, for John Harrel, the missing guide, knew the cave well and natives of the vicinity scouted the idea that he might be lost. Inspired by the large reward offered by the father, fresh parties began to explore the unknown portions of the cave. And then came the second tragedy. Two of the searchers failed to return. This time there seemed to be little doubt of violence, for screams and a pistol shot were faintly heard by other searchers, together with a peculiar 'screaming howl,' as it was described by those who heard it. A search was at once made toward the spot where the bracelet had been picked up, and the gun of one of the missing men was found within fifty yards of the spot where the bracelet had been discovered. One cylinder of the revolver had been discharged."

"Were there any signs on the floor?"

"The searchers said that the floor appeared to be rather more moist and slimy than usual, but that was all. They also spoke of a very faint smell of musk, but this observation was not confirmed by others who arrived a few moments later."

"What happened next?"

"The Governor was appealed to and a company of the National Guard was sent from Louisville to Mammoth Cave. They took up camp at the mouth of the cave and prevented everyone from entering. Soldiers armed with service rifles penetrated the caverns, but found nothing. Visitors were excluded, and the guardsmen established regular patrols and sentry posts in the cave with the result that one night, when time came for a relief, the only trace that could be found of one of the guards was his rifle. It had not been fired. Double guards were then posted, and nothing happened for several days—and then another sentry disappeared. His companion came rushing out of the cave screaming. When he recovered, he admitted that both he and the missing man had gone to sleep and that he awoke to find his comrade gone. He called, and he says that the answer he received was a peculiar whistling noise which raised all the hair on the back of his neck. He flashed his electric torch all around, but could see nothing. He swears, however, that he heard a slipping, sliding noise approaching him, and he felt that some one was looking at him. He stood it as long as he could and then threw down his rifle and ran for his life."

"Had he been drinking?"

"No. It wasn't delirium either, as was shown by the fact that a patrol found his gun where he had thrown it, but no trace of the other sentry. After this second experience, the guardsmen weren't very eager to enter the cave, and the Governor asked for regulars. A company of infantry was ordered down from Fort Thomas to relieve the guardsmen, but they fared worse than their predecessors. They lost two men the first night of their guard. The regulars weren't caught napping, for the main guard heard five shots fired. They rushed a patrol to the scene and found both of the rifles which had been fired, but the men were gone.

"The officer of the day made a thorough search of the vicinity and found, some two hundred yards from the spot where the sentries had been posted, a crack in the wall through which the body of a man could be forced. This bodycrack had fresh blood on each side of it. Several of his men volunteered to enter the hole and search, but the lieutenant would not allow it. Instead, he armed himself with a couple of hand-grenades and an electric torch and entered himself. That was last Tuesday, and he has not returned."

"Was there any disturbance heard from the crack?"

"None at all. A guard was posted with two machine-guns pointed at the crack in the wall, and a guard of eight men and a sergeant stationed there. Last night, about six o'clock, while the guard were sitting around their guns, a faint smell of musk became evident. No one paid a great deal of attention to it, but suddenly for no apparent reason at all one of the men on guard was jerked into the air feet upwards. He gave a scream of fear, and an unearthly screech answered him. The guard, with the exception of one man, turned tail and ran. One man stuck by his gun and poured a stream of bullets into the crack. The retreating men could hear the rattle of the gun for a few moments and then there was a choking scream, followed by silence. When the officer of the day got back with a patrol, there was a heavy smell of musk in the air, and a good deal of blood was splashed around. The machine-guns were both there, although one of them was twisted up until it looked like it had been through an explosion.

"The Officer commanding the company investigated the place, ordered all men out of the cave, and communicated with the War Department. The Secretary of War found it too tough a nut to crack and he asked for help, so Bolton is sending me down there. Do you think, in view of this yarn, that your experiments can wait?"

The creases on Dr. Bird's high forehead had grown deeper and deeper as Carnes had told his story, but now they suddenly disappeared, and he jumped to his feet with a boyish grin.

"How soon are we leaving?" he asked.

"In two hours, Doctor. A car is waiting for us downstairs and I have reservations booked for both of us on the Southern to-night. I knew that you were coming; in fact, the request for your services had been approved before I came here to see you."

Dr. Bird rapidly divested himself of his laboratory smock and took his coat and hat from a cupboard.

"I hope you realize, Carnsey, old dear," he said as he followed the operative out of the building, "that I have a real fondness for your worthless old carcass. I am leaving the results of two weeks of patient work alone and unattended in order to keep you out of trouble, and I know that it will be ruined when I get back. I wonder whether you are worth it?"

"Bosh!" retorted Carnes. "I'm mighty glad to have you along, but you needn't rub it in by pretending that it is affection for me that is dragging you reluctantly into this mess. With an adventure like this ahead of you, leg-irons and handcuffs wouldn't keep you away from Mammoth Cave, whether I was going or not."

It was late afternoon before Dr. Bird and Carnes dismounted from the special train which had carried them from Glasgow Junction to Mammoth Cave. They introduced themselves to the major commanding the guard battalion which had been ordered down to reinforce the single company which had borne the first brunt of the affair, and then interviewed the guards who had been routed by the unseen horror which was haunting the famous cave. Nothing was learned which differed in any great degree from the tale which Carnes had related to the doctor in Washington, except that the officer of the day who had investigated the last attack failed to entirely corroborate the smell of musk which had been reported by the other observers.

"It might have been musk, but to me it smelled differently," he said. "Were you ever near a rattlesnake den in the west?"

Dr. Bird nodded.

"Then you know the peculiar reptilian odor which such a place gives off. Well, this smell was somewhat similar, although not the same by any manner of means. It was musky all right, but it was more snake than musk to me. I rather like musk, but this smell gave me the horrors."

"Did you hear any noises?"

"None at all. The men describe some rather peculiar noises and Sergeant Jervis is an old file and pretty apt to get things straight, but they may have been made by the men who were in trouble. I saw a man caught by a boa in South America once, and the noises he made might very well have been described in almost the same words as Jervis used."

"Thanks, Lieutenant," replied the Doctor. "I'll remember what you have told me. Now I think that we'll go into the cave."

"My orders are to allow no one to enter, Doctor."

"I beg your pardon. Carnes, where is that letter from the Secretary of War?"

Carnes produced the document. The lieutenant examined it and excused himself. He returned in a few moments with the commanding officer.

"In the face of that letter, Dr. Bird," said the major, "I have no alternative to allowing you to enter the cave, but I will warn you that it is at your own peril. I'll give you an escort, if you wish."

"If Lieutenant Pearce will come with me as a guide, that will be all that I need."

The lieutenant paled slightly, but threw back his shoulders.

"Do you wish to start at once, sir?" he asked.

"In a few moments. What is the floor of the cave like where we are going?"

"Quite wet and slimy, sir."

"Very slippery?"

"Yes, sir."

"In that case before we go in we want to put on baseball shoes with cleats on them, so that we can run if we have to. Can you get us anything like that?"

"In a few moments, sir."

"Good! As soon as we can get them we'll start. In the meantime, may I look at that gun that was found?"

The Browning machine-gun was laid before the doctor. He looked it over critically and sniffed delicately at it. He took from his pocket a phial of liquid, moistened a portion of the water-jacket of the weapon, and then rubbed the moistened part briskly with his hand. He sniffed again. He looked disappointed, and again examined the gun closely.

"Carnes," he said at length, "do you see anything on this gun that looks like tooth marks?"

"Nothing, Doctor."

"Neither do I. There are some marks here which might quite conceivably be finger-prints of a forty-foot giant, and those two parallel grooves look like the result of severe squeezing, but there are no tooth marks. Strange. There is no persistent odor on the gun, which is also strange. Well, there's no use in theorizing: we are confronted by a condition and not a theory, as someone once said. Let's put on those baseball shoes and see what we can find out."

Dr. Bird led the way into the cave, Carnes and the lieutenant following closely with electric torches. In each hand Dr. Bird carried a phosphorus hand-grenade. No other weapons were visible, although the doctor knew that Carnes carried a caliber .45 automatic pistol strapped under his left armpit. As they passed into the cave the lieutenant stepped forward to lead the way.

"I'm going first," said the doctor. "Follow me and indicate the turns by pressure on my shoulder. Don't speak after we have started, and be ready for instant flight. Let's go."

Forward into the interior of the cave they made their way. The iron cleats of the baseball shoes rang on the floor and the noise echoed back and forth between the walls, dying out in little eerie whispers of sound that made Carnes' hair rise. Ever forward they pressed, the lieutenant guiding the doctor by silent pressure on his shoulder and Carnes following closely. For half a mile they went on until a restrainable pressure brought the doctor to a halt. The lieutenant pointed silently toward a crack in the wall before them. Carnes started forward to examine it, but a warning gesture from the doctor stopped him.

Slowly, an inch at a time, the doctor crept forward, hand-grenades in readiness. Presently he reached the crack and, shifting one of the grenades into his pocket, he drew forth an electric torch and sent a beam of light through the crack into the dark interior of the earth.

For a moment he stood thus, and then suddenly snapped off his torch and straightened up in an attitude of listening. The straining ears of Carnes and Lieutenant Pearce could hear a faint slithering noise coming toward them, not from the direction of the crack, but from the interior of the cave. Simultaneously a faint, musky, reptilian odor became apparent.

"Run!" shouted the doctor. "Run like hell! It's loose in the cave!"

The lieutenant turned and fled at top speed toward the distant entrance to the cave, Carnes at his heels. Dr. Bird paused for an instant, straining his ears, and then threw a grenade. A blinding flash came from the point where the missile struck and a white cloud rose in the air. The doctor turned and fled after his companions. Not for nothing had Dr. Bird been an athlete of note in his college days. Despite the best efforts of his companions, who were literally running for their lives, he soon caught up with them. As he did so a weird, blood-curdling screech rose from the darkness behind them. Higher and higher in pitch the note rose until it ended suddenly in a gurgling grunt, as though the breath which uttered it had been suddenly cut off. The slithering, rustling noise became louder on their trail.

"Faster!" gasped the doctor, as he put his hand on Carnes' shoulder and pushed him forward.

The noise of pursuit gained slightly on them, and a sound as of intense breathing became audible. Dr. Bird paused and turned and faced the oncoming horror. His electric torch revealed nothing, but he listened for a moment, and then threw his second grenade. Keenly he watched its flight. It flew through the air for thirty yards and then struck an invisible obstruction and bounded toward the ground. Before it struck the downward motion ceased, and it rose in the air. As it rose it burst with a sharp report, and a wild scream of pain filled the cavern with a deafening roar. The doctor fled again after his companions.

By the time he overtook them the entrance of the cave loomed before them. With sobs of relief they burst out into the open. The guards sprang forward with raised rifles, but Dr. Bird waved them back.

"There's nothing after us, men," he panted. "We got chased a little way, but I tossed our pursuer a handful of phosphorus and it must have burned his fingers a little, judging from the racket he made. At any rate, it stopped the pursuit."

The major hurried up.

"Did you see it, Doctor?" he asked.

"No, I didn't. No one has ever seen it or anything like it. I heard it and, from its voice, I think it has a bad cold. At least, it sounded hoarse, so I gave is a little white phosphorus to make a poultice for its throat, but I didn't get a glimpse of it."

"For God's sake, Doctor, what is it?"

"I can't tell you yet, Major. So far I can tell, it is something new to science and I am not sure just what it looks like. However, I hope to be able to show it to you shortly. Is there a telegraph office here?"

"No, but we have a Signal Corps detachment with us, and they have a portable radio set which will put us in touch with the army net."

"Good! Can you place a tent at my disposal?"

"Certainly, Doctor."

"All right, I'll go there, and I would appreciate it if you would send the radio operator to me. I want to send a message to the Bureau of Standards to forward me some apparatus which I need."

"I'll attend to it, Doctor. Have you any special advice to give me about the guarding?"

"Yes. Have you, or can you get, any live stock?"

"Live stock?"

"Yes. Cattle preferred, although hogs or sheep will do at a pinch. Sheep will do quite well."

"I'll see what I can do, Doctor."

"Get them by all means, if it is possible to do so. Don't worry about paying for them: secret service funds are not subject to the same audit that army funds get. If you can locate them, drive a couple of cattle or half a dozen sheep well into the cave and tether them there. If you don't get them, have your sentries posted well away from the cave mouth, and if any disturbance occurs during the night, tell them to break and run. I hope it won't come out, but I can't tell."

A herd of cattle was soon located and two of the beasts driven into the cave. Two hours later a series of horrible screams and bellowings were heard in the cave. Following their orders the sentries abandoned their posts and scattered, but the noise came no nearer the mouth, and in a few minutes silence again reigned.

"I hope that will be all that will be needed for a couple of days," said the doctor to the commanding officer, "but you had better have a couple more cattle driven in in the morning. We want to keep the brute well fed. Is there a tank stationed at Fort Thomas?"

"No, there isn't."

"Then radio Washington that I want the fastest three-man tank that the army has sent here at once. Don't bother with military channels, radio direct to the Adjutant General, quoting the Secretary of the Treasury as authority. Tell him that it's a rush matter, and sign the message 'Bird' if you are afraid of getting your tail twisted."

Twice more before the apparatus which the doctor had ordered from Washington arrived cattle were driven into the depths of the cave, and twice were the screams and bellowings from the cave repeated. Each time searching parties found the cattle gone in the morning. A week after the doctor's arrival, a special train came up, carrying four mechanics from the Bureau of Standards, together with a dozen huge packing cases. Under the direction of the doctor the cases were unpacked and the apparatus put together. Before the assembly had been completed the tank which had been requested arrived from Camp Meade, and the Bureau mechanics began to install some of the assembled units in it.

The first apparatus which was installed in the tank consisted of an electric generator of peculiar design which was geared to the tank motor. The electromotive force thus generated was led across a spark gap with points of a metallic substance. The light produced was concentrated by a series of parabolic reflectors, directed against a large quartz prism, and thence through a lens which was designed to throw a slightly divergent beam.

"This apparatus," Dr. Bird explained to the Signal Corps officer, who was an interested observer, "is one which was designed at the Bureau for the large scale production of ultra-violet light. There is nothing special about the generator except that it is highly efficient and gives an almost constant electromotive force. The current thus produced is led across these points, which are composed of magnalloy, a development of the Bureau. We found on investigation that a spark gave out a light which was peculiarly rich in ultra-violet rays when it was passed between magnesium points. However, such points could not be used for the handling of a steady current because of lack of durability and ease of fusion, so a mixture of graphite, alundum and metallic magnesium was pressed together with a binder which will stand the heat. Thus we get the triple advantages of ultra-violet light production, durability, and high resistance.

"The system of reflectors catches all of the light thus produced except the relatively small portion which goes initially in the right direction, and directs it on this quartz prism where, due to the refractive powers of the prism, the light is broken up into its component parts. The infra-red rays and that portion of the spectrum which lies in the visible range, that is, from red to violet inclusive, are absorbed by a black body, leaving only the ultra-violet portion free to send a beam through this quartz lens."

"I thought that a lens would absorb ultra-violet light," objected the signal officer.

"A lens made of glass will, but this lens is made of rock crystal, which is readily permeable to ultra-violet. The net result of this apparatus is that we can direct before us as we move in the tank a beam of light which is composed solely of the ultra-violet portion of the spectrum."

"In other words, an invisible light?"

"Yes. That is, invisible to the human eye. The effect of this beam of ultra-violet light in the form of severe sunburn would be readily apparent if you exposed your skin to it for any length of time, and the effects on your eyesight of continued gazing would be apt to be disastrous. It would produce a severe opthalmia and temporary impairment of the vision, somewhat the same symptoms as are observed in snow blindness."

"I see. May I ask what is the object of the whole thing?"

"Surely. Before we can successfully combat this peculiar visitant from another world, it is necessary that we gain some idea of the size and appearance of it. Nothing of the sort has before made its appearance, so far as the annals of science go, and so I am forced to make some rather wild guesses at the nature of the animal. You are probably aware of the fact that the property of penetration possessed by all waves is a function of their frequency, or, perhaps I should say, of their wave-length?"

"Certainly."

"The longer rays of visible light will not penetrate as deeply into a given substance as the shorter ultra-violet rays. This visitor is evidently from some unexplored and, indeed, unknown cavern in the depths of the earth where visible light has never penetrated. Apparently in this cavern the color of the inhabitants is ultra-violet, and hence invisible to us."

"You are beyond my depth, Doctor."

"Pardon me. You understand, of course, what color is? When sunlight, which is a mixture of all colors from infra-red to ultra-violet inclusive, falls oh an object, certain rays are reflected and certain others are absorbed. If the red rays are reflected and all others absorbed, the object appears red to our eyes. If all the rays are reflected, the object appears white, and if all are absorbed, it appears black."

"I understand that."

"The human eye cannot detect ultra-violet. Suppose then, that we have an object, either animate or inanimate, the surface of which reflects only ultra-violet light, what will be the result? The object will be invisible."

"I should think it would be black if all the rays except the ultra-violet were absorbed."

"It would, but mark, I did not say the others were absorbed. Are you familiar with fluorescein?"

"No."

"I think you are. It is the dye used in making changeable silk. If we fill a glass container with a fluorescein solution and look at it by reflected light it appears green. If we look at it by transmitted light, that is, light which has traversed the solution, it appears red. In other words, this is a substance which reflects green light, allows a free passage to red light, and absorbs all other light. This creature we are after, if my theory is correct, is composed of a substance which allows free passage to all of the visible light rays and at the same time reflects ultra-violet light. Do I make this clear?"

"Perfectly."

"Very well, then. My apparatus will project forward a beam of ultra-violet light which will be in much greater concentration than exists in an incandescent electric light. It is my hope that this light will be reflected by the body of the creature to a sufficient to allow me to make a photograph of it."

"But won't your lens prevent the ultra-violet light from reaching your plate?"

"An ordinary lens made of optical glass would do so, but I have a camera here equipped with a rock crystal lens, which will allow ultra-violet light to pass through it practically unhindered, and with very slight distortion. When I add that I will have my camera charged with X-ray film, a film which is peculiarly sensitive to the shorter wave-lengths, you will see that I will have a fair chance of success."

"It sounds logical. Would you allow me to accompany you when you make your attempt?"

"I will be glad of your company, if you can drive a tank. I want to take Carnes with me, and the tank will only hold two besides the driver."

"I can drive a tractor."

"In that case you should master the tricks of tank driving in short order. Get familiar with it and we'll appoint you as driver. We'll be ready to go in to-night, but I am going to wait a day. Our friend was fed last night, and there is less chance he'll be about."

The early part of the next evening was marked by howls and screams coming from the mouth of the cave. As the night wore on the noises were quite evidently coming nearer and the sentries watched the cave mouth nervously, ready to bolt and scatter according to their orders at the first alarm. About two A. M. the doctor and Carnes climbed into the tank beside Lieutenant Leffingwell, and the machine moved slowly into the cave. A search-light on the front of the tank lighted the way for them and, attached to a frame which held it some distance ahead of them, was a luck-less sheep.

"Keep your eye on the mutton, Carnes," cautioned the doctor. "As soon as anything happens to it, shut off the search-light and let me try to get a picture. As soon as I have made my exposures I'll tell you, and you can snap it on again. Lieutenant, when the picture is made, turn your tank and make for the entrance to the cave. If we are lucky, we'll get out."

Forward the tank crawled, the sheep bleating and trying to break loose from the bonds which held it. It was impossible to hear much over the roar of the motor, but presently Dr. Bird leaned forward, his eyes shining.

"I smell musk," he announced. "Get ready for action."

Even as he spoke the sheep was suddenly lifted into the air. It gave a final bleat of terror, and then its head was torn from its body.

"Quick, Carnes!" shouted the doctor.

The searchlight went out, and Carnes and the lieutenant could hear the slide of the ultra-violet light which Dr. Bird was manipulating open. For two or three minutes the doctor worked with his apparatus.

"All right!" he cried suddenly. "Lights on and get out of here!"

Carnes snapped on the searchlight and Lieutenant Leffingwell swung the tank around and headed for the cave mouth. For a few feet their progress was unhindered and then the tank ceased its forward motion, although the motor still roared and the track slid on the cave floor. Carnes watched with horror as one side of the tank bent slowly in toward him. There was a rending sound, and a portion of the heavy steel fabric was torn away. Dr. Bird bent over something on the floor of the tank. Presently he straightened up and threw a small object into the darkness. There was a flash of light, and bits of flaming phosphorus flew in every direction. The anchor which held the tank was suddenly loosed and the machine crawled forward at full speed, while a roar as of escaping air mingled with a bellowing shriek burdened the smoke-laden air.

"Faster!" cried the doctor, as he threw another grenade.

Lieutenant Leffingwell got the last bit of speed possible out of the tank and they reached the cave mouth without further molestation.

"I had an idea that our friend wouldn't care to pass through a phosphorus screen," said Dr. Bird with a chuckle as he climbed out of the tank. "He must have been rather severely burned the other day, and once burned is usually twice shy. Where is Major Brown?"

The commanding officer stepped forward.

"Drive a couple of cattle into the cave, Major," directed Dr. Bird. "I want to fill that brute up and keep him quiet for a while. I'm going to develop my films."

Lieutenant Leffingwell and Carnes peered over the doctor's shoulders as he manipulated his films in a developing bath. Gradually vague lines and blotches made their appearance on one of the films, but the form was indistinct. Dr. Bird dropped the films in a fixing tank and straightened up.

"We have something, gentlemen," he announced, "but I can't tell yet how clear it is. It will take those films fifteen minutes to fix, and then we'll know."

In a quarter of an hour he lifted the first film from the tank and held it to the light. The film showed a blank. With an exclamation of disappointment he lifted a second and third film from the tank, with the same result He raised the fourth one.

"Good Lord!" gasped Carnes.

In the plate could be plainly seen the hindquarters of the sheep held in the grasp of such a monster as even the drug-laden brain of an opium smoker never pictured. Judging from the sheep, the monster stood about twenty feet tall, and its frame was surmounted by a head resembling an overgrown frog. Enormous jaws were opened to seize the sheep but, to the amazement of the three observers, the jaws were entirely toothless. Where teeth were to be expected, long parallel ridges of what looked like bare bone, appeared, without even a rudimentary segregation into teeth. The body of the monster was long and snakelike, and was borne on long, heavy legs ending in feet with three long toes, armed with vicious claws. The crowning horror of the creature was its forelegs. There were of enormous length, thin and attenuated looking, and ended in huge misshapen hands, knobby and blotched, which grasped the sheep in the same manner as human hands. The eyes were as large as dinner plates, and they were glaring at the camera with an expression of fiendish malevolence which made Carnes shudder.

"How does that huge thing ever get through that crack we examined?" demanded the lieutenant.

Dr. Bird rubbed his head thoughtfully.

"It's not an amphibian," he muttered, "as is plainly shown by the shape of the limbs and the lack of a tail, and yet it appears to have scales of the true fish type. It corresponds to no recovered fossil, and I am inclined to believe it is unique. The nervous organization must be very low, judging from the lack of forehead and the general conformation. It has enormous strength, and yet the arms look feeble."

"It can't get through that crack," insisted the lieutenant.

"Apparently not," replied the doctor. "Wait a moment, though. Look at this!"

He pointed to the great disproportion between the length and diameter of the forelegs, and then to the hind legs.

"Either this is grave distortion or there is something mighty queer about that conformation. No animal could be constructed like that."

He turned the film so that an oblique light fell on it. As he did so he gave a cry of astonishment.

"Look here!" he said sharply. "It does get through that crack! Look at those arms and hands! There is the answer. This creature is tall and broad, but from front to rear it can measure only a few inches. The same must be true of the froglike head. That animal has been developed to live and move in a low roofed cavern, and to pass through openings only a few inches wide. Its bulk is all in two dimensions!"

"I believe you're right," said Carnes as he studied the film.

"There is no doubt of it," answered the doctor. "Look at those paws, too, Carnes. That substance isn't bone, it's gum. The thing is so young and helpless that it hasn't cut its teeth yet. It must be a baby, and that is the reason why it made its way into the cave when no other of its kind ever has."

"How large are full grown ones if this is a baby?" asked the lieutenant.

"The Lord alone knows," replied Dr. Bird. "I hope that I never have to face one and find out. Well, now that we know what we are fighting, we ought to be able to settle its hash."

"High explosive?" suggested the lieutenant.

"I don't think so. With such a low nervous organization, we would have to tear it practically to pieces to kill it, and I am anxious to keep it from mutilation for scientific study. I have an idea, but I'll have to study a while before I am sure of the details. Send me the radio operator."

The next day the Bureau mechanics began to dismount the apparatus from the tank and to assemble another elaborate contrivance. Before they had made an end of the work additional equipment arrived from Washington, which was incorporated in the new set-up. At length Dr. Bird pronounced himself ready for the attempt.

Under his direction, three cattle were driven into the cave and there tethered. They were there the next morning unharmed, but the second night the now familiar bellowing and howling came from the depths of the cave and in the morning two of the cattle were gone.

"That will keep him quiet for a day or two," said the doctor, "and now to work!"

The tank made its way into the cave, dragging after it two huge cables which led to an engine-driven generator outside the cave. These cables were attached to the terminals of a large motor which was set up in the cave near the place where the cattle were customarily tethered. This motor was the actuating force which turned two generators, one large and one small. The smaller one was mounted on a platform on wheels, which also contained the spark gaps, the reflectors and other apparatus which produced the beam of ultra-violet light which had been used to photograph the monster.

From the larger generator led two copper bars. One of these was connected to a huge copper plate which was laid flat on the floor of the cave. The other led to a platform which was erected on huge porcelain insulators some fifteen feet above the floor. Huge condensers were set up on this platform, and Dr. Bird announced himself in readiness.

A steer was dragged into the cave and up a temporary runway which led to the platform containing the condensers, and there tied with the copper bus bar from the larger generator fastened to three flexible copper straps which led around the animal's body. When this had been completed, everyone except the doctor, Carnes, and Lieutenant Leffingwell left the cave. These three crouched behind the searchlight which sent a mild beam of ultra-violet onto the platform where the steer was held. The engine outside the cave was started, and the three men waited with tense nerves.

For several hours nothing happened. The steer tried from time to time to move and, finding it impossible, set up plaintive bellows for liberty.

"I wish something would happen," muttered the lieutenant. "This is getting on my nerves.

"Something is about to happen," replied Dr. Bird grimly. "Listen to that steer."

The bellowing of the steer had suddenly increased in volume and, added to the note of discontent, was a note of fright which had previously been absent. Dr. Bird bent over his ultra-violet searchlight and made some adjustments. He handed a helmetlike arrangement to each of his companions and slipped one on over his head.

"I can't see a thing, Doctor," said Carnes in a muffled voice.

"The objects at which you are looking absorb rather than reflect ultra-violet light," said the doctor. "This is a sort of a fluoroscope arrangement, and it isn't perfect at all. However, when the monster comes along, I am pretty sure that you will be able to see it. You may see a little more as your eyes get accustomed to it."

"I can see very dimly," announced the lieutenant in a moment.

Dimly the walls of the cave and the platform before them began to take vague shape. The three stared intently down the beam of ultra-violet light which the doctor directed down the passageway leading deeper into the cave.

"Good Lord!" ejaculated Carnes suddenly.

Slowly into the field of vision came the hideous figure they had seen on the film. As it moved forward a rustling, slithering sound could be heard, even over the bellowing of the steer and the hum of the apparatus. The odor of musk became evident.

Along the floor toward them the thing slid. Presently it reared up on its hind legs and its enormous bulk became evident. It turned somewhat sideways and the correctness of Dr. Bird's hypothesis as to its peculiar shape was proved. All of the bulk of the creature was in two dimensions. Forward it moved, and the horrible human hands stretched forward, while the mouth split in a wide, toothless grin. Nearer the doomed steer the creature approached, and then the reaching hands closed on the animal.

There was a blinding flash, and the monster was hurled backward as though struck by a thunderbolt, while a horrible smell of musk and burned flesh filled the air.

"After it! Quick!" cried the doctor as he sprang forward.

Before he could reach the prostrate creature it moved and then, slowly at first, but with rapidly gaining speed, it slithered over the floor in retreat. Dr. Bird's hand swung through an arc, and there was a deafening crash as a hand-grenade exploded on the back of the fleeing monster.

An unearthly scream came from the creature, and its motion changed from a steady forward glide to a series of convulsive jerks. Leffingwell and Carnes threw grenades, but they went wide of their mark, and the monster began to again increase its speed. Another volley of grenades was thrown and one hit scored, which slowed the monster somewhat but did not arrest the steady forward movement.

"Any more bombs?" demanded the doctor.

"Damn!" he cried as he received negative answers. "The current wasn't strong enough. It's going to get away."

Carnes jerked his automatic from under his armpit and poured a stream of bullets into the fleeing monster. Slower and slower the motion of the creature became, and its movements again became jerky and convulsive.

"Keep it in sight!" cried the doctor. "We may get it yet!"

Cautiously the three men followed the retreating horror, Leffingwell pushing before him the platform holding the ultra-violet ray apparatus. The chase led them over familiar ground.

"There is the crack!" cried the lieutenant.

"Too late!" replied the doctor.

He rushed forward and seized the lower limb of the monster and tried with all his strength to arrest its flight, but despite all that he could do it slid sideways through the crack in the wall and disappeared. A final backward kick of its leg threw the doctor twenty feet against the far wall of the cave.

"Are you hurt, Doctor?" cried Carnes.

"No, I'm all right. Put on your masks and start the gas! Quick! That may stop it before it gets in far!"

The three adjusted gas masks and thrust the mouths of two gas cylinders which were on the light truck into the crack, and opened the valves. The hissing of the gas was accompanied by a thrashing, writhing sound from the bowels of the earth for a few minutes, but the sound retreated and finally died away into an utter silence.

"And that's that!" cried the doctor half an hour later as they took off their gas masks outside the cave. "It got away from us. Carnes, how soon can we get a train back to Washington?"

"What kind of a report are you going to make to the Bureau, Doctor?" asked Carnes as they sat in the smoker of a southern train, headed for the capital.

"I'm not going to put in any report, Carnes," replied the doctor. "I haven't got the creature or any part of it to show, and no one would believe me. I am going to maintain a discreet silence about the whole matter."

"But you have your photograph to show, Doctor, and you have my evidence and Lieutenant Leffingwell's."

"The photograph might have been faked and I might have doped both of you. In any case, your words are no better than mine. No, indeed, Carnes, when I failed to make the current strong enough to kill it outright I made the first of the moves which bind me to silence, although I thought that two hundred thousand volts would be enough.

"The second failure I made was when I missed him with my second grenade, although I doubt if all six would have stopped him. My third failure was when we failed to get a sufficient concentration of cyanide gas into that hole in a hurry. The thing is so badly crippled that it will die, but it may take hours, or even days, for it to do so. It has already made its way so far into the earth that we couldn't reach it by blasting without danger of bringing the whole place down on our heads. Even if we could blast our way into the place it came from I wouldn't dare open a path which would allow Lord only knows what terrible monsters to invade the earth. When the soldiers have finished stopping that crack with ten feet of solid masonry, I think the barrier will hold, even against that critter's papa and mamma and all its relatives. Then Mammoth Cave will be safe for visitors again. That latter fact is the only report which I will make."

"It is a dandy story to go to waste," said Carnes soberly.

"Tell it then, if you wish, and get laughed at for your pains. No, Carnes, you must learn one thing. A man like Bolton, for instance, will implicitly believe that a four leaf clover in his watch-charm will bring him good luck, and that carrying a buckeye keeps rheumatism away from him; but tell him a bit of sober fact like this, attested by three reliable witnesses and a good photograph, and you'll just get laughed at for your pains. I'm going to keep my mouth shut."

"So be it, then!" replied Carnes with a sigh.

FROM OUT OF THE EARTH
Ed Earl Repp
1931

As members of a scientific expedition exploring a newly found canyon in Death Valley, California, for the remains of a prehistoric
member of rhinocerotidae which we knew, by petrified bone fragments recovered from the float, lay somewhere ahead in the blazing silicious walls, we came upon a man, aged, withered, and almost dead from thirst and telling years.

At first glance we grasped that he was a prospector of the old
school, for somehow he had managed to cling to a shovel, pick and
empty canteen even in the face of death that yawned wide for him.

I was the first member of our party to reach his side as he lay
waiting for death to overtake him. Perhaps he was thinking seriously of the new world he was soon to visit, for he had not heard
our approach until I was within a dozen feet of him.

Then with the swiftness of a striking fer-de-lance he suddenly
found some hidden reserve strength in his brittle bones and
snapped himself into a setting posture to cover me with an old 1900
model pistol. Astonished at the unexpected display of hostility, I
halted in my tracks, holding up my hands wildly in a fearful gesture to impress him with my harmlessness. His eyes, half-closed
and filled with sand eyed me from head to foot. Then I spoke in a
trembling voice.

"Take it easy, old man!" I urged, forcing a smile. "We mean
you no harm. We spotted you a half-mile back and came up here to
see what was wrong. You look all in, old timer!"

The automatic pistol hanging at my belt caught his gaze. For a few seconds he appraised it blankly; then the clatter of the others coming up the float caused his eyes to become even more hard. I gaped fearfully into the muzzle of his ancient gun and saw him tug at the hammer with his gnarled thumb.

Realizing that the man meant to kill me, I watched almost in terror. The hammer came back perhaps a quarter of an inch and stuck there on the safety catch. Feebly he tugged at the death device, his strength waning rapidly. The hammer refused to move further, so weak was the thumb behind it.

With a guttural, resigned groan, he lowered his gun and sagged, finally to roll over on his side. His efforts had sapped his reserve strength. He began blubbering like a child in broken, sobbing words.

"Y-y-you've got me at last," he mumbled as I lowered my tired arms and glanced around for the others, "but I-I-didn't do it! I swear I didn't do it. They'll never h-h-hang me! They'll never . . . water . . . *water!*"

The gun dropped from his withered fist and slid down a short incline of gravel. I motioned wildly for my companions. They broke into a run, led by Dr. Frapin, paleontologist in charge, and soon reached the man's side.

As I bathed his wrinkled brow with water from my canteen, I wondered what he had meant by his suspicious words. My conclusion was inevitable that here was a man who had committed a crime; who had accepted us as officers come upon his trail to finally apprehend him.

After a time he ceased his blubbering, whereupon he informed us that his name was Jerome Ackerman. But I could see that it would not be very long until he carried it to his grave. His aged hands trembled and his lower jaw sagged weakly as he reiterated again and again that he had not committed the deed which had caused him, earlier in his life, to become a hunted man, a fugitive from justice. Time after time he asked us if we were officers searching for him. Informing him that we were scientists with no interest in his case beyond casual curiosity, his tongue, dampened with our water, gradually loosened and as though realizing that his end was near he began to unfold what I first expected to be a confession.

Frequently Dr. Frapin plied him with leading questions. On each occasion the dying man, now convinced that we were friends, the only ones he had met in many years of constant dodging his fellow beings, replied intelligently. Even with death standing in the offing, hovering over him like a grim, spectral shadow, he seemed to have full command of his faculties if not over his atrophied body.

Knowing that the man was soon to die, Frapin felt that whatever story he told, would interest the law and perhaps clear up an old mystery. And Dr. Frapin was the kind of a man to pry into the deeper things, being totally unsatisfied with surface indications alone. He was somewhat of a criminologist as a hobby, and handling the man deftly drew the admission that he would have killed me in cold blood, believing that I represented the law, had it not been for his weakness.

I offered a silent prayer of thanks that the hand of God had prevented that and listened, as under Frapin's urging, as he unfolded one of the most amazing tales that I believe has ever come out of the mysterious desert wastes of the Valley of Death. Being the secretary of the expedition, I jotted down, in shorthand, like a court reporter, every word the man muttered.

Presently Dr. Frapin ceased questioning the man. He offered him another drink of water which he refused with a feeble nod of thanks. Then from his parched lips came this tale of privation, death and horrible terror; of a pursuing menace that had plunged down upon him.

"I tell you," he began as soon as his waning strength would permit him, "that I did not kill my three friends, Gundelfinger, Crank and Bright! How can I convince the law and man that I did not kill them as I have been charged? I have told the true facts of the case only to be laughed at, sneered at and cursed. I will tell it again, to you, for as scientists you may believe in me. You may understand that such a thing that brought doom to my friends could materialize. I implore you to accept my word before God that my story is true from beginning to end. I did not kill Gundelfinger, Crank and Bright! Remember that!

"I first became acquainted with them at Tombstone, Arizona. They had prospected many miles of desertland thereabout for gold, with little or no success. Thereupon I befriended them, taking to heart their stories of bad luck, and gave them money until my pockets were almost empty.

"I took them into my confidence and we made plans to prospect in Death Valley, but Gundelfinger's wife lay ill and interfered with our departure. I knew that gold could be found in Death Valley and was anxious to be after it.

"Finally the woman recovered her strength enough to travel. At my expense we put her on a train bound for San Bernardino. We followed it on horseback, arriving at the California town two weeks later. From there the four of us went into hell, leaving the sickly woman in good care.

"It was she, incidentally, who made the first charges that I had murdered her husband and my other two companions to hide, for myself, the rich vein of gold. . . . This woman, whom I had befriended, whose expenses I had paid with the last dregs of my own money, was the one who falsely betrayed me into the hands of the law. . . .

"For weeks and months we wandered over Death Valley, digging here, digging there, the will-o'-the-wisp . . . gold, always beckoning us to peck at the burning earth beyond the next searing ridge.

"The heat was terrifying. The sun beat down upon us without mercy, causing our tongues to become parched and leathery on more than one occasion between distant waterholes.

"Day after day we struggled onward, up blind canyons, over searing flats and blistering mesas, down through dazzling coulees and out over the burning levels again. Always the yellow lure beckoned us to follow to the next saddleback. Death seemed, even as now, to tread the desert beside us. We drank sparingly of our water, half-dead with thirst, to save a few precious drops to dampen our leathery tongues when we attained the next ridge. On and on we went pursuing the mirage of gold.

"At night we heard strange sounds, weird, grotesque sounds, like the breathing of a monster bull, which at times sent us almost into stark insanity. But we managed to keep up our search day after day, my companions helping me, I in turn helping them. We shared together the terrors of Death Valley; we lay close together at night for warmth, for the desert nights are filled with a chill that bites to the marrow of the bones.

"Eventually we came upon a great streak of red tableland that stretched for miles, terrible, merciless miles, in either direction. We mounted a slight incline and entered upon it. As we gained the top it seemed that we had walked deliberately into an open oven, so hot was the terrible blast that struck us. Before long the heat of the soft red asphalt burned through our boots, cooking the soles of our feet.

"Our water began to evaporate in the canteens. Each time we removed the caps for a sparing drink, white wraiths of steam danced forth and escaped into the flaming air."

The Tracks!

He paused for a long moment to get his breath. His ancient lungs seemed to play out almost entirely every few minutes and he was forced to fight for wind. Frapin handed him a canteen and he drank sparingly from it as though hoarding the contents for a time of greater need. Finally he continued.

"For two days we trekked across that tableland toward the distant horizon that loomed up gray and ghostly in the eastern haze. Toward evening of the second day we came upon great, claw-marked tracks stamped deeply in the asphalt.

"They were the foot-prints of some tremendous beast that seemed to have dropped from the sky like a bird, landing on what must have been eight feet and went away again after a moment's pause. Each of its eight prints were imbedded inches deep in the asphalt, showing the great weight of the mysterious creature.

"'That's damn strange, Ackerman!' Gundelfinger said to me as we tarried to inspect the prints. 'I never heard of a critter as large as this!'

"'Nor I, Jim!' I told him frankly. 'And it had eight legs!'

"Crank and Bright appraised the tracks carefully, walked around them and measured the distance between the rear and the front prints. They looked up in astonishment, their faces pale despite their deep tan.

"'Twenty-three feet apart, partners!' they chorused.

"'Whatever made those tracks must've been a giant, Crank!' said Gundelfinger. 'Looks like some prehistoric, eight-legged beast has landed here from the air an' took away again. I think maybe the tracks were made thousands of years ago. I've seen some tracks in Arizony made by dinosaurs millions of years ago!'

"'I think you're wrong,' said Bright, shaking his head. 'Look here!'

"He walked the full length of the tracks, paused and pointed down to the hot asphalt. We followed and stared, Gundelfinger poking lightly at a conical heap with the toe of his boot. The stuff was soft.

"'Droppings!' he said, baffled. 'And no more than a few hours old, else they'd be dry!'

"'And another thing, Jim,' stated Bright. 'To prove that the tracks are not more than a few hours old, is that they're still sharp and clear. If they were old, the asphalt would have dripped oil into the holes, coverin' the prints, an' the edges would have overlapped by now!'

"'I guess you're right, Bright,' Gundelfinger acknowledged. 'They're young prints, by jingo!'

"'But we are getting nowhere, partners,' I reminded them harshly. I was impatient to get off that streak of red tableland. It was too damnably hot, too ghostly, and our water supply would hardly last to the next salt-hole.

"We departed at once and after a half hour's steady hiking we came upon another set of the tracks. Shortly thereafter we saw others until eventually we came upon a section of the tableland that was punctured by countless prints, making the going mighty hard. It was hard to go on without sinking ankle-deep in the holes in the bottom of which were exposed the clear imprints of the giant, clawed feet.

"The monster from hell must have done a dance of death there, else it was some kind of a roosting place for many of them. We hadn't a doubt in our minds but that the monster was from the air. The first set of tracks told us that much. If the thing had not come from the air, it would have left a steady trail as it walked across the blazing asphalt streak. As it was, it seemed to have landed here and there for a short period and then take off again, leaving conical piles that at times reached waist-high wherever it had come down.

"Fearful lest we encounter the monster itself, we banded close together and sped as rapidly as we could across the tableland. Night was falling fast. The sun was setting in the west like a blazing ball. A stiff breeze, as hot as the breath from a furnace, was sweeping over us. On it was an odor, tainting the air with a sickening sweetness, becoming at times, almost nauseating.

"Long after the sun had vanished behind the Funerals we kept on. But the hand of the devil seemed to interfere with our progress and we were forced to stop for the night on the fringe of a heavily tracked area. To go on in the darkness would have meant broken ankles, for the night was almost pitch-black and we could not have seen the deep holes.

"We did not build a fire for the evening meal, though we carried sufficient fuel to boil coffee. From the cans we ate cold beans that had long since been dried by evaporation. After that we placed our blankets close together on the asphalt, but we could not sleep.

"Terrifying sounds reached our ears, menacing hisses that cut the blackness like escaping steam, and dismal sighs that sounded like wind threshing through giant wings, made sleep impossible. The noises would cause any mortal to tremble in his books. They were blood-curdling.

"It must have been exhaustion that finally forced my eyes to close in a troubled, awful slumber. How long I lay in the throes of dreadful nightmares I do not know. But I suddenly awakened with a start.

"I knew that it was a beastly scream that jarred me to life. So human and terrible was it that my heart leaped into my throat as it came again followed by a thunderous roar sounding like stampeding cattle. In the blackness not far away I thought I glimpsed what appeared to be a ghostly monster hovering in the air, but laid the ghastly vision to exhaustion and fear. Then Gundelfinger suddenly spoke.

"'Where's Crank?' he asked in a low, terrified whisper.

"'Isn't he lying beside Bright?' I replied with a shiver.

"Bright emitted a frightened groan before he spoke. 'No, he's not here!' he said. 'He's gone . . . slipped away, for his gun is lying beside me!'

"'Good God!' I breathed fearfully. 'Do you mean that he slipped away with the monster prowling about?'

"'He probably went to investigate the noises,' said Gundelfinger, whispering softly. 'He'll come back!'

"'No, my friend,' I argued. 'Crank would not wander around here without his gun, unless something lured him away.'

"I felt Gundelfinger tremble suddenly as his hand searched for his pistol.

"'Lured away?' he inquired like a man dazed. 'Lured! Good God, I felt something trying to entice me away from here but I fought it off! I felt a terrible urge to go wandering around looking for the thing that seems to be hovering around us. I recall the sensation now. I must have been dozing when I felt it. It was like some invisible power, coaxing, pleading with me to follow an irresistible lure!"

"'Oh, Crank'll show up in time,' said Bright, trying to bolster his courage in the thought, though realizing full well that Crank would never be seen again alive.

"For the rest of the night we lay in breathless terror and listened to the terrifying sounds. I heard no more screams such as come from a human throat. I had no doubt but that Crank had been lured away and sent to his doom with the death cries that had jarred me to life. We listened tensely for sounds of his return and heard no human footfalls.

"Finally the desert became aglow with the rainbow colors of early morning. With the first streaks of dawn we stared around us, amazed that we had lived the night through.

"The tableland was deserted! There was nothing in sight that could have made such awful sounds as throbbed throughout the night in our ears. And Crank seemed to have been swallowed, for he had vanished entirely, leaving no trace.

"What had been his actual fate we could not know then. We did know that he was gone. We could see thirty miles in either direction and not a speck bespoke his presence anywhere on the flat. I did not doubt but that something awful had befallen him, though with the arrival of daylight we felt somewhat secure, and at a loss to know what to do next, we began hiking away from the spot.

"The new day was begun almost as the rising sun came over the eastern ridges. It seemed to pop up suddenly. Then the desert became an oven. As we went away hurriedly we ate dried prunes for breakfast, washing them down with a scant drink of water.

"The tracks were everywhere now. The conical piles of droppings were like prairie-dog mounds, though somewhat higher and more pointed at the top. Somehow Gundelfinger stumbled over a pile of the dung, fell on his face and swore.

"But in falling he had kicked off the top of the pile. We were mystified to find exposed a great, egg-shaped object weighing at least twenty pounds. So hard was it that the butt of a gun could not smash it. The thing was like an oval stone and as white as flour!

"After trying to smash the shell with a gun-butt, Bright finally succeeded in breaking it on a chunk of red rock. To our utter surprise we found, within the thing, a tiny animal scarcely larger than a newborn pup, with eight legs, a dragon-like head and thin, almost undeveloped wings on its sides like the membranes of a flying squirrel.

"It was a vicious little devil and very much alive, as Bright discovered when he tried to fondle the little beast. It opened its savage little mouth and sank needle-like teeth into his hand. With an oath he hurled it from him, killing it instantly.

THE STRIKE!

"'I think I know what it's all about, partners,' he growled. 'Some giant beast, possibly from another world, has been planting its eggs here on this tableland to hatch under the heat of the sun! This is the hottest place this side of hell and from the thickness of the shell it would take a helluva heat to hatch the filthy critters! Let's get away from here before we follow poor Crank!'

"'You're suffering from hallucinations, Jim!' I managed to laugh. 'The heat's got you by the ears! It is not possible for a beast to come here from another world!'

"'Dammit, Jerome!' he snorted heatedly. 'Where else could such an egg-laying monster come from?'

"'I admit it is a mystery, partner,' I told him. 'Yet it does not seem possible. I for one, do not believe that it came through space to this spot.'

"'Maybe Crank was so scared that he just up and bolted,' put in Jim Gundelfinger, squinting at the distant horizons.

"'No,' I said. 'Crank would not dare start across the desert without water.'

"'That's right,' acknowledged Gundelfinger. 'He did not take a canteen!'

"After another five hours of continuous hiking we came to the end of the tableland. Below us stretched the eastern rim of the desert as far as we could see. Our water had given out at noon and now we were burning up with thirst.

"We made our way down the buttresses and started across the scorching sand. In the evening we encountered a spring, running pure water as cold as ice. It was hidden in a little box canyon and we had accidentally stumbled upon it while searching for an easy way out.

"Gundelfinger, his tongue as hard as sun-toughened leather, made a dash for the little pool. I yelled at him to wait until we had tested the water before he drank.

"Having been born and raised in the desertlands of the west, I knew well the danger of drinking water that bubbles up from saline soils. My companions, raised in the east, could not know that nine out of every ten desert springs contain the deadly arsenic poison.

"'Jim!' I called. 'Do not drink the water until we have tested it!'

"'You go to hell!' he rasped back, his voice sounding ghostly as they formed on his dry, leathery tongue. 'You want it for yourself!'

"Despite my warnings he drank deeply and as I watched him for convulsions, he buried both his hands suddenly in the spring and shouted like a mad man.

"'Gold! Gold! Gold!' he cried frenziedly, dousing his hands in the precious water time after time, letting the silt of the bottom dribble through his fingers. The spring became a hole of mud before we recovered from our astonishment and made for it.

"And true enough, the silt was thick with sands of glittering gold! We had accidentally stumbled on life and wealth at the same time, lying together in the bowl of a bubbling spring of pure, untainted water! It was as pure as any I had ever tasted, but we drank it, red with mud.

"After a time the spring cleared. We filled our canteens from it, then with heavy hearts over Crank's disappearance, we began searching for the mother lode from which the particles of gold had come. After a little work we located it several feet above the spring and right under eight inches of volcanic shale.

"It was the richest strike ever made! I know it! The vein where we encountered it was two feet wide and only God knows how deep it ran! We patted Gundelfinger on the back and gave him credit for the strike. He accepted it modestly and together we staked out the claims, including one for Crank. Bright made a map of the location and stuck it in his pocket. Then we started to work on the vein of yellow, virgin gold.

"With my knife I peeled off long slivers of the metal. How brilliantly it glistened in the light of the westering sun! Never had I beheld such a yellow, shining wealth. It made our blood run high in spite of what had befallen our party on the tableland. But Crank was gone and it was beyond our power to bring him back to us."

Dr. Frapin eyed me curiously as the prospector and murder suspect paused again for a drink of water. I shook my head dubiously and tapped my temple significantly with a pencil to denote my belief that the man was perhaps more than a trifle cracked. The scientist's eyes hardened for he nodded in defense of the man's story. Then the dying man resumed his tale, drawing our attention to him.

"For five days," he continued in wheezing gasps. "We stayed at the spring, digging like mad men, into the yellow vein. We watched our pile grow from a few miserable nuggets and scrapings to a heap that would require a mule to transport it. Then to our disgust and chagrin we discovered that our provisions were almost gone, with only a few cans of beans remaining to see us to Barstow.

"We debated on the question of one of us returning to Barstow for more provisions and a string of burros. But each was so eager to return to civilization that we decided that all should go.

"Hurriedly we covered our discovery with shale and piled rocks over the spring to hide it from any wandering prospector. After posting our location notices all along the vein we filled our canteens and started once again across that terrible red tableland, weighted down with as much gold as we could carry.

"Night and day we traveled until finally exhaustion halted us in the middle of the vermilion streak. Scarcely had we lain down than we were fast asleep.

"Suddenly we were awakened by the most hideous roar that ever grated on the ears of man. The ground under us seemed to tremble from the terrific concussion of the sound.

"'Good God!' Gundelfinger exclaimed, sitting erect.

"Bright, beside me, gave a snort of terror and shot a hand for his gun. His eyes glittered with an ungodly fear and his teeth clattered in his mouth. He seemed speechless. I was appalled.

"It must have been close to midnight when we awoke. But a crescent moon, standing in the heavens to the eastward, bathed the blistered tableland with a pale, ghostly light. Stars glimmered overhead like fiery pinpoints. The tableland seemed to roll and sway as though under the influence of some dreadful underground upheaval.

"In stark terror we sat deathly still on our blankets, pistols ready, to get our bearings. The streak, with its monster imprints and piles of dung, was aglow with the pale, ghostly light of the dim moon and stars. Not a living thing was visible on it, yet we knew that something awful hovered perilously near. The terrifying roar thundered down again and again causing goose-flesh to stand out on me like itching hives. My blood curdled in my veins.

"Almost together we gathered our legs under us and stood up, each holding his gun ready for instant use. Then Bright's eyes searched the air above us. What he saw there caused him to recoil with a fearful scream. He hurled himself flat on his face and buried his head in his arms. We looked up, appalled.

"Directly over us, huge, membraned wings flapping dismally, ready to charge down upon us, was the monstrous beast whose tracks had punctured the red asphalt all around us! It loomed overhead like some gargantuan thing of a forgotten age, its eyes bulging and flashing fire, jaws dripping with red, flaming saliva.

"God, what a terrible thing for a man to behold! What a terrible smell for a man's nostrils to inhale! The beast stunk like the dead, but with a nauseating sweetness that made us violently ill.

"I hope to God that none of you gentlemen will ever see such a beast! Even now as I tell of it, I recoil at its haunting vision dancing before my eyes. My stomach revolts at the smell which has never quite left my nostrils. I can never get that vision erased from my mind. It is stamped so firmly there that only death, which beckons to me now, can erase it!

"But so huge was the flying monster that it cast a black shadow over us. It floated lightly between us and the moon, engulfing us in a terrifying gloom. Yet we could make out distinctly almost every detail of the thing.

"It was much like the little creature we had taken from the great egg previously. But how could a tiny little savage like that grow to such monstrous size, we asked ourselves?'

"The beast opened its dragon-like jaws, rolled its horn-studded head and roared at us. The concussion nearly knocked us flat on our backs. Then the monster flapped its great wings slowly and slid through the air, circling us. It dragged a monster tail behind it.

FLIGHT!

"Fascinated, we watched, insanity striking threatening blows at our reasoning. Bright began to blubber suddenly like an imbecile. Then he arose from the ground and stood trembling beside us. After a moment he seemed to crack under the strain and began to run wildly.

"Instantly the creature lashed out its long, flat tail. It curled around Bright's body like a python, lifted him high in the air and as we pumped shot after shot into it, hurled him to the asphalt with a sickening thud. Hardly had his broken body stopped rolling than the brute was upon it.

"Too appalled and stupefied to run, we watched the beast swing downward and land on all its eight feet, jabbing the asphalt deeply with them. It stood over Bright's body and proceeded to gobble it before our very eyes!

"I have always been a religious man and I got down at once on my knees to pray. Some strange, powerful influence urged me to do so. Sobbing, I offered my prayer for safety.

"'Shut up!' Gundelfinger hissed at me. 'Keep shooting the thing! Prayin' ain't going to save our hides! Shoot its eyes out!'

"The beast was facing us now, watching every move we made. But Gundelfinger snapped up his gun again and fired straight at the creature. With a savage roar it lifted its head, its eyes flashing like twin fires. From its jaws hung what remained of Bright, a mass of bloody, horrible flesh!

"Gundelfinger's gun blazed again. I knew that his aim was true, for he had been known to shoot silver dollars out of the air. But the eyes of the beast still flamed! He could not have missed his mark because of his excitement. No better marksman ever lived than Jim Gundelfinger, but the creature's eyes must have been protected by a shield of thick, transparent bone of a strength to resist even a bullet from a .45! It was like trying to shoot out a light protected behind a slab of transparent steel.

"I aimed quickly and fired again and again, thumbing the hammer in a way that had won me the title of expert gun-fanner. As true as my aim was, no damage had been done to the brute's flaming eyes. They continued to spray us with a deadly light that seemed to overcome, to hypnotize me.

"Slowly the winged terror came toward us. It hovered perhaps ten feet above the asphalt, its scaled legs almost dragging, its flat tail writhing like a serpent in the air. From its jaws dripped vermilion. Terrible shreds of flesh and bone clung to its saw-like fangs.

"I must pause here to comment upon the nerve of Jim Gundelfinger. If ever a man possessed the courage to stand before such a terrifying assault, Jim Gundelfinger was the man. I cannot praise him too highly for his bravery in the face of almost certain death.

"He stood his ground as the beast approached, holding his fire for a killing shot. I backed away fearfully. Then his pistol cracked three times. I saw him draw his arm back to hurl the empty weapon into the awesome face of the brute. The gun collided with the bony nose, bounced off sharply and clattered on the ground. His bullets ineffective, he turned on his heels and ran off to the side.

"Instantly the beast lashed out its tail and hurled him flat. I saw him lifted high in the air and thrown with a thump to the asphalt. He writhed in the throes of death for a moment and then lay still.

"In stark terror I began to run, it did not matter where. With my pockets filled with gold, the going was hard. My canteen was almost full and further hindered my race for safety. Yet I managed to run, filled with a deep-rooted horror and fear that brought insanity to my brain, expecting with every step to feel that awesome tail snap around my body like a steel spring.

"Then it came! It seemed to lash out for me like the tongue of a monster ant-eater flicking for an insect. I heard it drone through the air with a menacing wail, and then it snapped like a whip-lash just behind me. I was hurled flat on my face, but the tail had missed. I was a scant foot beyond its reach!

"Quickly I arose, blubbering like an imbecile, and continued my frenzied flight. Glancing fearfully over my shoulder I glimpsed that terrible tail again. The beast was curling it up for another thrust at me. I saw it, on second glance, spring outward. Again it snapped just behind me as though some monster was in my rear snapping a black-snake whip at my back. It missed by a mere fraction and once again I glanced back. I saw the brute's jaws close over the prostrate form of Gundelfinger. It began to gorge on its victim, now apparently unmindful of me, knowing evidently that my capture was but a matter of minutes.

"Like a madman I ran as fast as my legs could carry me. I leaped over narrow gaps, tripped in holes and prayed often for deliverance from the horrible creature that had so suddenly blasted our lives.

"Presently, in the dim moonlight, I saw a narrow gap loom up. I bunched my muscles to make a leap over it. As I sailed through the air I had a sudden thought. It came to me like a voice from the air.

"'Crawl into the chasm, Jerome!' something advised me plainly. 'Crawl out of sight and the beast can't get you!'

"I paused and looked back at the yawning abyss.

"'Hurry, hurry!' the strange voice urged. 'Crawl into the abyss and you will be delivered!'

"I shot a hurried glance at the star-studded dome of Heaven and mumbled my thanks. With lungs ready to explode from exertion, veins threatening to split, I ran along the edge of the abyss, searching for a place to go down.

"Finally I discovered a narrow shelf of rock five or six feet from the top. Without hesitation I leaped down to it, slipped and almost rolled to my death in the bottom far below.

"The moon's pale light struck the shelf just right, revealing it to me clearly. Far below I could see the bottom of the gorge, widening into a great pit. The shelf gradually descended down to it. Taking my life in my hands I raced downward, hugging the wall closely. It was sheer and smooth, but frequently great boulders projected outward to interfere with my escape. I had to pause and wiggle under them like a snake. On one occasion a rock was hidden in a black shadow. I did not see it until too late.

"My pounding feet collided with it and I went sprawling, clutching madly for a hand-hold to save myself from falling into the abyss.

By some miracle I saved myself even as I fell over, by clutching at the edge of the shelf. How I managed to pull myself back onto it, I shall never know.

"From overhead came a sudden burst of thunderous roars that lashed my faculties into a maniacal madness. The terrifying sounds crashed through the abyss like the explosion of a thousand cannons, echoing and re-echoing on every side. The horrible beast was on my trail at last!

"A dark hole yawned presently in the sheer wall of the shelf. It was the entrance to some underground cavern, leading from the shelf and created probably by some freak of nature. I dashed into the inky blackness without hesitation. Far within the tunnel I crouched. The heat was unbearable and little wisps of sickening, sulphurous vapors played around my nostrils, causing me to cough violently when I wanted only to be silent and still.

"Where was I? I had lost all sense of direction and might have been at the entrance of hell for all that I knew. As I lay I decided that somewhere near must be a sleeping volcano from which probably flowed the red asphalt that formed the vast, blistering tableland.

"The place was filled with savage, bestial roars. I shrank fearfully against the hot, steaming wall, gun in hand, ready to blow out my brains should the beast manage to get at me.

"Suddenly at the opening of the tunnel, I beheld a snake-like object sliding, gliding along the moonlit shelf. It was the long, flat tail of the beast, searching me out!

"I placed the muzzle of my gun to my temple, hammer back, to send a messenger of death crashing through my brain. How good it would feel to die by my own hand rather than follow my three companions! I waited and watch the outcome of the sudden appearance of the creature's tail.

"It curled restlessly into the tunnel, searching blindly for me. The beast seemed to know that I crouched there somehow and was trying to ferret me out with its long, terrible tail. But something whispered to me that I was beyond its reach.

"Fascinated, I watched the serpent-like thing. It curled and uncurled like the sensitive feelers of a butterfly, searching here, searching there, ever reaching out to clutch me in a grip of doom. It could drag me out of my hiding place with little effort and lift me into those awful jaws! I shrank farther away from it.

"On sudden impulse I leveled my gun at it and fired. The tunnel trembled under the explosion. My head swam, my senses reeled. Yet I saw the ghastly tail jerk back suddenly and then lash out toward me again. It seemed to glow with a strange, phosphorescent luminosity where my bullet had struck. It must have been the creature's blood that caused it to glow like that.

"But closer and closer it came toward me. From it radiated a sickening odor that I could detect even above the sulphurous stenches engulfing me.

"'Oh, God!' I cried out feverishly, as the tail came within five feet of me and paused, writhing frenziedly. It seemed alive with an undying craving to clutch me and haul me out of my place of terror.

"I watched it as I would the ugly head of a rattler. It writhed, stretched and lashed out, but after it failed to reach me, I laughed, insanely, madly. Then gradually my senses cleared and I realized that it could not touch me. I was beyond it! Finally it withdrew slowly and limply like an injured reptile. I breathed a stream of prayers and intoned my thanks to the invisible Protector.

"All night I crouched in the tunnel. Frequently I dozed off with a certain sense of security, awakening again and again with a jerk as I heard the terrible roars reverberating through the abyss. The earth shook when the raging beast stamped along the edge of the chasm, filling the skies with its seemingly disappointed bellows while it searched, I thought, for an opening large enough to admit its gigantic body.

"Gradually the mouth of the tunnel brightened with the approach of another day. Slowly the cave filled with murky light. I listened hard for sounds. The desert, with the dawn, had suddenly become quiet and still. Then I realized that the beast must have gone with the first light of day.

"Where had the great, interplanetary beast, as it must have been, gone? Had it left the tableland to bed down somewhere until the arrival of another night to lay its great eggs? Or had it flown into space to another world beyond our own? Was it safe to venture into the open or was the beast lying calmly, waiting for me to appear?

"I could not remain in hiding forever! My water could not last and hunger was already crying to be appeased. I must get out. I must get back to San Bernardino to tell Gundelfinger's poor woman what had happened, and give her some of the gold from my pockets!

"Cautiously I emerged from the cave and stood upon the shelf. The abyss was bathed in the brilliant sunshine of the new day. The sun was dazzling, blinding and it made my eyes smart. I felt the weight of the gold in my pockets. But the wealth was remote from my mind now. Life was more important. I could come back later with many men and guns if I was spared.

"As I looked down the abyss along the wall my blood seemed to coagulate in my veins, for there was that appalling tail in full view, though the beast itself was hidden. The tail was curling and un-curling like a writhing reptile. I recoiled in fear and shrank against the wall lest the beast sense or see me.

"But the winged terror was sleeping, its body hidden from my eyes by the curve of the walls, its tail lashing sharply from side to side as though watching for me to come out of my hiding place.

"It dawned upon me suddenly that I had taken refuge right in the lair of the beast! But after a few moments of breathless sus-pense I decided that I was reasonably safe for the time. The crea-ture could not, I realized, crawl down into the chasm from above and it was too far down to reach me with its tail, which must have been at least seventy-five feet in length. The beast must have entered its lair by another entrance. But was I safe, I wondered?

"The desert seemed as deathly quiet as a lifeless world. Not a sound stirred the stifling air. Slowly and silently I picked my way along the shelf, glancing often into the abyss to keep an eye on that writhing tail. It seemed unaware that I was escaping. The beast evidently slept during the day and prowled about only when evening came.

"Finally after what seemed hours of tortuous stealth, I reached the highest point of the shelf and glanced over the tableland. It seemed as deserted as the chasm, it was silent and ghastly. The asphalt surrounding the abyss was beaten into a jagged field. The great tracks were everywhere.

"A little pile of rags not far away held my gaze for a moment. With a start I recognized the trousers that had been worn by Crank. They had been of checkered weave, but now they were blood-stained and ragged. After devouring my partner, the beast must have later coughed up the clothing.

"It struck me then that the location of our precious claims had been lost in the destruction of Bright. But seeing those ragged shreds of clothing spurred me to the grim realization that I had not yet escaped the possibility of a similar fate. Sick and afraid I crouched down for an instant's rest. Sight of the stained garments completely unnerved me. I glanced again to the bottom of the abyss. The writhing tail was still there, awakening me again to the fact that my life was still in terrible danger.

"I pulled myself up from the shelf and entered upon the red streak of tableland. Without a pause I started due west away from the sun. I had a vague sense of direction now and felt more secure in the daylight, for it seemed that the beast was about only at night.

"More days of torture followed. The sun beat down upon me with the fire of hell. But I kept on toward San Bernardino, avoiding even Barstow in my haste to reach Gundelfinger's wife. I selected a shortcut through the blazing hills and with a leathery tongue in my mouth, and my body weighted down with many pounds of gold, I finally reached the town and went straight to the home of the woman.

"There I was given water to drink and to wash the sand from my eyes. Then I told my terrible story to the woman and gave her half of my gold. I could see, as I related my sad tale, that she disbelieved me. Certainly I had no witnesses or anything to substantiate my story and I would scarcely have believed it myself had it been told to me.

"But she became more and more suspicious of my weird, astounding narrative and suddenly she accused me of murdering her husband and the others to gain possession of the mother lode for myself.

"'My dear woman,' I told her frankly. 'Had I murdered your husband and the others for possession of the claims, I would not have come here to share my gold with you! No! I would have remained away forever!'

"'You are trying to protect yourself by your actions of generosity!' she snapped. 'I know what you did, you cold-blooded killer! You all found the gold and you weren't satisfied with a share, so you killed three men in cold blood for all of it!'

"'But, my dear Mrs. Gundelfinger . . .' I stuttered, appalled at her accusations.

"'You are a murderer!' she blazed heatedly. 'Your silly story is really amusing but not convincing! You shall hang for your deed, and I shall laugh in your face as you die!'

"Such was my reward for my charity and generosity toward the woman and her husband. The hands that I had aided, the mouth I had fed had turned suddenly against me. Before I recovered my senses, she had called a man from the street and I was arrested.

"I was charged with the murder of my three companions, and tortured by unscrupulous officers who sought to learn the location of the gold strike. But I could not tell them, for no man had ever been there before and my sense of direction was totally gone. I would not have yielded even had I known where the strike lay.

"My story was branded a lie. I was charged with the triple murder and languished in prison waiting until the searching parties sent out, ostensibly to find the *corpus delicti*, but really to locate the gold mine, came back to report.

"But public sentiment flamed against me, principally because I would not reveal to these hungry, greedy people the source of my wealth.

"Finally on an agreement to tell where the strike was, I was spirited away from jail by a band of men. I even gave them a false map by which to locate the place should anything happen to us.

"It happened as I expected. They got me into the desert, and then one night abandoned me, leaving me water and food to last only a few days. What happened to them I never knew. Probably they perished, following blindly the lure of the desert and the false clues I gave them. Perhaps they returned, realizing I had played them false, to hunt for me.

"So, I escaped into the Valley, and here I have been. For years I have been a hunted dog. I have watched the Valley year by year becoming inhabited until I felt that soon there would be little place for me in which to hide. I have become like the coyote, hiding by day and prowling about by night, seeking always seeking for the mine . . .

"Now I am done out . . . . my friends," he breathed heavily. "Let me have another generous drink from your canteen so that I can go on with ease. The nearest spring is forty miles from here and I can't make it."

The dying narrator tipped the tin to his lips. His Adam's apple bobbed up and down as the water trickled down his ancient throat. I studied him carefully during that moment and his gaunt, weather-worn face was pitiful to behold. And I suspected that that would be Jerome Ackerman's last drink on earth.

He waved a feeble hand at Dr. Frapin who held the canteen for him. His hands had grown suddenly weak and the container would have dropped to the ground but for Frapin's alertness.

"Let me repeat, friends," he smiled a ghost of a smile and squared his jaw firmly, "that I did not kill those three men. Nor will I hang for it! The same Invisible Protector who saved my life on the tableland and who interfered with the hanging, is again stepping in. I will not hang, for I am at last a free man, for death releases us from all obligations in this life.

"But before I go I'd like to learn where that beast come from. I've tried hard to figure it out and concluded that it had flown here from the moon. You men are scientists, can't you enlighten me?"

Dr. Frapin looked at the prone prospector for an instant and then nodded.

"I think we can, partner," he said with a shrug. "It is the theory of many scientists the world over that the earth on which we live is hollow. Marshall B. Gardner, in his papers, 'A Journey Into The Earth's Interior,' points out the possibility of life within the earth, with the earth's polar caps as possible entrances. Many of us believe that this is correct and your narrative tends, to some extent, to prove it . . . ."

"You believe me, then?" the prospector's eyes flashed dully.

"Of course," Dr. Frapin patted his gnarled, bloodless fist.

"Then I can die in peace," Ackerman wheezed.

"But to go on," continued Frapin, watching the man's wrinkled face. "It is entirely possible that the great beast to which you refer, entered into Death Valley by earth-faults or fissures leading from subterranea or the earth's interior. From your description I can recognize no such a creature as ever having existed on the surface. It must therefore have come from within and was unable to return, probably because the fissure might have closed up behind it due to earth movements, thus making it a surface inhabitant by necessity.

"I do not believe that there is anything to fear from it or from the creatures within its eggs as a menace to humanity. They have probably died out in the intervening years."

The old prospector emitted a weird groan. Across his withered visage flashed a sudden pallor.

"I guess that's all, gentlemen," Frapin said in a whisper. "He's gone . . . dead. We'll bury him here."

"You—you believe his story, doctor?" I inquired, folding my shorthand record.

The others in the party searched his face quizzically. Frapin eyed us solemnly.

"I do!" he said emphatically. "From what I've heard from this man, he never told an untruth in his life. He strikes me as an honest man. . . . Now let us get busy. We've got to find that streak of red tableland."

But a month's search availed us nothing, yet we live in hopes of locating it eventually. We are preparing now for a more extensive search, this time by airplane. But some day, some how, we believe we will find it, limitless wealth, and close to it the bones of the terror that came from within the earth. When we do, we will bring them back to San Bernardino and present them to the city, as a memento of a tale that no one believed!

GREAT GREEN THINGS
Thomas H. Knight
1931

Mac Randall lounged in a chair in his room, his feet upon the table, his long slim pipe emitting vast clouds of smoke. Over in the window upon the wide sill sat his friend, Edwin Ray, idly and somewhat crossly tapping his fingers upon the window screen as he gazed out over San Francisco's bay.

"So you don't believe, Mac," challenged Edwin across the room, "that there are insects or bugs in the world as big as a small man? That these ugly, ferocious things run around on two legs and stand up the size of a pigmy?"

Mac hesitated a moment before he answered, then he said: "Ed, let's talk about something else. I hate to see you getting this way, old timer. You musn't let your love of entomology go to your head. Don't let it actually get you 'bugs' . . ."

"I wish I could show you," interrupted Edwin. "I wish—I wish . . ." He paused and, looking from the window again, lapsed into silence, thinking.

The two men had been close friends ever since the war, and now Mac was worried about his pal. This was not the first time Edwin had spoken so foolishly of insects, enormous only in his own mind, and Mac did not like it. He arose from his chair and took a turn about the room.

Tall, straight and broad, Mac had, during those days of hate in 1940, piloted a fighting *Kling* across the air lanes of Eurasia and had come home with a double handful of medals to his credit. And while he had been hearing the "zing!" of bullets through his wings above, Edwin had been doing his bit—a good, stout "bit"—down below in the mud.

Since the war Mac had indulged his love for aviation in one form or another, fortunately having the necessary means; while Edwin had gone in for science—chiefly bugs. Bugs! Mac didn't like it. Edwin had bugs on the brain!

"Mac," began Edwin again, strategically taking up without his friend's realization the subject of bugs as large as little men, "tell me about your new plane."

Mac took the bait at once. If "bugs" were Edwin's weakness, certainly the air was Mac's.

"Ed, it's the best plane I've ever flown," he announced whole-heartedly. "I'm rather nutty about it. All metal, you know. Only one motor, but a beautiful thing of power and flexibility. Fine large cabin. Boy! I'd take her anywhere."

"What have you on your schedule for the next week or so?" asked Edwin, following up his strategy and clearing the way for the plans he had just formed.

"Not a thing. Would you like a trip somewhere?"

"Yes. Got a map?"

"Scads of 'em."

In a few moments Edwin was pointing to a spot in the upper portion of Brazil just a little above the Rio Negro. "I've got it plotted out to a dot on a big map I have at home, Mac," he explained, "but speaking roughly, how would you plan to fly from Frisco to right here where my finger rests?"

"Easy. Hop down along the coast and make our last filling at Panama Field," answered Mac, measuring with a practiced eye. "My plane is equipped with land gear and pontoon combination. I'd make the Rio Negro the next leg—(it looks about eight hundred miles)—and stay there overnight. Then I'd cross this Sierra Parima mountain range here next morning and land on your spot—that is if a guy *can* land—in about two hours."

"Mac, if you'll take me there I believe I can prove to you that there *are* insects as large as small men!"

Mac was silent. He was disappointed. He had not thought Edwin was still on the subject of bugs. "Ed, you're an idiot! This thing has got you," he exclaimed when at last he spoke. Then, with another thought appealing to him he went on, "but I'd like that flight all right, and it'll get your mind straight again maybe. Anyway, it would do us both good. Let's make our plans."

"You make your plans about the plane, Mac," agreed Edwin, "but let me tell you what you *must* take. Take along a good high-powered rifle, also a pistol on each hip; I'm going to. You don't know what we might find down there. Because I know of some of the things those jungles do hold, it makes me wonder what else lurks in the forests. You might say these swamps and jungles are almost completely unexplored. No telling what we may run up on. Not just in insects but in animals. Mac, did you know that during the Coal Age dragonflies had wings two feet across?"

"No. I didn't. And my ignorance makes no difference anyway. Your idea is all bosh. But I'll take a rifle and a pair of gats simply because I like to have those things around. Would you also recommend a machine gun and a poison gas outfit—or a tank?"

Edwin paid no heed to Mac's friendly sarcasm, but in just a little while both young men would have given everything they possessed for those same impossible articles of war.

It was not many days before Mac's sturdy plane lightly lifted from the field at Panama and presently came over the dense jungles of South America where, beneath them, they saw Mother Earth spread out like a thick green carpet. Here and there a river, winding and treacherous, broke through the green blanket to be seen for a moment and then lost.

Tall, bare peaks reached for the skies, while deep chasms with sparkling falls of far tumbling water showed bright beneath them. Then they planed over the black Rio Negro, that thick-looking river of tar. Mac adjusted the pontoons into position now instead of his wheels and, aided in his judgment of distance by a ripple on the dark surface, put her smoothly down.

They rose with the sun next morning and, leaving the river, crossed the Sierra Parima range, flying east and north. Edwin had his map across his knees and in a little while he said, "Set her down anywhere you can now, Mac. These are the forests we were in when I came with Doc Winters and his party. Here's where they are."

"Put her down?" mocked Mac. "Where? On which particular tree-top do you suggest we drape our . . . ? By Jimminy! there's a lake, though, at that. Let's swing around and see if we can get in on it."

He dipped for the lake, a circular green spot in the dense jungles. Then as they came in low again for the landing, Edwin cried excitedly, "Take her away! That's not water. Holy smoke, Mac, that's grass!"

"Whew!" whistled Mac as he gave the engine the gun. "That was a close one! I had the wheels drawn up, the pontoons down. Wouldn't this particular part of South America have made a messy mess of us?"

They swung over the green circle below them the second time. Then, skillfully handling the big ship into the restricted space, Mac landed, his plane taxiing through the thick grass and coming to a stop on the edge of the circle almost against the trees of the forest.

"We're here, Ed," he announced. "We're in. Pretty good! I believe we can get off when it comes to it. That'll be good, too. If we can't, we'll have to walk out and leave the ship behind. You know what that'll be. Come on, hop out, and let's swing her tail around all ready for a getaway."

They jumped from the cabin and swung the plane around. Then for a little while they investigated the opening in the forest where they had settled. They went back into the plane, and after some food and thermos bottle refreshments—(for lack of anything better to do)—fell to talking of their trip. It was still early morning.

"We'll stick around a bit," said Mac a little later, "but we'll pull out of here in plenty of time to make the river before nightfall. I don't like your jungle, Ed. It's creepy. I don't see a moving, living thing. But I bet that black tangle of trees holds everything from snakes to lizards."

"I don't know what family these bugs belong to," said Edwin in a low voice, enlarging upon Mac's train of thought. "That's why I should like to take a specimen back with us. I have an idea they are a species of giant *Pulchriphyllium bioculatum*, more commonly known as 'Walking Leaf.' You know, naturalists claim that years ago some vertebrates kept growing larger and larger in their fight for existence and their protection from each other until they finally disappeared. Perhaps these insects down here are doing the same thing."

Besieged!

Mac said nothing. There were, of course, no such giant insects. On this one thing poor old Edwin was off and Mac, his friend, was sorry about it. They sat silent for a long while, Mae wondering how long before it would be safe to suggest pulling away. But they were not to go yet!

Everything was as silent as death. Not the faintest quiver of a breeze stirred the dark wall of foliage about them. Not a whisper or sign of any form of life, despite their silence, had they seen. The sun beamed upon them and their ship. It was hot with a close-pressing heat. And yet Mac experienced a chill of dislike, mixed with not a little fear, for the clammy, tomblike spot.

Suddenly Mac felt Edwin's warning hand upon his knee. "Don't give a sign, Mac!" he whispered. "Turn your head slowly. Look! Over near the trees on the right!"

Mac looked. "Don't see a thing," he muttered from the corner of his mouth.

"That big leaf!"

"Yes. I see that. Looks like a big elephant-ear plant or whatever we call 'em back home," he agreed. "But that's nothing."

"You bet it is!" insisted Ed. "It wasn't there two minutes ago!"

Mac looked again. The plant, with its big leaf divided down the middle, looked to him a great deal like a large bird. Perhaps a heron. The two halves of the leaf looked like the two wings covering the body. The stalk of the plant, protruding below, even looked like legs. But there was no neck, no head. The plant was absolutely motionless. Certainly it was nothing to get excited about.

"Aw rats!" exploded Mac in disgust.

"Watch it!" commanded Edwin. "I've seen them before. *I know!*"

So Mac watched it for a while longer, then his interest and his gaze wandered. It was time to be going. Edwin was apparently losing his mind. Mac was just about ready to say he was pulling out when again his pal's hand fell upon his knee.

"Look!" he whispered in a hiss. Mac obeyed. And as he did his blood ran cold; prickles of surprise and horror ran up his spine. The hair on his head tingled his scalp.

The leaf had moved! It was standing upright upon two squat legs. From somewhere in its hideous green, slimy body it had thrust out an even more hideous head. A head upon which a face was formed of great hanging beak and bulbous, staring eyes!

The creature stood gazing at the plane that had, like a still more enormous insect, invaded its domain. Then, while the two men watched spellbound, it slowly advanced toward them.

"Ed," whispered Mac quietly reaching for his sporting Army Springfield, "tell me something about 'em. I'm sorry I doubted you. I apologize absolutely. They're worse than you said they were. They're devilish! Ugh! Where should a fellow shoot? In the face or through the body? Have they a heart?"

"Yes. Insects have what passes for a heart," whispered Edwin, thrilled almost into inability to act at sight of this great specimen. "That one's heart most likely lies, as he now faces us, near the surface of his back. But a bullet from your rifle would go through fifty of them. Don't shoot, though. Let's look him over."

"You'll have your chance before *this* party's over," grimly answered Mac. "They're coming out the forest by the dozen now."

"My gosh, Mae, by the hundreds! Maybe we'd better start up and get away. Look! There's a horde of them. Suppose they should swarm all over us like ants overwhelm a beetle!"

Just at that moment a multi-colored parrot—perhaps alarmed by the movement of the green creatures broke from the trees and flew toward the plane. Instantly one of the horde sprang a full twenty feet into the air. Its long arms and talon-like claws clutched the bird with lightning-like voracity, and even as the green beast fell back to the grass it had thrust the parrot into its loose-hanging mouth. One gulp and it was gone, feathers and legs and tail!

Mac reached for his starter. But before he could turn the engine over, five or six of the things had hopped up onto the wing of the plane.

"Thank your stars, Ed," he said as he turned off his switch again, "that we're all metal. I'm afraid to start the propeller now. It's metal, of course, but I don't want to risk those devils flying into it. We'll just have to wait until they've looked us over and passed on."

They could hear the things up on their wing, could hear the clamping of those horrid mouths as they attempted to bite through the aluminum alloy metal.

"How about our tires?" reminded Ed.

"Gosh, yes!" agreed Mac, at once admitting his plane's weakness. "You lean out your door and shoot 'em away from your tire. I'll keep 'em off my . . ."

"Crack!" Mac's rifle cut short his words as his first bullet through the face of one of the things saved his tire for the moment.

Edwin's rifle was a highly prized thirty-eight Winchester, and his first bullet, clean through the body, proved as effective as Mac's headshot.

After that they fired as rapidly as they could operate their weapons. A moment or two ago they had had no warning of danger. Mac had even not believed that such creatures existed. But now, with the advent of their hideous numbers, they realized that swarming death assailed them. Almost every shot counted, but still the horde marched on. They swarmed upon the wing and upon the body of the plane until Mac became alarmed as to whether or not the wing could stand the strain. He opened a door in the roof of the cabin, and, firing rapidly, dropped a number of the green bodies from the wing. Then just in time he lowered his head and slammed shut the door. A dozen of the beasts had pounced at him!

"Ed," he said, openly admitting their plight, "we're in a bad way. They've got brains—those slimy devils!—and they use 'em. They jumped at me."

Just as he spoke the disaster they feared overtook them, for there came from their landing gear two separate explosions. The men looked at each other, their faces pale.

"Gone! Now we're on our rims. Can't get out on flats through this thick grass," Mac said simply.

"Damn them!" cursed Edwin through clenched teeth, leaning far from his cabin door and pumping his Winchester at the great insects still gnawing at the tire on his side. His anger was his undoing. The giant things flung themselves upon his head and shoulders from above, and, as he toppled out the cabin, more of the beasts seized him from beneath the plane. In an instant Edwin was covered with them.

Mac shut his door, then sprang out after his friend. He drew the two pistols and, following Edwin closely, shot the things away from him so that he was able to regain his feet. Edwin fought bravely, swinging his rifle with telling effect. Mac felt them swarming upon his own shoulders until he was forced to shoot himself free of the devilish things.

Then Edwin was down again, driven to earth by the ferocious insects that pounced and hopped from every direction. Mac fought his way back to the plane, his empty pistols and his fists sinking into the soft faces before him.

In the cabin again he feverishly reloaded and fired, pouring shot after shot into the green bodies dragging Edwin away. But he could not check that mass of clinging, swarming devils that, before his horrified eyes, dragged off his friend. When his rifle stretched out a giant insect, three pounced in to take its place.

Mac waited then, his Springfield ready, to do for his pal if opportunity offered, the only thing left. He was determined, with a bullet, to save Edwin from the torture of their terrible mouths. But not until the great green things had their victim some fifty yards in front of the plane did Mac obtain a glimpse of him, and then, because of the movements of the things, Mac held that merciful bullet.

Edwin was flung flat on his back on the grass, and across his body, backward and forward, a number of the filthy things hopped and strode. At first Mac could not understand. Not until he saw that Edwin's body was becoming covered this way and that by a network of yellowish strands did he realize that the green things were weaving a net across their captive, securely tying him down to the long grass. Then they left him. Left him, decided Mac, until they were more ready for their horrible feast than they were just at present.

He groaned aloud in his plight. What could he do? He cursed his utter helplessness. What could he try? Even if he had box after box of ammunition for the Springfield he could not hope to shoot away the thousand brutes still surrounding him. But his ammunition was running short. There were still a lot of Edwin's cartridges, but the rifle Edwin so treasured was fifty feet from the plane. And fifty feet . . .

STRATEGY!

What *could* he do? He racked his brain, looking around the cabin of the plane for inspiration. He had rope. How could he use that? He thought of the things he might be able to use—if he only had them! A machine gun. Hand grenades. Dynamite. Poison gas. Oh, what was the use! All he could do was save one bullet for Edwin and then, after he had proved his engine's inability to get him out, to starve to death in his cabin, or to fling himself—insane—into their waiting mouths.

"I wonder," he said aloud, "how tough that web is across Ed? I've got to find out if I can, 'cause I'm going to try to cut him loose if it's the last thing I do."

He took his rope and made a running noose in the end. Watching his chance he dropped it about one of the big insects and dragged it to him.

He lifted the enormous bug into the cabin, fighting down its clawing talons, avoiding its snapping mouth, and securely wrapping it in his rope. Trussed and bound he flung it on the floor of the cabin. And there the creature, helpless and fear-filled, exuded from its body the ropish material with which Edwin was bound.

Mac watched it harden. Then he tested it. It was tough and strong to the pull, but when he took a long knife he found it severed like so much dough.

If he could reach Edwin he would soon cut him loose. But how could he get there? He would not get twenty feet toward him before they would drag him down; then both of them would be helpless, bound victims, lying waiting for the green things to come to the feast. To help Edwin, to outguess the devils, seemed as far away as ever.

But after a while, desperate, Mac went into action. Part of their supplies had been carried in a good-sized box. Mac dumped these. Then he filled the box full of waste, stuffing his sweater in for good measure. Then with wire he encircled the box so that the contents could not fall out. He tied a light cord into the waste, coiling it on top of the sweater. From a gasoline supply tank he ran in perhaps three gallons of the fuel and then, working quickly, he put his plan into action.

He saw there were no green things dangerously close at the moment; so, stepping from his plane and holding the end of the light rope coiled in the box in his left hand, he ran quickly as far as he dared beyond his wing-tip and hurled his box toward the heavier mass of the creatures. Then he sprang to his plane again.

He heard the sharp buzz of their wings as they leaped at him; felt them alight upon him. The long knife from his belt sunk deeply and easily into the filthy, clinging beasts. He fought them off, regained his plane. Then at once he touched a match to the rope he held in his hand.

He saw the flame rush along the saturated rope like the spark follows a train of powder; saw his box break into swirling flame greater than even he expected.

Pandemonium broke loose then. Into that great flame the green things leaped to be burned to a crisp on the instant as though their oily bodies, too, were gasoline saturated. The air was full of a roar as of a thousand motors as the infuriated insects, scorched and maddened, flung themselves to the flames like so many foolish moths.

Mac dropped from the cabin, raced under his wing to Edwin. Some of them barred his path but he shot and cut them down. They pounced upon him but his knife took its toll.

Reaching Edwin he slashed the soft rope woven about him in two long cuts, then with one movement flung him to his shoulders. The few green things that were not still flinging themselves to the flames challenged his path again, but they could not stop him. Their soft bodies offered no resistance to his knife.

Mac reached the plane and pushed Edwin in upon the cabin floor, then clambered in himself. At once Edwin sat up.

"By Jupiter, Mac!" he cried, "that was splendid. I thought I was gone. But I don't believe—I believe I'm not even hurt."

"Hurry up and find out, Ed, old boy," Mac insisted. "Let's see if there's a possible chance of getting away. Here, take my rifle. Don't lean out too far, but keep 'em from the propeller. I'm going to start the motor."

The flames from the box were dying down, but they still kept most of the devils interested. Mac started his motor, quickly giving her a generous throttle so as to speedily get her to her full power. Only an occasional shot from Edwin was necessary to keep a green thing from the whirling blade. Then as soon as he could, Mac gave full throttle. But the plane wouldn't move!

Mac clenched his teeth and cursed. "No good, Ed," he said. "We're trapped. Your damned devils will get us! Tires are flat; grass is heavy. Hell's Bells!"

"Can we get out and push?" asked Edwin.

"Yes, we'll try it. Take a knife to fight 'em off. Keep your eyes open. I'll give her full gun. Push like blazes and don't get left if she starts to roll. We do have a bit of a down-grade in our favor."

They sprang out again, the engine roaring wide open. They pushed and lifted at the plane until the veins in their foreheads stood out hard. They rocked the flat tires out of the hollows they had formed in the lush grass.

The plane rolled ahead an inch; then inches; then feet. The boys still pushed fiercely. She rolled faster, gathering speed. They pushed and strained and lifted, then sprang aboard.

Mac forced his engine to the limit, then the plane rolled smartly over the spot upon which Edwin had been so recently tied. It increased in speed until Mac, knowing he had to take the air or crash into the trees ahead of him, risked everything when he asked the ship to rise.

She bounced sluggishly once or twice, then she was riding smoothly in the free air, her roaring engine now bravely and rapidly increasing their speed.

Mac banked a bit and swung for a thinner and lower part of the forest. Only by inches they skimmed over. Then they were clear—gone—free!

They did not say much until once again the inky Rio Negro lay beneath them. As Mac adjusted his pontoons for a landing he said, "Close enough, Ed. We just got out. We've a story the world won't believe, though. I didn't until I saw 'em. Say, hold on! I forgot that we have one to take home with us to prove our story. The one I lassoed."

But next morning, before they left the river for the hop to Panama, they consigned the hideous green thing to the depths. Its condition made it everything but a desirable companion; it was rapidly getting worse.

"We're well rid of all of them," Edwin said. "There's just one thing I regret."

"What's that?"

"My rifle. I'd had it a long while. I'm sorry I lost . . ."

"Edwin Ray, my boy," broke in Mac, "would you suggest we go back for it?"

"No, Mac, we won't go back. Panama, James, then home!"

THE SARGASSO MONSTER
Edsel Newton
1931

I

For the tenth time within an hour and a half, the pilot of the Tilden Twin amphibian reached for the radio-telephone and called the Bermuda station, and for the tenth time he placed the 'phone back on the hook and sat there staring almost frantically before him. Something had gone wrong with the radio. As the plane moved slowly north he had been trying for almost two hours to pick up Bermuda over the nose. The compass indicator needle said so. The gasoline left in his tank said so; it was only a matter of a few minutes until the last drop of the precious stuff would ooze through the lines to the carburetors of the two singing Rickman-Conroff Hummingbirds. Then they would settle through the cushioning tropical atmosphere down to the surface, to drift there until aid reached them. That would be a gamble, since the radio was out.

Campbell's eyes took in all the instruments. They rested on that compass before him. It wobbled, suddenly. Yet the plane did not turn. She rode evenly, smoothly, through the air, like an ocean liner on a glassy sea. Over his shoulder he saw one of the seven passengers rise and go aft. Then the needle turned again, righted itself.

The pilot started up at the man. A hundred thoughts rushed through his mind. His jaw set. There was something familiar about the passenger. Campbell had seen him somewhere before. Could he be one of the spies of the company's rival? Anything to play hell with the Tilden liners.

Two of the ships had been thrown off their course that way, had drifted at sea for days and days while patrol boats hunted for them. This would be the third within a week. Demoralization. Yet Campbell, or any of the others, for that matter, could prove nothing. Hard luck, the company heads had admitted.

But the pilot of the *Bolivar* believed differently, now. He was almost certain of himself. Yet it was too late to do anything about it. He was over the Sargasso,* already. Too late had he asked the compass station for his bearings, for he had not suspected anything. The amphibian had been flying smoothly. He had been trying to pick up the 4hore for two hours. And now the passengers were looking at him inquiringly. One of them, a girl, young and slender, found her way up to his side and asked. "Aren't we off the course, Captain?"

He looked upon the brown mass that fringed out into the blue off there before him. Then his eyes wandered to hers, for the second time that day—the first time had been at Rio—and he said evenly, "Compass haywire." His voice lowered as he saw that she took it calmly. "Help me keep up the morale of the passengers—we'll get out O.K."

"I'll do all I can," she answered simply. She asked no further questions. Like a thoroughbred, she walked gallantly back down the aisle, giving the questioning fellow passengers an answer that apparently satisfied them.

Then the two Rickman-Conroff Hummingbirds coughed and their steady drone died down to a despairing wheeze. Campbell pulled back on the wheel and held the big plane at the stalling point. He picked up the transmitter and called shore. It didn't answer. He tried it again. Nothing more than the rattling buzz of his own generator unit greeted his ears. He slammed the transmitter down and looked to his plane.

He was gliding swiftly through the light mist that hung like a veil over the mysterious Sargasso. He could see only the long expanse

---

*A great floating sea of dense weeds in the North
Atlantic between 16° and 38° N, and 30° and 50° West.

of seaweed, with an occasional break of blue where the weed did not cover the surface. He turned the nose of the plane toward a likely looking spot and drifted gently down to it. Soon the spray was fountaining about the plane and she was checking speed.

The *Bolivar*, of the Tilden Airlines, was down in the Sargasso, out of gasoline, and her radio transmitter out of order.

Captain Campbell waited until the plane came to a stop on the surface. Then he turned to look squarely, accusingly the man who had returned to the front seat. His eyes blazed on the suspected man's hands, which went to the pockets of a sport coat, and the pockets bulged threateningly.

Campbell had to admit to himself that he knew nothing yet, that he had no real grounds to accuse the man of anything. Yet the passenger's eyes avoided his. Campbell got to his feet, revealing six feet of lithe youth in a neat uniform. His first thought was of his passengers.

"We have been thrown off our course. Something went wrong with the compass," he began. "It should not be long before we are rescued. In the meantime, there is little danger. We are out of gasoline. I shall repair the radio and get in touch with shore."

They plied him with questions, which he answered as best he could. On his way back to the rear, he saw the girl comforting an elderly lady who had receded into the cushions of the seat and started weeping. The girl gave him a trusting look and he smiled.

He stopped before the water fountain where the man had gone for a drink. Glancing beneath it, he saw a pair of common wire cutters lying there, and he also observed the counterpoise aerial that he used for transmitting messages had been torn away. He thought of connecting the transmitter to the receiving aerial, but upon examining the conduit that had contained the wires he saw that they had been ripped out.

His body came to a standing position. He whirled to see the man in the front seat suddenly turn from watching him. Then it occurred to him that he had not yet looked over the passenger list to see who the man was. He took a card from his pocket and checked it. Of the four men and three women aboard—a scanty list, to say the least—he determined the man was Bunyan. His jaw snapped when he saw the name. The Tilden lines had once discharged him for "doctoring" a plane. Paid by the rivals. He started forward again. The girl stopped him.

"That man up forward has been acting queerly all along the trip," she whispered, while the elderly lady at her side listened closely to gather what was being said. "He went back there several times. The last time he dropped a pair of pliers. He started to pick them up when he saw me looking at him, so he returned to his seat. Just now he threw something out of the window. It looked like a ring of iron."

"A magnet!" said Captain Campbell.

"I'm not sure," said the girl. But Campbell did not hear her. His hand suddenly shot under his thin coat and whipped out with an automatic, thinking to arrest the man and put him in confinement without any argument. But Bunyan turned as suddenly as he, and there was a gun in his own unsteady hand. Campbell leaped aside and a shot rang out. The passengers dropped down between the seats. The elderly lady fainted. The girl did not scream. Then the pilot's gun went into action. But already a bullet had torn along his wrist, cutting and burning deep into the flesh. Three times his gun blazed. Bunyan lay still, forward of the front seat.

There was a sudden scurrying of passengers as the pilot-captain started forward. They leaped from their seats, men and women, and ran aft. Just then Campbell sensed danger. But before he could move to a position of vantage, Bunyan's gun barked again. A bullet stung Campbell's side as he darted between the seats. Then Bunyan emptied his automatic. Campbell heard the familiar click after the last bullet had been spent. He leaped from his kneeling position and ran forward. He was upon Bunyan in an instant.

His hands gripped the vandal's arms like the talons of an eagle. He threw all his weight upon the man, bearing him down upon the seat. Bunyan's knee came up and dealt him a fierce blow in the groin. It stunned the captain for a moment, with a terrifying pain. Yet he managed to deal a fierce blow upon Bunyan's face. He had all but subdued his man when there came a terrifying scream. He lifted himself up to follow the eyes of his passengers who were staring out the windows. He relaxed his grip upon Bunyan and leaped for the steering wheel.

The plane was being carried along in a swift current, through a channel of the dreadful Sargasso. Yet nothing he could do would check its speed. He kicked the rudder, hoping to turn the nose of the plane into the seaweed on either side of the channel. But the plane did not respond. Instead, the current swept them along with ever increasing speed.

They were as helpless as if they had been in a canoe without a paddle.

Campbell called to the passengers, "Some of you come forward and give me a hand!"

The three men passengers besides Bunyan started toward the captain's cockpit, but a nasal voice ordered them to halt. It was Bunyan, who, automatic in hand, stood against the panel between the captain and his passengers. He had Campbell's gun, too.

"But we want to hoist the outboard motor into place!" said Campbell. "What do you mean, anyway?"

"A lot of help that outboard motor will be with no fuel!" snapped Bunyan. "We're going to stick it out, Campbell, including the ladies. Tilden paid me to check on you, and I'm on the job."

"That's a lie!" said Campbell. "Old man Tilden is the squarest shooter that ever lived. You're working with that Inter-Continental gang, Bunyan. You're a pirate. You're trying to demoralize my passengers, to make them think I'm incompetent. The rotten literature your outfit distributed around Buenos Aires and New York didn't work, at least not altogether. We still get a few passengers, and we're going to protect them."

"That's strong talk, Campbell, but it won't get you anywhere," answered Bunyan, a sneer on his lips. His eyes were bloodshot from the scuffle of a few minutes before. He raised the gun and pointed it at the defenseless pilot. Before Campbell could duck there came a deafening roar, then another. . . .

II

IN THE MAELSTROM!

"He didn't hit you that time?" he heard the girl ask as he opened his eyes to see her bending over him. He was lying across one of the wide seats, and she had been washing his face with cold water.

"I don't think so," he said, blinking. "It was the one that hit me a few minutes ago. Broke a rib, I think. I'll be O.K. What happened?"

"This little lady put him out of business with a little pearl handled .22," said one of the three men who were looking on. "When the maniac started to shoot she simply let him have a dose of his own medicine."

Campbell rose to a sitting position to see his enemy sitting across the aisle, bound hand and foot. A bandage encircled his head. His sullen face scowled when Campbell arose and started toward him. But the Captain stopped, suddenly, and said, "I'll handle you later, Bunyan. But if you don't tell me where the wires you pulled from the conduit are, I'll choke you to death." He stepped forward again, his fingers bent as if ready to clutch the neck of the vandal.

"They're back there somewhere in the ocean," said Bunyan wincing.

The passengers gasped. Anger beyond words welled up in the captain. Yet he held himself in check, and he said, "Bunyan, I'll make you pay for this if it's the last thing I ever do."

With that he turned to look out the window. The horrified eyes of the passengers were already taking in the situation. The plane was being carried along at terrific speed, and a tailwind was blowing down upon her.

Campbell hurried forward. He unlocked a box in the cockpit and began looking around for spare pieces of wire. But to no avail. He finally gave it up and turned to give the steering wheel another last despairing turn. The plane did not respond. He swore under his breath and started to open the window before him. The wounded arm pained as he held it up and he winced. Then a pair of feminine hands reached forth and raised the glass.

"Thanks," he said, looking around at the girl. She stood close to him like a guardian angel. "And thanks for saving my life," he continued.

She sighed heavily. "I couldn't have done anything else. It was the most cowardly thing in the world. One of the men is a doctor. He'll dress your wounds."

"But we've got to stop this drift," he explained. "If we could manage to nose the ship around into the seaweed we'd have a chance. As it is, God only knows where we'll end up. I never knew there was such a thing." He indicated the seemingly endless channel that cut through the seaweed before them. The growth on either side was becoming thicker and thicker.

"But you can't stop a heavy ship like this, surely—in so swift a current."

They stood looking at each other. Something about her thrilled the captain. It must have been her pluck. She wasn't too timid to shoot a murderer. She wasn't afraid of wherever they were going.

"You aren't afraid of anything!" he said. "What's your name?"

The straightforward manner of the captain brought a smile from the girl. She held out her hand.

"A physical coward is generally a moral coward, Captain Campbell. The name is Rickman."

"You astound me!" he exclaimed. "I'll bet my wings you're Marcine Rickman!"

She nodded. "My father designed those two motors out there," pointing to the great pair of Hummingbirds that hung forward. "But they won't run without gasoline!"

"Hardly!" he laughed. "Well, we've got to think up some way of getting out of this." He started to climb up the steps to the deck on the bow. She assisted him, for he was obviously weak from loss of blood. One of the men had wrapped a handkerchief around his wrist to stop the flow from the deep wound therein. That was perhaps all that saved him.

As they reached the deck, the girl started suddenly and gasped. He followed her staring eyes ahead of them. They were bearing down upon a whirlpool, a literal maelstrom. The channel widened about it. It swirled threateningly, carrying with it bits of seaweed and debris. Even in this twilight hour he could see it whirling like a gigantic animal, waiting there to take the great plane in its grasp and pull it down into the depths of the sea. And here even the wind seemed to give way to the rush of the water.

There was no longer the singing sound in the struts and braces. Only the lash of the eddying current broke the silence. Before they could dash below and close the hatch, the plane had nosed into it. Pandemonium broke loose among the passengers, the elderly lady and another woman screaming.

The three men sat pale-faced and helpless. Bunyan sneered and laughed in turn. And while the captain and the girl stood there before them, the swirling eddy took hold of the plane. As the screams of the two women reached their highest pitch, something above them shattered into a wing, broke through, and came crashing down upon the top of the cabin. It was a moment when all were lost, when only the miracle of an unforeseen providence could help them.

"Here, you men! Jump there and close the ports!" Captain Campbell barked, as he himself began closing the windows forward. "Every one of you sit tight—" He saw the girl as she was pitched across the cabin. Others followed her.

He had held to the top of the seat when the eddy turned the ship about. Now he too was lying sprawled upon the deck. Before he could rise and assist Marcine and the other two women, he was against hurled downward, this time to lie still, until the movement of the plane pitched him forward among the terrified passengers. Before he could get to his feet again, the plane was standing on her nose, and they were all thrown together before the door that opened into the cockpit.

Campbell made a desperate plunge for a stanchion, caught it on the swing as the plane reeled to port, wrapped his feet about it, and reached for Marcine. Her hands were outstretched to receive his. He pulled her toward him. She grasped the stanchion and held on. He then dived for a seat, reached it, and pulled her after him. While the plane was steady for a moment he strapped her in. Then

he picked the elderly lady from the deck and did likewise with her.
One of the men managed to place the other woman in a seat. Then
when the women were assured the maximum of safety, the men
sought their own seats, gaining them only by leaps when there came
a lull in that everlasting tossing and pitching. But it did not last
for long. As darkness fell upon the plane only hopeless despair
prevailed in their spirits. Yet the girl smiled when Captain Campbell looked anxiously in her direction.

The maelstrom was tossing them around now, its whirl increasing in speed as the plane was pulled toward the vortex. In that awful
spiral the great amphibian was twisted about, now on her nose,
now on her side, with her wing down in the wash, and again with
her gallant bows in the air like a whale leaping to the surface. It
would be a matter of only a few minutes, the captain thought. He
might have had a chance to save his passengers but for the crafty
Bunyan, who, by all the laws of all the lands, was a pirate.

His company had sought at great risk to disable the Tilden line.
It had begun by placing Bunyan in their employ in the early days
of the line, when Lawrence Tilden had sent the first big twin amphibians southward on the trade routes between North and South
America. Bunyan had been a traitor; though he had failed in an
effort to wreck the first Twin that went out on the long trek to the
lands beyond the equator.

For two years Bunyan had waited. Then something seemed to
have struck every Tilden plane on the line. He remembered now,
how Jimmy Trevelyn was lost, and turned up six days later to say
that a little two-seater had come to take a single one of his passengers off the disabled plane there in the Caribbean, leaving a dozen
more starving passengers staring at the fortunate man for whom
the plane had come. And Jimmy's radio had been disabled.

Well, there was one thing for which Captain Campbell could be
thankful. Bunyan would share the fate of the rest, whatever it was.
And it seemed certain that it would be terrible. Perhaps the bottom of the sea . . .

The captain started and looked at the girl. Her eyes were burning into his, as if she wanted to say something to him. He went to

her side, risking being thrown against the deck or overhead, and while he braced himself to look down into her appealing face she still smiled. There was nothing to be said. This was one of those unearthly moments when conversation was out. But as far as that went the girl told him all with her eyes. She was telling him that she admired him for having done his best to avoid the disaster, that she was not afraid, that they would be together wherever they went.

But the swirl of the vortex did not take them down. By a miracle, just as they gained speed a wind caught the plane and lifted it up. It seemed to tremble unsteadily for a moment, nose upward slightly, and drift back under the pressure of a sudden gust.

The amphibian landed tail down with a resounding smack, and lay quite still upon the southernmost side of the open channel, beyond the vortex, beyond the rushing current, and beyond human aid.

Again the wind took her and tossed her about. It screamed down upon them, as Captain Campbell made an effort to open the forward hatch and go out on the deck, and shook the amphibian from nose to tail. It blasted against the helpless plane until it had to move and then carried it along with ease across the darkened mass of brown, finally landing it nose downward into something that gave enough to prevent a crash. Even then something crackled and broke until the strain, and the great plane seemed to fall upon its side. It righted itself when it struck the soft bed of weeds, and at last lay still there in the dark night, while the fierce tropical wind howled about them.

III
THE CONTINENT OF SEAWEED

They remained awake almost all the night. The women did not sleep. Two of the men dozed. The others, including the captain and Marcine Rickman, probed the darkness beyond the windows. But it was useless. The sky overhead was inky. Even Campbell's penetrating flashlight revealed nothing more than a wide cushion of seaweed. The stuff had grown so thick that it could have supported a ship. It had drifted together at the edge of the whirlpool, thrown clear, and accumulated.

Campbell searched the plane for wire, with which he hoped to repair the radio, the new sleeping Bunyan had wrecked. But he found that every piece of wire had been pulled from the conduit. The cables in the steering apparatus wouldn't work. They were of common wire. Even then, he discovered that all the aerial wire in the world wouldn't help them. In the fall of the plane against the seaweed, a strut had broken through the forward end of the cabin, just above the water line, and torn away the transmitter. What a complete misfortune! A few hours before they had been flying safely. Now they were cut off from communication with the civilized world, lying on a bank of seaweed in the mysterious Sargasso, in the dead of the night.

"It looks like a diet of seaweed, Captain!"

Campbell, startled, looked again at the girl.

"Oh, I forgot. We can have some sandwiches. They're in the buffet—already prepared. There's coffee, too."

"That's luck," she said, turning aft to get them. While Campbell flashed his light through the inky darkness to determine whether the motors were still holding, she served the other passengers with food. She brought delicate portions forward, and they sat side by side in the pilot's seat eating them. Her presence seemed to assure the captain that he would come through. Yet when he realized the apparent hopelessness of the situation he shuddered. He marveled that even the women could sleep. But Marcine herself was soon dozing.

He woke with the sun in his face, streaking through the window at his left. His right arm was around the girl's shoulder. He withdrew it when he heard footsteps back of the curtain in the main cabin. Two of the men were pacing back and forth, their faces white and unshaven, a worried look in their bloodshot eyes.

Campbell rose and looked over the bow. And utterly strange sight met his eyes. He gave a startled gasp that aroused the girl, so that she too stood up and looked. They were on an island of seaweed. It piled up in mounds and cliffs as far as they could see. It steamed like the jungle they had seen when flying over Brazil. And it was silent like a Pleistocene swamp—silent and dead.

"At least we aren't sunk!" exclaimed Marcine, as if this were a commonplace adventure.

Campbell lost all sense of anxiety then, save for the immediate comfort of his passengers.

"We'll come out," he said. "Will you continue to help me with the passengers? You know, even those men are frightened out of their wits."

"You forget the passengers!" she laughed. "I found some more excellent emergency rations in the buffet, and there's water enough to last awhile. While you're exploring the surrounding country I'll prepare breakfast." She turned suddenly and went aft, leaving him staring across the wastes, of seaweed. A literal continent of it.

He was inspecting the broken radio transmitter when she came with his breakfast. After drinking the coffee, which was excellent, he looked aft. All the passengers were silent. Unlike most crowds in a crisis, they did not talk of their troubles. The men scowled at Banyan. One of them, Carter of the Metropolitan and International Bank, threatened to smash Bunyan's face after having taken the thongs off his legs and wrists. Thomason and Mills, the other two, were chatting with the two woman, the elderly lady and the middle-aged woman who had screamed so loudly.

When the captain went back into the cabin they all looked up, as if they expected him to work some sort of a miracle and take them on to their destination. He tried to smile at them, but he could not bring himself to meet their tragic stare. While he stood there, they began to venture timid questions.

"I'll be frank with you people," he said finally. "I know no more than you do. The radio is out. It is doubtful that we'll be able to get out of this mess without outside help. The left wing, as you see, is crumpled. It's fortunate that the cabin is left intact. We'll have to work together and make the best of it. I'm going to explore the surroundings. If you wish, two of you may follow me. The others will remain aboard."

Thomason and Carter rose to their feet and stepped forward. The banker handed Campbell one of the pistols he had taken from Bunyan, which the captain pocketed, glancing sidewise at his enemy.

"There won't be any plane to come out and pick you up, leaving the rest of us to drift," the captain told him. "If you had one following us, its pilot was too yellow to set down where we did."

With that, the captain, followed by the two men, turned and climbed through the hatch. But out on deck, he thought of Marcine. He had not seen her inside the cabin after breakfast. Hurrying back down the steps he called for her.

"The young lady went outside while you were talking to us," said Mills.

Campbell turned on his heel and ran back to the bow. He told Thomason and Carter of Marcine's disappearance. The three of them leaped to the matted seaweed and started off at a run toward the mounds that lay before them, Campbell searching for traces of her footsteps. But so tangled was the mass that he could distinguish nothing.

The three halted when they came around the second mound and listened. Campbell yelled the girl's name. They waited, but there came no answer to their calls, only the scurrying of several strange reptile-like monsters broke the silence that hung over them.

An iguana, the size of a Florida alligator, lay blinking at them from one of the smaller mounds. A giant sea turtle, twenty feet across, with a head over three feet in diameter, advanced toward them. Its great soft body ambled over the tangled weed. Even three shots from Campbell's automatic did not stop the turtle. Thinking to save their ammunition, the men hurried on. But ere they had advanced twenty yards they were stopped suddenly by a woman's scream which came from ahead of them. Then shots rang out and all was silent once more.

THE SARGASSO MONSTER

Campbell ran forward and topped an. other mound of seaweed. From there he looked southward. On the top of another mound he saw the girl and called to her. She did not answer. Instead, she leveled her gun at something below her and pumped several shots at it. She screamed again as he darted forward. Dashing ahead, Campbell came upon the mound just as she finished emptying the .22 again. She turned like a helpless child and ran to him. As he caught her up, she looked over his shoulder and screamed again. He turned and what he saw chilled his blood and froze him to inaction.

It was a nightmarish monster, seventy feet long and built like an eel. Its huge mouth could easily have swallowed five men at once. And it was emerging from the slimy depths of a swamp and encircling the mound. Thomason and Carter also froze when they saw it. Their advance was cut off by its threatening jaws. It raised its head toward Campbell and Marcine and came slowly toward them.

In an instant, Campbell reloaded his automatic and leveled it at the monster. Three shots seemed to take no great effect. In fact they only antagonized the thing. Its tail, which was blunt and almost as big around as its body, came swishing out of the slime. The monstrous jaws were open, and it was not more than fifteen feet from them. Before Campbell chanced another shot, the automatic that Marcine had now reloaded came into play. Then what happened amazed the captain.

The plucky girl had shot the monster's eyes out!

He leveled his own gun down upon the same spots, sending shot after shot from his heavy .44 into the thing's mouth and to a tiny round bump on the top of its head. But those immense slimy jaws were coming down upon them.

They backed off the other side of the mound together, leaped sideways just in time to avoid a brush of its heavy tail, and scurried to cover behind another mound, leaving Thomason and Carter to shift for themselves. More shots rang out, presumably from the banker's gun. There was a terrifying yell. It died suddenly.

"We've got to watch our step," said Campbell calmly. "Let's make our way back to the plane."

"But it's on the end of a peninsula and we're cut off by that thing," objected Marcine, loading her automatic with deft fingers.

Campbell pushed up the side of another mound. From its top they could see Carter making his way back to the plane. Thomason was not in sight.

"What could have happened to him?" said the pilot. The girl groaned and pointed to a spot just behind the retreating Carter, where a giant turtle was struggling with something in its jaws. They turned their eyes, terrified beyond speech.

"Why couldn't that have been Bunyan?" thought the pilot, shuddering because he could not avoid it. Marcine was clinging to his arm, sobbing hysterically. Together they found the power to turn and look again. Carter had disappeared over a mound in the direction of the plane. The turtle lay still. Their eyes followed the ground over which they had escaped the terrible jaws of the Sargasso monster. It lay very still, its head upon the mound. From the relaxed position of its body, Campbell concluded it was dead. Taking Marcine silently by the arm he suggested that they return immediately to the plane.

But before they had gone ten paces a new horror gripped them. What they saw as they came upon a new mound of seaweed struck terror to their souls and sent their blood running cold. Their senses reeled and they stood there frozen to the spot.

An animal of such proportions that the largest African elephant would have looked like a pigmy at its side was slowly creeping up from the slime of a nearby marsh. If it was a saurian it was of a species different from anything in the records of any museum of natural history or archaeological research. It was over a hundred feet in length, and lay like a huge worm, a great, leather-like, bloated, beastly thing with a head slightly smaller than its body and eyes that glared out from the great sockets.

Only one thing the captain had ever seen could have so reminded him of its shape was a long, flexible sausage, save for the head and the mouth, which was round and so big that it could have swallowed the two of them without the slightest effort. Even as they watched, one of the great sea lizards that resembled an iguana darted by and was quickly covered by the cup-like lips of the monster.

And while the victim uttered a piercing scream, much like a captured rabbit, only louder—much louder—it was drawn into the jaws of the monster and swallowed.

The thing gulped with a satisfying blink of its hideous eyes, and then advanced upon them.

Marcine screamed. Campbell steadied her and looked around. Behind them, in the opposite direction from the plane, was only the waste of the Sargasso. There might be waiting for them there terrors far greater than those they had already experienced. But he must take a gamble with fate.

Speaking as calmly as possible as they hurried back down the mound, he said, "Steady, Marcine! We'll find our way out over there, ahead of us."

He was pointing to the southeast. He did not realize that something unexpected awaited them just over the next mound. And the monster was coming toward them, slowly emerging from the marsh and revealing several fin-like feet that slapped against the weed with each lumbering step. They gained the top of the largest mound in the vicinity, stopped a minute to look around at the advancing monster, which was over two hundred yards away, and then started on down the slope. They stopped suddenly as if they had confronted a brick wall and looked with stark amazement at the sight before them.

IV

A WORLD OF MONSTROSITIES

Before the pair on the mound was stretched a level plain that reached out to the horizon and probably beyond, a literal island of seaweed, thrown up here by the numerous whirlpools and decayed as the years fled. On either side of the island were tangled masses of the weed, reaching out into the sea, but apparently always thrown back to the main mass by the tides and the currents that

rushed toward the different whirlpools about it. Vegetation grew
here, much as that of the Amazon valley. A few palms dotted the
landscape. A myriad of colors told of flowers in profusion.

Great flocks of birds lifted from the ground near Campbell and
Marcine, and fluttered into the sky and off with the wind to the
opposite shore. But what struck them most at this moment were
the thousand round-shaped objects that rolled about the surface
of the water at the edge of the island, some of them being thrown
ashore by the tide, others rolling across the island as if propelled
by the wind. Yet no wind was blowing.

They did not stop long to view the strange land. That hideous
monster was behind them. It had gained and was now only a hundred yards behind them. Its great bulk loomed up over the mound.
Now its huge cup-like lips were extended and it was puffing as if
from exertion. The two ran down the hill before them, reaching
the level ground just as the monster gained the top. They kept fleeing, not daring to waste a minute or a single breath in speech. Yet
when Marcine chanced a glance backward she screamed hysterically and pointed. Even while gathering her limp body into his
arms, Campbell saw that the thing had turned sidewise, was beginning to roll down toward them! His own sense of action left
him for a second. His brain failed him. His memory was gone. He
was stunned to insensibility, yet that powerful something that lies
deep down in the being of a man caused him to move, to try to run,
to realize his position with the girl to protect.

Still that mountain of flesh was rolling down toward them, was
almost upon them before the captain realized it. With the very last
ounce of his strength called upon to aid him in flight, he leaped
with his precious burden out upon the level plain. He was seventy
or more yards away when the beast crashed down the slope, only
to break through the thin crust that formed the island and disappear with a few gurgling sounds below the surface.

Campbell heard it and turned to see that the weight of the
gigantic monster had caused its own defeat. "How heavenly fortunate!" he gasped.

"Floating islands are like that," said a voice near his ears.

He looked up into the girl's eyes.

"Gosh, I thought you were out!" he said quickly, thankful that her swoon had not lasted longer.

"Gee, but you're a man!" she said. "You saved our lives!"

"We save our own lives every day; we leap from before automobiles and street cars; we make forced landings and make medicine—what's the difference?"

"You ask that question because you don't know the difference—because you don't see the difference. If you were some other sort of a man, like Bunyan, you'd know what I mean. Or if you were a timid woman—"

"Timid!" he laughed. Then he realized that his heart was pounding. He tried to lie to himself and say that it was because of the scare the monster had given him. He let her slide gently to her feet.

"Let's not get into a discussion on psychology. We'll find a way to get out of this if I have to build an airplane."

She looked at her wristwatch. "Why, we been out here only three hours! It seems like an age ago since we left the plane."

"And it's likely only a split second in the time of those monsters. They must be thousands of years old. I'm trying to make out what those round things can be." He pointed across the seaweed island. Several balls, the height of which looked to he about ten feet, were rolling slowly upon the beach.

Marcine studied them a minute. "It must be some sort of vegetation peculiar to this strange land," she speculated.

But as they looked they saw that the things were propelled by a sort of tentacle arrangement, a band of them extending around the leathery ball. As two of the strange things moved in their direction, they saw that the balls never touched the ground, but were held up in the air by the tentacles. As the ball rotated, the tentacle-legs reached forward, carried the weight until another leg came around, and then receded, to lie flat against the sides of the ball.

The two that were coming toward them were moving with express train speed.

"Monsters—of some sort!" gasped Campbell. "We've got to dive back up the hill. Watch your step!"

"I won't faint again," said the girl, gathering her breath. They skirted the edge of the hole where the gigantic monster had disappeared and started up the incline. Even as they ran they looked back to see the balls gaining upon them. But something moved in the weeds in the path of one of them. It looked like a sea lion. It could not move swiftly.

The ball bore down upon it. Then it opened on one side like an orange being cut in two, and the great mouth closed down upon the unfortunate seal. The other monster continued to roll toward Campbell and Marcine, but when it reached the incline it slowed down.

At close range, Campbell took careful aim and sent two shots from his .44 Colt at the thing. It stopped, dead still, and its tentacle-legs lowered it to the ground. It rolled back into the same hole wherein had disappeared the gigantic monster and lay very still upon the surface of the water. The other ball was also motionless. It was satisfied with the meal it had obtained.

"A world of monstrosities!" exclaimed the captain.

The girl did not answer. He looked at her suddenly, and he saw that she was reeling as she walked. He caught her up in his arms as her limp body gave way to the strain that had been upon it. He hurried quickly toward the plane.

But before the captain, on his way back to the plane with the burden of the lovely Marcine in his arms, lay hazards that come under the heading of things hideous and terrifying. Only the intelligence that held forth above the universe could know how he managed to escape the threatening jaws of another of the great monsters that looked like an eel. Or how his gun, in his free hand, happened to stop the charging trunk turtle that was so large it could have swallowed him with one gulp. The crocodiles and gigantic iguanas were like so many pets in comparison to the greater animals that had threatened their lives.

Yet it was not long before Campbell topped a mound to see the plane lying there, motionless. Tears filled his eyes as he looked at his great amphibian. She had been the pride of his heart. Now she lay with one wing dug deep into the mass of seaweed and crumpled, the other extended to the sky to invite the first fierce gust of wind that came down upon the Sargasso.

He collapsed as Carter and Mills hurried out to the listing deck to meet them. The strain of the past twenty-four hours left him weak and near to helplessness. Yet within an hour he sat up in his improvised bed and inquired about his passengers. Carter hesitatingly told him of Thomason's death. It was not until then that he learned that the unfortunate passenger was the doctor Marcine had mentioned the evening before.

"But you have a nurse, Captain," said Mills, smiling.

"And what a nurse!" said Campbell, looking up to see Marcine standing over him.

"She didn't say anything bad about you," continued Mills. "How about those monsters—are we in any danger?"

"Imminent danger," said Carter, looking to Campbell for confirmation.

"If one of those things finds us here we're sunk," agreed Campbell. He sat up, suddenly, and demanded, looking about him, "Where is Bunyan?"

"When Carter got back he sent him for a walk," said Mills dryly. There was just a faint trace of a smile on his lips.

"For—" Campbell stopped suddenly. There wasn't really any use to start an argument. He shrugged his shoulders. "Well, all of you saw how he tried to kill me."

The two men nodded and walked away. The two women, the elderly one and the middle-aged one, were preparing food over the emergency gasoline stove. They brought a bowl of milky soup and placed it before Campbell on the hinged table.

As he slowly sipped it, he thought over the circumstance that confronted them. It was likely that other planes of the Tilden lines were searching for them. But would they come far off the course here, beyond the latitude where he had been forced down? Would they discover the rushing current that carried everything far into the dark and mysterious Sargasso and follow it across the maelstrom?

They could only hope for rescue. Somewhere out there on the opposite shore of the strange island might lie a disabled ship. There might even be human inhabitants. But to reach them was something like old Lawrence Tilden would term "flirting with Hell," and that would be foolish. Those ball monsters would rush even a dozen men. The gigantic eel-like things, the turtles and that nameless creature so big that it would pigmy a whale, stood in the way.

Campbell's thoughts were interrupted by a single glance at the figure of Marcine outlined against the silken curtain up forward. But they were interrupted for only a minute. The sight of her made him all the more determined to effect an escape. He arose in spite of the warning of the two women and hurried into the pilot's cockpit. An idea occurred to him.

There were rockets, in the cabinet behind the fire extinguisher. He took his keys and unlocked the cabinet, bringing forth a dozen of them. Why hadn't he thought of them before? Where had been that pilot's sense of responsibility? Why, there was little need of a plane being entirely lost, of its crew and passengers being hopeless. He placed an armful of the rockets before the astonished girl. She picked one up and examined it, but did not speak.

"Send up three every five minutes," he said under his breath. He took out his cigar lighter and held it ready. He placed one of the rockets in the slots that had been provided on the side of the cabin for that purpose, and then touched it off. It hissed for a second, and then leaped into space, sailing high into the sky and bursting. A prolonged flame hung where it exploded. Then the flame died suddenly, and a black cloud took its place, so black and dense that it could not help but attract the most casual glance of a lookout or a cruising plane. Several minutes passed before the cloud dissolved into the blue of the Sargasso sky. Then one after another of the rockets were dispatched, some going higher than others, some lasting longer. After an hour, he looked at the number that lay before them.

"We'll rest a while," he announced. "You'd better go below and take it easy, Marc—Miss Rickman. I'll have Carter and Mills on watch up here."

"If, anything happens you can depend upon me," she said, and her hand brushed his ever so slightly as she turned to go.

But she did not reach the cabin hatchway before she screamed and pointed off to the starboard side of the plane. Campbell followed her gaze. What he saw so terrified and unnerved him that he was frozen in his tracks. It was one of those huge monsters, like the one that had rolled after them down the slope. But this one was much bigger and looked more ferocious as it ambled toward them, its fin-like feet slapping against the cushioning seaweed, and its gloating, monstrous eyes fastened upon them.

V

THE LAST STAND

"Get below—quickly!" snapped Campbell. He followed Marcine down the steps and closed the hatch after them. "Close all the ports," he snapped again. "That thing means business. Every one be still and silent. If it sees you move it will crush this cabin between its jaws."

The middle-aged woman sobbed. The older one fainted. The former became mad with fright.

"Take care of her," ordered Campbell to Marcine, who, smiling bravely, went aft to the stricken woman and took her hands and held them gently. Merciful oblivion took possession of her. Carter and Wells were running about the cabin aimlessly, like frightened inmates in a cell of death.

"Snap out of it, fellows—I'll need you!" sang out the pilot. "If anyone here has to die I'll go first and show you how easy it is!"

Carter looked up. Something of the fellowship of men, that kindred feeling that too seldom motivates the acts of men in desperate situations seemed to have crept over him.

Easy to die the words of Service. Both of the men looked up. Then they stood calmly before him. Campbell simply glanced between them and Marcine Rickman. He thought they caught his meaning.

"Drop to the floor and lie still. If it menaces the plane use these." He handed each of them several of the rockets. They took out matches and made ready.

Marcine, having disposed of the two helpless women by leaving them relaxed in utter abandon upon the soft cushions, came forward and followed the example of the others, taking a handful of the rockets. Campbell knelt beside her. A single open porthole kept their attention.

"I hope it swallows one of my dad's motors and chokes!" whispered the girl at the pilot's side.

"One of them running," added Campbell.

The monster of the dim past came closer and stopped. It raised its gigantic head like a conquering monarch. Nothing they had ever seen or dreamed of having seen was so gigantic or repulsive. Its great cup-like mouth was pink inside. The lips were extended toward the plane, a dozen feet from it. It loomed up over the helpless ship, its fin-like feet slapping the ground. An amphibious carnivore, Campbell knew, for his learning in ancient and natural history had taught him something of the animals of ancient seas. This giant saurian ate flesh. Perhaps it could smell them, if it had enough instinct to know that they were inside the cabin.

It ambled forward, two lumbering steps bringing it directly over the plane. Its mouth was open and its gigantic lips were almost touching the skylight directly over Campbell and Marcine. Slowly, the head descended upon them. Part of the upper wing crimpled as if it were made of tissue.

Terror struck the souls of them. Panic seized them. One of the woman screamed. Wells dived beneath a seat and lay there sobbing. Campbell whispered for them to be silent. Someone fell over his feet. It was Marcine. She got up and ran aft, opened a porthole, set a rocket in it and touched it off. There was a blinding flash, a hiss, and the rocket was gone.

Campbell reached for his own bundle of rockets. He held one in his bare hands and sent it up through the skylight, into the mouth of the monster. Another and another he let go as the great lips began to close. The rockets burst inside the saurian. There was a resounding blast, and then another that was muffled when the lips closed upon the fourth rocket that entered its mouth. The head swung away on the bulging neck, and the thing started on.

As it lumbered by them, one of its great feet crushed a motor off the wing and into the soft weeds. Campbell discharged his automatic into the side of the monster.

The foot barely missed the forward end of the cabin. Like a huge sea lion, it dragged on past. The panic-stricken women were shrieking. They were pointing out the portholes toward the saurian's tail. It was held high, ready to crush down upon them. Several rockets blinded the captain's eyes.

The tail swung closer and splintered the wing. One of those ten-foot-wide finny feet scraped the nose of the cabin, breaking it off. A huge claw a foot thick and four times as long was sunk through the deck. But it was soon raised and the beast moved again.

But the rockets were bursting beneath it, where they had fallen to the ground. Where was Marcine? She was not in the cabin! Campbell hurried aft, calling for her. Through the porthole aft, he saw her shadow. She was standing on the tail of the plane, letting the rockets fly away at the touch of a match. One after another they hissed and flew away as Campbell climbed through the hatch and started to pull her down into the cabin.

"Get your people aft!" she yelled. "Look!"

Following her finger, he saw a black speck in the sky off there to the north. It was far away and so small that he could not determine whether it was a seaplane or a dirigible. But it was surely coming toward them.

"Bring more rockets!" pleaded the girl.

Campbell dropped through the hatch.

As he herded his passengers aft, the tail of the monster struck. It splintered through the top of the cabin, breaking off the nose, the pilot's cockpit and the other motor. But the lumbering mass of the thing was moving away. Its leather-like sides were heaving and its feet were slapping the ground. Its great length dragged by them slowly. It was several yards away when the first blast of the Rickman-Conroff Hummingbirds on the big Tilden Twin came to their ears. While they stood there elated beyond words, the big amphibian slid gently down across the whirlpool, swayed over the mound, and went into a turn. When it came back it landed in the water not a hundred feet from the plane.

"Hey, Campbell! What the devil's that?" yelled Jimmy Trevelyn of the Tilden Airlines, super-pilot and an all-weather airman, from the cockpit of his amphibian as the six people came toward the plane. He indicated the monster.

"I think it's Bunyan's grave," answered the now elated Campbell, dragging his heavy feet forward to shake Trevelyn's hand.

"Let's get out of this mess—you can tell me all about it when we've lifted," said Jimmy, opening the door of the cabin. The two women and Carter and Wells hurried inside. All dropped to waiting seats in complete exhaustion. Campbell and Marcine followed into the pilot's compartment.

"I had a line on Bunyan," explained Trevelyn. "He was the fellow who was picked off my plane that day, leaving the rest of us to drift. That scuttler went ashore and disappeared. It was three days before the base knew our location, and he had promised to send a plane after us the minute he landed. The fellow who picked him off claimed to have been following my ship so as to be certain of keeping on the course. But that magnet story of yours explains things. I was out in the Caribbean, over a hundred miles off the course and bearing West, when the compass should have read Northeast."

"Well, he won't play that game again."

Strangely, it was not until that moment that he thought of introducing Marcine to the pilot. She had stood there listening, without comment. "I beg your pardon, Marcine," he said. "This is my old flying mate, Jimmy Trevelyn. She can send rockets higher than any one I know, Jimmy."

"That's how I found you," said Jimmy, bowing as the plane leveled off far up over the brown and blue Sargasso. "I cruised all day. When I was about to give it up and go back to Key West I saw one of those blackball rockets you sent up burst out over the most unlikely looking part of the whole ocean. I'll bet my wings there's something more in the story than you've told me."

Automatically, at his words, Campbell and the girl looked into each other's eyes. After that, for a full twenty minutes, Jimmy Trevelyn gazed straight ahead over the nose of the amphibian. Nor did he turn his eyes when he said, "There'd almost have to be."

THE DEADLY YAPPERS
Max Overton
1942

I

Vacationing along the seacoast I happened into Greencliff on a day
of excitement. The legend of the purple yappers was in the air!

"Two fresh skeletons in the cavern!" I overheard someone say.
I cocked my ears. Everyone on the street was talking about it.

"*Two* again! Who were they?"

"Nobody knows. Vacationers from up the coast, I reckon."

"Of course the local authorities won't do anything. They're
afraid to go near the place."

"And why shouldn't they be, considerin' what the yappers feed on?"

The curious superstition was that the deadly yappers fed on
evil thoughts!

I had heard that story a hundred times. The old sailor, Libinger,
who had once taken me for a day's fishing along the reefs below
Greencliff, believed it implicitly.

The yappers were said to be shaped like butterflies, but they
were more deadly than any plague of locusts. I can't give you their
scientific classification, for our attempt to capture a specimen was
ill-fated, as I shall relate presently. At any rate they were luminous purple insects of an unknown variety, and were never seen
except in the dark, when their double wings would float about like
illuminated dominoes swimming through the blackness.

I had learned about yappers from Libinger. On our aforemen-
tioned excursion he had talked of them from the minute we pushed
off in our rowboat.

"On evil thoughts they feeds," he had repeated, grunting at the oar. "And I'm thinkin' it's well fed they be."

"But why does anyone ever go near them?"

He spat at a wave and squinted his eyes. "No one does 'cept drifters, pullin' along this coast fer the first time, who don't know. Them an' the lovers."

"The lovers?" I asked in surprise.

"Sure. They're the ones that's really pie fer the yappers. Them that's tender and juicy. God only knows where they come from. Vacationers, I reckon. Skimmin' down the coast lookin' fer a trystin' place, an' here's this nice secluded cavern, yawnin' at 'em. So they ties up and goes ashore, not knowin' that these devilish yappers is hoverin' over 'em invisible, waitin' and workin' up their appetites fer the moment that they gits carried away by sinful thoughts."

Old Libinger was utterly serious, so I had him take me around the cape to see the place. It was a three hours' row, and might have been worth it if we had tied up and taken a look at the skeletons. But Libinger wouldn't hear of it. So all that I saw was the cavern, as big as a schooner, that opened a little above the water's edge.

"Those yappers may be over us right this minute—" he had insisted that they were invisible in the daylight—"and I'm not fer takin' no chances."

"I don't hear them yapping," I said.

"They don't yap except when they're about to go for you. Then they yelp like a flock of geese. I heard 'em one night and I kin tell you I rowed like a demon to git away. Never let up till I got clean around past the Mad Hermit's. Then a few days later I heard what happened."

"Another skeleton?"

"Two of 'em."

As we pushed on back around the promontory, I turned these weird notions over in my mind. "Strange no one's taken the trouble to exterminate these pests," I said, but the old fisherman shook his head. He was sure anyone who ventured into the cavern and glimpsed a pair of skeletons locked in each other's arms would turn into yapper bait on the spot.

"Nobody but what has sinful thoughts sometimes," he said, and he was so deadly in earnest that it was almost comical, "and I'm not havin' mine in reach of them deadly beasts."

No use trying to shake him from his phobia, so I turned to other subjects. I asked about the Mad Hermit, and he rowed me in close to shore so I could glimpse that curiosity.

The Mad Hermit proved to be a heap of bones and rags sitting on a stone in front of a small cave that penetrated the rugged rocks of the promontory. We were close enough to see his large white eyes following us as we rowed by. Libinger hailed him but he didn't move.

"Pleasant guy," I said. "Good fisherman?"

"Never knew him to fish," Libinger muttered. "I reckon he lives on what the sea tosses up to him."

The yappers were still gnawing at my mind, I guess, for I said, "Funny the yappers have never got him."

Libinger jerked his thumb over his head, saying, "They're clean on t'other side of the cape. I don't reckon they ever fly around—or over the top either—though if they ever did, they'd find a good fat meal."

Libinger said it seriously and I looked at him, puzzled. "I thought he was just a pile of skin and bones," I said.

"Your eyes are bad," said the fisherman, scowling at me. "He's fat as a drum."

Well, others told me similar things about the yappers, so I wasn't entirely in the dark when, during my present chance visit to Greencliff, I heard echoes of more yapper trouble.

I wondered if something couldn't be done, wondered if I had the nerve to try to do something. Then, strolling into the post office, I saw an eccentric looking old gentleman stamping about on a peg leg before the bulletin board. This grizzled, bespectacled person was tacking up a card.

The curious onlookers ogled. He finished, turned, and tapped off on his wooden leg. They closed in on the bulletin board. The message glared at them in red ink. It read:

THE YAPPERS MUST GO. WILL YOU VOLUNTEER
TO HELP EXTINGUISH THEM? IF SO, MEET AT
SAMPSON'S BOAT HOUSE FRIDAY NOON. I WILL
LEAD YOU.

HARRISON K. MERIWETHER,
AGENT OF THE GOVERNOR.

This announcement had the right tone. I was gratified. The
excited citizenry seemed ready to rally, were already counting the
hours till Friday noon, and generating plans to wipe out this menace. I had no thought but to join them.

As the hour approached, I wended my way to Sampson's boat-
house.

II

The Party Goes Forth

The day was blustery, and the tepid winds promised a storm. Between the weather and the superstition, only a handful of volun-
teers appeared.

It was just as well. A small party was preferable, I thought, and
I said so to Harrison K. Meriwether, who pranced about nervously
on his peg leg.

"Just so no more drop out," he said somewhat bitterly. It was a
blow to his pride that the whole town had not turned out. He was a
coddled hero of the governor's, a man of many past glories, but
now beyond his prime. No doubt the governor had set him on this
case to give him something to do, assuming it would be a wild goose
chase. Few people outside the realm of Greencliff took the legend
seriously.

The sea was rough. Meriwether decided we should not chance
the boats, so we set forth on foot.

Our by-road skirted the shore line for half a mile, then wound
inland, around a cove and up a ravine, then back to the sea. We
passed a small board sign, "Beware Yappers."

By now, we trailed in groups of twos and threes, Meriwether doing his best to hold the party together. He was not successful. Our numbers dwindled from the moment the walk began.

Now, three husky lads at the end of the procession stopped to throw rocks at the signboard and as we rounded the bend they turned back.

There were only six of us left: the two men in the lead, wearing khaki for the first time and wearing themselves out like two eager boys on their first hike; a young lad of fifteen named Monty, who strolled along by himself, cracking the trees and rocks with his bean shooter and seldom missing; the one girl who stayed with the party, Lucia Fontaine, with whom I struck up an acquaintance; the hobbling Meriwether, who now brought up the end of the line; and myself.

Lucia Fontaine was an attractive thing. She was just out of school, a few years younger than I, the first girl whose appeal for me had grown rather than diminished in the first hour of acquaintance. I kept saying to myself, here at last is the unbelievable—the sort of girl I thought came only in dreams.

She fitted in well with the rugged scenery we were passing. Her black hair floated in graceful waves as the rising gale blew against us. Her green sweater and slacks, her full blown orange blouse made her a colorful figure.

There was determination in her smooth even features. She was on a mission for her brother, a zoologist. He had heard of the yappers and was half convinced that a new, rare species might have come into existence out of some curious circumstance.

Lucia was to capture a specimen to take back to him.

"Aren't you afraid?" I asked her.

"Why should I be?" she laughed in her musical voice. "Of course I don't believe in the legend. But even if I did, I would have no reason to be afraid. I haven't any evil thoughts." She laughed again.

Suddenly a sharp crash of thunder brought our party to a halt.

The two men in the lead were bluffed out.

"This is no time to be getting farther from shelter," one of them said. "We're turning back before it storms."

Our gallant leader with the wooden leg was too fagged to dis-
suade them. He made a feeble protest while they marched off.

"We should have started earlier in the day," I mentioned,
noting how the black clouds were gathering. Then I saw that Meriwether was looking at me contemptuously, as if I had exceeded my
authority. He grew arrogant. Now that his force had dwindled to
Monty, Lucia, and myself—all of whom he knew would stick and
see this thing through—he began to strut his old importance. A
couple of sandwiches had restored his energy.

Food did us all good and we moved along again.

The skies grew darker, and rain began to spatter.

We looked about for a sheltered nook to duck into while the
first torrent poured down, and lo! right ahead of us in the crook of
the bend, was a cave. Now I knew where we were, for I had seen
that cave before. It was the Mad Hermit's! Moreover, there sat the
old boy himself, a lean, gaunt mass of skin and bones heaped on
the big rock outside the cave entrance, watching us with his big
white eyes!

III
THE MAD HERMIT'S CAVE

It would not be pleasant for me to describe in much detail the repulsive feelings that came over us as we approached this miserable sight.

Whether it was his actual appearance or his bestial manner that
caused the chills to creep through our spines, I do not know; but I
could see from the pallor that came over Lucia that she was expe-
riencing a wave of terror. Her shuddering body was close at my
side as we stopped before the Mad Hermit

Now that we were faced with him, I suddenly realized that I
knew nothing about him—his name, his language, his manner of
life, or why he was called the *Mad* Hermit. When I had seen him
before, I had been at a comfortable distance and it had not occurred
to me to inquire whether he was really mad.

His eyes were not actually white. They were yellow, upon closer inspection, surrounded by massive white eyeballs protruding from their sockets. Those eyes turned outward, and it was impossible to tell whether either of them was seeing us. They blinked slowly like an owl's. Wiry hair was scattered over his sallow greenish face and bony head. The wrinkled skin gathered on his hard cheekbones, and his black lips spread to reveal three big jagged teeth.

This we took to be his smile. Meriwether addressed him, told him we wanted shelter from the storm. He made a slight nod toward his cave which we took to be his welcome. We went in.

There he continued to sit as the clouds poured their flood down over him. I called to him to come in with us, but he didn't seem to hear. His dark body remained silhouetted against the splashing sea. Now and then a flare of lightning would illuminate the pockmarks that covered his loose copper skin, and the rotting threads of the blowing, tattered garment about his waist.

It was an unpleasant half hour, and as soon as the crest of the storm had passed, and the skies settled down to a slow, drizzling rain, three of us were anxious to get on. The lad, Monty, was impetuous and ready for adventure. Lucia and I agreed we had come too far to turn back. But Meriwether's humor had grown steadily worse. He was sick of the whole deal and he blamed us for his troubles. He cursed me for all his bad judgments, and raved because we hadn't made better time.

We let him rant, for we all knew that we had lost at least an hour holding back for him, and doubtless he was nearly exhausted from a strain he never should have undertaken.

As we picked up to move on, there was just enough daylight left for a glimpse of the map Meriwether drew from his pocket. It showed the promontory around which we were circling. There was the Mad Hermit's cave on one side, the cavern of the yappers on the other.

There was a curious fact I had not known before. The cavern of the yappers, according to this map, was directly opposite the Mad Hermit's cave where we now rested. Only a very narrow neck of this mountainous promontory divided the two points. And the caves led in toward each other. But the mass of wall that divided them would necessitate our hiking another two or three miles around the end of the point and back.

The curiousness of this arrangement caused me to flash my light around the rear of the hermit's dwelling to gauge its depth. The glimpse told me nothing, for the room tapered off into three or four obscure corners that my light could not penetrate.

So I assumed there was no way through. My next thought was that perhaps we could clamber over the top of this mountainous neck of land; but as we emerged from the cave I saw in a glance that it would be impractical to make such a suggestion. The rocks were high and rugged, and it would be hard enough for Meriwether to get around by the footpath.

"How far around to the yappers?" Meriwether shouted to the Mad Hermit, still sitting in the rain. The old scarecrows eyes blinked a little faster. To my surprise, he spoke an answer.

"Two mile." His voice was tight and squeaky. He made a slight nod in the direction of our course. Meriwether thanked him. He spoke again. "Look out for 'em. They feeds on evil."

His eyes were actually glittering now, and one of them was certainly on Lucia.

She clung to me fearfully, and I led her away, out of this sickening presence. A cackling laugh echoed after us.

"Did you see the way he looked at me?" she asked in a quaking voice, as soon as we were out of hearing. She was still trembling, and I must confess the gruesome sight which had unnerved her was not easy to forget. As we hiked along. I talked glibly of many things, but those glittering yellow eyes kept burning into my mind.

"Do you think he liked it when we went into his cave?" Lucia asked. "He looked positively wild when you shot your flashlight around."

"Did he?" That was something I hadn't noticed.

"He acted as if he were about to leap off his perch. And then all at once he tamed down and began batting his eyes again and twisting his lips and showing his big ugly teeth. Ugh!"

Impulsively my arm went around her waist as I tried to reassure her. I knew what was in her mind, now. Sooner or later we would be returning past his cave, and already she was beginning to dread it. So was I. As darkness came over us, our, outlook for the night's adventure grew more ghastly.

Something made this night different from anything in my previous experience—different in the most fearful way; and I knew it was more than the blackening skies and the sea, and terror waiting somewhere around the promontory. It was my realization that whatever gruesome adventure befell me must also befall this beautiful girl whom I had just found.

For her, everything mattered. I wonder now, as I look back, that I did not seize her by the hand and flee back to Greencliff to safety, for every step of our progress was haunted by more terrifying premonitions of evil.

Before we rounded the point of the cape, Harrison K. Meriwether dropped by the wayside. His body was aching sorely, he said, and he would have to rest. He was willing for us to go ahead.

"Wait for me at the cavern," he said. "I'll come as soon as I'm able."

"We'll kill off the yappers before you get there," I boasted, "but you can come and make an official count of the skeletons if you want to."

He protested. He didn't want us to kill any yappers till he got there. Stubborn old cuss. He wanted to commandeer the slaughter. Besides, he had brought some torches that he wanted to use. I offered to take over his torches and do the dirty work. Save him the trouble.

"No, no! I've got to see this through myself. I'm not hanging back and letting the rest of you horn in on the governor's re—"

He stopped short, then tried to cover up what he had said, but the cat was out of the bag. Somewhere there was a reward waiting for the extermination of the yappers, and Harrison K. Meriwether expected to cop it.

Well, he deserved it at that, I thought, tramping all over this rocky seacoast on a wooden leg.

Certainly the reward didn't interest either Lucia or me. We each had our private motives for going ahead: hers, to capture a rare specimen; mine, to protect her.

But there was Monty, game little scout. His eyes blazed bright at Meriwether's tongue-slip. A reward sounded good to him, all right, and, he was on his way toward earning a share of it.

Consequently, as we rounded the cape, Monty chuckled to hear Meriwether's voice, still calling at us out of the blackness against the slushing of the sea, ordering us to do nothing until he came.

In due time the three of us came to a stop before a ghostly black opening in the side of the promontory which we knew to be the dreaded cavern of the purple yappers.

IV

THE HUNGRY YAPPERS

The soft lavender lightning playing over the skies showed us the way into the cavern, but we were not quick to enter. We stood huddled close together, talking in low tones. The rain had ceased. Our clothes were soaked. We were chilled to the marrow. But most of our chill was not from the rain, for the air was still warm.

"I wonder how soon old Meriwether will catch up with us," I said. "I'm ready to go on in, myself—"

"So am I," chimed in Monty, spirited as ever. The lad was plainly eager for a sight of the skeletons he had heard so much about.

"But the instant we enter we may have a battle on our hands, Monty." I warned. "Those yappers may not like us. If they come our way we'll be forced to start swinging paddles at them, regardless of Meriwether's orders."

"Then you don't take any stock in their hunger for evil thoughts and nothing else?" the boy asked.

"Certainly not. Do you?"

Lucia and Monty both said no, very decisively. Thank goodness, we were free from superstition.

"It's beyond me," Lucia said, "how these insects can kill a person anyway. That's another part of the legend that bothers me. But I've come prepared."

She was drawing some glittery sheets from her haversack which proved to be cellophane hoods. A very ingenious precaution. We hooded ourselves snugly and put on gloves. Now that our bodies were completely covered, we crowded toward the entrance of the cavern more confidently.

We were keenly curious for a glimpse of the little purple devils. We held back only long enough to halloo for Meriwether, and getting no response, agreed to make the break.

We edged under the blackness of overhanging crags, single file. Lucia was following me, Monty in the rear.

"Listen!" I hissed.

There was a fluty musical tone echoing from those black depths, a velvety "Yeep, yeep, yeeple, yeeple, yeeple—"

Lucia caught my hand.

"They're yapping," I whispered. "Crying for food!"

We were breathing excitedly.

"Yeeple, yeeple, yeeple—" now louder as if coming toward us, now softer from a distance. We had seen nothing but jagged stones and wet shrubbery under the, intermittent streaks of lightning.

But the next bright glare from the skies penetrated every crevice in the hollow room before us, and what a sight! A graveyard of unburied dead! Glistening white human skeletons strewn about in grotesque positions. Lucia stifled a gasp. Monty's startled curse was uttered half in delight. The lightning was gone but the white figures still hung in the blackness.

The thunder echoed away and the weird yelping filled the cavern again.

"Where are they?" Monty whispered. "I thought they were supposed to be luminous."

His answer came from the yappers themselves, for suddenly, out of a crevice high in the wall, a dazzling purple stream poured forth. It was like a serpent of light, weaving through the blackness, sweeping down over the skeletons, yelping like little starved dogs.

But it was not a solid stream. It was hundreds—yes, thousands of floating purple spots, luminous wings, none of them as large as a half dollar, melted together in a glowing chain of purple fire. Now, they massed together on a single skeleton, turning it into a body of shimmering color.

Abruptly they rose and floated to the next bodies—a pair of skeletons, their bones intertwined. Then to the next, and the next.

We waited breathless, our weapons ready. As they finished their round of skeletons they circled about the cavern, throwing their ghastly lavender glow over the walls.

They swept down toward us, hesitated momentarily as if to light; then, as we drew our paddles, they yapped away again.

"God's sakes," Monty grunted, "I never saw anything like that before."

"The strangest sight I ever saw," Lucia breathed, as the purple host began another tour of the skeletons.

"Bird, beast, or fish?" I asked.

"A rare variety of locust, I think," Lucia answered. "My brother will be amazed." She was holding a small movie camera, catching some slow-motion shots. "Strange about these skeletons," she added, growing more perplexed. "The yappers don't seem at all inclined to attack us."

We stepped over the jagged pathway to the out-of-doors again, shouted for Meriwether, but got no response.

"He must have taken off his wooden leg for a rest," Monty cracked. "I wish to gosh he'd get here. I'm anxious to plow into these purple demons with a torch and see what happens."

It. was hard to be patient, especially after Meriwether had been so disagreeable, but I argued that we had just as well wait an hour or so, for the night was yet young. We loitered back along the footpath a hundred yards to a protected spot of ground under a cliff, and scraped together enough dry wood to build a fire.

We ate, and toasted our feet, dried our clothes, and warmed our spirits. It was curious, the change that had come over us. As if the dreaded menace of the cavern had already been conquered. As if these weird, yelping creatures were no longer anything to be afraid of. We pondered the matter. Their very attractive beauty, it seemed, had softened our feelings toward them. Lucia and I had no more desire to destroy them than one has to crush a lovely flower. And yet it was plain, from their rounds of the skeletons, that they had been guilty of feasting on human flesh.

Our fire burned low. The restless slapping of waves grew fainter. The storm rumbled away. Our talk ran out. Still Meriwether did not come.

"Musta gone back to the Mad Hermit's," Monty said carelessly.

Lucia nestled closer in my arms, and I knew her memory of the yellow eyes must have caused the momentary tremble that passed over her body.

"I don't see how that creature exists," she said with a shudder. "There wasn't a thing in his cave, no food, no fishing nets, no weapons—nothing except that big rusty knife."

"I didn't see it," I said.

"Neither did I," said Monty.

Silence fell again. It was a restless silence. The recollection of the mad man somewhere on the other side of this hill was disturbing, especially to this lovely, sensitive person huddled close beside me

At length our impatience for Meriwether reached a limit. It was nearly midnight.

"One of us better go back and look for him," I said.

"I'll go," said Monty, grand little fellow. He picked up his bean-shooter. "I figure you folks can take care of yourselves without me."

"I think so," I laughed.

"We'll be at the cavern," Lucia said. "I might as well get my specimens."

So Monty whistled his way back toward the point of the cape and we kicked out the fire and strolled in the other direction. Again the cavern yawned before us, black and silent.

V

Meriwether's Wooden Leg

We donned our cellophane hoods and went in.

There was very little yapping now. The chorus of "yeeple, yeep, yeep" had lost all its sharpness; it was no more than a low, contented, musical murmuring—strangely charming.

The glowing purple spots had ceased their agitation and were settled in a complacent mass over what we assumed to be one of the skeletons. Cunning, attractive little things. Gradually they began to stream upward toward the crevice in the wall from which they had originally appeared. But not all at once. The great host of them continued to hover over the object on the floor, from which a thin stream was constantly rising toward the crevice, and another thin stream constantly descending.

It was a beautiful sight. Lucia said it looked like a two-way waterfall into a pool of magic light; and it was hard for us to remember that each of these pairs of purple spots flowing through the blackness was a deadly enemy of man.

I took the glass jar which Lucia had brought, and picking my steps to the illuminated wall, I had no trouble in capturing a few of the specimens as they emerged from the crevice.

We settled back in a secluded nook near the cavern entrance to await the arrival of Monty and Meriwether. Nothing more to do until they came. What could be keeping them?

Lucia was very happy. She had her specimens and her motion pictures, the two goals of her coming. She rested contentedly. I think she even forgot her fear of the Mad Hermit as she yielded to my eager embrace.

"What a strange night," she murmured.

What a strange night! A few hours earlier I could not have dreamed that such an entrancing moment as this was drawing near. The soft rippling of the waves sounded from the misty rocks below us. The fresh, rain washed air wafted through our corner of the cavern. The masses of white along the floor were only dull blurs in the velvety blackness. The only light that played over the lovely feminine features beneath my gaze came from that magic pool of purple across the cavern floor.

The spell of beauty was upon us, but it was more than that. It was the first blush of new-found love, and our awakened passions knew no bounds. While the little purple killers murmured contentedly a few feet away, we dared to forget them for the moment. I had shed my own cellophane hood; now I removed Lucia's gently, and my lips sought hers.

I was inflamed. I was finding life anew, a world of rapture I had scarcely dared to dream of, and I thanked the strange stars that had brought Lucia to me.

Then, as we clung in close embrace, breathing together, my thoughts reverted to the legend. What a fantastic thing that was, and yet—!

No, I swore to myself. It could never have touched us! Even if it had been true, even though the deadly yappers had chosen to feast upon evil, Lucia and I could never have been harmed in such a moment as this! Our love was the real, the beautiful; the truest and strongest passion of life!

And then I wondered how many of these skeletons about us had been lovers who had believed that same thing about themselves—who knew the legend and believed it, but were too sure that their own rapturous moments could not be evil.

"Lucia," I whispered, "You don't believe in the legend, do you?"

"No, dear," she answered, and again her lips lifted to mine.

It must have been two hours or more past midnight when Monty at last returned to us. He was alone and I sensed that he was troubled. The complacent, chirping yappers were not disturbed by his entrance. They were still streaming to and from the crevice in the wall. I had ceased to wonder at their strange, industrious behavior.

"Did you find Meriwether?" I asked.

"No," said Monty. "I guess he's gone."

There was an ominous tone in his voice. I questioned him. He had trailed the footpath back to the Mad Hermit's, calling all the way without an answer. Now he breathed excitedly as he related his encounter with the Mad Hermit.

"There was just enough light that I could see his shadowy form coming down toward me. I was scared. I asked him if he had seen Meriwether—"

"Yes, go on."

"At first he didn't answer, except to give a hideous laugh. He kept coming closer and I kept backing up, asking him the same question. Then he told me he had seen two men come along in a boat and pretty soon three men went back, so he knew one of us had hailed a boat ride back home."

We breathed with relief. "All right," I said, "if that's the case—"

"But I don't think it is," Monty was still breathing hard. "I think he was lying."

"Why?"

"Because of the funny way he acted. He kept coming upon me, closer and closer and—you're right, lady," the boy blurted, "he does have a knife!"

"Oh!" Lucia gasped.

"And it was bloody!"

"What?" I snapped.

"I saw it—in the lightning—as plain as I'm seeing those yappers this minute. It was hanging right above me in his long bony hand. Believe me, I made tracks. I spilled over some rocks, and here he was, coming toward me again. I let fly with my bean-shooter. He let out an' awful yowl. By that time I was on my feet again and I had a club in my hand. Just in case I couldn't outrun him."

"But you did!"

"Yeah, it was easy, once I got back on the path. But the club—that's what I started to tell you about." He hesitated.

"Well, what about it?" I demanded.

"I brought it back with me. Thought you might want to see it."

I snapped the flashlight on. The object he was holding out to us was Meriwether's wooden leg

"Does that mean anything to you? That, and Meriwether gone, and the Mad Hermit running wild with a bloody knife?" The boy's lips were white. No doubt we were all three as pallid as those skeletons surrounding us, as these terrifying thoughts struck home. For a moment we were silent.

"What do you think he's done with the body, Monty?" Lucia's voice trembled finally.

"That's what I've been asking myself all the way back," said Monty through tight lips. "I can't figure it out. It doesn't make sense. The Mad Hermit's got nothing to gain by murdering people, so far as I can see. It's got me going."

He was no more exasperated than we. A heavy silence fell again. There were no sounds from the sea. Nothing but the contented yeeple, yeeple, yeeple from across the big open room—as if these busy little purple beauties were sending out their soft music to distract us from the awful reality we were facing. But we would not be lulled. The facts were coming out into the open at last.

"Did either of you notice that map Meriwether had?" I asked.

"What about it?" said Monty.

"It showed this cavern to be right over the ridge from the Mad Hermit's—at the narrowest width of the cape. These two caves run in toward each other. Why couldn't there be a connecting passage?"

Monty grunted an oath. "I get it."

"Then the yappers didn't kill these people!" Lucia exclaimed, "but simply fed on them after the Mad Hermit put them here!"

"That sounds like a safe hunch to me," I said, "if we can prove this grave yard is connected with his cave."

There was a tense silence as I shot the flashlight along the rear walls of the cavern. We were wearing our cellophane hoods now, so we didn't mind disturbing the traffic of the yappers. It was curious to see them turn invisible under the beam of light as it shot past the crevice.

None of the black shadowed corners appeared to be openings on casual examination.

"Let's take a look at the skeletons," Monty suggested. "If they're really the Hermit's, the bones should show some scars from his knife."

It was gruesome business, surveying these bleak human relics one by one under the sickly yellow glow of the flashlight. The three of us stalked along past them, one after another, catching a hint of knife scars here and there, trying not to notice their grotesque positions or their occasional signs of freshness. Finally we came to the object over which the deadly yappers had been hovering for the past two or three hours.

Lucia uttered a little outcry before my light turned on this object. Realization was a moment ahead of the senses.

Under the dim glow the pool of yappers went transparent, and our eyes beheld the form of a naked man, his features partially obliterated, his flesh partly consumed. But one thing was unmistakable—his right leg ended at the knee.

VI

The Hermit at Dawn

Before I had the presence of mind to swing the light away from this terrifying scene, Monty bent down to the object and put the wooden leg back in place.

Whether he did it out of a sense of returning lost property, a sense of reverence, or a morbid sense of humor, or whether he was so shocked by the spectacle that he did not know what he was doing, I do not know.

At any rate I flashed off the light at once, and the three of us at once slunk back toward the out-of-doors, speechless with horror. Now, looking back at the pool of purple dots, and the chains of purple dots floating up and down between the pool and the crevice, we were mortified to recall that this same sight had entranced us with its magic beauty only a few minutes ago.

Without a word we moved down the bank to the water's edge, breathing deeply of the fresh air, trying to rid ourselves of the sickening image that burned upon our eyes.

Stars were visible, now. Mists hung over the water. The next hour would bring the gray of approaching dawn. We talked again, in low tones.

"So, while we toasted our toes waiting for Meriwether, the Mad Hermit was placing him in the museum," I said. "He evidently murders for sport, and hides his crimes by dragging the bodies to the cave of the yappers. How—I don't know. But it's plain that's what he's done with Meriwether. As soon as we get back to town we'll send a boat out."

In this much, the three of us agreed. But as to our immediate course of action, we were thinking in three different directions.

I was in favor of finding the Mad Hermit without further delay, before he found us—Monty's one purpose was to exterminate the yappers. He remembered Meriwether's words about a reward.

Lucia saw reason in both of these plans, but she pointed out that there was still a baffling puzzle here that her scientist brother would wish her to solve.

"Before we exterminate the yappers, shouldn't we learn what it is they are doing? Why are they consuming that body so ravenously? Where are they storing their food when they pass through the crevice in the wall? If we can first answer that question, then I'm ready to see them destroyed."

Monty and I gallantly acceded to her wishes. None of us, of course, anticipated that we were bargaining for an even more gruesome climax to our night's discoveries. But once we had agreed to strike out for the answer, to this scientific mystery, we shut the horror of Meriwether out of our minds and went to work.

In the cavern I held Monty up on my shoulders and he put the dying flashlight to the crevice in the wall, but he could see nothing. The darkened room told us the yappers were working as industriously as ever.

"We've got to get to the other side," I declared. "There's a chance we'll find their depository if we do."

We surveyed the remote corners of the cavern again without results.

"Then it's over the top we go," said Monty.

"And keep eyes sharp for the Hermit," I warned. I patted my pockets to be sure the essentials were there in case of an emergency—my revolver and some light rope.

Half an hour later the three of us had crossed the rocky backbone of the promontory and were making our way down on the other side—the Mad Hermit's side of the cape. It was slow traveling, picking our way through the dark over this precipitous mountain ridge. Suddenly a gasp from Lucia froze us in our tracks.

"The yappers!" she uttered.

There they were in a brilliant purple heap not twenty feet below us, their illumination casting a soft glow on the waters a few feet farther down, on the hermit's side of the promontory.

We crept a little closer. Now, we could see the double stream that led to this purple mound—yappers going and coming. The slight buzz near my ear told me that Lucia was catching pictures of this end of the procession.

"What are they doing?" I asked. "Depositing their food right out in the open?"

"I don't understand it," said Lucia, "unless—"

"Unless what?" I asked.

"Unless it might be a very peculiar instance of symbiosis."

I turned the word over in my mind and was as puzzled as ever. I had a hazy idea of balanced aquariums in which one form of life helped to support another form, to the mutual benefit of both—or certain kinds of trees that support clinging vines which in turn give them life. But I couldn't see how these ideas helped to explain why purple yappers should carry their food through a tunnel of rock to deposit it by the seashore on the other side.

Monty emitted an exclamation. "Look! That mound of yappers is in the shape of a man!"

Lucia answered coolly. "It is a man. It's the Mad Hermit."

Monty was beside himself with excitement. "But why—?"

"They're feeding him. That's the way he lives," Lucia replied.

"You mean—?"

"On the transfusions of nourishment the yappers bring him." Her words were authoritative. The ghastly evidence was before us. Still, the very thought took us a staggering blow. A thousand questions leaped into our minds. Curiously we found some of the answers already there—the barren cave with no signs of food or fishing nets or hunting weapons—the blotched, pockmarked skin that covered the hermit's hideous body—the steady stream of yappers passing back and forth—and, in my own experience, Libinger's mysterious statement that the Mad Hermit was fat as a drum!

We whispered some of our questions to Lucia and stood amazed as she told us some of the fantastic-sounding cases of symbiosis that are a matter of scientific record.

Monty brought us back once more to the task at hand—to exterminate.

"Do you think a torch would attract them or repel them?" I asked.

Once more, Lucia's scientific knowledge came to the rescue. In her opinion, insects of this type were probably as combustible as so many capsules of explosive gas. Monty was eager to start back to the other side.

We reasoned that as soon as their food supply had run out they would still hover over the bones. That would be the chance to catch them all in a body.

Already the stream of purple leading to the hermit was thinning down; and now as the gray of dawn spread across the skies, rendering the yappers nearly invisible, we caught on film the awesome picture of the Mad Hermit—a changed creature—a huge bulbous mountain of swollen flesh sitting motionless below us, apparently half asleep.

We crept away silently. With the aid of growing daylight we were soon again over the mountain top and back to the dreaded cavern. The horror of what we had seen clung in our minds. It was plain to us that the Mad Hermit had somehow stumbled upon a hideous means of subsistence unlike that of any other human being.

So that was why he killed; that was why he could live in a barren cove by the sea where the dead fish washed up: to let the feasting yappers pass their nourishment on to him. These skeletons, then, had somehow fallen victim to his knife; and after he had killed them and placed them in the yappers' cavern, the deadly insects had done the rest. And all the while the superstition about the yappers had protected him in his ghastly business.

We paused before the cavern entrance. We told ourselves that we had looked upon the Mad Hermit for the last time in our lives. Never, we thought, would that repulsive bestial face ever confront us again. For now we would apply the torch to the yappers and be on our way. We would report our findings to the authorities and they could deal with the mad murderer and his trophies as they saw fit.

We steeled ourselves to look upon the remains of the unfortunate Meriwether once more. The little purple beasts had made swift work of him. Already he was scarcely more than a barren skeleton.

Even as we entered, I was still half-consciously gripped by the feeling that there had to be a passage somewhere in this cavern that would let the hermit through from the other side. We had failed to find it, but the presence of Meriwether's skeleton, and the others—

The yappers began to scramble for places over the surfaces of the bone. Their food was nearly gone. The outgoing stream of light ceased; the incoming stream was coming to an end. Though the blackness of the cave was fading to dull gray, the floor still blazed with purple light. A pool of thousands of illuminated dominoes. Here was our chance to catch them all together.

Before Monty lit the torch I made sure that Lucia still had the glass jar of specimens.

Then Monty marched in toward the pool of purple light with a burning stick.

"Yeeple, yeeple, yeep, yeep, yeeple!"

The ravenous creatures set up a sharp chorus as the last of the food vanished. Louder and louder, like survivors from a famine clamoring to be fed.

Strange illusion, I thought, the way that yapping was echoing through the cavern, but it did sound to me as if the loudest yeeple of all was coming from a point at the farther end of the rock-walled room, not far from the big open entrance. That single voice was so loud and harsh that I glanced in that direction. Something in the formation of the rocks, half visible in the dawn, told me that I should have searched there for the hidden passageway. I wondered—but I saw no yappers.

All that I saw was Lucia standing just outside the cavern, her lithe figure silhouetted against the pink sky, the jar of specimens in her hand. Then—

Crackle! Crackle! Bang! Pop! Poppety! *Pwoo-o-o-of!*

The flame touched the purple mass, and in less time than it takes to tell it, the deadly yappers were a thing of the past. A horrid stench rose out of the cloud of smoke, and Monty and I rushed out for fresh air.

I heard a frantic scream. Lucia's scream. It paralyzed me with terror. I froze to the spot, but only for an instant. Then I saw what her wild eyes were seeing—a mountain of bloated human flesh hovering over me—two great mad yellow eyes coming down upon me—a bloody blade swishing through the air.

There could be only an instant of time between that falling blade and my death. It was a lucky instant for me. A sharp *wham!* and the upraised steel swerved. Glass crashed against the cavern wall as the specimen jar glanced off the blade and flew to its destruction. In that flash I was out of reach.

The huge body charged at Monty. He ducked out of reach and fled. The fumes were so dense that I lost sight of the Mad Hermit for the next moment. Then I saw him bolt out of the cloud of smoke toward Lucia.

The girl did not scream. She ran—almost flew—but her third step was fatal. Her foot slipped on a stone, she went down. Two more steps and the Mad Hermit would be over her. My revolver went into action—once, twice, three times.

With each bark of the gun the mammoth form drew up straighter. The knife slipped from the upraised hand and slithered down over the back. The bloated form slumped backwards with an unearthly groan. The last sounds to pass the contorted lips were "Yeeple, yeeple!" the high pain-stricken call to the vanished yappers.

The Mad Hermit was done.

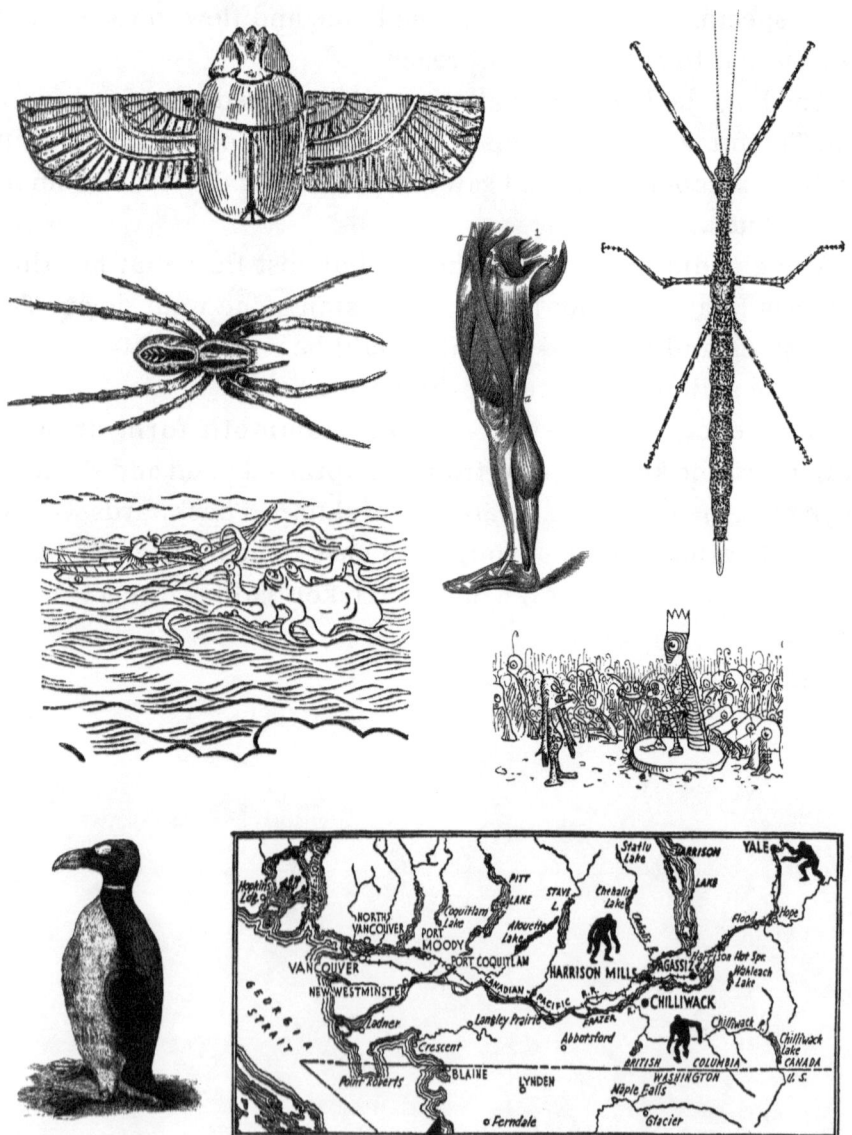

COACHWHIP PUBLICATIONS

COACHWHIPBOOKS.COM

Bestiarium
Cryptozoologicum

Mystery Animals and Unknown Species
in Classic Science Fiction and Fantasy

BESTIARIUM CRYPTOZOOLOGICUM
MYSTERY ANIMALS AND UNKNOWN SPECIES
IN CLASSIC SCIENCE FICTION AND FANTASY

COACHWHIP PUBLICATIONS
COACHWHIPBOOKS.COM

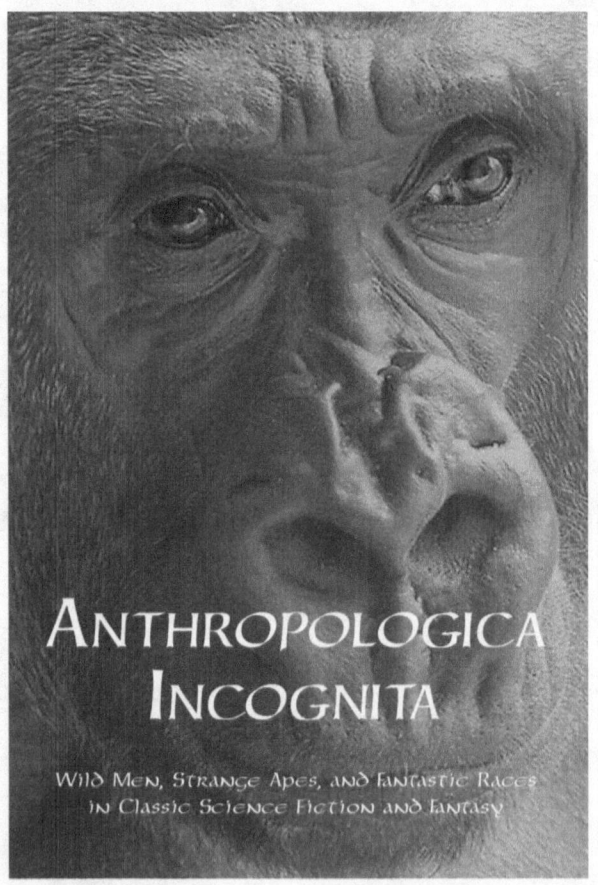

ANTHROPOLOGICA INCOGNITA
WILD MEN, STRANGE APES,
AND FANTASTIC RACES
IN CLASSIC SCIENCE FICTION AND FANTASY

COACHWHIP PUBLICATIONS

COACHWHIPBOOKS.COM

SAURIA MONSTRA

DINOSAURS, PTEROSAURS,
AND OTHER FOSSIL SAURIANS
IN CLASSIC SCIENCE FICTION AND FANTASY

COACHWHIP PUBLICATIONS
CoachwhipBooks.com

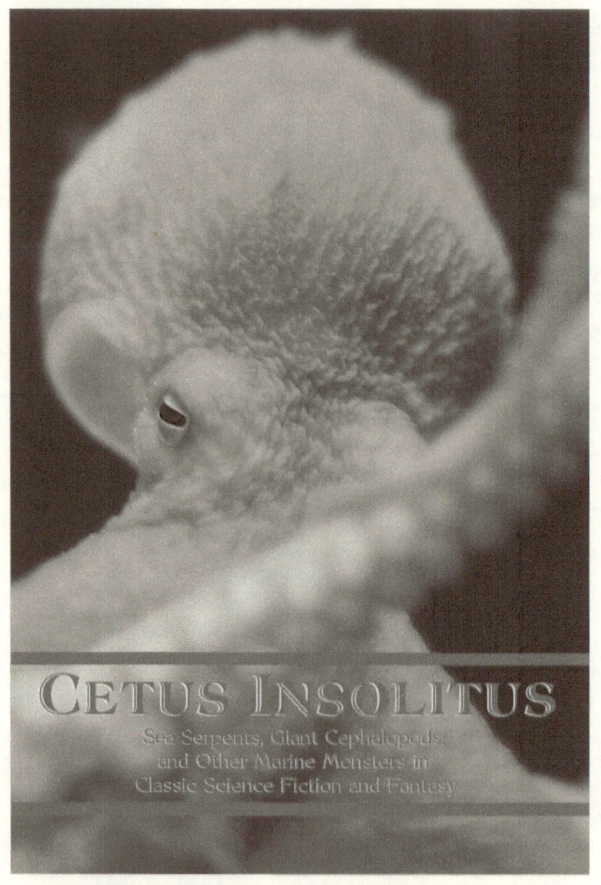

CETUS INSOLITUS
SEA SERPENTS, GIANT CEPHALOPODS,
AND OTHER MARINE MONSTERS
IN CLASSIC SCIENCE FICTION AND FANTASY

COACHWHIP PUBLICATIONS
COACHWHIPBOOKS.COM

INVERTEBRATA ENIGMATICA
GIANT SPIDERS, DANGEROUS INSECTS, AND OTHER STRANGE INVERTEBRATES IN CLASSIC SCIENCE FICTION AND FANTASY

COACHWHIP PUBLICATIONS
COACHWHIPBOOKS.COM

Flora Curiosa

Cryptobotany, Mysterious Fungi,
Sentient Trees, and Deadly Plants
in Classic Science Fiction and Fantasy

CHAD ARMENT, EDITOR

FLORA CURIOSA
CRYPTOBOTANY, MYSTERIOUS FUNGI,
SENTIENT TREES, AND DEADLY PLANTS
IN CLASSIC SCIENCE FICTION AND FANTASY

Coachwhip Publications

CoachwhipBooks.com

BOTANICA DELIRA
More Stories of Strange, Undiscovered, and Murderous Vegetation

www.ingramcontent.com/pod-product-compliance
Lightning Source LLC
Chambersburg PA
CBHW030555020726
47494CB00005B/1620